Nathan Burrage lives in Sydney, Australia with his wife and two daughters. He is the author of *FIVEFOLD*, a supernatural thriller first published by Random House and subsequently translated into Russian, and *Almost Human* a collection of short fiction published by IFWG.

A graduate of Clarion South—an intensive, six-week residential writing program based on the famous US workshops of the same name—Nathan has been shortlisted for both the Aurealis Awards and the Ditmar Awards in Australia.

Intermittent transmissions can be intercepted at www.nathanburrage.com

T0043987

The Hidden Keystone

Book 1 of the Salt Lines

by
Nathan Burrage

The Hidden Keystone

All Rights Reserved

ISBN-13: 978-1-922856-26-5

V.1.0

Printed in Palatino Linotype and Amarante.

IFWG Publishing International
Gold Coast

www.ifwgpublishing.com

For Liz, Liana, and Brielle.

A *Cast of Characters* can be found on page 297

A *Glossary of Terms* can be found on page 301

First comes the Shroud,
Second the Keystone,
Third the Test,
Unto eternity,
'Til we may rest.

Translated from Hebrew.
Author unknown.

CHAPTER 1

12 October 1307

Commanderie, south of Brienne-le-Château

During the coldest part of the night, well before the morning bell of Matins, Bertrand de Châtillon-sur-Seine knelt in the Chapel of St Anne and silently begged for forgiveness.

An icy draft whispered across the green tiles. Even though it was only October, the chapel was quick to forget the kiss of summer. His habit of thin black wool and linen breeches provided scant protection from the chill. Thankfully, he had been given a strip of lambskin to kneel upon. If it was not for that concession, he might never be able to straighten his legs again.

Bertrand faced the simple wooden altar. The Lord's Table stood before the stained-glass windows that faced east. Dawn's first light would end this all-night vigil, and if he proved worthy, see him join the ranks of brother-knights. However, that moment seemed an eternity away.

He drew in a ragged breath.

The vigil had sounded simple enough when Laurent, the Chaplain, had explained it. *Utter no word other than prayer throughout the night. Commend your spirit into the safe keeping of God. Then take the vow at dawn, arise, and be reborn.*

There had been no mention of how the stillness magnified doubt or how the silence echoed with the sins of the past. After all, would the Order really choose to elevate someone stained by disgrace so early in life? Could he really claim to be of noble spirit when all he could find in the quiet places of his soul was the memory of a woman's face?

Justine.

No, he must not think of her. Not now.

Her name was a promise on his lips, awaiting only breath to take life in his imagination.

Bertrand's gaze slipped past the altar to the three panes of stained glass. Instead of glorious depictions of the Bible like those in the great cathedrals of Troyes and Reims, the brothers had to be content with a simple border of green vines that occasionally sprouted a dull flower. A hint of the Garden of Eden perhaps, long since dimmed after that ancient fall from grace.

Once again, his thoughts returned to sin. Refusing to give in, Bertrand chanted the Prayer of the Heart, the words a plea for purity and strength.

"Domine Iesu Christe, Fili Dei, miserere mei, peccatoris." *Lord Jesus Christ, Son of God, have mercy on me, a sinner.*

This was his chance for redemption, an opportunity to weave a new life from the tatters of his past mistakes. But how was he to be reborn when Justine haunted him still?

Memories wove through his frosting breath. Pale, soft skin sliding against linen sheets. Slender, deft fingers clutching his curly brown hair, guiding his explorations. The soft gasps as he pleased her and the leap of his heart in response.

Justine was the widow of his father's former vassal. As the third son, it fell to him to collect the tithe from her estate in exchange for his father's protection. Bertrand had understood what was expected of him and had been prepared for any attempts to negotiate a reduction in what was owed. He had not been prepared, however, to find her quite so sophisticated and alluring. Young, and unfamiliar with the ways of women, he had ended up in her bed on the second night of his visit and remained there until it came time to depart. He liked to believe they had taken unexpected delight in one another, although in hindsight he could no longer be sure. It was only when he returned to his father's castle with a lighter tithe than anticipated that he realised the extent to which he had been manipulated. Furious, his father had shipped him off to the Commanderie three days later. On the morning of his departure, Armand—his eldest brother—told Bertrand what the entire household knew: Justine had been having an intermittent affair with his father even before her husband died.

Bertrand directed a silent appeal for strength at the three windows. If only his spirit could be gathered up into the dark, inert glass. When the sun rose, he would be wrapped in light, protected forever from temptation.

A candle on the altar suddenly flared. Strange, silver sparks crackled and snapped through the flame. The hiss and splutter were loud in the stillness of the chapel. A second taper flickered into silver, followed by the remaining candles.

Bertrand sat back on his heels in astonishment. Silver lines and whorls had appeared in the dark glass behind the altar. The vines, normally so wan in candlelight, sparkled a vivid green. Each flower had become a burst of yellow petals.

The silver threads combined to form a tree whose slender trunk rose from the base of the central window and brushed the uppermost arch. Five circles glistened in the central bole, spread evenly from apex to base. Two boughs split off from the main trunk, each stretching up the panes on either side to support three more of the strange circles.

Bertrand recalled Brother Laurent's words as the old Chaplain left him to his solitary vigil. To see clearly, you must first gaze within.

Had Laurent known this vision would appear? If so, what did it mean?

The silver sparks in the candles began to fail. Already the unearthly tree was fading. Bertrand noticed the second circle in the central pane had remained darker than the rest. By day, this part of the window was marred by a brown stain that resisted all attempts at cleaning. Now a ruby glow infused that blemish, revealing a rose with five petals.

The candles gave a final sputter, and the tree sank back into the depths of the glass. Forgetting his vow, he murmured, "A tree with the heart of a rose."

"Extraordinary, isn't it?" The words were gruff, and pitched low, as if the speaker was trying to mask their true voice.

Bertrand twisted towards the sound. After remaining still for so long, his back cracked at the sudden movement. A figure leaned against the south wall, just beyond the circle of candlelight. Dressed in an ordinary black habit, the speaker was slight and had drawn the cowl low to hide his face. Bertrand gaped, shocked at the blasphemy of this intrusion.

"You show restraint. That's good."

The priest skirted the candlelight. "Judging from your expression, you have many questions. An inquiring mind can be a dangerous trait."

The only warning he had was the soft scuff of leather on the tiles behind him. Bertrand rose into a crouch as strong hands seized him. He flung an elbow at the second intruder, but it failed to connect. Tiles slammed into Bertrand's face. Before he could recover, his arms were pulled back and efficiently bound together.

"Forgive these precautions," the first man said, "but it's important that I have your attention." Footsteps drew closer. With his face squashed against the tiles, Bertrand could see nothing.

"You're weary and no doubt berating yourself at having broken your silence. So, I'll be brief. Despite your past disgrace, I've come to offer you a choice. Say nothing of this visit and you'll be welcomed into the Order as Chevalier Bertrand."

Shame prickled across Bertrand's scalp. Did this stranger know about Justine?

"Or you could aspire to something far greater. You could bear witness to a deeper truth, known only to members of the Salt Lines."

Bertrand stilled.

The Salt Lines.

He had caught whispers about the secret Fraternity. Sometimes a snatch of conversation from the top of the stairs in his father's chateau, other times late at night, when troubling dreams had woken him and he went unnoticed by powerful relatives who had drunk too much wine.

The Salt Lines were part of his ancestry and never to be spoken of. Questioning his father had taught him that much. But he had gleaned enough to know they involved the deeds of his ancestors in Outremer, the fabled Holy Land. No doubt Armand had been initiated into their mysteries, but his brother had also refused to speak of them.

"We require a commitment," the priest said. "A statement of good faith."

An object slid across the floor and stopped in front of Bertrand's face. It was a simple wooden cross, unadorned, like those pilgrims or penitents might carry.

"If the cross remains whole and undamaged by dawn, we'll know you've chosen not to join us. There will not be a second invitation."

How could they ask him to defile the cross? Bertrand ached to denounce this sacrilege but that would mean breaking his vow of silence again.

Slow footsteps paced across the tiles. Bertrand caught the sound of the latch of the door in the south wall. "A good Christian would think ill of me for what I've asked of you. Believe me when I tell you the Salt Lines are the foremost servants of God. Remember, a tree that bends in strong winds won't snap."

The door creaked and a gust of wind swirled through the chapel. "We'll leave you now, as we found you. If you try to follow us, your vigil will have been abandoned and you'll never wear the white of a chevalier. Do keep that in mind."

The hands pinning Bertrand untied his bonds. Heavier footsteps hurried across the tiles. Bertrand rose to his knees and caught sight of a large shadow passing through the doorway.

He glanced around the chapel, but all remained still.

Bertrand picked up the cross. Should he tell Laurent?

No. If one of his brothers had asked him to deny Christ, the repercussions would require careful consideration. Better to remain silent for now.

Bertrand squeezed his eyes closed and pressed the cross against his forehead. What did the Salt Lines want with him when his own father refused to speak of them?

And what of the tree that still glittered in his mind?

Suddenly, he was glad of what remained of the night and the solitary contemplation that it offered. He began his prayers anew, this time asking for guidance as the wind moaned outside.

CHAPTER 2

12 October 1307

The Commanderie

Bertrand's thoughts swung between his complex feelings for Justine and the unexpected offer from the Salt Lines. Try as he might, he could not dispel either from his mind.

The bell tolled outside, striking five times in its tower. Doors banged in the distance. The brothers would be filing from the dormitory in dutiful silence, responding to the call of Matins, the morning devotion. Frost crunched underfoot in the courtyard.

Bertrand straightened with a wince. He only had a few moments to muster a semblance of calm.

A door at the back of the chapel opened with a creak. The scrape of one shoe across the tiles could only belong to Brother Laurent. Bertrand closed his eyes and exhaled slowly. Despite all that had tormented him throughout the night, he must strive for worthiness now. His future as a chevalier depended upon it.

A light touch on his shoulder interrupted his fervent thoughts. Bertrand's neck cracked as he looked up at the Chaplain.

Brother Laurent was lean to the point of infirmity. Unlike the chevaliers, he was clean-shaven. The little hair that Laurent's tonsure allowed him was white and so fine that it wafted about his head whenever he moved.

Laurent smiled before noticing the simple wooden cross lying on the tiles before the altar. Using his fingernail, Bertrand had scratched a second cross into the soft timber. Did Laurent recognise the significance of this message?

Laurent's wispy eyebrows bunched together as he shot Bertrand a quizzical look. Bertrand dropped his head. It was obvious that Laurent was not his night-time visitor, nor had he instigated the mysterious offer.

"Shall we commence?" another person murmured. Bertrand knew

that voice, although he was more accustomed to hearing it raised in command.

"Are the brethren assembled?" Laurent asked.

"They are. In fact, they've probably been awake almost as long as poor Bertrand here." Bertrand's tension eased as he caught the amusement in the Preceptor's voice. If his commander, Everard de Chaumont, was in good spirits, it boded well for the rest of his initiation.

"Then please bid them enter," Laurent replied.

Bertrand caught the faint sound of Everard striding back down the nave.

Moving slowly, Laurent bent down on his good leg and retrieved the wooden cross. He turned it over in hands dusted with white hair. "I would very much like to know where these keep appearing from. At least this one isn't damaged." Laurent gave Bertrand a sharp look.

The slap of leather shoes and the rustle of habits filled the chapel. This small Commanderie only boasted six brother-knights at present, so the initiation of a new chevalier was a rare deviation from routine.

Bertrand suppressed a shiver. A least two people entering the chapel at this moment had visited him last night. They knew about his passion for Justine. And they were part of the Salt Lines. Who were they?

He pictured the serving brothers in their brown tunics and leggings gathering against the south wall. Was it one of them?

The sergeants and squires would be forming ranks on the northern side of the nave. The front rows belonged to the Preceptor and his key aides: the Marshal, Steward, and Almoners. Surely, it couldn't be one of them?

Once the entire community had gathered in the chapel, Brother Laurent began the usual dawn service in a strong voice. Bertrand's attention wavered as Laurent began the recital of the required twenty-eight Pater Nosters. Faces paraded through his mind, each a possible candidate for his nocturnal visitors.

Eventually, Laurent rose, blessed the kneeling congregation, and bade them rise except for Bertrand. Standing before the altar and facing the assembly, Laurent said, "There is one here, known to all of us, who seeks admission to the rank of brother-knight."

Bertrand thought he caught a hint of pleasure in Laurent's serious expression.

Laurent spread his hands wide. "Are there any gathered among us with cause to deny that request?" Bertrand's breathing became fast and shallow. Would his mysterious visitors choose this moment to denounce him?

"Very well." Laurent motioned for Everard and his six chevaliers to approach. "As the shepherd of Bertrand's soul, I confirm that I have no objection to his petition."

Laurent limped to one side as Everard's bulky figure moved in front of the altar. Flanking Bertrand on either side was a row of three chevaliers, each dressed in the pure white cassock with the Cross Pattée on their left breast, signifying their rank as knights of Christ.

Everard gazed down at Bertrand with a serious expression. Time had salted his beard and left white streaks at his temples. "Brother Bertrand, do you come before us, willingly, and free of encumbrance or obligation?"

"Willingly and humbly, do I come before you," Bertrand replied. "Free of encumbrance, both physical and spiritual." The practiced words slipped from his lips, yet he felt like a fraud. He had looked into his heart and found Justine, not God.

Bertrand focused on the cord knotted around Everard's waist and kept the guilt from his face.

"Then Brother Bertrand," Everard said in a loud voice, "repeat after me. I, Bertrand de Châtillon-sur-Seine, do solemnly swear to observe my original vows of poverty, chastity, and obedience."

Bertrand repeated the vow in a clear voice.

"Further," Everard continued, "I swear to renounce all ties to secular life that might tempt me, including any lands, chattels, family inheritance, and all other worldly possessions in favour of my service to the Lord God, and to the knighthood of the Temple of Solomon of Jerusalem, for howsoever long I may live."

Bertrand repeated the words.

"And I shall live in accordance with the Rule of our Order, defend those pilgrims who seek the Holy Land to the utmost limit of my endurance, rewarded only in spirit as a humble soldier of Christ and the Lord God."

Bertrand finished his recital in a rush. No one cried out to declaim him. If anything, a heavy cloak of silence had settled over the chapel.

"Having heard your vows," Everard continued, "and calling all present to bear witness, I confer upon you the title of brother-knight of the *Ordre du Temple*. Arise, Bertrand de Châtillon-sur-Seine, now reborn into the service of God."

Everard gestured discreetly to his two most senior chevaliers, Roland and Arnaud. Taking an elbow on either side, they helped Bertrand struggle to his feet. Pain throbbed through his numb legs. Everard grinned as he drew Bertrand into a rough embrace. Each of the other six chevaliers embraced him in a public sign of acceptance.

Laurent blessed the assembled brothers and said, "Go about your daily business and remember; *laborare est orare*. To work is to pray. God be with you."

"And also with you," the brethren replied.

"Brother Laurent," Everard called, "I wonder if we may have a moment alone with our newest member."

"Of course." Laurent dipped his head, clearly not surprised by the request. Gathering his priests, Laurent limped towards the chapter house to prepare for the new day. The remaining brethren filed from the chapel.

Everard drew his Marshal and Steward outside. A quick exchange between the three men ensued just outside the doorway. The conversation was too low for Bertrand to catch. Both men hurried off with purposeful strides. Everard returned to the chapel and closed the door behind him. His expression had clouded over.

Bertrand glanced at Roland and Arnaud. Roland's expression was dour at the best of times. He was a big man and certainly possessed the strength to hold Bertrand down. Was he one of the visitors?

Arnaud was lighter in both frame and character. He was known to enjoy a jest and had tolerated Bertrand's presence with an easy disposition. Neither man met Bertrand's gaze now.

Everard nodded. The brother-knights formed a ring around Bertrand. Like the Preceptor, their expressions were grim. Panic fluttered against Bertrand's ribs. Roland grabbed Bertrand's habit by the nape and pulled him backwards. Arnaud kicked the back of Bertrand's knee.

Pain jolted down Bertrand's leg as he collapsed. Roland shoved him down onto the tiles and grabbed a fistful of Bertrand's hair.

Arnaud squatted in front of Bertrand and slapped a bible on the floor. "Spit on it," Arnaud ordered.

Bertrand stared in astonishment. "What?"

Arnaud back-handed Bertrand. The blow stung like a whip and blood filled his mouth.

"Spit," Arnaud demanded again. Roland's grip tightened until Bertrand feared chunks of hair would be torn from his scalp. The big chevalier's knee sent jagged pain rippling down Bertrand's spine.

"No."

Arnaud struck him again. The blow was savage, especially since Bertrand couldn't turn his head to absorb the impact. Blood and saliva spattered across the tiles and the bible.

"You vowed *absolute* obedience," Arnaud snarled. Roland hauled

Bertrand to his knees by the hair and swung him around.

"Kiss my feet," Roland ordered.

Bertrand squinted up at the brother-knight towering over him. Arnaud was positively amiable next to this man who never smiled. No one trifled with Roland. Not even the other chevaliers.

Was Arnaud right? Did he owe these men total obedience?

Roland kicked him in the stomach. Bertrand doubled over and gasped for breath.

"Kiss my feet or I swear they'll have to carry you out of here," Roland growled.

Bertrand bent over and pecked the top of Roland's leather shoes. He gagged at the stench.

"Now here." Roland lifted the hem of his habit to expose dirty breeches and a hairy stomach. He pointed at his navel.

"No," Bertrand said in revulsion.

A moment later he lay sprawled sideways on the tiles. A dull roar echoed in his right ear. His vision blurred and the side of his face throbbed.

Rough hands yanked him upright. Fingers wound through his hair again. Dragging him across the tiles, they pressed his lolling head against Roland's stomach. The big chevalier stepped back, apparently satisfied. Bertrand tried to focus on the men surrounding him. Even though he squinted, his eyes refused to cooperate.

Through the ringing in his ear, Bertrand heard Arnaud's next command. "Repeat after me: Christ is not the son of God, he was merely a fisherman."

Bertrand blinked in utter amazement. How dare they utter such heresy inside a consecrated chapel? He shook his head to deny what was happening.

Bear witness to a deeper truth.

That's what the priest had said during Bertrand's vigil. Is *this* what he had meant?

"I can't...hear." Bertrand coughed up saliva flecked with blood. He was going to die here. Suddenly, it all made twisted sense.

"Christ is not the son of God, he was merely a fisherman," Arnaud repeated. "Say it."

Bertrand finally focused on the blurry outline of Arnaud's face. "No."

Arnaud bent down and grabbed Bertrand's habit. He cocked a fist and said in a soft voice, "Last chance."

Bertrand spat in Arnaud's face. The chevalier sucked in an angry breath through his teeth and drew his fist back.

"Enough," Everard said. Arnaud immediately released Bertrand who slumped to the floor.

"See to his wounds," Everard ordered. "Then have him brought to my Lodge. And make sure that he's treated with respect."

Bertrand was lifted off the tiles, gently this time, and carried out into the dull grey light of an autumn morning. Someone murmured, "Well done," although Bertrand was not sure if the comment was directed at him or the brothers who had beaten him.

A light rain was falling. The fine mist soothed the fiery pain that throbbed across his face while the rest of him ached. He sagged in their grasp as they dragged him to the infirmary.

CHAPTER 3

12 October 1307

The Commanderie

"You handled yourself well in the chapel." Arnaud clapped a hand on Bertrand's shoulder.

Bertrand did not know how to respond, so he remained silent.

"However, it would be a mistake to think your trials are over." Arnaud gave Bertrand a mirthless grin. "As chevaliers, we're constantly tested. You'd do well to remember that. Especially now."

Arnaud turned and banged on the heavy, iron-bound door of the Preceptor's Lodge. Set in a wall of stone black with age and rising damp, it was the only entrance to Everard's private domain.

Feet shuffled on the far side of the door. Metal bolts rasped in their housings. Thibauld, the Preceptor's Seneschal, appeared in the doorway.

"Inside, quickly," Thibauld snapped. "Before the warmth escapes."

Bertrand limped after Arnaud. His head throbbed and every part of him ached despite having his injuries tended to.

The door opened into a small antechamber. A wooden staircase led upstairs while worn stone steps dropped beneath the stairwell into the cellar.

"Not you," Thibauld said, pointing an ink-stained finger at Arnaud. "Only the new one."

Arnaud's customary grin faltered at the dismissal. "Get some rest after you've seen him," he said to Bertrand with a wink. "No one will begrudge it after what you've been through."

Bertrand nodded. He was not sure how to respond to Arnaud's sudden concern for his welfare.

"Off with you," Thibauld said with a flutter of his bony hands. Arnaud slipped back out the door with a jaunty wave.

"And Everard says *I* need to learn humility," Thibauld muttered as he bolted the door. "That one could do with lessons in it, not me."

Thibauld glared at Bertrand with his watery blue eyes. "I see they made you earn your promotion. Hmph. Mind what you touch and speak with respect. This isn't the stables or armoury." He poked Bertrand in the chest to emphasise his point. "You'll find him in the main hall," Thibauld said with a nod before retreating into his study.

Bertrand entered the dining hall. Two rows of pillars supported the ribbed vaults of the ceiling whose arches appeared to spring from the top of each column. A long table ran down the central aisle of the hall, stiff-backed chairs flanking it. The table was empty except for the remains of three meals nearest to the hearth. Bertrand frowned. All brothers were obliged to dine together in the refectory, except on special occasions. Had Everard been entertaining guests?

He took a tentative step into the hall. Banners hung from the ceiling. The standards alternated between the *Beauseant*, the white and black battle flag of their Order, and the gold fleur-de-lis on a field of royal blue to honour the Capetian Kings who ruled France.

Pride stirred within Bertrand. He was part of a great legacy now. The Order had achieved famous victories over the last two centuries, even if Outremer had been lost.

"Bertrand." Everard's voice drifted from the far end of the hall. Although his name was spoken softly, it still conveyed a command.

Bertrand hurried towards the hearth as quickly as his aches allowed.

"Here, drink this." Everard emerged from behind a pillar and handed Bertrand a tin goblet. Dark red wine rippled just beneath the rim.

"Drink," Everard urged. "It's ill-mannered to refuse an apology once offered."

Bertrand rubbed his thumb against the side of the goblet. "Is that what this is?"

Everard grimaced. "Should anyone have to apologise for necessity?" He crossed his arms and sighed. "Should I make amends for preparing men for the possibility of failure?"

"Failure?" Bertrand repeated. "How does that justify blasphemy? To even—"

Everard turned his piercing stare on Bertrand, who wisely fell silent.

"People forget that our Order held the Holy Land for nearly two hundred years," Everard said. "Many chevaliers became martyrs in its defence. Many more were captured." He seized a poker and stabbed the embers in the hearth. The ruddy glow of flames flickered across his bearded face.

"In the beginning," Everard continued, "the Saracens thought they could convert our brethren to Islam. After a time, they learned we couldn't be turned from Christ, no matter what they tried. Eventually, capture by Saracens resulted in instant death for any member of our Order. This is our legacy, our history writ in blood."

"So, the initiation is a form of preparation," Bertrand said in sudden understanding. "A test of faith."

Everard placed a hand on Bertrand's shoulder. "At some point, every warrior must look into the face of defeat. Some find defiance in that moment. Others despair. If a man rides beside me in battle, I must know what strength lies within him." Everard squeezed Bertrand's shoulder. "Only faith can sustain us in such moments."

"I understand." The relief that swept through Bertrand was dizzying. Everard was not guilty of heresy, he had simply tested Bertrand's faith.

"Good." Everard smiled although it seemed tinged with sadness. "The initiation is difficult for everyone involved. Especially those who remember their own experience with shame." His gaze returned to the flames.

Bertrand took a sip of the undiluted wine. Plum and oak flavours burst across his palate.

They stood that way for a time in silence; Everard lost in the flames, Bertrand sipping from his goblet. The wine numbed Bertrand's aches and a tide of weariness washed over him.

Everard eventually folded his hands together. "Bertrand, Brother Laurent tells me he found a cross lying on the floor of the chapel. Can you tell me how you came by that cross?"

Bertrand wrapped his free hand around the goblet to stop it from trembling. Uncertain how to respond, he chose to feign ignorance. "I'm not sure how it came to be there. The chapel was dark. Perhaps one of the clergy left it by accident."

"I see." Everard studied his hands. "While the cross was scratched, it wasn't badly damaged." A wry note entered Everard's voice. "I'm sure Brother Laurent would've been upset if it had been broken."

"I'm sure he would." Bertrand avoided Everard's searching gaze.

"It would rub salt into the wound, would it not?"

"Not if there was no wound to offend," Bertrand murmured.

Everard laughed in surprise. "True." His expression became thoughtful. "Although we can't escape what we are, Bertrand. The lines of history that lead down to us can never be erased, much as we may wish to. You'll find your path in life will become easier if you accept that this is so."

Bertrand had no answer to this, so he remained silent. Had his father sent him to this Commanderie knowing that Everard was a member of the Salt Lines? Was the course of his life still being manipulated? Bertrand's grip tightened around the goblet.

"You'll recall that our families are distantly related," Everard said into the awkward silence.

Bertrand nodded, not trusting his voice. Everard had commented on it once before, when Bertrand was first presented at the Commanderie. The statement now took on new facets of meaning.

Everard rubbed one thigh as if it pained him. "Bertrand, we share the same ancestry. The same heritage marked in salt. I don't understand your reluctance to embrace it."

Bertrand drew a deep, steadying breath. Talk of family and inheritance always invoked the sour taste of bitterness. "Whatever legacy my family inherited, I wasn't deemed fit to be instructed in it."

"*We* are your family now." Everard gestured at the hall. "Whatever the shortcomings of your old life, they are done with now. Today is the beginning of your new life."

He wished it were that simple, but how could he forget requesting a tutor only to be summarily refused by his father? Or watching his older brothers receive a new saddle or accoutrements made especially for them, while Bertrand only warranted their cast-offs. How could those moments, and a thousand like them, be forgotten or forgiven through a single gesture?

Everard nodded in understanding. "I see this is difficult for you. Perhaps that's for the best." He prodded the fire again. "Let me ask you this: can a man claim to be virtuous if he stands idle in the face of evil?"

The shift in topic caught Bertrand by surprise. "No. Of course not."

"What if he's powerless to prevent it?"

"Then he should tell his master or lord," Bertrand replied.

"And what if *they* are part of that evil?" Everard glanced sideways at him.

Bertrand groped for answer. "Then he should inform the Church."

"Yes, he should." Everard rubbed his cheek. "I will tell you two things about the Salt Lines, Bertrand. First, they have always believed every man must answer to his conscience before his master or priest. And second, they believe it is the duty of the strong to care for the weak. Think on that."

Bertrand frowned. What was Everard trying to say? Obedience was the first rule of their Order. "I will."

Everard sighed. "You're weary. Get some sleep. We'll speak on this again."

Bertrand placed his unfinished wine next to the bowls on the table and walked back down the hall. After growing up in the shadow of his father's disapproval, he was well versed in recognising a dismissal.

Thibauld grumbled as he bolted the door to the Lodge behind Bertrand. A breeze blew in from the north-west. Each fresh gust carried a chill edge. Brothers hurried about the courtyard, going about their daily labour. Bertrand dallied a moment beneath the wide lintel, luxuriating in his newly won status.

He was a brother-knight. A chevalier of Christ. The thought was like wearing a new garment: it did not seem to fit properly, yet he was determined to grow into it.

The image of the tree with the heart of a rose came to him. What did it mean? And what was Everard trying to suggest about the Salt Lines?

Bertrand shook his head. It was all too much, too soon.

For now, surely it was enough just to be counted a chevalier. His new pallet in the dormitory beckoned, but Bertrand was not ready for sleep yet. He needed to share this triumph with someone.

With the recent rain, the ground had become soft and muddy. He kept to the cobblestones that skirted the main courtyard, walking gingerly to avoid mud splattering his white cassock. Walking parallel with the chapel, Bertrand passed the chapter house and the circular tower of the dovecote.

Dark plumes of smoke rose from the kitchen's twin chimneys. The main meal of the day was some time away yet, although the smell of baking bread that wafted on the biting breeze was tantalising.

Bertrand cut through the gap between the kitchen and the under-ground cellar. Emerging from the narrow lane, he stopped at the edge of a large garden. Lay brothers, distinguishable by their brown tunics, were hard at work, spreading manure across the moist earth.

Closer to Bertrand, the garden had been divided into small plots bordered by wickerwork fences. A profusion of herbs and plants grew in each section. The outer wall of the Commanderie curved around the garden and back towards the stables. Not a proper fortification, the stone and mortar fence still stood well over the height of a man.

He passed the garden and caught sight of the long, timber frame of the stables. A man stood in the shadow of the doorway, hands on his hips, examining Bertrand critically. "Well now," he said gruffly. "Doesn't the lordling look fine today?"

Bertrand squinted. "Rémi, what are you doing skulking about like that?"

"Skulking, he says! I call it working, as opposed to tottering about with a head too heavy for my body."

Rémi emerged from the gloom of the stables. The sergeant was a full head shorter than Bertrand and blessed with exceptionally broad shoulders. Barrel-chested and heavily muscled from years of practice in the weapons yard, Rémi was shaped like a boulder. His thick black hair, cropped short, resisted all attempts to govern it and his beard was a shade or two lighter than on his head.

"I was looking for *you,*" Bertrand countered.

"Come to gloat, eh?"

"Of course not. Is wanting to share my happiness against our Rule as well?" Bertrand's tone was sharper than he had intended.

"I was only jesting, cub." Rémi glanced about. Seeing they were alone, he stepped closer and squinted at Bertrand's bruises. "Did they hurt you bad?"

"Not really." Bertrand glanced away from the sudden concern in Rémi's dark brown eyes.

While Rémi might be content to play the dullard, he was smart enough to conceal his intelligence and his fierce protectiveness of Bertrand. Once, long before they had joined the Commanderie, three serfs had accosted them on a forest path. When they threatened Bertrand, Rémi flew into a murderous rage. He snapped the first peasant's neck with his bare hands. The second serf slashed Rémi's arm with a hunting knife. Rémi struck the man such a blow that it crushed his nose and left him senseless on the ground. Seeing the fate of his companions, the third serf had fled.

After it was over, Rémi had stood over the fallen men. Blood dripped from his elbow and a terrifying ferocity had blazed in his eyes. For a long moment, Rémi did not even seem to *recognise* Bertrand. Then the man Bertrand knew returned. There was no other way to describe it. Rémi shivered, looked at Bertrand, and suggested they move on in a quiet voice. They had never spoken of the incident again, but Bertrand would never forget the naked ferocity that he had glimpsed in Rémi that day.

"Doesn't look like they were playing," Rémi said with a scowl.

"It doesn't matter." Bertrand drew a deep breath. "I'm a chevalier now."

Rémi grunted. "You've always been a chevalier. I've known that from the first day your father sent me to watch over you. You don't need the Preceptor to say it's true."

Bertrand flushed. "It's not the same."

Rémi shook his head. "Take it from someone who has seen enough to know the difference between a title and nobility." He glanced about again. "If you court the good opinion of others, you'll pay for it with your conscience."

"I swear you're wasted here," Bertrand said with a laugh. "You should be helping Master Thibauld translate the great Greek and Roman philosophers."

"There's no call to mock."

"I'm not mocking." Bertrand sighed. "I just haven't had much cause for mirth of late."

Rémi's thick eyebrows knit together.

"Don't worry." Bertrand patted Rémi's shoulder, which felt like a slab of shifting rock. "They've just given me a lot to think about."

"They?" Rémi's frown deepened into furrows. "They who?"

Bertrand glanced around. "The Salt Lines."

"What?"

"Everard's one of them. He told me himself." Bertrand savoured the look of shock spreading across Rémi's face.

"And I suppose he had a good reason for telling you that." Rémi gave him a keen look. "Mind you, that explains the new horses."

"Horses? What new horses?"

"A big bay charger and a mare." Rémi hooked a thumb in the direction of the stables. "Just appeared in the stalls overnight. The Marshal told the head groom to mind his own business when he asked who they belonged to."

"That explains the meals on the table," Bertrand mused.

Rémi would have asked more but the squeak of a wheel warned him to remain silent. A serving brother emerged from the stables. He was pushing a cart with a wide, wooden draw. Balanced on top was an iron-pronged pitchfork.

"I thought you were going to collect hay," he said to Rémi.

"Was and still am." Rémi nodded at Bertrand. "Just explaining to the new chevalier here that he'd need permission from the Preceptor to examine the horses."

"Or the Marshal." The man turned his disapproving stare upon Bertrand.

After a quick glance at Rémi, Bertrand said, "I'm well aware of the protocol, brother. I merely wanted to ensure that the mount I donated to the Order is being well cared for."

The man frowned. "I know that mare. It joined our stable back at the end of last summer. You haven't tried to see her once since then, so why the sudden interest?" His suspicious gaze flicked between Bertrand and Rémi. "If you're malingering, the Preceptor will hear of this."

"You needn't worry," Bertrand replied in a tone that he had learned from Everard. "The Preceptor has already given me dispensation for today. As to why I am inquiring after the horse I once owned, it's quite simple really. Chevaliers are entitled to choose a mount for training. Is that not so?"

The serving brother glanced between Bertrand and Rémi. "That's true," he admitted reluctantly.

"Well and good." Bertrand gave him a bright smile. "Perhaps you'd be so kind as to pass my request to the Marshal for consideration then."

"I will." He glared at Rémi before retreating into the stables.

A quirk of Rémi's lips suggested he was stifling a laugh. The sergeant lifted the handles of the cart and pushed it towards the mounds of hay.

Bertrand threaded his way back towards the dormitory. The courtyard was bustling with activity. The ring of hammer striking metal drifted from the forge. He crossed the driest section of the courtyard and tramped up the wooden stairs of the dormitory.

His pallet had been moved to the section reserved for chevaliers. He unknotted the cord about his waist and lifted the white cassock over his head. Mud had dirtied the hem despite his best efforts. If he was not so tired, he would have washed the wool before the mud dried into a hard crust. Instead, he neatly folded the habit and placed it on a wooden stool next to his dirty leather shoes.

Bertrand sank into his straw-filled mattress with a groan. He had never felt so exhausted. A sharp object prodded his cheek as he burrowed into the goose down of his pillow. He sat up and pulled the pillow aside.

Lying on his mattress was a small cross carved from wood stained almost black. Someone had gouged furrows into the timber and smeared blood into them.

He turned the desecrated cross over and over in his trembling hands. Eventually, he slipped it under his pallet and lay down again. Despite his fatigue, sleep took a long time to find him.

CHAPTER 4

13 October 1307

The Commanderie

"Wake up." Rough hands shook Bertrand awake. A shadow moved above him in the darkness.

"Who's there?"

"Out of bed. Now."

Bertrand sat up and blinked.

Almost all of the candles in the dormitory had been extinguished. He caught whispers of movement in the gloom.

"What's going on?" Bertrand pitched his voice low so that it wouldn't carry.

"Keep quiet or I'll have your hide," the man whispered into Bertrand's ear.

Bertrand recognised Roland's voice. The big chevalier hauled him out of bed. "Armoury. Preceptor's orders. Now move." Roland gave him a shake.

Bertrand felt for his leather shoes and pulled on his habit. Throwing back his cowl, he stumbled after the line of men creeping through the dormitory.

A few solitary candles cast enough light to find their footing. Some of the brothers stirred at their passing. Most continued to snore, exhausted from their labours.

Why had Everard summoned all his chevaliers? The dawn service was hours away yet.

Bertrand followed his brother-knights down the creaking stairwell. A smaller figure at the head of the line, possibly Arnaud, slipped into the cramped sleeping quarters of the lay brothers. Were they to be woken too? What was going on?

Roland led the rest of the chevaliers outside into the courtyard. The heavy clouds from the day before had largely blown over. A few wisps curled about the familiar constellations like a fleece of wool that had been torn up and scattered about the heavens. The damp odour of churned mud and the rank smell of old sweat from the chevaliers jostling Bertrand was overpowering.

They were tense, he realised suddenly. On edge and expectant. Like before a battle.

A tremor of anticipation tripped down Bertrand's spine.

He knew better than to ask why they had been summoned. Discipline, unity and obedience: that's how the chevaliers of the Order fought. With a single purpose and to the glory of God.

Whatever they were about, he had earned his place. No brother could deny it. The exhaustion that had plagued him the day before had evaporated. He would show them he was ready...for whatever needed doing.

Arnaud emerged from the dormitory. Three men followed, rubbing their eyes and stretching. Like Bertrand, they were obviously confused at being woken. Rémi's broad figure was instantly recognisable in the moonlight. Bertrand took comfort from the sergeant's presence.

The other two men Arnaud had collected were also experienced sergeants. Everard had clearly picked his most seasoned warriors. No squires or lay brothers, only men accustomed to fighting on horseback. Bertrand realised with a jolt that he was the youngest man there.

"If you need to piss," Roland said quietly, "do it now and be quick about it. Against the wall," he growled when some of the men moved towards the privy. Bertrand hesitated, as did a number of the brothers.

"Quickly," Arnaud whispered. He waved them towards the wall of the dormitory. "Do it now or piss in your saddle later."

A brother would normally be punished for soiling any of the Commanderie's buildings. What could possibly be so urgent?

Bertrand joined the line of men fumbling with their breeches.

Afterwards, Roland led them along the courtyard to the armoury. Candlelight glimmered through chinks in the narrow windows. Someone must have covered up the glass with cloth.

The Marshal emerged from the doorway of the armoury and waved them inside. "Quickly," he ordered. "Full battle dress. As fast and quietly as possible."

Bertrand followed the other chevaliers inside. Racks of weapons—lances, pikes, stands of swords and stacked shields—lined the low chamber. In the centre, a dozen wooden stands supported hauberks of chain mail. Next to each stand was a bascinet, the pointed kettle helm worn over the top of the mail coif.

The chevaliers cast off their habits and began dressing for battle.

Bertrand shared a brief, questioning look with Rémi. The sergeant shrugged, although Bertrand detected concern beneath his nonchalance.

He squirmed into his padded under-tunic with practiced ease and pulled on thick woollen leggings. Sturdy boots, with spurs attached, protected his feet. The hauberk of chainmail was heavy as he struggled into it. A squire would normally tighten the leather cinches that ran down his side. Bertrand found it difficult without assistance, but he managed.

"No tabards," the Marshal ordered.

Even Roland and Arnaud looked surprised. Only men without allegiance, such as outlaws and mercenaries, dispensed with wearing the colours of their lord or Order.

The Marshal grimaced. "Preceptor's orders."

Bertrand strapped a wide belt around his waist and placed a leather cap on his head. He reached up and pulled the mail coif over the cap. Despite the strangeness of this summons, the scent of iron, boiled leather greased with pig fat, and the tang of old sweat were familiar companions.

Selecting a plain sword and long knife, he rammed them into the sheaths that hung from his belt. He cradled his bascinet in one elbow while he hooked a plain kite shield over his other arm. Despite his haste, Bertrand was one of the last to finish dressing.

"Do you know where to meet the Preceptor?" the Marshal asked Roland.

Roland nodded; his expression grimmer than usual.

"Good. May God be with you." The Marshal glanced about the room. "All of you." Bertrand thought he detected a hint of sympathy in that look.

"And with you," Roland replied.

Arnaud led the armoured chevaliers back into the courtyard. The three sergeants, who wore lighter leather armour, followed. Bertrand found it difficult to remain quiet. His shield and bascinet kept bouncing against his armoured hips. The resulting clink of metal earned him a sharp look from Arnaud.

Roland led them towards the cellar. Peering into the dark, Bertrand saw figures stirring in the deep shadow of the dovecote. Everard emerged from the gloom. He was also dressed for battle, and like them, had forgone his usual surcoat. Even his shield was devoid of markings. Painted entirely black, it looked like he had carved out a piece of the night sky and draped it over his arm.

"This way." Everard strode through the gap between kitchen and cellar. Bertrand caught the stamp of feet as Everard descended the steps to the cellar. Why in heaven's name were they going down there?

Two new figures emerged from the deep shadow that had concealed Everard. One was clearly male. He was as large as Roland and moonlight glinted off his mail-shirt. The second was smaller and covered head to foot in a shapeless cloak.

Bertrand caught a good look at the second stranger's feet. The leather riding boots were small and narrow for a man of his apparent height. A jolt of recognition shot through Bertrand. He remembered marvelling at Justine's petite, narrow feet. They were so soft and delicate. Justine had laughed at the time, low and at the back of her throat, before demanding that he kiss each toe in turn.

The memory left Bertrand trembling. He stared at the cloaked figure as she swept past, for he had no doubt that it was a woman. Even the lightness of her step was feminine. He forgot about his bascinet and it clinked against his leg. Someone behind him hissed at the noise. Bertrand focused on remaining silent as he followed Everard and his mysterious companions into the cellar.

The presence of these strangers explained the unfinished meals in the Lodge and the new horses Rémi had noticed, but how had they arrived unremarked? Visitors to the Commanderie weren't unusual, particularly members of the Order who were travelling. However, any disruption to their daily routine was noteworthy.

Besides which, it was *unthinkable* that one of them was a woman.

All brothers were expressly forbidden to have contact with any women, even their own sisters and mothers. To think that a woman had been secreted inside the Lodge was a direct contradiction of their Rule. Why would Everard allow a woman into the Commanderie?

He stopped. Could she be involved with the Salt Lines?

Someone nudged Bertrand in the back. He turned to find Rémi waiting behind him. Rémi pointed at the stairs. The angle was steep and the stone damp. Bertrand descended, making sure of his footing before committing his weight.

The press of bodies magnified the smell of oil, leather and nervous sweat. A number of candles had been lit and placed inside lanterns. The light flickered up and down the curved stone walls of the cellar. Sacks of grain and jars of preserved food had been carefully stacked together. Haunches of salted pork and a side of beef hung from iron hooks in the ceiling.

"Bolt the door behind you," Everard ordered. The sergeant at the back of the queue hurried to obey. Bertrand counted their number.

Including Everard and his unnamed guests, the company was composed of seven chevaliers and three sergeants. So, they tallied thirteen in total. He doubted that was an accident given the Order had always revered the number thirteen in honour of the Saviour and His twelve apostles.

"I know you have questions," Everard said in a low voice that nevertheless carried.

Bertrand strained to get a good view. Fortunately, he was one of the tallest present, apart from the new chevalier who towered over Everard. The stranger was fair-haired and his cold, restless blue eyes scrutinised the men assembled before him. Bertrand straightened beneath that gaze.

"I must ask you to remain silent," Everard continued, "and remind you of your vow of obedience." He glanced at someone Bertrand couldn't see. Probably the cloaked woman. "If we're attacked, don't hesitate to strike back. No matter who they claim to be, or whose authority they might be acting under." Everard's expression darkened. "It's vital to our Order that we protect these guests. Do whatever you must to keep them safe."

Everard turned to the back of the cellar and muttered a command. Roland moved past Everard and disappeared into the adjoining chamber. No one spoke, although Bertrand burned with questions. Where were they going?

Wood scraped against stone. Someone, presumably Roland, grunted with effort.

Everard raised his lantern so he could peer at the assembled company. "Not a single word." He ducked down and the light from his lantern faded.

Bertrand had been in the cellar countless times. He knew this main chamber connected to a smaller one stuffed with jars of preserved fruit, cuts of meat covered in salt and barrels of wine. The chevaliers shuffled forward over the plain tiles into that small space. Surely there was not enough room to contain them all?

Arnaud had remained behind to direct the flow of men. When Bertrand reached the entrance, he saw a narrow passage gaped in the far wall. Roland must have shifted aside the barrels stacked there to reveal the tunnel. A wooden board, painted to look like stone, lay discarded on the floor.

Where did this tunnel lead?

Bertrand pictured the layout of the Commanderie. Of all the buildings, the cellar was closest to the outer wall. The purpose of the tunnel suddenly became clear.

Arnaud hurried Bertrand into the tunnel.

The passage was too low to stand upright. Bertrand crouched down and shuffled forward, dragging his shield on the ground while clutching the bascinet to his chest. It was an awkward position to hold. He began to sweat beneath his padded jerkin.

The nearest lantern was at least two men ahead, so it was hard to see much. Uneven chunks of stone jutted overhead. The tunnel was damp from the recent rain and stank of mould.

Someone ahead was breathing hard, as if they couldn't get enough air. Bertrand's arms and lower back ached from stooping. Yet no brother voiced a complaint. Bertrand felt a surge of pride. Despite the strangeness of this mission, he felt honoured to be included among them.

A gust of fresh, cooler air wafted down the tunnel. Bertrand caught sight of a pair of legs climbing upwards. As he staggered closer, he saw a rough, wooden ladder leading up a vertical shaft.

The chevaliers in front of Bertrand negotiated the ladder with some difficulty. Roland had remained at the bottom to pass up their shields and helms. Bertrand did not have long to wait. Wordlessly, he handed his shield to Roland and dumped his bascinet on the packed soil. It was a squeeze to get past the big chevalier. Bertrand tucked his gauntlets into his belt and climbed up the ladder.

Strong hands helped Bertrand over the lip. Roland passed up his bascinet and shield.

Bertrand moved aside to make way for Rémi. They had emerged in a dense thicket of poplars and birch trees, not far from Commanderie. In the dark, the glorious colours of the leaves had dulled into a patchwork of greys and charcoal. Bertrand could just make out the dark line of the outer wall.

If Everard wanted their departure to be kept secret, he must suspect the Commanderie was being watched. Bertrand's eyesight was keen: he had proven that beyond question on the archery field. Staying low, he moved quietly through mottled silver trunks in the moonlight and crouched at the tree line. The dark fields were still. Bertrand strained to detect any sign of movement.

Nothing.

If someone *was* watching, they were well hidden.

Bertrand quietly re-joined his companions.

The last of the sergeants had emerged from the tunnel. Arnaud covered the entrance with wooden boards and a pile of branches and leaves. Roland led them down a path through the trees. After forty paces, they emerged into another clearing.

Horses whickered. Bertrand held out his hand to the nearest one, a bay standing at perhaps fifteen hands. The horse muzzled his hand and snorted. Wisps of its steaming breath twined through his fingers.

Everard and the two strangers choose their mounts. Once the entire company was in the saddle, Everard led them away from the Commanderie without a word of explanation.

CHAPTER 5

8 July 1099

Mount of Olives

Heat shimmered above the bleached, stony ground.

Godefroi de Bouillon, Duke of Lower Lorraine, paused in his march up the steep slope of the Mount of Olives. Sweat soaked his linen undergarments and the padded tunic beneath his hauberk. His blond head, uncovered as a mark of humility, felt like it was slowly boiling. Dust coated his lips and the pebbles that turned underfoot scorched the bare soles of his feet.

Long lines of fellow pilgrims struggled uphill. Urged on by the clergy, thousands of voices were raised in prayer in dozens of tongues; French, English, Flemish, Frisian and many others he did not recognise.

They were like the Tower of Babel collapsing to earth, thought Godefroi. The drums and taunts of the Saracen garrison inside Jerusalem had fallen behind them on the far side of the valley.

Godefroi cleared the dust from his throat. "No wonder the Saracens are so fond of their robes and turbans. I swear I'm slowly roasting."

"Take some water, messire." Achambaud de St Amand, his dark-haired bodyguard, offered him a flask. Sweat trickled down the olive skin of Achambaud's face and into his neatly trimmed beard, but he paid it no heed. Hugues de Payens, Godefroi's personal chaplain, wiped sweat from his tonsured skull. Even though his beardless face was bright red from the heat, his expression was fierce, almost exultant. The rest of Godefroi's escort stopped at a respectful distance. Groups of pilgrims trudged past them. Each knot followed a priest clutching a reliquary or ornamental cross.

"Thank you." The water was warm and tasted of leather. Godefroi was grateful for it, nonetheless. He was painfully aware of how scarce water had become since the Saracens poisoned the wells outside the walls. Only the pool of Siloam remained uncontaminated, although it lay within bowshot of the gate. So far thirst had claimed the most casualties during this siege.

Godefroi gazed at the city of Jerusalem on the far side of the Kidron Valley. Sunlight gleamed across the gilded domes of mosques and blazed across the tempered bronze that reinforced the inner citadel known as the Tower of David. His pulse quickened at the sight.

"The navel of the world," Godefroi murmured. "After imagining it for so long, it feels like a dream to finally gaze upon it."

Hugues made the sign of the cross. "Soon, if God wills it, we'll get a much closer look."

Godefroi's gaze shifted beyond the walls. The besieging Christian army was divided into two opposing camps. To the north-west of Jerusalem, the tents of his encampment dotted the plain. South of the Sion Gate, the Provençals had established their smaller camp under the banner of Count Raymond de Toulouse.

Godefroi sprinkled water into his palm and rubbed his neck. "After the debacle at Arqa, Raymond will be desperate to reach the Holy Sepulchre first."

"True," Hugues agreed, "although the approach to the Sion Gate is narrow and heavily defended. You'll enjoy more success against the northern wall."

Achambaud nodded, his long black hair framing his lean face. "Especially if Etienne's plan with the siege tower works."

Godefroi waved their speculations aside. "The city's already ours. It was the moment we set out from Lorraine. What is still to be decided is *who* takes it." He squinted uphill. Three separate columns of pilgrims converged upon the summit.

A motley assortment of poor folk followed the ragged figure of Peter the Hermit up the steepest incline. The Tafurs, wild zealots dressed in little more than rags, followed close on Peter's heels. They leapt and brandished their weapons in frenzied excitement. Godefroi's shoulders tensed at the sight. The Tafurs had stooped to cannibalism outside the walls of Antioch. They were like rabid dogs; ferocious in battle but not to be trusted.

A large, gilded cross swayed at the head of Godefroi's column. Arnulf de Chocques, chaplain to the Duke of Normandy, strode next to it. Bible in hand, Arnulf recited psalms that were repeated down the procession.

The third and final column was led by Raymond's pet clergy. The Count's tall figure was not hard to locate. He followed the priests a few yards back, surrounded by his personal guard. Raymond's mail glinted in the harsh sunlight. He had chosen a white tabard with a red cross stitched above his heart.

Godefroi ground his teeth. He would worry about Raymond once the city had fallen.

His attention shifted back to the distant walls of Jerusalem. The barrage of burning dung from the trebuchets had ceased when they moved out of range.

"Godefroi?" Hugues called him back to the present.

"What?"

"Did you hear what I said?" Hugues' forehead was creased with concern.

"Forgive me. I was wondering how we must seem to our enemies."

Hugues raised his eyebrows. "Formidable, I hope."

Godefroi's expression became grim. "Courage can be born from desperation."

"Which brings me back to my original point." Hugues threaded his fingers together as he always did when he was about to preach. "You can't claim the Holy Sepulchre if you die leading the first charge."

Godefroi frowned and lowered his voice. "The Salt Lines chose me to recover the holy places. Now that Jerusalem is within our grasp, you can hardly expect me to leave it to others." He shrugged his heavy shoulders. "Besides, *fortis fortuna adiuvat*."

"Fortune may indeed favour the bold," Hugues replied, "but let's not put it to the test. I beg you: choose a contingent of chevaliers to take the wall. Any one of them would kill for the honour. Don't risk years of planning in a fit of pride."

Godefroi's frown deepened into a scowl. "Leading by example is not pride."

Hugues waited for another party of pilgrims to overtake them. "If you fall, Raymond will claim the city. None of the other princes are strong enough to resist him. He'll appoint a Patriarch and the holy places will be closed to the Salt Lines forever. You know what a catastrophe that would be."

"I won't fall," Godefroi replied. "My fate has already been charted in the stars."

"Messire," Achambaud interrupted, "please listen to Hugues. In the days that follow the city's capture, people will remember that it was you who obeyed the Pope's command to seize the Holy Sepulchre for all of Christendom."

Godefroi rubbed his beard in irritation. "It bodes ill for me when the guardians of my spirit and my flesh agree. Very well, I won't join the vanguard. But we three *shall* be the first to enter the site of Christ's resurrection."

Hugues shook his head. "No. There must be five of us. Always there must be five."

<hr />

Five days after the ceremony on the Mount of Olives, Hugues woke in the small hours before dawn. Despite the merciless sun that bore down by day, the cloudless nights were surprisingly cold.

He rolled out of his woollen blanket and adjusted his habit. Careful not to disturb his sleeping brethren, he slipped out of the tent.

The night was still. Small pinpricks of light winked down from the vault of heaven. He pulled on his worn shoes and went in search of the one man he knew would already be awake, apart from the sentries guarding their camp.

His quarry was not hard to locate. A tall figure, already dressed in chain mail with an anonymous surcoat of grey, stood on a slight rise just outside their camp.

Hugues joined Godefroi in companionable silence. Watch fires twinkled along the northern wall of Jerusalem, but the city was cloaked in darkness. Further to the south and west, the campfires of Count Raymond's forces were a distant glow.

"Many faithful Christians will die in the days ahead." Hugues addressed his comment to the city.

"As have many already." Godefroi's gaze remained fixed on the wall. No doubt he was picturing the siege as it unfolded. Somewhere in the darkness, near the centre of the city, lay the Church of the Holy Sepulchre.

A breeze ruffled Hugues' cassock. In the distance, horses whickered. The world turned, yet the stillness between the two men was a fixed point.

"It would be best if you didn't number amongst them," Hugues said eventually.

Godefroi turned towards him, amusement and irritation warring across his features. Tall and fair, his blond hair was cropped short. His beard hadn't been trimmed for some time, lending him the look of a fierce Norseman. Summer blue eyes softened his otherwise hard face. Heavy-set, broad of shoulder and thick of limb, Godefroi commanded a physical presence few men could match.

"Haven't we had this conversation already?" Godefroi asked. "Halfway up the Mount of Olives, as I recall."

"We did, yet Achambaud tells me you still plan to lead the assault."

"My bodyguard should learn to keep his lord's counsel."

"Be that as it may, I thought we had reached an understanding." Hugues held his breath. Godefroi had little patience for being corrected.

"I must lead if we're to counter Raymond's claims to the city." Irritation pinched Godefroi's face. "I shouldn't have to explain this to *you* of all people."

Hugues rubbed his hands together for warmth. "Be that as it may, all our plans will fail if you die making a pointless gesture."

"It's not pointless," Godefroi growled. "One decisive victory is all Raymond needs to regain his prestige. *I* must be first inside the city. *I* must take the Holy Sepulchre. You said as much only days ago."

Hugues turned towards Godefroi. "Jerusalem is merely a step towards our goal. An essential one, yes, but we lose the path entirely if you die."

"I haven't come all this way for that."

"Not all can be foretold or anticipated, Godefroi. Pride is the first step before a fall. Complacency is the second."

Godefroi stabbed a finger at Hugues. "Men fight better when their prince leads them. And a quick victory means Christian lives spared. That's not pride, it's compassion."

Hugues tucked his hands into the sleeves of his habit. "At least promise not to be in the first wave. Make it seem like you're bestowing the honour upon your bravest chevaliers."

Godefroi folded his arms across his broad chest. "I promise nothing other than to consider what you've said."

Hugues plucked at the rough wool of his sleeves. "Godefroi, you can't do this alone. Regardless of what some seer predicted when you were born. There are five sacred points, each bound to the other. If one fails, all do."

Godefroi gave him a cool, appraising look. "We may be bound, you and I, but I will not be dictated to. Not by you, or those who stand behind you."

Hugues stiffened. Given Godefroi's mood, any response would be a mistake. Instead, he nodded and left Godefroi to his contemplation of the city.

The camp was stirring when he returned. Perhaps Godefroi was right. A quick victory *would* save lives, but was that worth risking the mission the Salt Lines had entrusted to them? Hugues chewed the inside of his lip. He could lose days debating the dilemma.

Instead, he went in search of Achambaud. Godefroi might heed a fellow warrior.

The argument with Hugues weighed on Godefroi's mind long after his chaplain had departed. What he needed was a solution that would save lives *and* gain him entry into Jerusalem before Raymond. Winning the city was one thing, holding it was another.

All of his hopes rested with two men.

Godefroi strode down the rise towards his camp. The sun rode the sky behind his right shoulder. The hills to the north shimmered in the growing heat. The sirocco, the hot wind that sometimes blew from the deserts of the Sahara, snapped at the pennants of his nobles. Acrid smoke from cooking fires twisted and scattered before it.

A large wooden tower dominated the tents and banners. It was twenty yards high and rested on four large, wooden wheels. Carpenters and craftsmen already swarmed around its base, applying finishing touches. The bulk of the activity was centred on attaching thick animal hides and wattle screens to protect against hurled fire.

A small circle of inactivity followed Godefroi's progress. A youth ran ahead, no doubt to warn the engineers of his approach. He strode around to the back of the siege tower.

The bottom section of the tower had been left open and there was no floor, save for a shelf at the front that was two yards deep. Ceramic jars and wineskins had been stacked on this footboard. Two sturdy ladders led to the upper levels.

A pair of men descended the left-hand ladder as Godefroi studied the tower.

Gaston de Bearn was a tall man, overtopping Godefroi by half a head. He was lean for a chevalier with light brown hair and a perpetual frown. The nobleman had been in Raymond's service until the disastrous siege at Arqa had seen him fall out of favour.

Etienne de Champagne trailed Gaston as a servant might follow his master. Dressed in the brown tunic and leggings of a lay brother, he reminded Godefroi of a bird with his curly black hair, long neck and expressive dark eyes. His manner was self-effacing to the point of invisibility. If Hugues hadn't recommended Etienne, Godefroi would never have assumed the man knew anything about weapons of war.

"Is the tower ready?" Godefroi demanded.

"Almost, messire," Gaston replied. "It will be finished by nightfall, as promised."

"Good. What of Raymond's tower? I hear it nears completion as well."

Gaston grimaced. "So, I believe. The Genoese engineer he employed is gifted. Their tower rivals ours in size, if not design."

Godefroi frowned. "Meaning our design is superior. How so?"

"When constructing a rolling tower," Gaston replied, "one must balance the need for durability against manoeuvrability. The stronger the structure, the heavier it is and hence harder to direct." Gaston glanced at Etienne, who stood to one side, head cocked as he listened. "Etienne here has had some quite innovative ideas for improving both."

"Show me."

Gaston gave an order to open some of the screens before ushering Godefroi inside. Etienne trailed after them.

"Do you see these bars attached to the three walls?" Gaston pointed out iron beams jutting from the side of the tower. The thick iron bars were about chest height.

"I assume these are for pushing the tower forward," Godefroi said.

"Correct. However, they serve a second purpose." Gaston rotated the nearest bar and pulled it inwards. It thudded into place, now about a forearm longer. He leaned on the end with all of his weight. The wooden frame beneath the bar shifted a fraction, allowing in a glimmer of sunlight. Gaston released the bar and the chink of light disappeared as the frame settled back into place.

"I don't understand." Godefroi looked to the two men for an explanation.

"Etienne has placed levers throughout the tower so that each storey can be prised from the one beneath. Once raised off the—" Gaston turned to Etienne. "What did you call them?"

"Locking pins," Etienne murmured.

Gaston turned back to Godefroi. "Having levered each storey off its locking pins, the entire tower can be disassembled, portaged across the ground, and reassembled at will. In all my years of campaigning, I've never seen such a thing."

Godefroi rubbed his bearded chin. "Do you mean to tell me we can move this tower to a new position?"

"Within reason, messire." Etienne directed his reply at the ground.

Godefroi turned to Etienne. "How long would it take?"

"With sufficient men and favourable terrain?" Etienne considered for a moment. "The tower could be moved from here to a point east of the Gate of St Stephen overnight." He glanced up at Godefroi. "If it pleases you."

A slow smile spread across Godefroi's bearded face. "So instead of attacking the Quadrangular Tower, we can approach the wall at its lowest point. The Saracens will concentrate their defences in the wrong place. By the time they realise their mistake, it will be too late. Can you imagine their shock?" He laughed in delight.

Etienne's face shone.

"There's more, messire." Gaston gestured outside.

Godefroi raised his palm. "A moment, Gaston. Etienne, how many chevaliers can the tower support?"

"The upper landing can accommodate a score, although I'd caution against attempting more. The tower is already very heavy. I couldn't afford to reinforce the floor as well."

"I'll need more troops than that to take the wall."

"Yes, messire." Etienne gestured outside. "Perhaps I could demonstrate?"

"Lead on."

Etienne escorted them to the front of the tower. "Do you see the shutters on the second and third landings?" He pointed to the wattle screens Godefroi had noticed earlier. "They're designed to swing inwards, allowing crossbowmen to target enemy archers. The shutters will swing back while reloading, thus protecting against counterattack."

"Archers can't storm walls," Gaston muttered.

"Agreed," Etienne replied, "but they *can* hamper Saracens on the wall."

Godefroi chewed the inside of his lip. "I'll still need at least two score chevaliers to take the parapet and force the gate open."

Etienne nodded. "Once the tower is secured against the wall, reinforcements can climb the ladders within the tower. I've also placed a number of looped ropes on the upper landing, which can be thrown over the battlements to allow your men to haul the tower even closer. As an added measure, the wattle screen at the very top has been strengthened. Once your men are close enough to the wall, it can be dropped to form a bridge between tower and parapet."

"Like a drawbridge." Godefroi stared at the top of the tower. "We could rush across en masse."

"Exactly, messire." Etienne shifted on his feet. "I have one further proposal."

"We've been through this," Gaston said with a quelling gesture. "The risk is too great."

"Let him speak," Godefroi commanded.

Etienne clasped his hands together. "The Saracens will attempt to destroy the tower before it can reach the wall. Compounding the problem is the ground rises against us as we near the wall. The tower will make a large and slow-moving target for catapults and Greek fire."

"And we have little water to waste on dousing flames," Godefroi added.

Etienne nodded. "Better to evade Saracen rocks and fire by approaching in haste."

Gaston shook his head, his lips pressed together.

"How is that possible when pushing the tower uphill?" Godefroi asked.

Etienne turned towards the Gate of St Stephen. "Do you see that low rise east of the gate?"

Godefroi squinted against the rising sun. "What of it?"

"If we reassembled the tower on its summit, the tower should roll in a straight line, gathering speed. Provided it remains on course, it might reach the main wall without stopping. Even if it didn't, the Saracens won't be able to adjust their catapults in time."

Godefroi considered Etienne's proposal. "A bold idea fraught with risk. The tower could topple. The wheels might collapse. If the tower falls, Raymond will seize the city while my men rattle the gates and die beneath Saracen arrows."

"Exactly, as I have said on numerous occasions." Gaston glared at Etienne.

Etienne bowed his head. "As you say. Yet a slow march uphill will be met with stones and fire the whole way. I can't promise the tower will endure such punishment."

"We'll still have the advantage of surprise," Gaston countered.

"True, although I believe it will be short-lived." Etienne addressed Godefroi. "You asked for a strategy that would give you the city at the cost of the fewest lives. This is the best solution I've been able to devise."

Godefroi sucked his teeth in thought. Etienne's proposal was dangerous, a calculated gamble at best. He scrutinised the two men. Gaston shook his head. Etienne's face held a fierce confidence at odds with his earlier timidity. Hugues had vouched for Etienne, which counted for much. And yet the entire outcome of the siege might rest upon this decision. Was saving lives worth the risk of failure?

There could only be one answer.

"Etienne, make sure the wheels are reinforced with iron. And clear any obstacles along the tower's path during the night." Godefroi stabbed a finger at the engineer. "Since this is your plan, you must eliminate every possible way it can fail. Understood?"

"Yes, messire." Etienne bowed low. "I won't fail you."

"Gaston, you'll oversee the diversion before the Quadrangular Tower. Spare as many lives as you can whilst still being convincing."

"As you command." Gaston sketched a bow, disapproval etched

into the lines pulling at the corners of his mouth.

Godefroi, you can't do this alone.

While Hugues might be right, he did not have to like it.

Biting down on his frustration, Godefroi went in search of breakfast.

CHAPTER 6

13 July 1099

Outside Jerusalem

Just over five thousand fighting men, and almost as many camp followers, had assembled to hear Godefroi speak. The sea of faces rippled in the heat of the mid-morning sun. Hugues probed his dry mouth with his tongue. It was a trick he had learned from his early days in the monastery, a way of keeping the body active when it had to remain still during long ceremonies. He had seen grown men faint during the mild summers of Payens and that was nothing next to the heat of the Holy Land.

Godefroi emerged from his tent and strode to the top of a low, wooden dais. He had changed from the dull fighting armour he had worn in the morning to a burnished coat of mail that glinted in the sun. His surcoat was black with a white cross that ran from neck to crotch.

Achambaud stopped at the foot of the dais. His dark eyes flickered across the crowd, searching for possible threats. Not as tall as Godefroi, Achambaud was almost as broad but darker of skin. His black hair was unusually long for a chevalier, cut just above the shoulder. A neat beard followed the curve of his jaw. Achambaud's hauberk was made from dark rings of iron and his tabard was black, relieved only by a small red cross above his heart.

The remaining nobles who had aligned with Godefroi stood on the left side of the dais. Key members of the clergy, including Hugues, had gathered on the other side. The message was clear; the temporal and spiritual leaders were united behind Godefroi.

"Good folk of Lorraine and fellow Christians," Godefroi called out in a voice that carried. "I know that you have all suffered. Many have succumbed during our great journey to reclaim the holy places. But now, at long last, the fulfilment of our vows is within reach!" He gestured towards the distant walls of Jerusalem. A hoarse cheer rolled across the gathering.

"We have fasted. We have prayed. We have honoured those pilgrims that preceded us by marching barefoot around the walls of Jerusalem. Cleansed before God, we are now ready to enter His most holy city." The approval was stronger this time. Dust ballooned as the crowd stamped their feet.

"The final steps we take tomorrow will be our hardest yet. Many of us will surrender our lives unto God's care. However, know that whoever falls will be honoured in heaven as martyrs. For we are about God's work." Godefroi spread his arms wide. "His representative on earth, his Holiness the Bishop of Rome, has blessed our cause. How can we not succeed?"

A resounding roar greeted Godefroi's words. Many faces in the crowd turned to the heavens. The people began to chant "Deus vult." *God wills it.*

Hugues kept his expression blank. While the masses believed they were serving God, the astute understood that Pope Urban wanted a Latin Patriarch sitting upon the throne of the Jerusalem See. No doubt the Eastern Churches would protest, although victory here would reinforce the Pope's claim of being the preeminent representative of God in all of Christendom.

No, the only holy quest being pursued was a secret one, known to but a few.

"Arnulf de Chocques, will you lead us in prayer?" Godefroi asked.

The attention of the crowd shifted to Arnulf, Chaplain to Robert of Normandy, one of the princes who supported Godefroi.

Arnulf mounted the dais with exaggerated gravity. Sweat beaded his broad face and trickled down his thick neck. Hugues noticed his hands trembled as he clutched his Bible.

"Brothers and sisters, let us pray."

A wave of hats rolled across the ocean of heads and dropped beneath the swell.

"Our Father," Arnulf began, "who art in Heaven, protect Thy children who have sworn to serve the cross, who fight in Thy name, and that of Thy Holy Son."

After all the planning, all the agitating for this pilgrimage, the whispered conversations and coin that had changed hands, they finally stood upon the threshold of victory. An unexpected chill swept through Hugues.

"We beseech Thee to embrace those lost fighting to recover Thy most holy city."

The tip of a thousand quills pressed against Hugues' skin. His chest tightened and he felt…

"Our lives are in Thy hands, our souls indebted to our Saviour, our souls beholden to the Holy Spirit."

…like he had stood here before. Listened to this sermon. Sweated beneath this sun.

"Look down upon our toil and suffering o'merciful Lord," Arnulf continued, "and have pity, as Thou didst upon Thy Son. For Thine is the Kingdom, and the Power, and the Glory evermore. Amen." Arnulf made the sign of the cross and blessed the entire gathering.

The crowd replied, "Amen."

Hugues' stomach muscles knotted. His throat tightened until it became hard to breathe. The ground trembled beneath God's scrutiny. Hugues glanced at his brethren. None of the other clergy seemed to notice.

This reaction, this *acknowledgement*, was for him alone then.

Somehow the city, or the ancient land beneath it, was aware of why he had come, of the claim he hoped to stake. He flinched at the recognition.

Godefroi returned to the dais. "Well done," he murmured as Arnulf made way. A pleased grin split Arnulf's coarse features.

The strange sensations lifted as suddenly as they had arrived. Hugues felt like a wine skin emptied of its contents. His legs trembled and he remained upright only through sheer force of will.

Godefroi's voice soared over the crowd. "Tomorrow, we'll stand upon those battlements." He flung an arm at the high wall encircling Jerusalem. "Together, we'll take back what belongs to all humble Christians. And we will avenge those pilgrims who were slaughtered on their way to the holy places."

The elation of the crowd changed to a dark muttering. Men gripped their weapons. Camp followers clutched at their loved ones. Devotion devolved into the ugly threat of violence in a matter of heartbeats.

"Good folk of Lorraine and fellow Christians," Godefroi called. "No matter what the days ahead bring, your deeds will echo through the halls of history. God be with you."

"And with you," the crowd responded.

Godefroi stepped down. "May God forgive me for those who never live to pray at the Holy Sepulchre." He scowled at Hugues as he marched towards his tent. Achambaud gave Hugues a brief nod before following Godefroi.

Let Godefroi think they were ready. Hugues knew a final task remained.

CHAPTER 7

14 July 1099

Outside Jerusalem

Achambaud leaned against one of the timber poles supporting Godefroi's tent. The council of princes had ended, and the weary nobles had retired for the night. Only Baldwin de Bouillon, Godefroi's younger brother, remained along with Godefroi, Hugues and Gaston.

"I don't care what you think you deserve." Godefroi stabbed a finger at Baldwin. "You're not entering the siege tower until we've secured the parapet." Old sweat had stained the collar of Godefroi's linen undertunic. His black *bliaut* had faded badly throughout their travels and showed signs of much repair.

"There's no honour in waiting for others to clear a path for you." Baldwin's cold, blue-eyed gaze did not waver in the face of Godefroi's anger. Dark of hair and slighter in build than his older brother, he wore a grey *bliaut* with gold thread stitched through the sleeves and hem. A leather *ceinture*, also chased in gold, cinched his waist.

"This isn't about *honour*," Godefroi protested.

"It is for you."

The fair skin above Godefroi's beard flushed with anger. "Have you forgotten how much I've sacrificed to fund this campaign? The Church holds the titles to all my estates."

"I forget nothing," Baldwin replied in a cool voice. "What *I* remember is being offered the chance to claim an inheritance in the Holy Land. Instead, I find that I'm prevented at every turn. If you wanted to render me irrelevant Godefroi, why didn't you just leave me in Lorraine?"

While Achambaud was wary of Baldwin, he understood the younger man's complaint. He knew only too well the limited prospects of a youngest son. After all, how many times had his father locked him in the musty, unlit cellar of their castle? Too many to count. Yet it was in that darkness Achambaud had learned to touch the awareness of a passing hound or a horse champing at the bit. He had even discovered the superstitious, fearful places behind people's eyes were not beyond his reach. That was why he always wore black. The darkness was a comfort, a place where he belonged.

"Holding the County of Edessa is vital in maintaining the road to Constantinople." The flush of anger had spread to Godefroi's neck. "Why are you never content?"

Achambaud glanced at Hugues. The Chaplain's head was bowed and the bare skin above his tonsure glistened in the candlelight. It seemed he was either deep in thought or prayer, although Achambaud suspected he was listening closely. The rigours of the journey had hollowed out Hugues' features. Since yesterday's sermon from Arnulf, Hugues had become withdrawn and introspective. Surely, he did not begrudge Arnulf for leading the prayer?

"So, you'll accept the largesse of my new county," Baldwin said, "but not allow me to share in the glory of taking Jerusalem. Is that the way of it?" Baldwin pushed away from the table in disgust.

Hugues lifted his head with obvious weariness. Dark circles ringed his brown eyes. "Baldwin, you know very well that whatever food Edessa supplies today will be rewarded a hundred-fold in years to come. Our position in the Holy Land is precarious. If Baghdad and Cairo ever settle their differences, none of us will survive. So, you must live to hold Edessa while we tame Jerusalem."

"Your concern for my person is heart-warming," Baldwin replied. "But I do find it strange that one of the clergy is advising me not to fulfil my sacred vow."

Hugues gave Baldwin a knowing look. "And I find your sudden devotion out of character. Nevertheless, you'll get your chance to pray alongside us at the Holy Sepulchre."

"Enough." The table shuddered beneath Godefroi's fist. "Baldwin, you'll direct our forces into the tower. You will *not* mount the wall until the parapet is taken. No, don't argue with me. Etienne tells me the floor won't support more than twenty at a time anyway. You'll just have to wait your turn. There'll be enough spoils inside the city to satisfy even you."

Baldwin pressed his lips together, wisely choosing not to argue any further.

Godefroi addressed Gaston. "Are you convinced the Saracens have been deceived by our diversion?"

"I believe so, messire." Like Achambaud, Gaston did not hold sufficient rank to earn a seat at Godefroi's table. "The Saracens concentrated their forces at the Quadrangular Tower, as expected. Their archers slew many of the Tafurs who helped to fill the outer ditch. Enough to convince them of our intentions."

Godefroi grimaced. The mounds of bodies littering the approach to the north-western wall were visible to any who cared to look.

"We'll fill the ditch between the Gate of St Stephen and the Gate of Flowers overnight," Gaston continued. "God willing, the Saracens won't expect a second bridge of stones."

"Good." Godefroi leaned an elbow on the table and cupped his chin. "Achambaud, how is Etienne progressing?"

Achambaud reluctantly stepped into the light of the lanterns. "Disassembly of the tower commenced as soon as the sun set, messire."

"Does Etienne have sufficient men to conduct the portage?"

"He believes so, although progress is difficult in the dark. Etienne remains confident the tower will be in its new position by dawn."

"So much rests upon his efforts." Godefroi shot a sharp look at Hugues.

"Have faith," Hugues murmured.

"Messire," Gaston said, "with your permission, I'll oversee his efforts."

"Go." Godefroi waved him out and turned back to the table. "Count Raymond's tower is also in position. I've heard the Saracen Governor was sighted directing the defences before the Sion Gate. If that's true, then Raymond's troops will face stiffer opposition than ours. We've reason for optimism."

"*You* have reason for optimism." Baldwin stood. "The rest of us must clutch at your stirrups in the hope of keeping up." He stalked out of the tent.

"Another reason to be careful," Hugues said in a soft voice. "If you fall Godefroi, Baldwin can't be trusted with our mission. The Salt Lines won't allow it."

Godefroi leaned back in his chair, which creaked dangerously. "I couldn't disagree with them in all honesty." He ran a calloused hand across his face. "I'm weary. Leave me to rest."

"There's one other matter we must attend to first." Hugues strode to the back of the tent, lifted the canvas, and called out in a low voice. Moments later, a hooded figure crawled through the gap. Achambaud gripped the hilt of his dagger. The stranger was lightly built and shorter than Hugues, and the cowl of his black habit concealed his face.

"What's this?" Godefroi demanded.

Hugues led the stranger to the table. "Godefroi, I told you there were five sacred points. Three are known to you and stand in this room.

The fourth is Etienne and this is the fifth. His name is Gondemar."

Godefroi rose from his chair. "I don't understand."

Hugues gestured to the stranger. "All five of us must be present when we enter the Holy Sepulchre. Otherwise, the way will remain closed." Hugues knelt before the lay brother. "In front of your peers, I beg forgiveness for how I've treated you."

Gondemar placed a hand on Hugues' head. Even for a member of the clergy, his skin was soft and pale. "There's nothing to forgive." Gondemar's voice was high for a man.

Hugues looked up at Gondemar. "Thank you, yet I fear you're being too charitable."

"What are you two talking about? Show your face," Godefroi demanded.

"You already know me, Godefroi." Gondemar drew back his cowl to reveal a thin, beardless face with brown eyes framed by dark lashes. Long braids of brown hair had been wrapped into a tight bun.

Godefroi took a step back in astonishment. "Godwera?" he whispered. "But...you're dead. Baldwin...he said—" Godefroi shivered. "This is a dream."

"No, Godefroi." Godwera shook her head.

He took a step forward and tried to touch her face. Godwera intercepted his hand and pressed his knuckles to her lips.

"I did die," she said. "Just not in the way that you think."

Achambaud concealed his shock. Godwera—Baldwin's wife—was supposed to have died of a fever after they left Constantinople. Hugues must have concealed her all this time.

"But how? We all thought you dead." The timbre of Godefroi's voice was rough with emotion.

"The Godwera you knew is gone. Now you have need of Gondemar, and that is who I've become. Don't speak the name of Godwera again, for she must remain buried."

She appeared thinner than Achambaud remembered. The gauntness of her face emphasised her lips, which had so often been pressed in a thin line of distaste in Baldwin's company.

"I don't understand," Godefroi said. "Have you been part of the Salt Lines all this time? Does my brother know?"

"He doesn't, nor must he ever." Fear flashed across her face at the mention of Baldwin.

Hugues intervened. "The Salt Lines arranged for Godwera to marry your brother, Godefroi. It was all planned long ago."

"But why?" Godefroi sank back into his chair. His troubled gaze flicked between Hugues and Godwera, perhaps trying to decide who was more responsible for deceiving him.

"It was the safest way to bring her to Jerusalem," Hugues replied. "And as your chaplain, none would question why I spent so much time with a monk. Although I fear our plan has caused more anguish than it should have."

"Please." Godwera held up her palm. "Let's not speak of it again. I've endured the marriage and moved beyond him, as he clearly has of me."

"*You* asked her to marry Baldwin so she would come to the Holy Land?" Godefroi's tone turned the question into an accusation.

Hugues shook his head. "Not personally, although I agreed the decision made sense."

"I see." Godefroi's expression remained hard. "And what need have we of a woman in battle?"

"Taking the city is only the first step," Hugues replied. "I've no doubt other trials will follow. Not every test can be overcome with a sword."

Godefroi's eyes narrowed. "You don't know what to expect, do you?"

"I know that what we seek is well hidden." Hugues spread his hands. "Only the five sacred points may tread the path of righteousness. We'll fail without Godwera. That much is certain."

"More evasions and vague claims." Godefroi pointed to the entrance. "Out. All of you. I wish to speak with my...sister-in-law. In private." Hugues made a noise of protest, but the look Godefroi directed at him was so fierce it brooked no argument.

As Achambaud left the tent, he saw Godefroi take Godwera's hand and murmur something to her. She listened attentively, her expression stiff and polite. To Achambaud's eye, she resembled a cornered deer.

CHAPTER 8

13 October 1307

The Commanderie

Roustan's charger shifted impatiently beneath him as he scowled at the closed, iron-bound gate of the Commanderie. A score of the King's Guard, each mounted and heavily armed, waited on the muddy road behind him. The jingle of tack punctuated the stillness of the dawn.

Mist hovered over the fields that surrounded the Commanderie. Trees jutted from the fog, their bare branches resembling agonised fingers clutching at the sky. The coming day would be overcast and foreboding. Roustan grinned. How appropriate.

The soldiers nearest to him shifted uncomfortably in their saddles. On the far side of the wall, the chapel bell tolled in the distance. The deep, reverberating sound sent a prickle of anticipation down Roustan's spine.

"You heard the call to Matins," Roustan said to the soldiers. "The brothers will be too busy with their devotions to open the gates." His observation drew a ripple of tense laughter.

"Captain, send your most agile man over the wall."

The captain of the King's garrison in Troyes hurried to obey. Roustan paid no attention. The guards were a necessary encumbrance. Later, if all went according to plan, they would become inconvenient witnesses. Why bother courting the respect of men who were as good as dead?

Roustan licked his upper lip. After searching for *her* for so long, it was excruciating to be this close. She was inside this pathetic little Commanderie. He knew that beyond any doubt. A skilled hunter always knows when its prey is within striking distance. Roustan felt the end of the chase in his gut, and he craved the release that it offered.

"What's taking so long?" Roustan snapped. Sensing its master's mood, his charger stamped its hooves.

"Guerin has just topped the wall, sir. See." The captain pointed.

Roustan wheeled his horse around with a savage jerk of the reins. A wiry soldier was indeed clambering over the lip of the wall.

Guerin dropped out of sight on the far side. Moments later a chain rattled. No cry of alarm or challenge greeted the noise.

This Commanderie was not even defended properly. Perhaps she thought anonymity might prove a more effective defence than seeking sanctuary in one of the Templars' great castles. If so, then she had badly underestimated the network of informants available to his master, Guillaume de Nogaret, Keeper of the Seals and the true power behind the French throne.

A bolt was drawn inside the gate. A second and third followed. The scrape of metal on stone, the press of eager soldiers, and the rapid pulse in his throat summoned memories of Guillaume's dungeon. He remembered...

...the horrified expression on his mother's face as Roustan bolted the door of her cell...Guillaume insisting that Roustan remain just outside the door, even when his mother's pleading turned to screams when she discovered that she was not alone. Meeting Guillaume's questioning gaze without flinching... earning the silent nod of approval...and God save his soul...the flush of pleasure at being acknowledged thus.

Roustan shivered in his saddle. Whatever sins he had committed had all been justified. Guillaume trusted him now and had even shared his plans with Roustan. Plans that would finally break the shackles the Papacy had wrapped around France.

Roustan fought down the sick feeling rising from the pit of his stomach. He was no longer the reviled son of a lowly merchant but the instrument of a king. A price had to be paid for such elevation, did it not?

The heavy timber gate groaned as it swung open. Roustan urged his charger through the gap. Guerin grinned at Roustan in triumph, perhaps expecting a word of praise. Roustan was tempted to kick the fellow in the teeth but refrained. He needed the soldiers' undivided support for what lay ahead.

After a short canter, Roustan and the column of guards entered the Commanderie's tight cluster of buildings. The courtyard was empty. No doubt the brothers were crowded inside their ugly little chapel.

"Set guards at each door of the chapel," Roustan told the captain. "No one enters until I'm ready. Search the remaining buildings. Bring anyone found to me. Use whatever force is necessary, although make sure they can still be questioned. Understood?"

The captain nodded and hurried off. Guards dressed in the tabards of the Capetian kings of France—gold *fleur-de-lis* on a field of royal blue—spread out through the courtyard.

Roustan dismounted and threw his reins to one of the soldiers acting as his bodyguard. This was a small Commanderie by Templar standards. Where would she hide? He stroked his beard in thought. The Preceptor's Lodge was the most likely place. After all, where else would you hide a woman amongst men who were sworn to celibacy?

Roustan sized up the building. The high, narrow windows resembled arrow slits. As for the main door, the heavy oak timbers were bound in iron. He did not doubt that it was well secured.

The captain strode over to Roustan. "No sign of anyone in the stables or the refectory. I'm just waiting for a report from the dormitory."

"What about the chapter house and cellar?" He couldn't afford any mistakes. Not now, with her finally in his grasp.

"The chapter house is connected to the chapel, so we didn't enter as you ordered."

"And the cellar?"

"Locked." The captain frowned. "From the inside, apparently."

Roustan stilled. "Are you sure?"

"I'll check."

Another guard raced over to report. "The dormitory is empty, sir."

Warning prickled the back of Roustan's neck. Something was wrong. Their arrival should have been noted by now. This determined silence felt deliberate.

"Leave a pair of guards outside the cellar," Roustan ordered. "Deploy the rest of your men at each entrance to the chapel. We'll enter via the chapter house."

The guards hurried into position. She was slipping away somehow. He could feel it.

Roustan ground his teeth together in frustration. Guillaume's messenger had been adamant that she was here. Had she outmanoeuvred him again?

Roustan ordered the guards inside. The captain and his men burst into the chapter house. Roustan touched the scroll case hanging from his belt for reassurance and drew his sword. A wail of protest erupted from inside the chapel. Something crashed onto the tiles. Men shouted in alarm. Roustan raced up the short flight of steps, strode across the muddy tiles of the chapter house and entered the chapel.

The King's Guard had forced the congregation back into a loose semi-circle about the altar. "What do you think you're doing?" a serving brother cried out.

An older priest pointed an accusing finger at the guards. "How dare you invade this house of God?"

The majority of the brethren stood in frightened silence. Roustan searched for the white cassocks of the chevaliers and found none. It was all the confirmation he needed.

She had slipped away with an escort.

Frustration boiled through Roustan. His knuckles cracked around the hilt of his sword. Yet another part of him silently applauded. Guillaume's best agents had been unable to catch her for almost a decade. She had eluded every snare and trap set for her. Why should now be any different?

Roustan exhaled slowly.

The truth was he wanted this chase to continue. Each near miss brought him one step closer. The gap was narrowing. He was certain of that. And each disappointment, each thwarted capture, would only sweeten his eventual triumph.

He moved into the centre of the chapel. The protests faltered and fell silent. Ignoring the brethren, Roustan grounded the tip of his sword and knelt on the tiles. Facing the altar, he made the sign of the cross and bowed his head.

Every eye was fixed upon him.

This was power. The fate of every single man in this chapel hung from the scroll that swung at his belt. Each breath they took was at his sufferance.

Roustan rose to his feet. Serving brothers and chaplains trembled beneath his stare. "Strip them," he ordered.

The captain motioned to his soldiers. One group levelled their spears while a second group seized the nearest brethren and tore off their clothes. Despite a fresh round of protests, the task was completed with brutal efficiency.

A sneer nestled in Roustan's mouth. He let the silence draw out, knowing that their leader would emerge eventually.

Never strike at a snake without knowing where its head lies.

Guillaume's words, yet Roustan had never truly understood their meaning until this moment.

An elderly priest emerged from the knot of terrified brothers. He was lean to the point of emaciation. Stringy muscles sagged from his protruding bones. The little hair that age and tonsure had left him was white like snow. Some of his brethren tried to hold him back but the old priest brushed them aside. Judging from the deference shown to him and the small iron cross that he held in one hand, this was probably their head chaplain.

Roustan cocked his head and waited. Someone in this room knew where she had gone. That someone was unlikely to be this pious old fool.

"By what right do you invade this house of God and treat His servants so roughly?" The old priest's rasping voice was even and unafraid.

Roustan gestured and his bodyguards allowed the chaplain to approach. Roustan unclipped the leather cylinder from his belt and withdrew its contents. He lifted the scroll that bore the King's seal over his head so that all could see it. "This is a warrant from Guillaume de Nogaret, Keeper of the Seals and chief adviser to King Philippe."

He pitched his voice so that it filled the nave. "It empowers me to place all assets and members of your Order in the custody of the King of France, as agent of Pope Clement, until such time as your leaders answer the charges of heresy levelled against them."

Murmurs of surprise swirled through the congregation. Their astonishment seemed genuine.

Roustan waited until the whispers died down. He offered the scroll to the priest with a flourish.

The chaplain ignored the gesture. "The King has no authority here. Our Order is only answerable to his Holiness."

Roustan had expected defiance and outrage, not disdain from a priest with one foot in the grave.

"His Majesty, long may he reign, is acting on behalf of Pope Clement in this matter." Roustan offered the scroll again with an impatient shake.

"Then such an order would've been delivered by members of the Inquisition, not by a lackey of Guillaume de Nogaret." The chaplain gazed at the soldiers that hemmed in his brethren. "I say again, you have no jurisdiction here. Leave us in peace or risk the Lord's wrath upon your immortal souls."

Fear flickered across the faces of the more pious guards. Roustan slid the scroll back into the leather cylinder and refastened it. "Twice you've refused to follow the instructions of your sovereign king, who is acting on behalf of the Holy See. You stand accused of heresy and your current actions only demonstrate the validity of this charge. I ask you a third time, will you yield to this warrant, validly enacted and served upon your Commanderie?"

"My son, we answer to God first, the Pope second, and to our conscience last." The priest closed his eyes, as if in pain. When he opened them again, he blessed Roustan with the iron cross. A calmness had settled over the chaplain, as if he *knew* what was about to happen and had accepted it. "I pray that one day you may come to realise the error of turning aside from that holy trinity, as will your masters."

The old priest had refused him three times. Any resistance had to be crushed, no matter how harmless it might appear. Roustan drew his knife, took a short step forward and thrust the blade up under the chaplain's ribcage.

The priest gasped and clutched at Roustan. The old fool's fingernails clawed at his chainmail. Someone cried out "Laurent"!

Blood bubbled from the old priest's mouth, robbing him of any final words. But Roustan had caught the shape of them: "I forgive you".

Bile rose up Roustan's gorge, which he quelled savagely. Yes, he had killed an old, unarmed priest. The chaplain probably didn't even know of her existence, but he had questioned Roustan's authority. Guillaume had taught him respect and fear were far more valuable tools than compassion.

Roustan ripped his dagger from the priest's chest and the body crumpled to the tiles. He spoke in a flat, inflectionless voice. "Your chaplain has gone to God now. Unfortunately, for all of you, you remain here. With me." Roustan pointed at the shocked brothers with his bloody knife. "So, who wants to tell me where your Preceptor has gone?"

The growing horror of their situation seemed to have struck all the prisoners dumb.

Roustan glanced about the chapel. "No one?" Tongues would loosen as the depth of their plight became apparent. However, if she was fleeing the Commanderie—and he did not doubt that she was—time was too valuable to waste.

He allowed a thread of reason to weave through his voice. "They did abandon you, after all. Left you here, undefended." Roustan spread his free hand in a gesture that invited them to explain. "Why show *them* any loyalty?"

A murmur passed through the gathering. The serving brothers glanced at each other in what appeared to be genuine confusion. Hidden among the ignorant was at least one dedicated to the cause of salt. While he might be a willing a martyr, would he allow his fellows to be slaughtered?

"I'm afraid I simply can't wait for you to decide. Captain, seize that one." Roustan pointed out a youth. He was probably too young to know anything of value and that made him expendable. The captain and a second guard seized the lad and dragged him, squealing with terror, in front of Roustan.

Roustan squatted in front of the kneeling youth and placed the flat of his knife against the boy's lips. "Quiet now."

The boy stilled with a whimper and a puddle of urine pooled on the tiles beneath him. "There now." Roustan wiped his dagger clean against the boy's tunic, rose to his feet and sheathed the blade. "I will show you what will happen to every one of you until someone tells me where your Preceptor has gone."

The captain tied a rope around the boy's wrist and drew it tight while the second guard held the youth in a headlock. The lad's outstretched arm trembled.

Once, when Roustan was very young, a group of older boys had tied him by the wrists and dragged him through the mud behind their plough horse. Even though it was a score of years in the past, the humiliation and helplessness of that moment still filled him with such rage that it became hard to breathe.

That was when he had learned there was no such thing as pity.

Roustan drew his sword and swung it in a smooth arc.

The boy's severed hand flopped to the floor and he screamed at a pitch Roustan hadn't believed possible. Dark blood spurted across the tiles. Many of the brothers turned as pale as the white habits of their missing chevaliers. Others were violently ill. The stench of urine, vomit and blood thickened the air.

The boy curled into a ball as he cradled the stump of his arm. Some of the braver brothers tried to reach him. The soldiers' spears forced them back.

"Who will speak?" Roustan's voice rang with power. He would have the truth, no matter what the price.

"We don't know where they've gone," someone cried.

"Captain, the other hand." Roustan raised his sword and resumed his position over the boy. The brethren cried out to God to protect them.

"Perhaps if your Order hadn't turned to heresy," Roustan shouted, "He might answer you. Instead, He sent me."

A shocked silence fell over the chapel. Roustan was panting. The beginning of an erection throbbed through his loins.

"Stop! I beg you in the name of all that's holy and sacred!'

Roustan turned with exaggerated slowness. "Show yourself."

One of the men reluctantly parted from his brethren. He was thin with an unkempt tonsure of grey hair. Watery blue eyes squinted at Roustan. This was no warrior. He had the look of a scribe.

"Thibauld," someone hissed.

"Please, no more," Thibauld pleaded.

"Speak," Roustan demanded. The captain looped the cord around the boy's remaining hand and drew it tight. Roustan raised his sword. A glaze of shock had set over the boy's ashen features. Roustan recognised that look from prisoners in Guillaume's dungeon.

Thibauld glanced at the boy. "How do I know you won't mutilate the rest of us?"

"These guards have orders to bring you to Troyes for questioning," Roustan replied. "*My* orders are to find your Preceptor." He lowered his blade and took a step towards Thibauld. "So you see, I've no interest in what happens to you. None whatsoever, so long as you tell me what I wish to know."

"No, Thibauld," someone whispered.

"I'll not see innocents slaughtered," Thibauld snapped over his shoulder. "Whatever the Preceptor has done to bring these soldiers down upon us, he wouldn't see us mutilated for it."

"Exactly," Roustan agreed. "Now, the next man who speaks out of turn will have his eyes put out and lose every finger and toe, before being crucified upside down upon the front gate. Am I clear?"

"He left the Lodge in the middle of the night," Thibauld blurted.

"So I gathered." Roustan motioned the guard to release the youth and to drag Thibauld before him. Up close, the scribe's fear convulsed through the muscles of his face. "Where did he go, *Thibauld*, and who was with him?"

Thibauld swallowed and hunched inwards. "The other chevaliers met him in the courtyard. They entered the cellar. That's all I could see from my window."

"You're his Seneschal?"

Thibauld's tongue darted across his upper lip. "Yes."

"Did your master have visitors? A woman and a big chevalier with fair hair, perhaps?"

"I never met them." Thibauld avoided Roustan's searching look. "The Preceptor wanted them kept secret though. That's all I know."

"The cellar is locked from inside." Roustan rested the flat of his sword on Thibauld's bony shoulder. "Do you really expect me to believe they've barricaded themselves inside?"

"There's a hidden tunnel." Thibauld finally looked up, trying to gauge Roustan's reaction. A flicker of triumph twitched across his narrow features.

Of course.

A bolt hole.

Clever...and infuriating.

Roustan pursed his lips. "Captain, I'll need two of your men to accompany me and Thibauld here. Make sure they bring axes. The rest of your men remain here, guarding the prisoners. If the good Seneschal is lying, or should anything happen to me, kill every one of them. Then burn this cursed place to the ground."

CHAPTER 9

14 October 1307

The River Marne

" **I** still think it would've been easier to bring the horses to the riverbank." Bertrand gestured towards the Marne. Thick mist had gathered above the surface of the river and rolled into shore, dampening sound and blanketing the landscape. "An entire army could march past not a stone's throw away and we wouldn't know."

Rémi finished filling his water-skin and drew the leather cords of the neck tight. "Smart, if you ask me." He lifted the bulging skin and waded to the bank. "This one's for you." He thrust the skin at Bertrand.

Bertrand staggered under the sudden weight of the sloshing skin. Rémi had handled it as casually as if it were a horse's nosebag. "Why is blundering about in the mist smart?"

"Use that lump on your shoulders you call a head."

Bertrand eased the skin onto the ground while he waited for Rémi to fill the second one. His back was stiff with knots of pain that hadn't loosened from the beating he took during his initiation. A long day in the saddle had not helped either.

"Everard's using the mist to hide our tracks," Bertrand said. "That's why we've avoided the roads all day."

"Sense at last." Air bubbled up to the surface as Rémi squeezed the second skin.

Bertrand glanced around the riverbank. Evasion suggested pursuit, but there had been no sign of any. "But why? Who are we avoiding? And why should *we* hide from anyone?"

"All fine questions, the lot of them. Hold onto them for a while. Maybe you'll get an answer."

"Aren't you even curious?"

"What's the point?" Rémi shrugged. "Questions rarely put food in bellies, whereas doing as you're told does."

Bertrand crossed his arms. "We've known each other far too long for you to convince me you've no interest in such things."

"Bide your time is all I'm saying." Rémi deftly tied the cords and hefted the skin over one shoulder. "There's plenty of trouble to be had without inviting it through your door." He waded out of the water. "You coming or did I fill yours up too much?"

Bertrand grinned at the familiar banter. "I'll try not to walk too fast." He lifted the bulging skin and slung it over one shoulder. Rémi snorted at Bertrand's transparent attempt to conceal the effort that it took.

Everard had decided to camp within the woods rather than open ground where it was easier to tend their horses. The flat, marshy shore of the river quickly gave way to stands of elm and beech wrapped in their autumn coats of gold, orange, and russet. The occasional fir tree stood out, their dark green needles resisting winter's advance.

The land rose steadily upwards as they moved away from the shore. Despite the chill in the air, Bertrand broke a light sweat as he kept pace with Rémi.

Eventually, the land evened out into a flat hilltop. The trees were thinner here, although the campsite couldn't be called a clearing. The horses had been tethered to the boughs of saplings. They nuzzled nosebags and whickered to each other in the gathering gloom. Everard had forbidden a fire so only half shuttered lanterns provided illumination.

Rémi and Bertrand moved in opposite directions around the camp, watering the horses. Most of the brothers were either grooming their mounts or checking their saddle and tack. A few nodded thanks as Bertrand passed by but none spoke. The camp was eerily silent, cloaked in mist and anxiety.

Towards the back of the camp, furthest from the Marne, a jagged spike of weathered stone presided over the knoll. Wedged upright in the ground by ancient tribes long since forgotten, the menhir was taller than two men and too wide for Bertrand to wrap his arms around. Spirals and cup marks scarred the dark stone. All of them were old and worn, except for a symbol that reminded Bertrand of a flower. A vertical furrow like a stem ran through a series of small concentric circles.

The sound of movement deeper in the forest drew Bertrand's attention. He moved past the menhir and listened carefully. Whatever it was, it was big. Leaves rustled ominously. The nearest horse snorted and stamped one foot.

"Rest easy," a voice said to Bertrand's right.

He turned quickly. Arnaud was crouching a few feet away in the growing dark. He was so still, Bertrand had failed to notice him earlier.

Arnaud stood. "The Preceptor has set a watch. Unfortunately, they're not skilled woodsmen." He nodded towards the trees. "Get some rest. There'll be no Vespers tonight and you've drawn the dawn watch."

"Yes, brother." The water-skin was almost empty and Bertrand's mount was already groomed and hobbled for the night.

"Why are we hiding?" Bertrand asked in a whisper.

"It's not for us to ask why." Arnaud stroked his beard as he stared into the woods. Bertrand strained to see what he was looking at.

"Sleep while you can." Arnaud moved off.

The centre of camp was a loose ring of brothers who had found places to sleep on the ground. Hides greased with animal fat on one side kept the damp at bay, while their saddle blankets cushioned the uneven ground. Armour and equipment had been stacked in two careful piles at each end of the camp and covered with sheets of canvas in case it should rain.

Bertrand chose a spot not far from Rémi. He settled into a comfortable position on his side and closed his eyes. Water dripped through the forest and a stream gurgled in the distance. Everything seemed peaceful, although Bertrand couldn't shake his uneasiness.

What was Everard hiding?

He opened his eyes. The mysterious cloaked woman had already retired for the night near the menhir. As far as Bertrand was aware, she hadn't spoken to anyone apart from Everard and the big chevalier who seemed permanently stationed half a step behind her.

Bertrand craned his neck. Everard was still awake. He sat on a low rock and passed a strip of salted pork to the fair-headed chevalier, who chewed on it contentedly. The exchange was so mundane, so familiar, that Bertrand felt sure they had shared food together a thousand times before.

Whoever these people were, Everard knew them well. And it was obvious they trusted him. Maybe Rémi was right; perhaps asking questions was pointless. But if Everard was involved with the Salt Lines, it seemed reasonable to assume these strangers were as well.

A light sheet of rain drifted across the campsite. Bertrand settled deeper into his blanket. He continued to watch Everard and his mysterious guests long after Rémi's breathing became deep and even.

When sleep finally descended, Bertrand dreamt that he stood in a dry riverbed, turning over stone after stone in a futile search for something he couldn't remember.

The toe of a boot and a curt, "Your watch," woke Bertrand.

He sat up and stretched his arms overhead. The muscles in his back protested and his bruises ached. Dawn had just begun to stain the sky with deep shades of purple. The air was cold and the fog had thickened during the night. It looked like a cloudbank had descended upon the forest. Smoky tendrils wrapped around dark trunks, making them appear suspended in mid-air.

Bertrand rolled to his feet and chafed his arms. Despite his sleeping hide, damp had crept into his padded tunic and saturated his leggings. A fire and a warm broth would have banished both problems, but neither comfort was to be had.

He moved quietly to the cache of weapons. On his way past, Bertrand noticed that Rémi had left his bedroll. Perhaps he was already on watch.

Roland was up as well. The tall chevalier gave Bertrand a curt nod before continuing to gaze into the shifting banks of mist. Roland had donned his hauberk and wore a sword at his hip. He carried a bow and had slung a quiver across his back. The fletching jutted behind his right shoulder. Watching Roland, Bertrand was reminded of a stag scenting the air for danger.

Bertrand licked his lips. Both Everard and his senior chevaliers were acting in a manner that suggested they expected an attack. Who would dare such a thing and why? It didn't make any sense.

A figure moved through the trees on the far side of the camp. Probably one of those on watch. From this distance, movement was easier to detect than actual shapes.

Bertrand donned his hauberk and secured the clasps. Trying to remain quiet, he sheathed his sword and following Roland's example, strung a bow and slung a quiver over his shoulder. His bladder was full but not insistent. Like all the brothers, he was accustomed to not eating until noon, so his stomach did not complain. He moved into the trees and entered a different world.

Overnight rain had saturated the forest floor and the scent of rotting leaves filled the air. Only the chink of chainmail and the scrape of his scabbard on rocks marked his passage.

Bertrand leaned against a thick elm and peered into the wood. This forest felt older and denser than the one near his family's estate. Perhaps it was because of the elm and beech. They were thicker trees than the poplars and birch he was accustomed to. Older and more imposing too.

He caught the muffled sound of a splash in the distance. Bertrand eased an arrow from his quiver and nocked his bow. A thread of tension wound through his chest and drew tight around his thudding heart. He crouched down to reduce the target he presented and peered into the fog.

Perhaps he should report back to Roland, although he was reluctant to leave his post. Fear soured Bertrand's mouth. It could be just a deer or a wild boar rooting through the forest. Imagine calling Roland over only to discover that? He would rather die than be called craven.

Bertrand clenched his teeth and tightened his grip on the bow.

"Steady," someone breathed on the far side of the elm. Bertrand swung his bow towards the voice. Rémi emerged from the far side of the trunk. He was dressed in his customary boiled leather armour and carried an axe and buckler.

Bertrand released his breath. "Where have you been?"

"About." Rémi's gaze did not leave the forest. "I don't know what trouble your precious Everard has led us into but it's following close behind."

"What?" Bertrand swung his bow back in the direction of the splash. Or at least the direction he thought it had come from. "Who's following?"

"Not sure. They're well equipped though."

"We've got to warn the others." Bertrand rose from his crouch. Rémi pulled him back down with a firm grip.

"Already done. Told Roland I'd bring you back while he prepared our defence. But when the fighting starts, you just head that way." Rémi pointed deeper into the forest with his axe. "Most of them are coming up from the Marne, so deeper into the woods should be safest."

"I'm not going to abandon our brothers."

"And I'll not see you dead on account of getting mixed up in someone else's affairs. Made a promise to your father, didn't I?"

Your father.

Rémi was still acting on his father's orders? He had assumed Rémi had accompanied him to the Commanderie because of their friendship, not because he had been ordered to.

Before he could question Rémi any further, four men clad in chainmail emerged from the mist. They rushed forward when they spotted Bertrand and Rémi. Two carried spears, while the other two brandished axes.

"Run." Rémi shoved Bertrand towards the camp and moved to intercept the soldiers. Yells erupted behind them, followed by the clash of metal and screams.

Bertrand stepped to one side and drew the fletching to his cheek.

His first shaft flew too high and to the left of the nearest spearman. His second arrow thudded into the gut of one of the axe-wielders. The man went down with a cry and he thrashed on the forest floor, almost tripping one of his companions.

Rémi blocked a spear thrust with his buckler and severed the wooden shaft with his axe. The second axeman hacked at Rémi's head, who twisted away from the blow. Bertrand hurled his bow at the third soldier. It earned him enough time to draw his sword. He wished he had retrieved his shield.

A spear tip flashed towards Bertrand's face. He parried but it was already darting at his groin. Bertrand dodged away from the lunge. The soldier was light on his feet and maintained his advantage of reach. Every time Bertrand tried to move inside the range of his spear, the man retreated.

Rémi was fully engaged with the remaining soldiers. As strong as he was, it was unlikely he could overcome two soldiers working in tandem. Plus, his leather armour wouldn't protect him from a heavy blow. Bertrand had to disable his opponent as quickly as possible, otherwise they were both dead.

He swung his sword at the darting spear in an attempt to sever the shaft. His opponent spun the spear away and then thrust at his face. Bertrand ducked and charged beneath the tip. His opponent lurched back and slipped on a patch of moss. Bertrand slashed at the man's thigh. The spearman tried to block the blow with the butt of his spear. Bertrand's sword struck the man's fist and severed his fingers.

The soldier staggered backwards with a cry. Bertrand leapt forward and cut him down with a blow to the neck. Blood sprayed outwards in an arc. Bertrand wiped the gore from his eyes with a trembling hand.

Rémi was holding his ground, although blood trickled from a superficial cut on his forearm. The spearman had forsaken his ruined spear for a mace, which he smashed into Rémi's buckler. The axeman was limping and seemed less keen to press his attack. Bertrand darted forward and hamstrung the man wielding the mace. Swinging his blade on the return arc, Bertrand took off the top of his head.

Seeing his comrade fall, the remaining soldier fled. Rémi flung his axe with such force that it lifted the man off his feet before he crashed face-down into the ground.

Bertrand staggered against the elm, his chest heaving for breath. Tiny points of fire pricked his lungs. He couldn't drag his gaze away from the soldier's broken skull. Glistening pink coils dribbled from the wound and wisps of steam joined with the mist.

Bertrand dry-retched and the taste of vomit stung the back of his throat.

He had never killed a man before, let alone two.

"Thought I...said...run." Rémi rasped for breath.

"No time."

Rémi squinted at Bertrand. "You hurt?"

Bertrand ran a hand across his face. Blood dripped from his fingers and ran down his chin. *Not mine*, he tried to say. He emptied the contents of his stomach on the ground instead.

"Best be off." Rémi strode over to the fallen axeman and braced his foot on the rump. The axe came out from between the soldier's shoulder blades with a horrifying sucking sound. Bertrand thought he might be sick again.

"This way," Rémi motioned deeper into the forest.

"What about...the others?"

The sound of battle still echoed through the trees. It was impossible to tell how close they were or who was winning.

Rémi shook his head. "Done our share. No sense dying for someone who hasn't done right by you. Let's go."

"They need us." Bertrand sucked in a lungful of air. "How can you just abandon them?"

Rémi grimaced. "Your precious Everard hasn't been honest. Those are king's men we just killed. Look at their tabards. Whatever he's mixed up in, we're well clear of it."

Bertrand stared at the bodies. The attack was so sudden he hadn't registered the gold fleur-de-lis on the field of royal blue.

"We took an oath of obedience."

"*You* did," Rémi replied. "Me, I'm just an armed servant."

Bertrand ground his teeth. Rémi had a point, although he simply couldn't believe that Everard would play him false. If he ran now, he would be a fugitive whatever the outcome of the battle. Plus, he would never learn the truth. Strangely enough, that outweighed anything else.

The sound of fighting drifted closer. "I'm not leaving." Bertrand hefted his sword. "You head back to Châtillon and tell my father what happened. If I live, I'll tell him how you protected me. No one will think any less of you."

Rémi spat. "Stupid cub. I'm going to beat some sense into you when this is done."

Bertrand grinned and threaded his way back through the trees. The clash of steel and cries intensified. He almost tripped over a fallen body. Crouching down, he saw it was one of the King's Guard. Bertrand stripped the shield from the corpse and stood.

A horse raced past, emerging from the fog and disappearing again like an apparition. The menhir loomed out of the mist, the scarred pillar of stone indifferent to the chaos surrounding it.

Someone nearby yelled out the Order's battle cry: "Beauseant! Beauseant!'

"That way," Rémi indicated with his axe. A group of figures emerged from the dense fog. The cloaked woman hurried towards them, followed by the hulking figure of her bodyguard. Everard accompanied them. He cried "Beauseant" again.

Roland was at Everard's side and Arnaud staggered into view. His shield arm was limp and blood stained his hauberk. Roland caught Arnaud as he nearly fell.

The cloaked woman spotted Bertrand and Rémi and slid to a stop. "Roard," she cried. Her bodyguard swung about and strode towards them, his long blade raised.

"We're friends," Bertrand called.

Everard turned and called out to the big chevalier. "They're mine, Roard. Get her to the menhir."

The twang of a bowstring sounded in the fog. An arrow sprouted from Roland's chest and the chevalier staggered backwards before falling to his haunches. Arnaud stumbled to one knee by Roland's side. More soldiers emerged from the bank of fog. Two converged on Arnaud, who struggled to raise his shield. The first soldier bludgeoned Arnaud's shield aside with his axe while the second slammed his sword into the chevalier's face.

Everard roared in anger and struck down the swordsman who had killed Arnaud. The axeman retreated as more of his comrades emerged from the mist. They approached Everard warily, fanning out to attack him from different angles. Bertrand and Rémi rushed forward, but the woman caught Bertrand's arm in a surprisingly strong grip.

"Have them fall back to the menhir," she snapped. "We can still escape."

Bertrand only had time to gather a few impressions before she thrust him towards the battle: high cheekbones, a bold, straight nose and long dark hair. Thin, pale scars covered her olive skin.

Rémi and Bertrand joined Everard in fighting a rear-guard action. Everard was in a murderous rage, laying about with his sword without any thought to his safety.

The large chevalier—Roard, the woman had called him—was reluctant to join them at first. He stayed close to the woman, but as the weight of numbers forced them back, he joined the fray with devastating effect. His two-handed sword whistled through the air with deadly precision.

The battle blurred into a sequence of crunching impacts and counter-blows. Bertrand's awareness contracted into thrust, parry, and counter-thrust.

A blow struck Bertrand on the hip. Spikes of pain lanced down his leg, but he set it aside as he had been taught to do. He focused on the opponent before him, gave thought to those on either side, and no more.

An arrow whined past Bertrand and Everard cried out. Bertrand glanced to the left. Everard teetered backwards, the shaft of the arrow jutting from beneath his collarbone. A soldier lunged forward, seizing his opportunity.

Bertrand's feet slipped on the wet ground as he charged towards Everard. The soldier slashed at Everard's unprotected thigh. His leg collapsed and Everard fell. Blood immediately welled from the wound. The soldier raised his sword overhead for a finishing stroke. Bertrand drove his blade into the soldier's side. The man tumbled to the ground and wrenched Bertrand's blade from his grip.

A second soldier hammered Bertrand's shield with a heavy mace. The blow forced Bertrand to one knee. He raised his shield, bracing it with both hands. Roard swung his sword over Bertrand in an arc that slashed open the soldier's throat. The man stumbled backwards, clutching at the ragged gash as blood poured between his fingers.

"Fall back," the woman called out.

Discarding his shield, Bertrand grabbed Everard by the armpits and hauled him towards the menhir while Rémi and Roard guarded their retreat. The remaining soldiers reformed into a single mass for a final charge.

"Quickly, Roard," the woman called. "I can't hold it open much longer."

The tingling, charged atmosphere of an impending thunderstorm filled the air. Everard moaned as Bertrand dragged him towards the standing stone.

"That's the last of them," Roard called out behind Bertrand.

The air throbbed and the mist rippled. The voices of the massing soldiers became distant, then surged close. Bertrand felt strangely dislocated, as if his place in the world had become detached. The finger of stone, the figures in the mist, everything felt distant. The world oozed through his senses and refused to settle into place.

Bertrand glanced at the menhir. The woman had sliced her hand open and smeared blood down the groove in the stone he'd noticed earlier. Each concentric circle rippled in the strange, pulsing light. She slid her finger down the groove and traced the curve of the innermost circle.

He glanced back at the soldiers. A new figure had taken charge. The man was of average height with a neat, black beard that framed the bottom half of his pale face.

Perhaps the man sensed Bertrand's scrutiny because their gazes locked. Pitiless, dark eyes assessed Bertrand in an instant. The man possessed the focused intensity of a predator stalking its prey.

The leader pointed his spear at Bertrand and cried out. The sound did not carry until a few heartbeats later. The soldiers charged through the trees, their movement slow, as if they waded through deep water. The man hurled his spear at Bertrand. It floated towards him impossibly slowly. Bertrand stared in astonishment. A few yards from the menhir, it suddenly shot forward and Bertrand ducked. The spear flew past him and caught Roard in the throat. The chevalier crashed against the stone, scrabbling at the shaft embedded in his neck.

The woman completed the circle on the menhir as Roard collapsed at her feet. Seeing him fall, she screamed in horror. The sound ricocheted through the charged mist and splintered in Bertrand's skull. The ground abruptly dropped away and the surrounding trees rushed towards him in a blur.

Sound, light and sensation imploded.

All that remained was a dizzying emptiness for Bertrand to tumble through.

CHAPTER 10

15 July 1099

Outside Jerusalem

Godefroi waited impatiently with the chevaliers and archers picked to man Etienne's tower. Night was giving way to dawn and the shadows were retreating. Achambaud and a large Flemish chevalier called Diederic waited with Godefroi while Etienne and Gaston completed a final inspection of the tower.

Almost fifty warriors had been selected for the vanguard of their attack. Two columns of archers and pedites, the regular infantry, flanked the siege tower. Many carried wooden ladders and knotted ropes that ended in metal hooks. The garrison would concentrate their efforts on the siege tower, but Godefroi was determined to force them to defend a broad section of the wall.

He took a deep breath. The air was thick with nervous sweat and choking ash. Godefroi lifted his gaze to the dark skyline of Jerusalem. Smoke crouched over the city, lit by the lurid glow of spot fires the inhabitants had been unable to put out.

Somewhere to the southwest, near the Sion Gate, Count Raymond's men were assembling. Was Raymond's heart pounding? Did he dream of the treasures that awaited them inside? Did he wonder what Godefroi was thinking at this precise moment?

Destiny prowled around the walls of Jerusalem. It was a caged beast waiting for someone strong enough to tame it. Godefroi gripped the hilt of his sword. His entire life had been preparation for this moment.

"Soon," Achambaud murmured at Godefroi's shoulder. "The garrison is focused on Raymond. His tower is closer to the wall. They won't expect us to suddenly appear east overnight."

Godefroi grunted in acknowledgement.

Etienne and Gaston emerged from the tower. Etienne wore plain leather armour and padded hose. A light sheen of sweat glistened on his forehead.

"We're ready, messire," Etienne said. "Your chevaliers may ascend the tower, although I'd advise them to kneel while moving. The ride will be bumpy."

"A few bumps will be the least of their concerns," Gaston noted.

"Pass the word to enter the tower," Godefroi told Diederic.

"Rings have been bolted to the wall," Etienne called after Diederic. "Tell them to loop their arms through." The Flemish chevalier nodded and moved off to spread the message.

"Is this going to work?" Godefroi was more nervous about rolling the tower down the low hill before them than the actual battle.

Etienne spread his hands. "I've done all that I can. Our path has been cleared of heavy stones and the wheels reinforced as you asked."

"Just how fast will we be going?" In his dark armour, only Achambaud's face was clearly visible.

Etienne ran a hand through his curly hair. "At the height of its speed, almost as fast as a horse at canter."

"Saints preserve us," Achambaud said. "Surely the tower can't withstand such pace."

"If I had more time—"

"Enough." Godefroi cut off the debate with a sweep of his mailed hand. "It's too late to change our plans. Etienne, remain on the ground level. If we fall short of the wall, you muster enough men to drive it forward."

"Yes, messire. God be with you and your chevaliers." Etienne hurried off into the shadowy recesses of his tower.

Godefroi signalled the commanders of his army. Baldwin stalked over, along with the Dukes of Flanders and Normandy, and other nobles. "Follow the tower as quickly as you can. Should we be delayed, don't attempt to scale the wall until the tower is in position."

"And what if it collapses or turns awry?" For once, Baldwin's expression was grave and not mocking.

"If the former, I'll likely be dead and expect you to avenge me." Godefroi gave Baldwin a savage grin. "If the latter, then we'll do our best to change course." The knot of nobles nodded and dispersed with brisk efficiency.

Godefroi caught Baldwin's arm. "Remember your promise."

Baldwin's blue eyes narrowed. "I'll hold to our agreement, though you shame me by insisting upon it." Baldwin shook him off and marched back to his contingent.

Godefroi's twenty hand-picked chevaliers clambered up the ladders to the top of the tower. Diederic had returned to his post behind

Godefroi's shoulder, silent and steadfast.

"Let's take our positions." Godefroi rolled his head to loosen the knots of tension drawing tight in his neck and shoulders.

The darkness was thick inside the tower. Weapons clinked, boots scraped on floorboards and the timber frame groaned beneath the shifting weight. Godefroi took a moment to allow his eyes to adjust, then slung his kite shield over one shoulder and climbed up the ladder.

"This way." Achambaud directed him to the back of the top platform. Godefroi gave him a hard stare. Achambaud shrugged. "Hugues said you promised."

"That monk only hears what he wants to," Godefroi muttered.

"Then he's no different to the rest of us," Achambaud replied with a wry smile.

Godefroi addressed the chevaliers on the top platform. "Soldiers of Christ, let us fulfil our vows."

"Deus vult," the chevaliers responded in low, fierce voices.

"Ludolf and Engelbert de Tournai, you may lead the first charge." The two chevaliers rose and bowed in recognition of the honour. They took up positions behind the reinforced wooden screen at the front of the tower.

"Here's your crossbow, messire." Diederic handed Godefroi his weapon.

"Thank you. Are they ready below?"

Achambaud strode across to the ladder and conducted a whispered conversation. "Yes. They await your orders."

"Good." Godefroi gripped his ring bolt and leaned over the side the tower. "Etienne? Can you hear me?"

"Yes, messire." The engineer's voice floated up from below. It was growing lighter by the second.

"Release the wheels and signal the catapults once we're away."

Etienne issued a set of instructions. Godefroi sank onto his haunches and threaded his arm through the ring bolt. It was done now. For good or ill, their course was set. No time left to offer a quick prayer.

Tremors vibrated through the tower as Etienne's workers struck the wooden stays with heavy mallets. Dawn was staining the eastern horizon with hues of rose and lavender.

Thud—thud—thud.

The blows matched the drumming of Godefroi's heart.

Thud—thud—thud.

The tower lurched.

Thud—thud—thud.

Wood groaned and splintered.

"Look out," someone called in the darkness below.

Godefroi resisted the urge to peer over the side. The wheels groaned and the tower swayed to the right. Only one of the wooden anchors had given way. This could set them off course before they had even begun.

Etienne's voice rose over the confusion. The tempo of mallets striking timber increased.

Thud — thud — craaack.

The tower lurched forward, wheels groaning ominously like distant thunder.

A flaming arrow arced through the air. Heavy stones followed in its wake as the catapults released their loads at the signal. Distant cries of alarm sounded from the walls. The tower picked up pace, lumbering down the rise Etienne had chosen.

The iron bindings on the wheels squealed as they crushed rocks beneath the enormous weight of the tower. Every jolt and bump was magnified as the top platform swayed. Godefroi held on grimly, hoping the rest of his troops could keep pace. Cool air whipped past his face.

For the first time on this pilgrimage, Godefroi wondered whether he was but moments from death. Imagine falling victim to his overly ambitious plan at the very foot of Jerusalem.

Godefroi laughed. Achambaud flashed a grin at him, although he seemed pre-occupied with holding on. Diederic stared at Godefroi wide-eyed.

The tower pitched forward. Godefroi used the motion to rise from his crouch to get a better view. Arrows whistled past or *thunked* into the wattle screens. The wall rose before him, much closer than he had expected.

The tower pitched alarmingly but kept rumbling forward. Slower now, the screeching protest of its wheels had become a protracted groan. In the distance, men shouted to each other in the harsh tongue of the Saracens. An arrow ricocheted off Godefroi's shield. He returned fire with his crossbow, although the jarring motion of the tower made it difficult to aim. Far off to the left, a rock from a Christian mangonel struck the main wall with a jarring impact. Two men in conical helmets fell off the parapet, their arms flailing uselessly.

Godefroi dropped back into a crouch and re-loaded his crossbow with another quarrel. It took enormous strength, which Godefroi had developed through long years of practice. Feet braced against the stirrup, he used both arms and shoulders to draw the stock taut and locked it into position.

The tower was slowing. The final rise towards the walls had robbed their speed faster than he had hoped. If they pulled up short and the drawbridge couldn't reach the battlements, they would have to hold out until the rest of the army arrived to push them up the final yards. He doubted Etienne had enough men to drive the tower forward unaided.

Godefroi chanced another look. The wall stretched out to his left and right as far as he could see, not twenty feet distant. Saracen reinforcements were rushing to intercept them from both directions. The new position of the tower and the speed of their approach had undoubtedly taken the garrison by surprise.

"Please God, just a little further." Godefroi ducked beneath another volley of arrows.

The tower shuddered and ground to a halt.

Wattle shutters in the front of the tower opened and a hail of quarrels raked the parapet. A handful of Saracen archers fell from the wall, screaming as they clutched at shafts protruding from their lightly armoured bodies. Godefroi leapt up, took careful aim at a large Nubian warrior carrying a poleaxe and fired. His quarrel punched through the warrior's chest and the man dropped from sight without a cry.

At ground level, some of Etienne's men would be risking their lives by placing wooden stays behind the wheels to stop the tower from rolling backwards.

Godefroi raised his shield and checked on the progress of his army. A ragged line of soldiers swarmed up the low rise towards the outer wall.

Now that the tower was stationary, the chevaliers on the platform rose and hurled spears at the Saracens or fired their bows. A hail of stones flew overhead, angling from the west where the garrison had mounted their catapults on the Quadrangular Tower. A stray rock struck a chevalier in the head, hurling him from the platform in a spray of blood.

The Saracens on the wall counter-attacked with mallets studded with nails and wrapped in burning rags. Burning arrows thudded into the timber frame of the tower. The wattle screens and thick animal hides deflected most of these attacks. Where fire did take hold, Etienne's men doused the flames with precious jars of water.

The leading sections of Godefroi's army began massing behind the tower while volleys of Christian arrows peppered the parapet. Pedites poured into the base of the tower, pushing against Etienne's iron bars. The tower shuddered and inched forward.

Godefroi fired another bolt at the Saracens. The quarrel glanced off the stonework and missed the archer he had targeted. A flaming arrow flew past his head and he ducked down again.

The wheels groaned and the tower rolled another foot closer to the wall.

"Achambaud," Godefroi yelled over the din. "Tell them to be ready for Greek fire." Achambaud scrambled to the top of the ladder and passed on the warning.

The Saracen catapults hurled another load of stones. Thankfully, they flew wide. Fixed to the parapet, they could not be readjusted, and Godefroi guessed the tower was inside their range now.

Another lurch forward. Flaming arrows swarmed about the tower like fireflies.

"Almost there," Achambaud cried.

Godefroi gave him a wolfish grin beneath the faceguard of his helmet. The desperate swarthy faces of the garrison became clear.

The defenders changed tactics. Many dropped their bows and hurled clay pots at the tower instead. Most shattered on impact, although a few were deflected by the animal hides. One particularly large Saracen heaved a wineskin at the tower. Fortunately, it fell short and burst open, black liquid staining the dusty ground.

Burning arrows and smouldering mallets followed in an effort to set the Greek fire alight. Flames erupted across the face of the tower. Godefroi felt a stab on panic. The fires had to be doused before they could take hold. Etienne's men opened the shutters and poured jugs of vinegar over the flames.

The pedites at the base of the tower surged forward. The wall was now so close Godefroi thought he could almost leap across the gap. A barrage of stones from Christian catapults slammed into the wall near the Gate of Flowers. The parapet collapsed under the impact.

Godefroi watched in astonishment as one of the wooden towers protecting the approach to the gate toppled over and crushed those Christians unfortunate enough to be directly beneath it. A few Saracens crawled from the wreckage, but they were slaughtered mercilessly.

"Now," Godefroi bellowed. Ludolf and Engelbert slashed the ropes holding the heavy wattle screen in place. It dropped with a crash against the lip of the battlements. Without the protection of the screen, Saracen arrows whined across the platform. Godefroi crouched down as arrows struck his kite shield.

Ludolf and Engelbert charged across the narrow wooden walkway with a roar and crashed into a knot of defenders. The rest of the chevaliers followed, leaping over struggling bodies to secure a foothold on the parapet.

Godefroi's world contracted to the length of his blade and the width of his shield. Time expanded and contracted with his movements: one moment his sword would describe a slow, deliberate arc overhead. The next moment it blurred into the ring of metal, the thud of shield against armour, and the wet *thwack* of his blade slicing through flesh. A brief, gasping pause accelerated into his next opponent.

Ludolf was face-down and still. Engelbert had engaged two Saracens carrying long spears. Their superior reach and synchronised attacks hampered his ability to counter-attack. Godefroi charged the spearmen with a wordless bellow. Distracted by the attack, one of the Saracens dropped his guard. Engelbert thrust aside the spear with his shield and severed the defender's arm.

The second Saracen flung his spear. Godefroi deflected it with his shield and cut down the defender before he could draw his scimitar.

Engelbert saluted Godefroi with his sword before re-joining the fray.

Godefroi held back to assess the situation. While they had secured a foothold, the narrow parapet prevented them from bringing their superior numbers to bear. Fortunately, the partially collapsed wall near the Gate of Flowers impeded reinforcements from the east. However, defenders from the Gate of St Stephen to the west were pressing against Godefroi's forces in a desperate effort to dislodge them. He needed to take the gatehouse and open the gate to the rest of his troops before the Saracens succeeded.

"Achambaud," Godefroi roared. The dark chevalier was suddenly at his side. Blood dripped from his sword and a long scratch ran the length of his black shield. Otherwise he appeared unscathed. Diederic flanked Godefroi, the big chevalier radiating menace. The ebb and flow of battle had moved on, creating a small pocket of calm.

"We must break their line," Godefroi yelled over the screams and clash of battle. He pointed towards the knot of Saracens attacking from the Gate of St Stephen.

Achambaud nodded to show he understood.

The first of Baldwin's troops crossed the tower's drawbridge. "Diederic," Godefroi yelled. "Order the Edessans to clear the parapet as far as the eastern gate." The Flemish chevalier gave him a curt nod and rushed back to the tower to relay the order.

Godefroi grabbed Achambaud by the arm. "I need your skills," he yelled.

Achambaud jerked back in horror. "Here, messire?"

"I must reach the Holy Sepulchre first."

Most of the Christians who had attempted to scale ladders or climb the knotted ropes looped around the battlements hadn't fared as well as Godefroi's heavily armoured chevaliers. Bodies littered the foot of the wall, the majority of them Tafurs or common pedites.

"Now, Achambaud."

"Over here, in the shadows at least." Achambaud drew Godefroi away from the bright sunlight and sank to his knees behind a pile of fallen bodies. He shrugged off his kite shield and dropped his sword with a clatter. Gauntlets and helmet followed before Achambaud bowed his head.

"What's he doing?" Diederic had returned from the siege tower and stared at them in confusion.

Godefroi cursed inwardly. Why had Hugues chosen a bodyguard from outside the Salt Lines?

"Praying," Godefroi snapped. "Guard my back." He shoved Diederic away.

Achambaud knelt in a puddle of blood. He bowed his head and pressed the fingers of both hands to his forehead. After a moment, his body stiffened. Achambaud grabbed Godefroi's ankle and his fingers wormed beneath the thick woollen hose and hard leather protecting Godefroi's shin. "Let this man be the face of vengeance," Achambaud said in a harsh voice. The sound of battle became muffled, as if Godefroi had suddenly plunged under water.

Achambaud's sorcery crawled beneath his skin like a swarm of biting insects. The prickling sensation swept up Godefroi's leg and all the way to the roots of his hair. He felt cold, and furious, and terrible beyond imagining.

Godefroi turned towards the Gate of St Stephen. Big, black-skinned Nubians wielding flails and poleaxes were using their superior reach to check the Christian advance. He trembled with the ferocity inside him.

"Diederic, protect Achambaud with your life." Godefroi's voice was cold and held echoes from beyond the grave. Diederic drew back in horror at Godefroi's appearance.

A distant part of Godefroi knew Diederic had witnessed too much. Godefroi dismissed the thought and focused on the Nubians. Howling with the rage of vengeance, Godefroi charged.

CHAPTER 11

15 July 1099

The sacking of Jerusalem

"What did you do?" Diederic stood over Achambaud, his sword half raised.

"I prayed that God would make Godefroi His tool of vengeance." Achambaud pulled on his gauntlets. He was unsteady from gathering so much hatred and wrapping it around Godefroi. However, the weakness would soon pass.

Diederic glanced towards the gatehouse. Godefroi's bloodied, frenzied figure was at the forefront of the battle. Christian troops rallied to him as he hacked through Saracen defenders who quailed at the sight of Godefroi.

Achambaud rose to his feet and donned his black helmet. He retrieved his sword and shield.

Diederic took a step back on the blood-slicked stone. "I know what I saw."

"And what was that?" Achambaud asked tiredly.

"Sorcery. You touched Godefroi and he…the Duke…his eyes were terrible. And his voice—" Diederic's vocabulary failed him.

"What you *saw* was a devout Christian asking for God's blessing. You should be protecting him, not questioning me. Your life will be forfeit if he falls."

A strange expression twisted across Diederic's face. Achambaud, for all his talents, couldn't interpret it.

"My life has been forfeit from the start." Diederic strode towards the battle, his shield lowered and a determined set to his shoulders.

An odd remark. Especially for a man Achambaud had always assumed lacked such complexity. It would need to be considered later, as would Diederic's claims.

A constant flow of Christian troops swarmed over the wall now. Some climbed up through the tower and used the makeshift drawbridge.

Others negotiated the precarious wooden ladders. These weren't chevaliers, but pedites and Tafurs. Dressed in heavy padded tunics or scraps of hardened leather, they wielded a crude assortment of weapons.

"Achambaud!'

He turned towards the voice. Baldwin beckoned to him. Achambaud trudged over.

"Where's my brother?" Baldwin demanded.

"Need you ask?" Achambaud pointed. "Over yonder, in the thick of it."

"And why aren't you with him?"

"I took a blow but have recovered." After so many years of practice, the lie came easily to Achambaud's lips. "Come. Godefroi could use our support."

The parapet was slippery with blood. A low bulwark, only waist high, protected against the long drop to the streets of Jerusalem below. Warriors from both sides had toppled over the breastwork and broken upon the unforgiving cobblestones.

Godefroi and his surviving chevaliers had routed the garrison from the wall. The remaining defenders had taken refuge inside the gatehouse. Christian troops milled around the heavy wooden door. Saracens harassed them with arrows and heavy stones from the roof of the gatehouse.

A shaft clattered off Achambaud's shield and ricocheted into an alley below. A pedite next to him screamed. The man dropped his spear and clutched at a feathered shaft that suddenly protruded from his shoulder. He stumbled backwards and a second arrow sprouted from his chest. Arms windmilling, he tumbled backwards and fell with a curdling yell.

"They've barricaded the door," Baldwin yelled beneath his shield.

Achambaud shouldered his way forward. Two chevaliers battered the locked door with battle-axes. The doorframe trembled with each blow.

The glamour Achambaud had woven around Godefroi had dissipated. Covered in blood and brimming with impatience, he was still a fearful sight.

Another volley of arrows peppered their shields. A heavy stone struck a chevalier only a few feet from Achambaud. The hapless warrior collapsed like an empty sack. Blood seeped from his crushed helmet.

Crossbows thrummed behind Achambaud. He chanced a look up. One of the Saracen archers tottered between the crenelations of the gatehouse. A ragged hole had opened in his chest. His dark eyes were wide in disbelief as he stumbled backwards and plummeted from sight.

Achambaud glanced back towards Etienne's tower. Baldwin had marshalled the Christian crossbowmen to concentrate their fire on the roof. With a quick series of gestures, Baldwin arranged to have some of the wooden ladders lowered to street level.

Scores of pedites clambered down the ladders. They charged towards the base of the gatehouse and attacked the Saracens reinforcing it. Outnumbered, the defenders quickly took refuge inside.

Achambaud gave Baldwin a quick salute. Godefroi's younger brother gave him a short, sardonic bow, before descending a ladder. It seemed Baldwin would be the first noble to set foot in Jerusalem. Not even Hugues had predicted that.

A loud crack echoed across the parapet. Wood splintered as the door succumbed to the axes. Surely, the Saracens had no choice but to surrender now?

The door caved inwards and chevaliers surged into the stairwell. The entrance was narrow, no wider than two men abreast. Achambaud lost sight of Godefroi. Screams replaced the sound of clashing swords. The press of men was so thick Achambaud was forced to wait his turn.

The carnage that greeted him inside was sickening. Hacked limbs littered the steps and intestines slipped beneath his boots. Wounded Saracens moaned piteously where they had fallen, only to be gleefully stabbed by Christian soldiers.

Achambaud dashed down the steps and leapt over bodies. The ground floor was just as bad; Saracen corpses strewn around the circular floor. Several pedites were already looting the bodies, even squeezing their entrails in search of swallowed coins.

The battle for Jerusalem was effectively over. Only Godefroi could stop this siege turning into a massacre.

Achambaud stumbled out of the tower. For once, he was grateful for the bitter taste of smoke that masked the smell of death. Godefroi bellowed at his soldiers in an effort to re-establish order.

"Godefroi!" Baldwin sauntered over to his older brother. "You took your time."

Godefroi removed his helmet and wiped sweat from his face. "As usual, you leave the hard work to me. What's happening inside the city?"

"The northern garrison has fled," Baldwin replied. "We control both the main gates. Our troops are flooding the city."

"We must hurry then." Godefroi gave Achambaud a curt nod as he joined the circle. "I've had reports that Raymond's tower had problems clearing the ditch, but they must be close to the wall by now." He glanced towards the southern part of the city. A long plume of smoke marked the Provençal assault. "We must reach the Holy Sepulchre first. Nothing else matters."

"And leave the riches of the mosques to the other nobles?" Baldwin shook his head. "Brother, you can have the accolades. I want gold and silver."

Godefroi grimaced. "There are more important riches at stake."

Baldwin was about to argue when Achambaud interrupted. "What of the slaughter?"

Godefroi frowned. "What of it?"

"Aren't we going to take any prisoners for ransom? Won't you offer your banner to the enemy?"

"Why should we when they've shown no mercy to Christian pilgrims?" Baldwin demanded. "Would they have accepted our surrender during the weeks we were besieged at Antioch? No. You've seen how they taunted us, burning a cross on the wall every night. I say we take this city and kill every heathen we find."

"Is this truly God's work?" Achambaud asked Godefroi. "Is this what we've come to do? To reclaim this city no matter how we stain our souls? Hugues would—"

"Hugues is huddling with the rest of the clergy," Godefroi snapped. "Whatever happens today is God's will, Achambaud." He shook his head. "I've no time for this. Baldwin, make sure we retain control of both gates. Delegate command to one of the minor nobles, if you must. Then pursue whatever goal seems fit to you. Achambaud, you're with me."

"You're leaving me behind *again*?" Baldwin's face mottled with outrage.

"Don't be an idiot," Godefroi snapped. "If we're ambushed, we'll need a place to regroup."

Baldwin turned on his heel and marched off without another word.

"Where's the Armenian?" Godefroi called. Word passed through the ranks until they located the guide. A small, nervous man, he had lived inside the city until the garrison evicted all the Christians before the siege began.

"Take me to the Holy Sepulchre," Godefroi ordered.

"This way." The Armenian pointed to a narrow alley that rose uphill in a series of steps and landings. Stone houses crowded the lane on either side. Sheets of canvas fixed between the roofs created the impression of entering a tunnel. The air was thick with smoke and fear.

Godefroi took the Armenian by the arm and began walking uphill. His most loyal men followed a pair at a time.

Further down a street that ran parallel with the wall, six Tafurs emerged from one of the poorer houses. They dragged a Saracen family out the doorway. Even from a hundred yards away, Achambaud could tell one of the two women was elderly. The three children wailed in fear. Achambaud watched in horror as the biggest Tafur calmly speared each child in turn. The women screamed and struggled to intervene. The Tafurs laughed before carelessly cutting the women's throats. They tossed the bodies on the ground before moving on.

A wave of paralysing terror struck Achambaud without warning. The stale taste of fear flooded his dry mouth. He trembled with the horror of it and was sure he would be sick.

The terror of an entire city poured into him. An endless torrent of misery churned through his flesh. Every Christian atrocity was being tallied and accounted for in his soul.

Achambaud staggered against the side of a house. He could not participate in this battle any longer. War was one thing; wanton slaughter was entirely another.

Those Tafurs must be punished.

He drew his sword. The hilt quivered in his fist with his rage and disgust. Not one of Godefroi's chevaliers had intervened. The band of six Tafurs moved further down the narrow street, heading east. Godefroi's troops continued south up the alley. He couldn't follow both.

Achambaud hesitated. After a moment of agonising indecision, he turned from the Tafurs and trudged after Godefroi's men. Each step was a new lesson in self-loathing.

CHAPTER 12

15 July 1099

The Holy Sepulchre

He was inside the city.

At last. After all the suffering, all the sacrifices, the end was almost within grasp.

Godefroi smiled. This day would be remembered forever.

"How much farther?" he asked the Armenian.

"Only a short distance, messire." The Armenian's accent was thick and he seemed afraid of the blood-drenched chevaliers accompanying them.

Almost three-score men had resisted the allure of looting to accompany Godefroi. Most were chevaliers and many carried injuries from the battle. The remainder of the contingent were professionally trained soldiers known as milites, many of whom belonged to Godefroi's household guard.

The Armenian reached a crossroad and glanced both ways down the intersecting street. The stone walls of old shops leaned in on all sides. Screams sounded to the south. Raymond's continued assault was a low rumble in the distance.

"This way." The Armenian darted forward and turned left into the new alley.

"Wait," Godefroi called.

The Armenian stopped and pointed. "Almost there."

"Where? Why can't I see it?" He knew the Saracens had desecrated the site, but surely it should be visible by now.

The Armenian waved him on. A few yards later, he turned and disappeared into another side street.

Godefroi cursed and hurried after the Armenian.

"I'll catch him." Diederic ran after their disappearing guide, moving quickly for a big man.

"Be wary of ambush." Heeding his own advice, Godefroi paused a moment to allow the head of his column to catch up. Engelbert was among them, even though he was limping from a nasty gash in his leg. Familiar, weary faces looked to Godefroi for guidance.

"This way. We're almost there." He hurried after Diederic and the Armenian.

The side street ran downhill and opened into a large square. Godefroi's first impression was of space, which was at odds with the rest of the densely packed city. The area had been razed. Mounds of grey stone littered the ground. Blackened tiles and a few charred timber beams, now grey with age, jutted from the earth. The destruction had been wrought by the mad Caliph, al-Hakim, ninety years earlier.

A terrible, choking disappointment tightened in Godefroi's throat. Surely, this couldn't be it?

Every Christian had heard of the magnificent church Emperor Constantine had built. Approaching from the east, a pilgrim would first enter the Triportico, an open-air atrium built around the Rock of Calvary where Christ had died. Then they would pass through the Martyrium, the basilica supported by wide colonnades of stone. After passing beneath the dome, the weary pilgrim would finally behold the Anastasis, an open-air rotunda centred upon the cave that was the site of Christ's resurrection. Constantine's men had laboriously excavated the entire hill that had once stood there to build the fabled church.

Godefroi opened his eyes. He hadn't deliberately closed them, yet the site before him bore so little resemblance to Constantine's glorious church it was the only way to picture it.

The reality of the desecration was worse than he could have imagined.

A low wall fenced off the church from the rest of the city. Attempts had been made to restore the *Anastasis* with stones salvaged from the ruins. An uneven square of flagstones was all that remained of the former courtyard. The Martyrium and Triportico had been completely erased.

Godefroi approached the rotunda. After the frenzy of battle, the desecrated grounds were an oasis of quiet. Some signs of care were visible. A narrow path wended through the ruined stone. The court-yard, when he reached it, had obviously been swept clean. Recent attempts had been made to patch the makeshift walls of the rotunda. A new looking dome had been added.

After all that he and his followers had suffered, they deserved something more…triumphant than these ruins. This was meant to be the navel of the world, the source of hope for all those doomed to sin.

The Saracens had done this. They had shattered the very cornerstone of the Christian world. He swore they would suffer terribly for this outrage.

Godefroi noticed an apse in the façade of the Anastasis. The recess contained a simple altar, although it was too dark to make out much more.

The Armenian approached Godefroi with tears in his eyes. "You see now, yes? You see what they've done?"

"Yes, I see." Godefroi cleared his throat. "Someone find my chaplain. Bring him here." His eyes never left the battered rotunda. "And make sure he arrives safely."

Godefroi stopped before the apse and took a deep breath. Despite its aged appearance, his pulse quickened. The circular design created an impression of being drawn inwards and a sense of antiquity infused the building. The tips of Godefroi's toes and fingers tingled with anticipation. When Godefroi sank to his knees and laid his sword on the ground to give thanks, the chevaliers and milites who had accompanied him followed.

No matter how it looked, this was the site where Christ rose again. No place on earth was holier.

Godefroi crossed himself and rose to his feet. He took a deep breath. This was the moment that would define his life. Savouring his triumph, Godefroi entered the apse.

"Duke Godefroi of Lorraine," a voice called from the shadows deeper inside the building. "Come no further."

Godefroi stopped, shocked at being addressed in French. He squinted into the darkness. "Show yourself."

"Careful, messire." Achambaud was suddenly at his side, his sword drawn. Godefroi could let his warriors rush the man but that would mean relinquishing his claim of being the first to enter the Anastasis.

No. This siege was pointless if he surrendered that honour.

"Stay back, Achambaud." Godefroi tightened his grip on sword and shield. Nothing, and no one, would keep him from his life's purpose. He moved from the doorway to allow more light into the apse. His opponent was large and armoured like a Christian. He couldn't make out a face beneath the helm.

"This holy place is reserved for another," the stranger warned.

Godefroi knew that voice. "Diederic? Is that you?" He peered into the gloom. "You're Raymond's man, aren't you?" Godefroi spat on the ground.

"I am." Diederic's guard never wavered.

"He sent you to kill me." Godefroi looked for an opening as he made the accusation.

Diederic glanced at Achambaud.

"Count Raymond de Toulouse is the rightful king of Jerusalem," Diederic called out in a loud voice. "You all know Bishop Adhémar, the Papal Legate, chose Count Raymond as our commander before he died. Entering this holy place without the Count's leave is defying the Holy See. I merely protect it in his name."

"Wrong," Godefroi replied. "Jerusalem has no king. And even if it did, he couldn't claim this place. It belongs to all Christians. Your master's pride knows no boundaries."

Diederic met Godefroi's gaze. Beneath his helmet, his broad face was implacable. "You've no right to judge Count Raymond. Not when you allow the vile touch of sorcery to stain your soul." Diederic's accusing gaze shifted to Achambaud.

"Either stand aside or die," Godefroi warned.

Diederic did not budge.

Godefroi rushed forward and swung his sword low, aiming for the thigh. Diederic blocked with his shield and counter-attacked with a high, overhand stroke. Godefroi caught the heavy blow on his shield and pain splintered through his shoulder. Godefroi pushed with his legs, forcing Diederic's sword up, and swung his blade in an underhand stroke. The tip of Godefroi's sword screeched against Diederic's chainmail as he jumped back.

"Godefroi!" Achambaud hesitated in the doorway.

"Hold," Godefroi commanded.

As Diederic moved forward to re-engage Godefroi, a second figure emerged from the interior of the rotunda. Dressed in black robes and with soot smeared across his skin, the newcomer was all but invisible. Diederic never saw the mace that crunched into the back of his helmet.

Diederic toppled at Godefroi's feet. Godefroi maintained his guard. "Who are you? What are you doing inside the Holy Sepulchre?"

The man threw back his cowl and gave Godefroi an impatient look. "There's more than one entrance, messire."

Godefroi gaped in astonishment. "Hugues?"

"May I suggest your men form a cordon around the Anastasis? No-one is to enter without your permission." Hugues took a step into a shaft of sunlight. "Hurry. There's not much time."

CHAPTER 13

15 July 1099

The Anastasis

"It was foolish of you to wander the streets before the city was taken." Godefroi sheathed his sword and removed his helmet and shield. His injured shoulder throbbed.

"A calculated risk," Hugues replied, "but not as foolish as it might first appear." He rolled up the sleeve of his habit to reveal a hauberk of chainmail underneath.

Godefroi shook his head. "Nothing is ever as it appears with you."

Hugues smiled grimly. "Believe me Godefroi, a time will come when we'll be stripped bare before each other in the sight of God." Hugues' gaze swept the remains of the once-great church. "If you would fear something, fear that day, for I certainly do."

Despite the growing heat, a chill brushed against Godefroi's skin. He shook it off with a shiver. "How did you reach the church before me? What were you doing inside there and who are we waiting for?"

Hugues laughed. The sound shocked Godefroi. The priest had always been so dour, or at best, practical. To hear his amusement, especially in this place, bordered on irreverence.

"Don't let it be said that I never answer a direct question." Hugues' eyes twinkled with what might be mistaken for excitement in another man.

"To answer your first question, I followed Baldwin. A wooden ladder gave me access to the street while you fought for control of the gatehouse. From there, I kept to the shadows and avoided everyone. As to your second question, I was eager to reach the Anastasis before any further damage could be inflicted upon it. And finally, we await Etienne and Gondemar. As I've said before, all five sacred points are required."

"What?" Godefroi asked in alarm. "You're bringing Godwera into the city?"

"*Gondemar*," Hugues replied with a warning look, "will be quite safe. He has Etienne for protection, along with a number of trusted servants loyal to the Salt Lines. It's Achambaud that I fear for. He's especially vulnerable to the pain this holy city is enduring."

Raging fires lit the sky and faint screams drifted across the rooftops. No doubt Moslem families were being dragged from their homes and slaughtered in the streets. Godefroi remembered Achambaud's agonised expression as he pleaded for mercy. "What would you have me do? Round up the civilians, expel them from the city and call it a kindness."

"It might prove a wise stroke," Hugues replied. "After all, what could galvanise the Caliph in Egypt more than the slaughter of an entire city? Would you let such an injury go unanswered?"

Godefroi grunted. It was a valid point. Retribution for sacking the city was inevitable.

"But no, that's not what I'd urge you to consider. Godefroi, all will be held to account before our lives are done. Our choices, even our inactions, will be weighed. Remember that."

"I hear that every time I enter a house of God," Godefroi replied. "Why should now be any different?"

"Because this is Jerusalem. The centre of everything." Hugues lapsed into silence.

Godefroi marvelled at his inability to understand Hugues. Here they stood at the brink of their goal and Hugues insisted they wait for a chevalier who disliked killing, a noblewoman who was supposed to be dead, and an engineer more at ease with tools than people.

"Ah," Hugues murmured. "Finally." He beckoned towards a group approaching the rotunda. A knot of milites surrounded Etienne and Godwera. The cowl of Godwera's habit covered most of her face.

"Quickly." Hugues beckoned to Achambaud. "With the garrison routed, it won't be long before Raymond is inside the city, if he isn't already."

Godefroi ignored Hugues and asked, "Gondemar, are you well?" Godwera nodded and kept her head bowed.

Etienne said, "All is well, messire. Both the Gate of Flowers and St Stephen have fallen. Your forces range throughout the city unchecked."

"And you, Achambaud," Godefroi asked, "I trust that's not your blood."

Achambaud glanced at the dark blotches staining his armour. He removed his helmet, as if the weight had suddenly become too much to bear. His face was pale and drawn. Black smudges underscored his dark eyes, which brimmed with misery.

"None of it is mine," Achambaud replied in an empty voice. "It only feels that way."

"You mustn't take the Saracen deaths to heart," Godefroi protested. "We fight in God's name and with His sanction."

"Do we?" Achambaud lifted his head and glanced between Godefroi and Hugues. "How can gutting defenceless women be called God's work? How can roasting small children on a spit and searching through the entrails of corpses for coin be called God's work?" His shaking voice rose with each question. "I've seen all of these things on this pilgrimage, and it makes me ashamed to name myself Christian."

A stunned silence settled over the group. Try as he might, Godefroi couldn't find a response.

"All my life," Achambaud continued in a raw voice, "I've been tormented for being...different. I won't become a persecutor like my father." He shook his head. "I couldn't live with that."

"Then trust me now." Hugues took Achambaud by the arm and drew him towards the apse. "I grieve for the sins committed as well." Hugues squeezed his arm. "Your conscience does you credit, but you must trust me when I say our cause is righteous. Gondemar?"

Godwera slipped her hand through the crook of Achambaud's free arm. He glanced down at her, almost surprised by her presence, before his expression softened. A pang of jealousy shot through Godefroi.

Hugues gestured towards the interior of the rotunda. "Duke Godefroi, you must be first to cross the threshold."

At last, something he understood: action, movement, leadership. Shaking off his concerns over Achambaud, Godefroi strode into the apse, passed the altar without genuflecting, and entered a low archway. A ring of shadow circled the space that enclosed the burial site of Jesus Christ.

Godefroi felt like he had stepped into another world. Perhaps it was the dome that curved overhead but remained open to the heavens at its apex. Or it might have been the soft sunlight that filtered into the chamber and bestowed a deep, lustrous glow upon the tiled floor. Whatever it was, no sounds of pillaging violated the cool serenity of this place. The air was sweet and free of smoke. While the stone of the rotunda was old and weathered, the light softened it, revealing hues of grey that reminded him of the morning mists in lower Lorraine.

In the centre of the Anastasis, the worn tiles gave way to rocky ground and a pile of jumbled stone. A simple wooden cross, taller than Godefroi, marked the site. He moved closer to examine the pile of stones. No cave or tomb was visible. The debris must have covered the opening.

"They've destroyed the Acdicula and filled in His tomb," Hugues said quietly at Godefroi's shoulder. "I knew this from the reports of pilgrims, of course. But to see it in person—" His voice trailed off.

"I don't understand," Achambaud said. "What is this Acdicula?"

"Back in the time of the Lord Jesus," Godwera said, "this whole area was a hill." Now that they were away from prying eyes, she had drawn back her cowl. "Back that way," she pointed towards the courtyard and the rubble, "was Golgotha, the site of the crucifixion. Emperor Constantine had the entire hillside excavated, levelling it so that his church could be built around the cave where the Resurrection took place. The Acdicula was an elaborate altar that protected the burial site."

"After Caliph Al-Hakim burned down the church," Hugues continued, "he ordered the tomb of Jesus be covered with rubble. It's somewhere beneath those rocks."

"Then what we seek is either buried or destroyed." Achambaud searched each face in turn. "All this death has been for nothing."

"It was always a possibility," Hugues replied, "but I don't believe so."

"Explain," Godefroi commanded. This was not the triumphant moment he had dreamed of. First the despoiled church, now the desecration of the Saviour's tomb.

"The Salt Lines came into possession of an ancient scroll from Judea some hundred years ago." Hugues replied. "It was just a fragment and badly damaged. Moreover, it was written in Hebrew and protected by a cipher, preventing our scholars from translating it. We only managed to decipher it with the assistance of Rabbi Ephraim ben Davide."

"Go on," Godefroi said.

"The text only contained a few lines. Even so, it remains a closely guarded secret. You must swear to never repeat what I'm about to say."

The others nodded.

Hugues closed his eyes and recited.

> *"Humble pilgrims from afar,*
> *With hearts steeped in honour,*
> *Remember who came before,*
> *Five as one forever.*
> *When sacred points are unified,*
> *O'er the ancient Sepulchre,*
> *Baphomet rises to once more,*
> *Her wisdom eternal's flower."*

The verse settled in Godefroi's mind, light and fragile as thinly spun glass.

After a long pause, Etienne said, "Who is *Baphomet*?" He frowned at the rotunda, as if the answer lay in its architecture.

"A reference to the Virgin Mary perhaps?" Achambaud suggested.

"A reasonable guess, but no." Godwera had released Achambaud's arm but remained next to him. "The reference to wisdom makes me think of Sophia, the Greek Goddess of wisdom. Some believe she's the feminine aspect of God."

Hugues grimaced. "A dangerous view."

Godefroi sensed an old argument resurfacing and a bitter tide of resentment rose inside him. Not only had Hugues arranged Godwera's marriage to Baldwin and then staged her death, it was obvious that Hugues had confided in her.

"This is all you have," Godefroi said. "This is the only clue to locating the great artefact the Salt Lines refuses to speak of. No wonder you need me to be crowned king. It'll take months to excavate the tomb with the clergy crawling over every inch of rubble. No secret can possibly survive such scrutiny."

"The verse was but the beginning, messire." Hugues crouched at the lip of the tiled floor. "Whatever the Caliph sought to destroy in this holy place, we must first believe that it endures. Second, we must trust the artefact never resided in such an obvious place." He reached underneath the tiles that jutted over the rubble and ran his fingers along the underside. "All I hope for is a marker." Hugues stopped. "Ah, the seventh. Godwera, please stand here."

Godwera moved to stand above the tile that hid whatever Hugues had found. Hugues paced around the edge of the circle, counting under his breath. He squatted again, searched beneath the lip of the tiles and placed a pebble to mark his spot. The process was repeated three more times as he circumnavigated the collapsed tomb.

"Etienne, your place is by that first stone. Achambaud, you take the second." After a brief hesitation, both men adopted their positions. The looks of bewilderment on their faces suggested only Godwera understood what Hugues was about.

"What is this?" Godefroi asked, refusing to budge.

"Ephraim, the Rabbi who helped us, warned that we'd have to assemble the Sacred Points in their correct positions," Hugues replied. "Godefroi, if you'll take your place by that third rock, we'll soon see if the way remains open."

Godefroi frowned but strode to the position Hugues indicated. He squatted and felt beneath the scorched tile. The ground was dry and dusty. The underside of the tile was covered in grit, except for a small, smooth section. Tiny grooves had been carved into the surface of the tile. Godefroi could not decipher them.

"What does it say?" He rose to his full height and directed the question at Hugues, who had taken up a position on Godefroi's left.

"It's the Hebrew numeral for ten, or in this case, the tenth," Hugues replied. "I'm standing before the eighth and moving around the circle to my left is the sixth, the seventh and the ninth."

"The tenth what?" Godefroi demanded. "Why have you never said anything about this before?"

"There was no need unless our siege proved successful." Hugues clasped his hands together. "I promise upon this holy site to explain everything I can, but we must complete the ritual before Raymond's forces arrive."

"What ritual?" Godefroi snapped.

"It stands for the tenth aspect of the Holy One," Godwera cut in. "Please Godefroi, Hugues is right. We must hurry."

"I need each of you to close your eyes and focus inwards," Hugues instructed. "Do it now."

Godefroi glanced at Godwera, who nodded in encouragement before clenching her eyes shut. He closed his eyes grudgingly.

"Picture your strength, your will and determination," Hugues said, his voice surrounding Godefroi in the circular chamber. "Gather it inside your body. Pull it inwards from your feet and hands. Feel it pooling in your chest, pressing against your ribs. Now imagine your strength transforms into light. It burns against your eyelids. It boils your breath and sears your scalp. The light is pouring forth from your skin. You're glowing brighter than a thousand candles. Now push the light out. Push it out into the place where Christ rose again. Release the light. Release it now."

Purple dots swarmed across Godefroi's eyelids. Despite his armour, he felt light enough to float above the tiles. The barest breath of wind would send him fluttering about the chamber. The light sank from his eyes, ebbing towards his stomach. It pooled in his bladder, hardening into a knot of pressure. For a moment he was afraid that he might urinate. The pressure between his legs became a physical weight pressing against his skin.

Release it now.

The knot split open and light surged outwards.

Godefroi's eyes flicked open in shock. He had never experienced anything like that before.

Floating above the rubble was a five-pointed star. The manifestation was faint, like a heat haze. Motes of dust floated through the pentacle, sparkling silver as they drifted through the connecting beams. Godefroi glanced down. One tip of the star radiated from just above his pubic mound.

"The Pentemychos," Hugues said in wonder.

The star wavered and drew inwards to the centre of the tomb. Godefroi experienced a sense of loss, a lessening, as it receded from him. Each of the points contracted into the centre of the rotunda. Only Etienne's lingered longer than the others, before collapsing into a single point and winking out.

The sound of horses clattering on flagstones and men hailing each other in French broke the spell. Godefroi stepped back from the tomb and immediately felt giddy. The disorientation passed after a few moments, leaving behind a cold certainty.

Count Raymond's retinue had finally arrived, so any further questions would have to wait.

CHAPTER 14

18 October 1307

Underground

The ground slammed into Bertrand's feet. He fell onto his side and lost his grip on Everard. The air throbbed again, an unearthly pulse that wrenched through his guts.

"Roard!" Grief splintered through the woman's cry.

Bertrand rose to his knees and blinked furiously. It was almost completely dark. Only a few rays of light filtered down from the left, about head height. He squinted. Where were they? He couldn't tell for sure. The air was musty and stale with a whiff of damp.

They had moved. Somehow—impossibly—the woman had transported them from their camp to this place.

Somewhere away from the soldiers. And his fallen brethren.

Bertrand sat in the dirt, too stunned to do anything else.

The symbol the woman had traced on the menhir glowed faintly in the darkness. The outermost circle around the flower stem was fading from silver to grey. It cast enough light for Bertrand to see that it was carved into a slab of rock like the one at their campsite.

Mercifully, the woman—the *witch*—had stopped screaming. She moaned "Roard" under her breath instead. The wheezing breathing of the wounded chevalier was thick and clotted with blood.

"Rémi?" Bertrand's voice was hoarse.

"I'm here, cub. Wherever that might be."

Bertrand released a pent-up breath. At least he was not alone with the witch and her fallen protector.

Everard moaned. Bertrand crawled across the hard packed earth, following a sticky trail of blood back to Everard.

"Rest easy," Bertrand whispered. "We're safe, I think." He lifted Everard's head into his lap. With the arrow lodged below Everard's collarbone, blood might be leaking into his lungs.

Everard moaned again. Was that an attempt to speak? He clutched at Bertrand's hand.

"Rémi, I need light to staunch his wound. Can you widen that gap to allow more sunlight in?" Bertrand pointed in the gloom.

"If I can reach." Rémi stumbled and something crunched beneath his boots.

The witch ignored them. Roard's breathing had become a horrible gurgle. "No, no, no," she whispered.

Bertrand clutched Everard in the gloom. So many of their brothers had died. Poor Arnaud and Roland. He pictured the savage intensity of the commander who had thrown the spear. The only reason Bertrand and Rémi had been spared was through witchcraft. He was not sure how he felt about that. Perhaps a clean death might have been better?

"Why would the King's Guard attack us?" Bertrand whispered, desperate to make sense of this situation.

A tremor shuddered through Everard's body. His breathing became shallow and fast. When Everard tried to reply, he gasped like a landed fish. Bertrand touched Everard's face and was horrified to find blood trickling down his chin. He knew what this meant.

"Rémi," Bertrand called. "I need more light. Now."

"I'm doing my best," Rémi snapped.

Metal struck rock. Another blow followed. Dirt and pebbles poured down onto Rémi, who spluttered.

"Careful," Bertrand called. "Don't bring it down upon us."

"Do you want out or not?" Rémi grunted and a boulder thudded onto the dry, packed earth. A cloud of dust billowed through the cavity and set Rémi coughing.

Tentative sunlight filtered through the breach. Bertrand blinked away the grit in his eyes. They had ended up in a chamber shaped like a beehive. Broad upright stones placed in a semi-circle supported the roof.

A large, black rock jutted from the centre of the chamber. Carved into the face of this stone was the stem-and-circles symbol that reminded Bertrand of a flower. Small cairns of rock had been placed between the makeshift pillars. Crude stone knives and wooden spears surrounded each cairn. A passage facing the central rock extended into the darkness.

The witch had brought them to a burial chamber.

Rémi retrieved his axe and staggered away from the breach. Dust had turned his bristly hair grey. Shards of pottery crunched beneath his feet.

"Help me," the witch cried out. She cradled Roard's head in her lap much like Bertrand held Everard.

"I don't want him dying where the light can't reach him," the witch said. "Please." Rémi hesitated, glancing between her and Everard.

"Help her," Bertrand said. "I can manage Everard."

Rémi nodded and strode over to the witch.

"Let's get you outside," Bertrand murmured.

With Everard's injured leg all but useless, Bertrand was forced to drag the Preceptor across the ground. Taking care to avoid the arrow, Bertrand looped his arms around the older man's chest. Everard moaned in pain.

The breach in the earth wall was narrow. Bertrand had to crouch down and drag Everard through the gap by his arms. Soil showered them as they passed through. Thankfully, the wall held, even when Everard's hip caught on a partially embedded rock and tore out a chunk of earth.

A chilly but fine autumn morning greeted them. Their makeshift tunnel emerged from a steep mound covered in thick grass. The sun sat low on the horizon, casting long shadows amongst the trees.

Bertrand dragged Everard away from the entrance and gently laid him out on the dewy grass. Blood oozed from the wound in his leg and the arrow quivered through the rings of his hauberk. Everard's face was a mask of pale, drawn skin. His eyes were sunken and bruised. More blood trickled from his mouth when he tried to speak. His eyes rolled in their sockets with desperation as he tried to force words past his throat.

"What is it?" Bertrand asked.

Everard tried again, but the guttural sounds he made were indecipherable.

"What would you have me do?" A tear ran down Bertrand's cheek. Everard saw it and smiled through his pain. The blood coating his teeth turned the expression into a grimace.

Bertrand gripped Everard's hand. "Let me carry your burden, brother."

Everard squeezed his fingers and fought for breath. His gaze flicked towards the hole in the side of the mound. Rémi emerged dragging Roard. The big chevalier was a dead weight that tested even Rémi's strength. The witch followed, staggering as she carried his feet. Roard was obviously dead and she knew it. Tears streamed down her face. In the sunlight, Bertrand saw faint white scars covered her face and hands.

Everard lifted a trembling hand towards the witch. Silent agony pulled at the corners of his mouth, but his eyes pleaded with Bertrand.

The strength left in the Preceptor in a rush. Everard's head lolled and his slack gaze found the sky. A final breath whispered through his lips in a long, low sigh of surrender.

Grief tore through Bertrand. A gaping emptiness opened inside him that was so deep and so wide, he feared he would tumble in and never escape from it. Bertrand tore furrows in the rich soil with his bare fingers. He ripped out chunks of grass and smeared dirt across his face. He took hold of Everard and shook him, demanding answers.

Why did this happen?

What am I supposed to do?

You were meant to be my new family!

Everard was gone and so were Bertrand's brothers. The thought of them watching him, judging, gave Bertrand the strength he needed. He arranged Everard's body into neat lines. Using dew from the grass, Bertrand gently wiped the worst of the dirt from Everard's slack face.

He said a short prayer over the corpse and rose to his feet. Rémi leaned against the slope of the barrow, watching Bertrand's ministrations. He nodded in quiet approval, his face impassive. Bertrand was grateful for that. Any expression of sympathy, no matter how small, would have shattered his fragile composure.

Bertrand's gaze slid to the witch. She had slumped over the body of Roard, sobbing softly into his chest. Everard had died because of her. And if the soldiers that attacked them truly were from the King's Guard, fleeing with her made him an outlaw. This was *not* the future he had hoped to carve out.

Bertrand took a step towards her. Grief switched to cold rage like parry to counter-stroke. "Who are you?" Bertrand demanded.

Rémi rose from his slouch and glanced between the two of them. "Have a care, cub."

Bertrand was beyond caution. "Answer me!" He took another step towards her. Fury prickled across his scalp and scalded the back of his eyes. "Look at me, witch."

She looked up at him, her face a mask of misery. Brown hair, almost black despite the sunlight, fell like a veil across one cheek. Her scars had faded since he first noticed them, now barely visible. Her dark eyes were wet with pain, and beneath that, something worse, something darker.

Here was the ill-omen, the one who had destroyed Bertrand's only chance of finding a place to belong. He gathered in his anger and grief and packed them into a tight ball in the centre of his chest. Each breath he took was fast and shallow, and filled with a satisfying ache.

The witch glanced at Everard, dropped her head, and she shuddered. She murmured something, too low to hear. Bertrand could almost see her gather in another shard of regret.

"I loved him too," she said quietly.

Whatever reply Bertrand had been about to make took flight.

"This is my true curse," she said to the ground. "Not to carry the wisdom eternal, but to be loved by those who cannot protect me. And to love them in return."

Looking up, she searched Bertrand's face. "Perhaps you can understand what that feels like now." She tilted her head as she examined him. "You ask who I am. I am *loss*, before anything else."

The emotions churning inside Bertrand refused to settle. He had a sense of the world contracting, as if the sum of his life was being drawn into this single moment to balance upon the knife-edge of his reaction. And in the churning confusion, all he could focus on was her face.

Her pain was too honest, too finely wrought, and yet brutal in its construction, to be fabricated. As he stared, he saw that she was a mirror to his feelings. She too had been isolated and lost all that she cared for. Yet most disconcerting of all, this woman, this scarred witch, was eerily beautiful in her sorrow.

His heart lurched, as it once had for Justine. He knew this delirium, this craving for approval. And it was accompanied by self-loathing that he should feel such a thing after so much death and loss. He would not be manipulated again.

"Who *are* you?" Bertrand repeated.

CHAPTER 15

15 October 1307

The River Marne

Roustan ground his teeth. His quarry had vanished. Cornered, on the brink of defeat, somehow—impossibly—she had engineered another escape. It was not the evasion that sent frustration sheeting through his veins. No, it was his inability to understand how it had been accomplished.

He closed his eyes and relived the final moments of the assault. Stupidly defiant to the end, the Preceptor had fallen, cut down by a stroke to his thigh. Roustan's spear had claimed the woman's Shroud. The hulking chevalier couldn't possibly survive such a terrible wound. So, she was all but defenceless, with only a squat sergeant and a young chevalier left to defend her. Then the ground had shuddered, the air had shimmered, and they were gone.

Roustan had given orders to search for any survivors. His remaining troops had shot him dark looks and more than once he caught someone muttering "witch". Not that he could blame them. He had arrived at much the same conclusion. Witchcraft was the only possible explanation.

Guillaume would need to know of this. Roustan paused as a new thought occurred to him. What if Guillaume already knew? Was that the reason he was hunting her so relentlessly?

Guillaume was careful in what he chose to confide: Roustan understood that. But did Guillaume understand what this witch was capable of? Eight guards dead, six wounded and another four still missing. How was Roustan supposed to explain such heavy casualties?

He needed to speak with Guillaume. He needed to understand what he was facing. Even if that meant temporarily giving up the search.

Roustan kicked the nearest corpse, not caring if it was one of his guards or a Templar. Damn that woman to the eternal fires of hell. He had been so close. What if another of Guillaume's agents located her? They would claim the priceless reward of Guillaume's lasting gratitude that he had rightfully earned.

"Pardon me, sir." The captain's tone was tentative.

"What?" It took all of Roustan's discipline to contain his rage. If only the soldiers had taken the camp sooner. He glanced at the large menhir looming at the top of the knoll.

No. She had chosen this place deliberately. The dice had been weighted in her favour.

"We have a prisoner."

Roustan regarded the captain, who watched him warily in return. "Have we now? Is he capable of being interrogated, or have your men shepherded him to death's doorstep?"

"We found him in the woods attempting to escape." The captain shifted on his feet. "He's sustained injuries, but he'll survive. If that's what you want?"

Roustan stroked his beard in thought. "Strip him and bring him to me."

"Yes, sir." The captain strode off, obviously relieved to have something to do. Roustan sat on a mossy rock. A Templar brother had fallen nearby. Roustan rested his boots on the rump of the corpse.

His back and legs ached, especially since the rush of battle had faded. He felt light-headed from lack of sleep and his eyes were gritty. The forced ride from the Commanderie had taken all day and a fair portion of the night. The guards would need rest, especially the injured, if they were to continue being useful.

Roustan chewed the inside of his lip. He needed rest too.

The captain returned with two of his soldiers. They dragged a forlorn figure between them. The brother had been stripped naked. Angry, purple bruises mottled his skin and long welts ran the length of his back, suggesting he had been beaten with the flat of a sword or a spear. A trickle of blood ran from a shallow scalp wound into his beard.

The soldiers released the brother. He fell to his knees and huddled against the cold, misty air.

"And who is this, Captain?" Roustan asked in a cheerful voice.

"Says his name is Amyon, sir. We found him dressed in a sergeant's garb soaked in his own piss."

Roustan addressed the prisoner. "Is that your real name?"

The sergeant shivered and avoided his gaze.

"Amyon, allow me to do you the courtesy of being forthright." Roustan leaned forward to gaze into his dirty, miserable face. The sergeant cringed like a beaten dog.

"You *are* going to die today," Roustan said. "There's no avoiding that fate, I'm afraid. However, some deaths are far harder than others. Especially those reserved for heretics. But as the Holy Church teaches, you can find salvation through repentance." Roustan lowered his voice. "So Amyon, where were you going?"

Amyon did not respond.

Roustan grabbed him by the beard. "If you've anything of value to say, I'd advise you to offer it now. Otherwise, I'll have my men shove a pole up your arse and slowly roast you over a fire."

The two soldiers laughed. Roustan ignored them.

"Name's Amyon, sir." He ducked his head as a peasant might when addressing his betters. "Begging your pardon, but I'm just a sergeant. I don't know why we snuck out in the middle of the night."

Roustan sat back and watched Amyon through slitted eyes. His speech was rough like a peasant's, but a clever man could fake that.

"Humble Amyon, if Everard de Chaumont brought you with him, it means he trusted you. Playing the ignorant fool won't wash with me." Roustan nodded at one of the soldiers. The man enthusiastically cuffed Amyon about the head. The sergeant did not whimper or plead for clemency.

"Where were you heading?"

"I don't know, sir."

"Who was the woman with you?"

"What woman, sir?"

"The woman in the cloak," Roustan snapped. "She was constantly being guarded by that lumbering chevalier I killed."

"Begging your pardon, but I don't know, sir. The Preceptor, he never explained who they were or what we were about. I swear it."

Roustan grabbed Amyon by the hair and jerked his head back. "Last chance," Roustan warned. The sergeant was forced to meet his gaze. Whatever he saw in Roustan's face made his brown eyes widen in fear.

"We never had time for talk or explanations," Amyon babbled. "The Preceptor, he just told us to remember our vows."

Roustan released Amyon with a snap of his wrist. "Captain, have your men build a fire."

"Yes, sir." The captain nodded at one of the soldiers who scurried off.

"And find me a nice, thick spear," Roustan called.

Amyon moaned and began to pray.

A thought suddenly struck Roustan. "Your company," he said. "They were all known to you, except for the cloaked woman and her protector. Correct?"

Amyon nodded miserably.

"Then you can tell me the name of the young chevalier who escaped."

"I—" Amyon hesitated. "Escaped?"

The man was feigning ignorance. Roustan was certain of it. Something more subtle than crude pain was needed to break his resistance.

"The young chevalier," Roustan repeated patiently. "With the curly brown hair and patchy beard. At least a head taller than me. You know him, don't you?"

Amyon's head dropped.

Yes, the sergeant knew the brother Roustan was referring to. "What is his name?"

"Can't be sure," Amyon said, "but that sounds like Guichard de Montbard."

"Guichard," Roustan repeated. "See, you can be helpful if you set your mind to it. Captain, would you be kind enough to retrieve the register I took from the Commanderie? It's in my saddle bag on the left flank."

Amyon stilled.

Roustan made a show of noticing his interest. "That's right. I took the register from your Seneschal. Let's see. I think that was right before I slit his throat. Made a terrible mess of his writing desk."

Amyon visibly paled. "Thibauld...dead?"

"Afraid so." Roustan smiled sympathetically. "Along with your Marshal, the Almoners and that insufferable Chaplain that should've gone to God years ago. The rest of your brothers are in chains awaiting the outcome of the charges lodged against them."

Amyon's defiance wilted. "But how?"

"By order of the King."

The captain returned with the leather-bound journal that recorded the names of all brothers who had joined the Commanderie.

"Excellent." Roustan took the register from the captain. "Let's find this Guichard of yours. Surely, he can't be hard to—"

Amyon leapt at Roustan. Caught by surprise, he tumbled backwards off the rock and something hard crashed into the side of Roustan's head. Amyon clawed at Roustan's armour as pink and green spots swarmed across Roustan's vision. He felt his belt knife drawn from its sheath. Alarm shot through Roustan's fog of disorientation.

The knife rose above him. Roustan tried to shove the sergeant away, but the man was too heavy.

The tip of a spear suddenly burst from Amyon's naked chest. The tip nearly caught Roustan in the face. As it was, he was showered in blood.

Amyon glanced down in shock. The knife fell from his grasp and he shuddered. He bared his teeth at Roustan, the expression both fierce and triumphant.

The soldier who had skewered Amyon ripped his spear out. Amyon collapsed on top of Roustan, his face locked in that terrible grimace. Roustan wriggled out from underneath the dead Sergeant and hands helped him up. The worried expression on the captain's face swam in and out of focus.

"You killed him." Roustan's tongue was thick in his mouth.

"No choice, sir."

Roustan supposed that was true. He sank against the boulder. "Give me a moment."

The spots eventually faded. His head pounded from the fall, although it could have been much, much worse. The soldiers lit a fire and brought warm water to wash his face. The captain offered a bowl of broth and a hunk of hard bread. Roustan dipped the bread and ate gingerly.

He had no choice now. Many of the soldiers were injured and needed rest. Trying to reach Guillaume on horseback in his current state was madness. Another fall could kill him. Besides, riding alone without an escort was unthinkable.

Once he finished the broth, Roustan picked up the register. He wiped off the worst of the mud and opened the stiff, leather cover. It contained a long list of names, starting with the inception of the Commanderie and moving forward in time. A cross next to those early names indicated they had passed into God's care.

Roustan flipped through the earliest pages until he reached the most recent entries. Thoughtfully, the Seneschal had instituted the use of four columns: one for the laity, one for the Armigeri Servienti—or sergeants and squires—one for the priests, and one for the chevaliers.

Roustan ran his finger down the last column. As expected, there was no Guichard. But a 'Bertrand de Châtillon-sur-Seine' was listed in the Armigeri Servienti column. A recent looking line had been placed through that entry and his name was the last to appear in the "Chevalier" column.

Squinting to decipher the small letters, Roustan read the date of Bertrand's initiation as a chevalier: 11 October 1307.

Only four days ago.

Roustan massaged his aching neck as he pictured the fear and determination mingling on the young chevalier's face. Yes, that one had only recently won his white habit. Perhaps there *was* something he could do while recovering from his ordeal.

Not long afterwards, a lone, disgruntled soldier rode out from the quiet camp with a hastily penned letter from Roustan. Instead of heading towards the road to Troyes, he turned south, in the direction of Châtillon-sur-Seine.

CHAPTER 16

18 October 1307

Grave mound

"Who am I?" The witch rose from her crouch over Roard's corpse and pushed her charcoal-coloured hair from her face. "Someone Everard chose to protect with his life."

Bertrand couldn't deny that, although it was hardly the answer he was hoping for.

Rémi coughed into the awkward silence. "Begging your pardon, but that's not what Bertrand here asked."

The witch's flat, dark-eyed gaze shifted to Rémi. "I suppose not, if you value names over truth." Tears still leaked from almond-shaped eyes.

Bertrand glanced at Everard's body lying on the grass. Some of his anger returned. Whatever she was suffering couldn't diminish the loss of Everard.

The witch was watching him again. A measure of thoughtfulness had entered her expression. Bertrand sensed she was assessing him, gauging his adequacy to a task that he couldn't begin to guess at.

She sighed and knelt by Roard. Her long, slim fingers stroked the chevalier's blood-spattered face. The mail coif was unnecessary now, so she lifted his head and drew it back. Roard's hair was dark blond under his padded cap and longer than typical for a chevalier. Sweat stained his temples. The witch brushed aside Roard's fringe and placed a chaste kiss on his forehead. Her fingers trembled and her lips became a taut, unhappy line.

"Farewell, my Shroud," she breathed.

Bertrand felt like he was spying on some intimacy he had no right to witness. He recalled the feeling of creeping through his father's chateau at night, keeping to the shadows so that he might eavesdrop upon discussions with powerful relatives. Members of the Salt Lines, he knew now. Only there was no excitement in watching her tenderness, no rush of fear at the thought of discovery. Just a sense of shame that lessened him.

The witch kissed Roard on each cheek. More tears slid down the faint scars on her cheeks.

Bertrand cleared his throat. "Rémi's right. You haven't given us your name or any explanation as to why we were attacked. Everard, I mean, the Preceptor—" Bertrand choked on a fresh surge of grief.

The witch ignored him. She touched Roard's forehead, closed her eyes and murmured words too low to catch. It might have been a prayer for his departed soul, but if so, it was brief. She rose to her feet, eyes still closed, and rocked from side to side. Bertrand had the impression she was drawing upon reserves of courage as a chevalier might before going into battle.

"You want my name, yet you fail to offer yours in return." She inhaled deeply and opened her eyes. "Tell me, what should I conclude from your lack of courtesy?"

Bertrand considered his options. Offering his name to a witch was dangerous. Whereas insisting on anonymity would make him appear evasive, even afraid. For some reason—heaven help him—he did not wish to appear either before her.

"My name is Bertrand de Châtillon-sur-Seine. This is my friend, Rémi. You'll forgive our lapse in courtesy given the situation, I hope."

"You've a talent for understatement, Chevalier Bertrand." Nothing in her expression softened, yet her formality relented. "My name is Salome, and I'll tell you no more than that until I know you to be a true friend." She drew a small pouch from inside her cloak and untied the neck.

Bertrand glanced at Rémi in concern. Rémi shrugged, although his fingers twitched, as if they were grasping for the haft of the axe he had left inside the grave mound.

Salome poured salt from the pouch into her palm. Bertrand frowned. She pinched the crystals into a pile in the centre of her hand and approached Bertrand. He was a full head taller than her, yet her proximity was unnerving. A faint scent teased him—cloves and cinnamon, perhaps— but he was afraid to inhale too deeply for fear of bewitchment.

She held her palm up. Bertrand gazed into eyes so dark he could see his reflection. Whatever she thought or felt was buried too deeply for him to tell.

Bertrand stared at the salt balanced on her palm. He had seen his father perform this ritual once when emissaries from the Count of Champagne had visited.

"Don't eat anything she gives you," Rémi warned.

"That's not what this is for." Bertrand placed the tip of his thumb in the centre of the salt with his fingers pointing to his left. Pressing down gently, he rotated his hand until his fingers faced right. Bertrand withdrew his thumb, leaving a circle in the salt.

Salome made a fist and dribbled the crystals back into her pouch. "Everard said you were descended from them." She drew the strings of her pouch tight. "But not educated in their ways. It seems he was misinformed."

"I was never good enough." The reply slipped out before Bertrand could stop it.

"Secrecy has always been our friend." A shadow of Salome's earlier grief flickered across her face. "Until now."

"The King's Guard," Bertrand said. "They're after you."

"Yes."

"Why?"

"Answering that question will raise many others." The pouch of salt disappeared back into her cloak. "If you truly wish to know, you must forsake your earlier vows and bind our fates together."

"Bertrand," Rémi interrupted. "Have done with her. You don't know who she is or what she wants, but look where it got that poor fellow." He nodded towards Roard's corpse.

Bertrand examined Salome's face for any kind of reaction. His gaze lingered on the dark sweep of her eyebrows, her high cheekbones, and the swell of her lips. Even the mystery of her faint scars was tantalising.

"Everard wanted me to protect her," Bertrand murmured.

"Maybe, maybe not," Rémi countered. "I doubt the Preceptor knew what hell she was leading us into."

"Rémi's right," Salome interrupted. "You must choose, Bertrand. One path requires courage, the other an ability to live with lasting regret. And you must choose now, once and for always." Her rich voice was spiced with just the hint of a foreign accent.

"Are you merely a chevalier or part of something greater?" Salome asked. "Will you bear witness to a deeper truth or feign ignorance?"

"How do you—" Bertrand took a step back. "That was *you* in the chapel?" Since leaving the Commanderie, there had been little time to consider the offer made during his vigil. It suddenly made sense: Roard had pinned him to the tiles while Salome had disguised her voice.

"Of course." She shrugged. "A man's voice and gait are not so hard to feign." Salome glanced at the sun. "We have no more time, I'm afraid.

Our escape is only temporary and purchased at the highest possible price. The man who seeks me won't give up, so you must choose now. Will you honour your heritage and become my Shroud, or will you turn your back on your ancestry?"

Bertrand took in the still figures of Roard and Everard. He glanced at Rémi who shook his head. He recalled the savage expression of the commander who cast the spear that had killed Roard. He did not doubt that man, whoever he was, sought them at this very moment. And yet...hadn't he always dreamed of emulating the mighty deeds of his ancestors? Perhaps this was his chance, although it had arrived in a way he had never imagined.

"I don't understand what you're asking of me," Bertrand replied. "Nor do I understand how we came to be here, away from the river."

"And I can tell you none of it until our fates become one." Salome clasped her hands together. "They'll find me soon if I remain alone and unprotected. If you'll not be my Shroud, I must find another quickly."

"This Shroud, is it some kind of bodyguard?"

"That, and more." Salome's tone hinted at complexities that Bertrand could only guess at.

"Bertrand, she's not for you." Rémi pointed a finger at Salome. "You can't ask him to make this decision. Bloodlines aside, he's barely into his manhood. I don't know what secrets you're hiding, and I don't care to. You've already brought us too much grief. Leave us in peace."

"If only I could," Salome replied sadly. "I wish Roard was still alive. I wish good, honest Everard hadn't left with him. I wish my need wasn't so great that I must ask Bertrand to shoulder a burden he is unprepared for. But wishing is for those who can't make decisions or have no choices left."

"I killed two men today," Bertrand said. "I might be young, but I'm not a boy anymore." Rémi tried to protest. "No, Rémi. I value your counsel, but you can't stand between me and my conscience. Everard wanted me to protect her. I owe him that much."

"Bertrand." Rémi strode forward and gripped his arm. "You can't know what's in a man's mind when he dies. That's between him and God."

Bertrand smiled. "Maybe not, but Everard died protecting this woman. If he believed her worthy of that sacrifice, then so do I."

Rémi's expression hardened. "Listen, I—"

"Enough." Bertrand shook of Rémi's hand. "What must I do?" he asked Salome.

"In the name of the holy blazing angels," Rémi cursed. "Why was

I ever saddled with the most obstinate, goat-bred, mule-born child that ever walked the earth?" He kicked the ground and a clod of earth sailed through the air. "If you must have this Shroud, at least pick someone who has a chance of defending you."

Salome laughed. Her mirth caught both men by surprise.

"Rémi that was perhaps the least gracious offer I've ever received." Her amusement quickly faded. "But you don't belong to the Salt Lines. I can see that from your features and bearing. I'd be honoured, and grateful, if you remained our companion though."

"Where he goes, I follow," Rémi said with a jerk of his thumb at Bertrand. "Despite what he might think of it."

Bertrand snorted. He had been afraid she would choose Rémi over him. For some reason, the mere thought of it sent a jealous twist through his gut. How could that be possible when only a few minutes ago he had blamed her for the death of Everard and the rest of his brethren? Had she bespelled him to create this sudden yearning to help her? Or was he just a fool when it came to women in need?

Bertrand sank to one knee. "What would you have me do?"

Salome smiled down at him. "Take my hand."

Her skin was hot and smooth. Bertrand was conscious of his rough calluses earned from training with sword and axe.

"Bertrand, repeat what I say," Salome said. "You must speak the words in your heart and your mouth. Do you understand?"

"Yes, I think so."

"Bertrand...don't do this," Rémi pleaded.

"I've set my mind, Rémi. That's the end of it."

"Then let's have it done." Salome took a deep, steadying breath. Her grip on his hand tightened.

In that pause, between his life before and what it was to become, Bertrand glimpsed the woman she must have been once, before the course of her life had led her to this point...

...a damp field with a barrow mound looming behind her like an omen. Hunted and alone. Stripped of protection and those dearest to her. Her only resources a newly made chevalier and his stalwart sergeant. How could any of them see the burden she carried safely to rest with all of the forces of Severity pursuing her? She was weary, so incredibly weary. Death and destruction followed wherever she went. When would it end? Could it ever, truly end?

Bertrand blinked in astonishment. Was he hearing her thoughts? He drew back but she did not release her grip. The bones in his hand ached from the building pressure of her touch. A cold finger of fear trailed down his spine.

Salome spoke. "I, Bertrand de Châtillon-sur-Seine, do solemnly swear before God that I renounce all previous vows, to act as both advocate and defender of the Lady Salome, until my mortal existence expires. In the name of the Holy *Shechinah*, let it be thus."

He repeated the vow, taking care to enunciate each word clearly.

The pressure of her grip intensified and a searing sensation burned through the webbing of his hand. Salome released him with a sad, knowing smile. Bertrand snatched his hand back and rubbed his skin. Etched into the webbing between thumb and index finger was a tiny rose. White scar-lines, like Salome's, had branded his blotchy flesh.

"My mark," Salome said in a tight voice. "It signifies that we're bound for as long as you draw breath."

"Bertrand, are you well?" Rémi asked anxiously.

"I—" He was not sure.

Bertrand gazed up at Salome. A subtle glow had infused her body. The radiance was strongest along her scars. Bertrand closed his eyes and shook his head in confusion. The glow did not diminish. If anything, it became stronger in his mind's eye. He was aware of her presence, whether he could see her or not.

"We are becoming attuned," she explained.

Bertrand opened his eyes. "Attuned?"

"You're the veil—the Shroud—that separates me from this world and…what lies beyond." The tip of her tongue moistened her lips as she chose her next words. An unexpected current of eroticism pulsed through Bertrand's loins.

"I'll explain as much as I can, but we must move from here. The agents of Severity know I can travel along the salt lines. They'll work out where we've gone soon enough."

"Wait. I thought the Salt Lines were a group of ancient families. Not…not this." He gestured helplessly at the grave mound.

"The two are inseparably linked," Salome replied. "The families you know as the Salt Lines descended from the ancients who built the great stone circles and menhirs. Using the heavens and sacred geometry, their seers discovered channels of power that criss-cross the land at regular intervals. The first menhirs were designed to mark such intersections. Devotees gathered around these markers, and villages grew around them. Trade soon followed, and since salt was the most important currency of that time, the channels became known as salt lines."

"And you've moved us along one of these *channels*," Bertrand asked with a frown.

"Yes, although it takes energy and we've lost more time than you realise. Three full days have passed." Salome glanced at the sky again.

"How is that possible?" Bertrand felt increasingly ignorant in her presence.

Salome touched his forehead with the tips of her long fingers. "I *will* explain, I promise. But we must leave immediately. The menhir at the river was damaged, as many of them are now. It only allowed me to move us south or north along the vertical. I fear they'll guess which direction I chose."

"And what direction would that be?" Rémi had folded his arms across his barrel chest. For once, Bertrand couldn't read his expression.

"South," Salome replied. "Champagne and Burgundy are no longer the haven they once were. My pursuers will expect me to head north in the hope of reaching the coast." She rubbed her upper arms. "A ship is waiting for me, but I dare not risk it now."

"A ship," Bertrand repeated. "With winter approaching? Where are you hoping to sail to?"

"England. A…sanctuary has been prepared for me." Salome twisted the sleeve of her cloak. "Everard was to escort us to the vessel."

Bertrand absorbed this news in silence.

"And who exactly is looking for us?" Rémi pressed.

Salome considered Rémi's question. "Across all of France, agents of King Philippe are taking the members of your Order into custody. No Commanderie or Preceptory or minor estate will be spared."

"That's impossible," Bertrand said. "Our Order is only answerable to His Holiness."

Salome dismissed Bertrand's protest with a flick of her wrist. "Rest assured Philippe will find a way to justify his actions. His Keeper of the Seals is sure to find some loophole in canon law. Now please. We must leave. No matter how hard it is to part with those we loved." She glanced at Roard and her bottom lip trembled.

"No wonder you were in a rush for Bertrand to swear his oath." Rémi hawked and spat on the ground. "We'll have to keep to the woods. I'll see what I can salvage." He returned to the barrow.

Bertrand shivered. Only a few days ago the path of his life had finally turned down a fork that promised fulfilment. Now he did not even know where they were or why they were being pursued.

"We can't leave them here." Bertrand nodded at the bodies. "And I take it we've no time for a proper Christian burial."

Salome shook her head.

"Then I think it best we leave them in the grave with our sincerest apologies." He did not wait for her reply. Bertrand gripped Everard by the wrists and dragged his corpse back into the barrow.

Rémi helped Bertrand drag Roard into the grave mound. The man was unbelievably heavy. Bertrand felt small and inadequate next to Roard's bulk. Rémi had managed to retrieve some of their supplies from the burial chamber along with his axe and Everard's sword. "Take it," was all he said when he offered Everard's blade to Bertrand.

The sword was the same length as the ones Bertrand had trained with, although the leather grip wrapped around the hilt was finer. Etched leaves curled around the quillons and an enamel version of the *Beauseant* had been set into the round pommel. The red cross, set on a field of black above and white below, gleamed dully.

Rémi set about breaking some of the pagan spears into pieces.

"What's that for?" Bertrand was pleased to find his voice was steady.

"Kindling. We won't find any dry wood to light a fire and come night, you'll be grateful for some light and heat."

Salome sifted through the sacks and saddle bags Rémi had found, sorting out essential items. By the time they were ready to depart, the sun was peeking over the top of the barrow. Despite her outward calm, Bertrand sensed a deep anxiety from Salome.

Rémi used the shaft of a broken spear to collapse the hole they had made in the barrow. Sods of grass tumbled into the breach. It was hardly a fitting burial for Everard, but it was better than leaving him outdoors to be mauled by wild animals.

They approached the tree line with the rising sun behind them. Clouds were rolling in from the south, promising further rain. Bertrand offered a silent farewell to Everard and plunged between the trees.

CHAPTER 17

15 July 1099

The Holy Sepulchre

An orderly line of soldiers emerged into the barren courtyard of the Holy Sepulchre followed by a handful of mounted nobles.

"At last," Godefroi breathed. "I'm going to enjoy this."

"Don't let him goad you into anything rash." Hugues moved back a step to leave Godefroi in clear possession of the Anastasis. Godefroi's men had assembled in a knot outside the apse. They muttered quietly and shifted their feet as the Provençals approached.

Count Raymond de Toulouse was accompanied by at least three-score men. Many of the Provençal nobles were known to Godefroi, but his gaze remained fixed upon Raymond.

"Raymond," Godefroi called out. "May I present what remains of the Holy Sepulchre." He gestured to the rubble and patched walls of the rotunda.

Raymond regarded the site with a dispassionate, one-eyed stare. He had lost the other eye fighting the Moors in Iberia. The long scar that cut across his eye socket and down his cheek was a constant reminder of his distinguished military record. Grey haired, hatchet-faced and lean, Raymond was like a thin blade of tempered iron.

"Godefroi, you're alive. How remarkable." Raymond dismounted stiffly from his black mare. Only the wealthiest of nobles still retained mounts. "Can we say the same of your ambitious sibling, Baldwin?"

"We can indeed. As we speak, he's driving through the city towards the Temple Mount."

"Ah, well he'll meet my forces there." Raymond removed his gauntlets with exaggerated care. "The Governor and his personal guard fled to the Tower of David before our onslaught. No doubt the panic spread north."

Godefroi suppressed a flicker of irritation. "I believe my men breached the northern wall well before your followers secured the southern parapet. News of *our* success probably convinced the Governor to abandon his post."

Raymond pursed his lips. "If the reports are to be believed, my men faced a far greater concentration of defenders. Therefore, any success you've enjoyed can be at least partially attributed to me."

"Come my lords," Peter Desiderius interrupted, "we shouldn't quarrel on this blessed occasion." The young priest and visionary stepped between the two men. He was accompanied by Peter of Narbonne, the Bishop of Albara. Awe softened Desiderius' expression as he gazed at the rotunda. "Haven't all good Christians dreamed of this day?"

Peter of Narbonne was older than Desiderius and walked with a slight limp. He kept his black hair short but had grown a beard, as there was not enough water to spare for shaving. "Peter's right," Narbonne said. "We should be rejoicing, not arguing."

Raymond ignored both members of the clergy. "Godefroi, have you crossed the threshold?"

Narbonne gave Godefroi a searching look.

"Only briefly, your reverence." Godefroi addressed Narbonne as the most senior member of the clergy present. "None of my men would loot or damage such a holy place." Godefroi glanced at Raymond. "Rest assured only those with devotion in their hearts will be allowed entry."

Raymond stiffened at the inference.

"Excellent." Desiderius dry-washed his hands as he gazed longingly at the rotunda. He seemed oblivious to the narrow look Narbonne directed at him. "The Holy Church extends its thanks for recovering the site of the Resurrection."

Raymond twisted the gauntlets in his hands. "Duke Godefroi, am I correct in understanding that you propose to determine who should be allowed entry into the Holy Sepulchre?"

Narbonne paled at this suggestion. He glanced at Hugues in concern.

"My lord, that is not correct." Hugues stepped forward and addressed Narbonne. "Your reverence, I can attest to the fact that it was Duke Godefroi who liberated the Holy Sepulchre. As his chaplain, I know it's his heartfelt desire to protect this sacred place. No lord, or member of the clergy, could lay claim to it when clearly it belongs to all Christians. Therefore, Duke Godefroi would welcome Count Raymond and his men in the spirit of the brotherhood of Christ."

Raymond gave Hugues a vicious look. If the Count entered the

Anastasis now, it would be under the auspices of Godefroi's gener-osity, even though Hugues had relinquished any claim to the Holy Sepulchre. But if Raymond refused the offer, he couldn't complete his vow to pray at the site of Christ's resurrection.

Narbonne considered Hugues for a moment, his thoughtful express-ion conveying depths of understanding that Godefroi hadn't expected. Eventually, Narbonne nodded gratefully. "The Church is indeed fortunate to have such devoted servants." He took a deep breath and avoided Raymond's furious look. "Until such time as the city is subdued, it would be wise to solicit the protection of such valiant warriors. Therefore, I accept your generous offer."

"You don't have the authority to appoint him as protector of this site," Raymond protested.

"I make no appointments," Narbonne replied. "I've merely accepted an offer of protection until the city is secure. The Council of Princes will determine the issue of secular leadership. Now if you'll excuse me, I wish to fulfill my vow and offer a prayer of thanks." Narbonne swept past them and entered the apse, followed eagerly by Desiderius.

Red blotches mottled Raymond's face. "This discussion is not finished, Godefroi."

"Of that, messire, I'm certain," Godefroi replied with a smile.

Raymond mounted his steed. "I will make sure the Governor cannot escape. He'll make a good hostage." Raymond gazed around the ruins in frustration before jerking his reins. The Provençals followed their leader through the southern entrance and back towards the Tower of David.

"The next battle begins," Hugues murmured.

"No." Godefroi shook his head with a rueful expression. "It has been waged constantly since we left Constantinople."

The last Provençal disappeared from sight.

Godefroi glanced at Hugues. "What of the tomb?" he asked in a murmur. "You've effectively handed it over."

"We had no choice." A look of excitement infused Hugues' face. "But we have what we came for, I think. Now we need a roof over our heads and a detailed map of the city."

CHAPTER 18

15 July 1099

The āl-Aqsa Mosque

His tenure had come to an end, at last.

The Sharif sensed it in the bones of the city and the currents in the wind. Deep within his body, in the sacred place of his being, the balance of things had shifted. His successor approached, vital and unpredictable.

As the fierce, fair-headed Franj conquered the city, the Sharif allowed himself a modicum of regret. Change was inevitable. He knew this from his long years. But he regretted the upheaval, the toll of lives it always exacted. Would mankind ever learn to embrace a lasting peace?

He knelt on his prayer mat and placed his forehead on the floor. His prayer was offered in the form that he had learned as a child, facing Mecca. He prayed for the inhabitants of Jerusalem, whose lives were being so carelessly shed.

For the Franj, he could find no prayer or forgiveness. How could such a wild, uncultured people be chosen to bear the weight of the responsibility he and his brethren had shouldered for so long?

Sandals clattered on the stone steps outside his private chamber. The door burst open. Kamil ibn Hasan gasped for breath. The Sharif knew who it was without looking. He knew Kamil's emanation. He knew every inch of the āl-Aqsa Mosque and its devotees as he knew his own body. Many of the faithful cowered inside the mosque above, hoping for mercy. They would ask him to protect them. Denying that request would be his most painful task.

"Apologies, ālim Sharif," Kamil said in a breathless voice. *ālim Sharif: learned noble.* Would they still think of him as such after today?

"The Franj are slaughtering everyone they find," Kamil blurted in fear. "It won't be long before they reach us. Will you not treat with them?"

The Sharif rose from his prayer mat. Facing the wall, he took a long, calming breath. He turned to Kamil and crushed all remaining hope. "I'm sorry you must bear this message, Kamil. I wish that it were another." A bitter taste curdled his mouth. "Tell them that I will not come. Tell them their lives are in the hands of Allah. All will be as it is written. Allāhu akbar." *God is great.*

Kamil's eyes widened in surprise and his thin shoulders shook beneath his robe. Respect for the ālim Sharif withered across Kamil's face and died. The Sharif tallied another regret in his heart, but he let none of it soften the stern expression on his face.

"I won't tell them," Kamil replied in a trembling voice. He shook his head, perhaps trying to dislodge what he had just been told. The Sharif waited patiently, although he knew little time remained. The Franj drew near.

Kamil gathered his composure and spat out the words the Sharif needed to hear. "Such a message must be delivered by the coward who spoke it."

The Sharif bowed his head. A lifetime of respect spent in a single moment. How could Mercy contend with Severity when it was so easy to destroy what had taken so long to build? He backed against the stone wall and pressed the concealed catch with a click. A draft of air brushed against his calves.

Kamil gaped at the hidden passage. His expression turned to fury. "You intend to flee? To abandon us when we need you the most?"

"No," the Sharif replied calmly. "I intend for *you* to flee. Go to the place of caves by the sea. Tell them—" The Sharif paused, choosing the right words, the ones that would convey enough but not too much should Kamil be caught. "Tell my brothers that the wind blows from the west and we are all dust before it."

Doubt eroded Kamil's anger. The Sharif shifted perception for a moment to examine Kamil's emanation. Spikes of fear still shot through his anger and disappointment. The core of Kamil's being, however, was hardening into something approaching determination. He would need every ounce of it in the days ahead.

The Sharif made Kamil repeat the message three times before he was satisfied.

"And what of you?" Kamil asked.

He noted the absence of his usual honorific but also caught a note of conciliation in Kamil's voice. Silently, he thanked Ein Sof, the Unknowable, for that small comfort.

"I will wait for the Franj in the place they seek." He retrieved his scimitar and dagger from where they rested next to the door.

The familiar weight of the blades felt good, although he was a shell of what he had once been. "Go now," the Sharif said. "Don't fail me."

He bustled Kamil towards the passage.

A scream echoed down the steps, followed by harsh battle cries that shattered the serenity of the mosque. Kamil stopped, half inside the tunnel, a question upon his lips.

"Quickly, now," the Sharif urged.

Kamil climbed inside with a grimace. "ālim Sharif, what place do the Franj seek?"

"Peace be upon you, my son." He slammed the stone facade shut and made sure that it had sealed properly. Only then did he answer the question in words spoken too softly for any to hear. "The place of Solomon, which I am sworn to defend until another takes my place."

CHAPTER 19

15 July 1099

The Temple Mount

Save us. Have pity on the children. Show mercy.

The voices whispering to Achambaud had become more incessant as the day waned. At first, they had only crept into his mind when he was idle. Now that the sacking of the city had begun in earnest, the cries invading his head had become increasingly desperate. Fearing for his sanity, Achambaud had found the one person who could help him.

"This way." Achambaud yanked on Hugues' sleeve as they moved down the narrow, abandoned street.

"Where are you taking me?" Hugues asked.

"You must see this."

"Achambaud, I hardly think it's safe to be roaming the streets."

He swung around to face Hugues. "All resistance ended when we took the wall. The only danger we need fear now is from our own people."

Hugues blinked in surprise. "What's happening to you?" he asked, placing one hand on Achambaud's mailed shoulder.

"Voices. In here." Achambaud tapped the side of his head. "Get out," he said through gritted teeth. "Get out! Get out!"

"Who's speaking to you?" Hugues demanded. "Tell me."

"I'll show you," Achambaud replied in a bleak voice.

The street intersected with another alley to form a small souk. Many of the stalls were overturned or damaged, their goods looted. A few bolts of undyed linen had been ground underfoot and a shattered jar of honey seeped into the cloth.

Achambaud spotted three headless Saracen bodies. Perhaps they were merchants caught trying to salvage their wares. Their heads had been stacked together on a wooden bench in a pyramid. Someone had cut out their tongues and arranged them neatly in a row. The tongues had blackened as they dried out. They reminded Achambaud of hideously swollen dates. Flies swarmed around the remains in a frenzy.

Have pity on us. Show mercy, Achambaud.

They knew his name now. Achambaud shivered in the deepening twilight. The incessant, desperate voices called to him from the east.

"This way." Achambaud wove through narrow alleys. His route took them south on occasion, but always east. The smell of death and decaying flesh made him gag. Voices buzzed inside his head like the flies at the souk.

"Achambaud, where are we going?" Hugues struggled to keep up.

He ignored the question and pushed on.

As they travelled deeper into the city, more bodies littered the streets. One Jewish family had been cut down in the doorway of their home. The man and woman lacked hands and feet, which had been arranged to cradle a dead child. The baby girl had been stripped and her soft skin was covered in shallow, cruel cuts. From the looks of utter horror etched into the faces of the parents, it was obvious they had lived long enough to witness the torture of their child.

"What d'you want?" a voice asked in harshly accented French. A sour looking pedite leaned against the doorframe while munching on an apple. Spittle dribbled down his unshaven face. His tunic and hose were drenched in blood.

"What happened here?" Hugues demanded.

"What d'you think happened? I killed them swine just like God told me too." The man's sharp gaze took in Achambaud's armour and sword. "And I claim this home by right of conquest."

"Did you slay the child as well?" Achambaud's voice was remarkably calm. Deep inside his skull, a man and a woman screamed at the murder of their child. The baby's piercing wails were heart rending.

The soldier's eyes narrowed. "Listen, I was at Civetot with the Hermit's lot when those Saracens slaughtered almost the lot of us. They didn't hesitate to kill good Christian women and children neither."

This man was no honest Christian. Achambaud did not need to touch his mind to know that. "I understand," Achambaud replied, "but they didn't cut off your hands before making you watch as they sliced up your child, did they?"

Achambaud drew his belt knife and rushed up the steps. The soldier hurled his apple at Achambaud and raised his axe, which he had hidden behind the doorframe. Achambaud caught his raised elbow with his free hand and plunged his dagger into the pedite's liver. A look of shock fractured across the man's face. He dropped to his knees and feebly clutched at the dagger's hilt. Achambaud drew his sword and hacked off the man's head with a single, furious blow.

"May your soul burn in the seven circles of Hell for all eternity." Achambaud spat on the corpse and wiped both blades on the dead man's tunic.

"That...was nobly done." Hugues looked pale and shaken.

He had forgotten about Hugues in his rage.

"Three less voices up here." Achambaud tapped his temple.

"This is what you wanted me to see," Hugues said. "The senseless cruelty. Our barbarism. Do you think me ignorant of it?"

"No." Achambaud shook his head and sheathed his weapons. "There's much more."

Expressionless, Achambaud led Hugues through a gate that connected to the Temple Mount. Here the voices swelled into an agonised chorus. Achambaud clutched his skull at the intensity of their anguish.

"Listen to me." Hugues gripped his shoulder. "You must shut them out. Listening to them will only drive you mad."

Achambaud stumbled forwards and caught his first glimpse of the Dome of the Rock. Rising above the flat quadrangle of paved stone, the mosque's golden dome curved gracefully into the air. The building was shaped like an octagon. Rays from the setting sun bathed the whitewashed walls in shades of red. Achambaud's gaze dropped to the courtyard. Saracen bodies covered the ground. Pedites and chevaliers picked through the piled bodies looking for valuables. They waded through pools of blood that were ankle deep in some places.

Misery and horror lifted off the killing ground. To Achambaud, it appeared as a crimson mist filled with hollow, accusing eyes and mouths that gaped in silent agony. The fog billowed across the ground, an enormous wound inflicted upon the marrow of Jerusalem.

They slaughtered us like animals.

They cut us down, even though some of your lords gave us their banners for protection.

"No," Achambaud whimpered.

"You must listen to me, Achambaud." Hugues clawed at his arm. "Shut out the voices of the dead."

We pleaded for mercy.

For salvation.

"I can't." Achambaud moaned in terror.

"Achambaud!" Hugues shouted in his face.

You must bear witness.

You must avenge us.

The fog darkened into the rusty brown of dried blood and drifted towards him. A face formed in the mist; a bearded face, with shoulder-length hair, a strong chin and haunted eyes. They were taking on his appearance as a way of claiming him.

"No." His denial was little more than a hoarse whisper.

The mist gathered around him. Long tendrils trailed from the bottom of the hideous cloud. Each tendril was connected to a corpse.

"Hugues?" Achambaud whimpered.

The death cries of thousands of murdered souls drowned out any reply. The world darkened around Achambaud. He lost sight of Hugues and the beautiful dome. The world was dying and only he could hear its dirge.

Not quite, brother, a clear voice spoke inside his skull. *We're always gifted with light, if we but choose to see it. You must shut out the grief of the slaughtered lest they overcome you.*

"Who are you?" Achambaud cried out.

Someone who understands your pain. Someone who can help.

"You're another one of them," Achambaud whispered. "Get out of my head. Leave me be."

Achambaud, you must focus now else the anguish of the fallen will drive you insane.

"How?" Achambaud asked desperately.

Imagine a circular mosque surrounded by five minarets. The muezzin calls you to prayer. Stand in the centre of the mosque within Allah's embrace. The prayer joins each minaret to the other, drowning out all else. Imagine that you now stand beneath the dome. This you must do now, before the voices of the dead become stronger than the living.

Achambaud did as the mysterious voice instructed. He pictured himself standing within the Dome of the Rock, except the interior looked like the Anastasis. The call of the muezzin wove through the slender minarets, overlapping until they formed a five-pointed star. The voices, the horrors that Achambaud had helped perpetrate, were forced from his mind.

The voice that had aided him was expelled as well. All that remained was a lingering sense of concern...and a strange sense of kinship.

"Achambaud? Can you hear me?" Hugues' anxious face swam into focus.

He must have fallen to his knees because they both knelt in Saracen blood. The voices of the murdered had finally stilled. Even the terrible mist that had borne his face had dissipated.

Achambaud blinked. "They're all dead. Cut down while praying in their mosques. The Jews too. Burned alive inside their synagogue while we stood outside singing *Christ We Adore Thee*." He shook his head, not understanding how this knowledge had come to him.

Achambaud clasped Hugues' forearms. "What good can possibly justify the sins we've committed here?"

Hugues eyes were filled with pain. "Achambaud, I swear good will come from the deeds of today. It's our duty to ensure it."

Achambaud searched his face. "I'll hold you to that promise."

The sun dipped below the horizon as Hugues led Achambaud in fervent prayer.

CHAPTER 20

15 July 1099

The Merchant Quarter

It was well into the evening before Hugues finally managed to coax Achambaud away from the Temple Mount.

A party of Tafurs stumbled into the alley ahead of them. They were singing *Christ We Adore Thee* interspersed by bouts of laughter. One man pretended he was on fire, running around in circles and trying to pat out the flames with his bare hands. His antics elicited a fresh round of hilarity.

Achambaud grasped the hilt of his sword. Hugues caught him by the arm and pulled him into the deeper shadow of a balcony. "Do nothing," Hugues whispered.

"Do you know how many Jews they burned alive today?" Achambaud murmured.

"The Rabbis are friends to the Salt Lines, so I mourn those deaths. But if you try to avenge them, you'll end up dead as well."

"Godefroi's right." Achambaud's dark eyes glittered. "You ask us to have faith, yet you don't show any in us. I always have the sense that you're holding something back." Achambaud removed a gauntlet and reached for Hugues' temple. "I have bared myself before you, but you remain closed to me."

Hugues backed away. "That's not true." He swallowed. "*I* found you, remember? I was the one who embraced your talents, who found you employment with Godefroi."

"I remember," Achambaud replied in a flat voice. "And I've served faithfully ever since. Now I need more."

It took all of Hugues' discipline to keep his voice steady. "I'll keep my oath to Godefroi to share all that I know. Just don't be disappointed if that is less than you expect."

"Then let's find out." Achambaud nodded towards the alley. The Tafurs had moved on, so he set out down the cobbled street.

Cold stole through the city as night deepened. They dodged two more bands of Christians in search of spoils before reaching the Via Dolorosa that led west.

"We're here." Achambaud nodded at a large house built from amber-coloured stone. Three stories in height, it overlooked the corner of a small square. Light glimmered between wooden shutters. A white banner hung from the balcony on the second floor. Emblazoned across the white silk was a square cross potent in gold cloth. Quartering the main cross were four smaller crosslets, also gold in colour.

"Godefroi has adopted a new banner," Achambaud noted.

"One cross for each of the wounds of Christ," Hugues murmured. "We'd best hurry. He'll be wondering where we are."

They strode across the square towards Godefroi's quarters. Members of his personal guard shivered on the steps before the main entrance. They stood and squinted at the new arrivals. A sergeant—Randolph, if Achambaud remembered correctly—pushed his way to the front. He scowled at them in suspicion.

"Duke's been looking for you," Randolph said to Achambaud. "And his Chaplain. Where have you been?"

"On the Duke's business," Achambaud replied. "Where is he?"

Randolph rubbed his bearded chin. "If he knew where you were, why did he send some of us out to find you?"

"We took longer than expected," Hugues replied. "Now we're back, he'll want to see us immediately."

Randolph grudgingly made way. "On the second level. With that engineer of his and that little monk who scribes for him. Hardly a way to celebrate if you ask me." Some of the guards muttered in agreement.

"I'll commend your caution to him." Achambaud clapped Randolph on the shoulder. "Don't let a single Provençal past this door."

"You needn't worry about that," Randolph replied.

Hugues and Achambaud climbed the steps, passed through the open door and entered a world of eastern opulence. Smooth white tiles flowed outwards from the worn doorstep, interspersed with patterns of black squares and ochre diamonds. A mosaic ran the length of the wall on their left. Candlelight glittered off chips of bright ceramic and coloured glass. Thick carpets and bright silk cushions littered the floor.

More of Godefroi's personal guard lounged amongst this finery. Their piles of weapons and bloodied armour jarred with the peaceful ambience of the residence. Achambaud stomped up the steps to the next level. Hugues followed him with an increasing sense of foreboding.

"Finally!" Godefroi's voice echoed down the steps.

Another sumptuous room greeted Hugues when he reached the landing. This one had been painted a pale shade of green, which reminded him of a shallow sea in bright sunlight. Candlelight wavered against the walls, creating the illusion of shifting water. Brightly woven carpets covered the tiled floor and more cushions swathed in silks of vivid yellow and deep purple were scattered about the chamber. The only piece of furniture was a low table of polished walnut.

Godefroi had risen to his feet, dressed only in a simple linen bliaut and plain woollen leggings. "Where, in God's name, have you been?" He waved them over impatiently. Etienne and Godwera sank back down when it became apparent that Hugues and Achambaud were joining them. A half-eaten meal of dates, unleavened bread and goblets of wine were scattered across the table.

"It's my fault," Achambaud replied. "I needed to show Hugues—"

"The importance of trust," Hugues cut in.

Godefroi's sharp gaze darted between the two of them. "What happened?"

"With your permission, messire," Hugues said, "I would fulfil my promise made at the Holy Sepulchre. Before I do, however, we must ensure we're not overheard."

"I'll see to it." Godefroi tramped downstairs. When he returned, he wore a grim look of satisfaction. "No one who values his manhood will mount those steps without first calling up for permission."

"What about those stairs?" Hugues pointed to a narrow set of steps at the back of the chamber.

"Sleeping chambers," Godefroi replied. "All empty."

"Etienne." Hugues nodded towards the stairs. Etienne rose without question and hurried up the steps to check the top level.

"Forgive the precautions," Hugues said, "but many lives have bought the knowledge I'm about to share."

Etienne returned to the table and shook his curly head. He still seemed in shock at sharing a table with Godefroi.

"The balcony as well," Hugues said.

Etienne unbolted the door at the front of the building and slipped out onto the balcony. He returned a few moments later, slid the bolt home and resumed his place at the table. "We're alone."

"Very well." Hugues dropped his voice a notch, forcing his companions to lean forwards. "The five of us are bound together after what we witnessed at the Holy Sepulchre. But you must swear upon your hope of salvation not to reveal any of what I'm about to tell you."

Achambaud was the first to take the vow, swearing upon his hope of eternal life. Godefroi followed, taking the oath in a solemn voice, his gaze never leaving Hugues' face. Etienne and Godwera repeated the vow.

"Each of you know the Salt Lines seek an artefact." Hugues threaded his hands together to avoid fidgeting. After maintaining secrecy for so long, it was no small thing to speak of these things. "I can't tell you the form this artefact takes, but I *can* tell you something of its nature."

Godefroi made an impatient gesture.

"I'm not dithering, messire, only trying to explain. Without a physical description of the artefact, the scholars of the Salt Lines were forced to track its effect."

"What effect?" Achambaud asked.

"The artefact is a catalyst of change," Hugues replied. "Whenever it has surfaced, the course of history has been altered."

"How?" Godefroi leaned back into the cushions, his big hands clasped around one knee.

"It's difficult to describe." Hugues stared at the ceiling as he searched for the right example. "The artefact has always caused a shift in power and influence. The dominant kingdom is overthrown. One doctrine of thought overtakes another. So it goes, endlessly throughout history."

"War is a part of life." Godefroi shrugged. "Only the strong survive. Every warrior knows this."

"Yet war need not define our days," Godwera replied quietly.

Godefroi favoured her with a dubious look.

"Please." Hugues held up both hands. "I'm referring to something much more pervasive than the rise and fall of kingdoms." He waited until he was sure they were all listening. "The earliest reference to the artefact is in the writings of Pythagoras, the ancient Greek philosopher and mathematician. The pentagram was a sacred object to him, which he called the Pentemychos."

"That's what you called the star in the Holy Sepulchre." A rapt expression lit Etienne's face.

Hugues smiled. "Yes. The doctrine of Pentemychos was written by Pythagoras' teacher, Pherecydes of Syros. Pythagoras and his followers subsequently expanded upon it. Pentemychos means five recesses or chambers. Pythagoreans believed that the first beings to exist were placed inside the Pentemychos, which gave rise to the cosmos."

"What do ancient Greek beliefs have to do with the artefact?" Godefroi asked.

Hugues sighed. "As I said, the artefact has shaped history. Its influence upon the rise of Greek civilisation is quite clear, as it was on the Roman Empire."

Etienne shifted on his cushion. "So the Romans believed in this Pentemychos too."

"They adopted some of the Greek beliefs," Hugues replied. "In particular, they venerated the mythical figure of Lucifer, who was the bringer of light and knowledge." Again, he paused to let the significance of that name sink in. "Lucifer is symbolised by Venus, the Morning Star. Roman astronomers knew that every eight years, the star of Venus charts a perfect pentagram around the Zodiac."

"Mere coincidence," Godefroi scoffed.

"Really?" Hugues countered. "Is that why the Emperor Hadrian built a temple dedicated to Venus on the very site where the Holy Sepulchre stands today?"

Godefroi frowned. Even Godwera—who was the most educated in such matters—looked thoughtful.

Hugues pushed on relentlessly. "The Saracens have five pillars of faith. Their call to prayer is issued five times a day. And in our faith, we venerate the five wounds of Christ, linking them to the five noble virtues."

"What are you saying?" Achambaud demanded.

"Only this." Hugues searched each of their faces. "All the great religions and civilisations have known there are five elements, or chambers, to the human soul."

Etienne shifted on his cushion. "And this has something to do with the artefact."

Hugues smiled. "Straight to the heart of the matter, as always." He smoothed the coarse wool of his cassock across his knees. "Do you remember the fragment of a scroll from Judea I mentioned? This scroll was written by a member of a sect known as the Essene. We know little about them, save they avoided the company of strangers. However, after careful research, we discovered the Essene believed they were the heirs of Abraham. Their writings refer to an ancient oral tradition that unlocks the secrets of the Torah, which are the first five books of the Bible. Furthermore, they refer to the five chambers of the human soul."

Hugues studied the expressions of his audience as he spoke. Godwera knew some of this, but she had never penetrated so deep into the mysteries. Etienne's shone face with fascination, which was to be expected. Achambaud's expression was more difficult to interpret, although at least he appeared willing to listen. Godefroi remained sceptical, however.

"Is that what we are about?" Godwera asked. "Unearthing the secrets of these Essene."

"Almost." Hugues clenched his hands together and forced out the words that denied all that the Church had taught him. "The Salt Lines have collected strong evidence. Evidence that suggests Jesus Christ was a member of the Essene. Not only that, but he was one member of the five sacred points along with John the Baptist. We believe that he used the artefact to shape the course of history."

Stunned silence.

Hugues knew it would only last a moment, so he hurried on. "That's why the star of the Pentemychos appeared to us above his tomb. The artefact recognised our presence and is showing us the way."

Everyone spoke at once, although it was Etienne who voiced the question that had vexed Hugues for so long. "Are you suggesting that Jesus is not the son of God?"

"I am not certain of anything, Etienne. Perhaps he *was* sent down to guide us. Or perhaps he was merely a great man, a leader who changed the course of history. Either way, the Salt Lines are confident he wielded the artefact."

"Your heresies will see us all burn." Godefroi shifted nervously on his cushion and glanced at the stairs.

"You said the artefact recognised us," Achambaud said into the silence that followed Godefroi's prediction. "How is that possible? Are you saying this artefact can think for itself?"

Hugues lowered his voice even further. "As far as we can tell, the artefact is the single point that the one, true God used to manifest all Creation. The Greeks believed it was a pathway to both Heaven and Hell. The Salt Lines want us to locate the artefact hidden by the Essene and to bring it back to Lorraine."

Godwera shook her head in wonder. "I never thought—" She shivered and searched Hugues' face. "Are you sure that's wise?"

Hugues gestured towards the balcony. "Would you rather leave it here for the Saracens to claim?"

"And do you know where these Essene people left it?" Godefroi asked.

"No," Hugues admitted. "But it's clear we must look for further signs in Solomon's Temple."

"King Solomon? What does he have to do with this?" Achambaud asked.

"Everything," Hugues replied. "The Seal of Solomon is normally depicted as a six-pointed star surrounded by two circles. But in some of the oldest references we've found, it was originally a five-pointed star. The sixth point was added for the divine."

"Of course," Etienne exclaimed. "The Anastasis is the outer circle with the star in the centre."

"With one point for each of us," Godwera murmured.

Hugues nodded. "Exactly so."

Achambaud gave him a strange look. "Do we know where the Temple of Solomon stood?"

"Yes, Achambaud." Hugues took a deep breath. "The mosque on the Temple Mount was built over part of Solomon's ancient temple. That's why I believe Etienne's point was the last to fade. If you take a map of Jerusalem and draw a straight line from the centre of the Holy Sepulchre through Etienne's fourth point, it intersects with the mosque. The next part of our journey lies there."

"You're sure?" Godefroi asked.

"I am not sure of anything," Hugues replied. "Although I don't think it coincidence that Achambaud was drawn to the Temple Mount earlier today."

"And that explains why you relinquished the Holy Sepulchre to Narbonne so readily," Godwera said.

Hugues smiled. "It will keep our brethren occupied while we seek the real prize."

"What happens if we find the artefact?" Achambaud asked. "We hand it over to the Salt Lines, then what?"

Hugues couldn't contain the excitement he felt at that prospect. "The Salt Lines will attempt to use the artefact to communicate directly with God. Achambaud, I promised you that the lives spent on this pilgrimage weren't wasted. Now you understand how I can make that promise. If the Salt Lines are successful in wielding the artefact, we may unlock the gate to Eden. Death, poverty, plague, all would be banished from this earthly realm. This is what we fight for. *This* is the great work we serve."

A rumble of voices reached them from outside. Hugues stood, alarmed at the sudden commotion. Achambaud jumped to his feet and raced to the top of the stairs. "What's going on?" he called down to the guards. The reply was muffled.

"Raymond?" Godefroi directed his question at Achambaud with a grim expression.

"No, something else." Achambaud strode to the balcony door and threw it open. The sound of singing rolled into the house.

Hugues followed Godefroi out onto the balcony.

A stream of people marched down the Via Dolorosa. Their torches and candles resembled a river rolling towards the Holy Sepulchre. Their voices swelled in adulation as they gave praise to God for their victory over the Saracens.

"The great and humble alike wish to fulfil their vows by praying at the Holy Sepulchre," Hugues said to Godefroi. "You must be foremost among them as the man who returned Jerusalem to Christianity."

"After what you've told me tonight, I'd feel like an impostor in their midst," Godefroi replied with a dark look.

"Serving truth is never deceitful," Hugues replied. "Even if it must be done in secrecy. Come, let's pray with our people."

CHAPTER 21

15 July 1099
The Holy Sepulchre

Diederic's eyes cracked open. Stars glittered across the canopy of a night sky. His head felt full of sand and a low whine filled his ears. Diederic groaned, rolled onto one side and dry retched. His body was so parched he had nothing left to vomit.

He propped himself up on one elbow and gingerly touched the back of his neck. His fingers came away matted with congealed blood.

His memories of the confrontation with Godefroi were hazy. The clearest picture that burned in Diederic's mind was the dark face of Achambaud as he prayed on the parapet of the north wall.

Sorcery.

It was the only explanation.

Dark magick had transformed Godefroi into a nightmare of bloodied iron and bellowing rage. Diederic lay back and made the sign of the cross.

Count Raymond had warned of a hidden sect in Godefroi's forces. Raymond suspected they had funded Godefroi's campaign to the Holy Land for some unknown, but undoubtedly heretical, purpose. Here then was the proof that Raymond sought. Godefroi's bodyguard consorted with the servants of Lucifer.

Raymond must know without further delay.

Diederic rolled onto his hands and knees. A fresh wave of dizziness swept through him. Ignoring it, he tried to stand. The ground lurched beneath him and he staggered against a broken column of stone. He closed his eyes and inhaled deeply, willing control of his body to return. The nausea eased as he counted out ten long breaths.

When he opened his eyes, the ringing in his ears resolved into verse.

Sanctus, Sanctus, Sanctus,
Dóminus Deus Sábaoth.

Pleni sunt cæli et terra,
Maiestátis glóriæ tuæ.

Diederic glanced around in confusion. Someone had dragged him to the furthest corner away from the Holy Sepulchre. Hundreds of people had filled the courtyard, ringing the rotunda as they gave thanks to heaven. Many bore torches or lanterns. Light spilled from the open dome and cracks in the walls.

What was going on?

He finally recognised the hymn: *Te Deum*. They were singing the Hymn of Praise.

The glorious company of the Apostles: praise thee.
The goodly fellowship of the Prophets: praise thee.
The noble army of Martyrs: praise thee.

Diederic staggered upright. His first steps were tentative, but they soon grew in confidence. Using his bulk, he pushed through the heaving mass of pedites and peasants who had gathered outside. All were covered in the filth of battle. Many clutched grisly prizes: silk robes smattered in blood, golden bezants and jewellery. Some even gleefully brandished rings by the severed fingers of their former owners.

While he had lost his sword and shield, Diederic's size and armour forced openings in the crowd where none had previously existed. Gradually, he moved towards the centre of the Anastasis. The singing continued, reverent and exultant.

Thou sittest at the right hand of God: in the glory of the Father.
We believe that thou shalt come: to be our Judge.
We therefore pray thee, help thy servants: whom thou hast
redeemed with thy precious blood.

The crowd became denser near the apse where he had fought Godefroi. Diederic elbowed his way forward. The rotunda was filled with milites and fellow chevaliers. He could no longer use rank to force his way inwards. However, he was tall enough to catch glimpses of the ceremony.

The hymn was swelling to its triumphant finale. Senior members of the clergy brandished their holy relics, resplendent in vestments edged in gold thread. A thousand candles dazzled the eye. Every face shone, bright with the knowledge that their vows had finally been fulfilled.

In te, Dómine, sperávi: non confúndar in ætérnum.
O Lord, in thee have I trusted: let me never be confounded.

The silence that followed the hymn was profound, a physical presence that touched every Christian who bore witness to it. Tears sprang to Diederic's eyes. The gratitude he felt at having survived long enough to be part of this was completely overwhelming.

His gaze lifted above the crowd to the centre of the rotunda. A dais had been erected so that the princes and the clergy were visible to all. Basking in the centre of the crowd's adulation was Godefroi de Bouillon. Golden-haired and smiling, he acknowledged the thanks of priests and chevaliers alike for having liberated Jerusalem.

Hatred hardened into a bitter knot inside Diederic. It was an unforgivable insult that this man—who treated with foul sorcerers—should be feted at the very site of the Resurrection.

Arnulf de Chocques stepped forward. The broad priest raised one hand in benediction as he recited the Lord's Prayer. The assembly repeated each line after him, finishing with a final joyous "Amen" that rolled around the courtyard. Tears flowed as warriors embraced each other.

Diederic stood outside the circle of the assembly's happiness. Instead, he bowed his head and uttered a short oath in the presence of the Holy Spirit that surely moved amongst them.

Godefroi de Bouillon would be cast down along with his pet sorcerer. This he promised in the presence of almighty God. And after that? Count Raymond would have no choice but to reward his most faithful subject.

CHAPTER 22

15 July 1099

Godefroi's quarters

The hour was so late it could be considered early. After the long day culminating in the ceremony at the Holy Sepulchre, a dull ache throbbed through Godefroi's limbs. His injured shoulder had seized up and his eyes were gritty with exhaustion. Yet sleep remained elusive.

Godefroi sat up and swung his legs over the low bed. Moonlight from a small window painted deep shadows across the opposite wall. His mattress was far more comfortable than what he was used to. Too much so. The softness was a distraction, a luxury he could not afford yet.

Too restless for sleep, he rose and crossed the room. He made no sound as he padded over the tiles.

Godefroi's sleeping chamber opened onto a narrow set of stairs. It was darker here, so he ran one hand along the wall while feeling for each step. The stairs descended into the main chamber on the second level. He still could not believe the Salt Lines questioned the divinity of Jesus. If the Inquisition were to ever learn of it…

He shuddered at the thought.

A pair of lanterns hung from metal brackets fixed to the walls. Crescent moons and tiny stars had been etched into the delicate glass. They appeared to flicker and dance as the tapers burned.

Godefroi skirted past the flat, broad table that was so different to the great tables he was used to in Lorraine and moved towards the balcony. It was not hard to picture the swarthy Saracens lounging on their cushions, escaping from the heat in their flowing robes, laughing and feasting. This was not the barbarism that the clergy had spoken of. Quite the reverse. The sophistication of this room left Godefroi feeling like an impoverished traveller who had barged in uninvited.

The acrid smell of smoke and the rank odour of death wafted on the night breeze.

"It would be safer if you remained inside, messire."

Godefroi froze. He reached for the dagger he normally wore on his hip and cursed inwardly when he realised that he had left it by his bedside. "Who's there?"

A figure stirred in one corner. Godwera's pale face emerged from the cowl of her habit that blended so well with the night.

"Now that the city has been taken, Raymond would have no qualms in killing you," she observed. "You mustn't give him the opportunity."

"I know that!" he snapped, angry at being caught unawares.

Godwera flinched.

"I'm sorry. You startled me." He glanced about to ensure they were alone. "Godwera. You need never fear me. I'm not like—" He swallowed. Baldwin's name was bitter on his tongue. "You mustn't think I'm like my brother."

Faint lines of pain drew tight across her face. "Please. Let us leave those days behind. Let us...forget everything."

He caught the appeal in her voice but could not accept it. "How can I leave the past behind when you constantly remind me of it?" He gazed angrily out the balcony door. Fires twinkled in the darkness. "I've been forced to let you go twice now. Once to Baldwin, once to death. Are you really asking me to accept a third loss?"

"We've never belonged to each other, despite what either of us may have desired." She clutched his injured shield arm. He welcomed the grinding pain. It had defined their relationship for as long as he had known her.

"Am I speaking to Hugues now?" Godefroi did not bother to hide the bitterness in his voice. "Have you no will of your own, no desires? Must every last part of us be given over to the Salt Lines?" He searched her face for some glimmer of the feelings he knew she harboured for him.

"Godefroi." She touched his cheek with trembling fingers. "This is so much more important than anything we might feel...or want."

Godefroi caught her soft hand in his calloused grip and kissed her fingers. "Godwera." His voice was suddenly hoarse. "Ever since I first met you, I have *known*—"

"Please." She pulled away.

He let her go reluctantly, bewildered by her reaction. Why did she keep shying away from what they both wanted?

Godwera took a step back and became a phantasm of the night that might vanish at the slightest movement. "You mustn't say it, Godefroi. You mustn't bring *us* into being. We mustn't...I can't—" She cast about the room in desperation.

A pounding, furious rage coursed through him. Words rose unbidden to his lips, drawn from the depths of frustration. "But you can with Hugues, can't you? He takes you into his confidences, he seeks your counsel, yet he is deaf to my requests. And you! You accept his protection. You heed his words, whereas I've always accepted you as a woman who knows her mind. No wonder you spurn me when you have given everything to another."

He must have taken an inadvertent step because suddenly he loomed over her. Each word was driven home by a pointed finger.

"Godefroi, no." A look of horror transformed her face. The lines of unhappiness he had observed earlier deepened and her bottom lip quivered. He saw fear too, cringing beneath her misery.

"You'd rather lie with a man of secrets, in thought if not in deed, than with a man who isn't afraid to tell you that he loves you, regardless of the consequences."

"That's not true," Godwera gasped.

"Then speak." Godefroi gripped her by the shoulders. It took an effort not to shake her. She flinched, her arms soft beneath his strong fingers. "Tell me the truth. Tell me how you feel when you look at me."

"I don't love you in the way that you wish," Godwera said. "You're a brother to me, no more."

How could she lie after he had reached out to her?

Godwera slipped from his grasp and fled across the cool tiles. Godefroi's hands twitched. The feel of her flesh still tingled through his fingertips, but he did not pursue her. He walked out onto the balcony instead and watched as Jerusalem burned. Like the city, his heart filled with ash.

CHAPTER 23

18 October 1307

The forest

Bertrand's body ached, the chainmail coif chafed his neck, and a hundred different bruises and scrapes throbbed. Compounding his misery was a constant, seeping rain that had settled in during the afternoon. He was splattered with mud and chilled to the bone.

"We can't continue like this." Coming from Rémi, who was also drenched, it was a statement of fact, not a complaint.

Bertrand was too tired to muster a reply. He dropped his sack and leaned against the mottled silver trunk of a birch.

"We need shelter," Rémi said to Salome. "Otherwise, your friends won't have to kill us. The cold and wet will save them the trouble."

The hood of Salome's cloak kept the rain from her face. Despite their trek through the woods, her stride had not shortened or faltered.

"You're right." She sniffed the air and glanced about the darkening forest. "They can't follow us in this weather. Hopefully the rain will wash away our tracks."

Salome peered at Bertrand. "You are suffering." She ran the back of her fingers across his wet cheek. The gesture was almost possessive, and he shivered at the contact.

"Take my hand," Salome said. Bertrand glanced uncertainly at Rémi.

"Woman, we've no time for your tricks." Rémi grabbed Salome by the arm and swung her about to face him.

Bertrand drew his belt knife and had it to Rémi's throat in an instant. "Let her go," he said in a snarl.

Shock spread across Rémi's face. He released Salome, who rubbed her arm and moved out of reach.

"Cub. What are you doing?" Rémi's voice was puzzled.

Bertrand stared at his blade. How did it come to be there? The edge trembled at Rémi's throat. He pulled away in confusion. "I'm sorry. Rémi, you know I'd never—" It was too awful to say. Too awful to even contemplate. Rain trickled through the hair plastered to his forehead. "I don't know what came over me."

"I do." Rémi's grim, accusing gaze slid to Salome.

"Bertrand and I are bound," she said. "He'll respond to any threat to me. In return, I'll protect him. And those loyal to him."

"You've bewitched him." Rémi's fingers tightened until his knuckles cracked. The scar in the webbing of Bertrand's hand tingled.

"That is an ugly description for a choice freely made." Salome tucked a loose strand of hair behind one ear. "Think of it more as a union. Like the outer pillars of the tree, the genders must be in alignment."

Bertrand stared between the two of them. *A union?* What was that supposed to mean? His imagination started down dangerous paths. With an effort, he forced his thoughts back to the present. "Rémi's right. We need shelter. The rest hardly matters if we freeze or die of a fever."

"Then let me help." Salome held out her hand again. Bertrand took it tentatively. Her skin was warm, unlike his fingers which were numb with cold.

Salome closed her eyes. Bertrand was highly aware of her proximity, the tilt of her head, the rise and fall of her chest. She was tall for a woman, overtopping Rémi by at least an inch. In a way, she reminded him of Justine: both women possessed a self-assurance that would be the envy of most men.

It might have been a trick of the rain, but Bertrand noticed that Salome's outline was hazy. He frowned. Even the hand he was holding was fuzzy. He shifted his gaze to the trees, which appeared normal. Even the billowing gusts of rain were visible if he concentrated. It was Salome who had become unfixed. Bertrand held her hand, so he knew that she was not moving. Yet for some reason he had the impression that she was drawing closer.

He closed his eyes to refocus and felt Salome shift upon her feet. Her smile curved upon his lips. She was not troubled by his aches and pains. While he was far stronger, she possessed a resilience that surprised him.

His eyes opened in astonishment. The impression of moving towards each other, of merging—*yes, that was the right word for it*—strengthened.

Bertrand trembled with the strain of keeping his sense of self separate from her. A loop had been created. Each sensation flitted between them. Seen from two different perspectives, the forest blurred, two views overlapping to become one.

Just as the disorientation became intolerable, his perspective snapped outwards. Instead of delving into each other, they swung outwards in an ever-widening spiral. A rush of images hurtled through Bertrand: branches whipped past, leaves shivered and twirled in the wind. They wove through beads of rain and skipped past rocky outcrops. They soared over banks of rotting leaves and skimmed past fallen logs.

The images flashed through Bertrand's mind. Yet the sense of movement, of spinning outwards, persisted. Finally, a collection of upright timbers whipped past, too ordered to be natural. Bertrand only caught fleeting impressions; timber covered with moss, the wind tugging at loose boards, dried leaves rolling through a narrow opening.

Salome released his hand. And Bertrand lurched back into his body.

Bertrand gasped for breath. The dual vision was gone.

Rémi caught him by the elbow. "What did she do?"

Bertrand blinked and his eyes reluctantly focused. Rémi looked worried. Almost afraid.

"I'm...not sure."

Rémi squeezed his arm. "You went into a trance. Didn't you hear me calling you?"

"Don't fret, Rémi," Salome said. "He'll be fine." She pointed deeper into the forest. "There's a hovel on the far side of the next ridge. It's unoccupied and mostly dry inside."

A jolt of astonishment shot through Bertrand. Yes, she was right. He *had* glimpsed a hut.

"How do you know that?" Rémi demanded.

He hid it well, but Bertrand caught a hint of fear in his gruff voice.

Salome's eyebrows lifted in amusement. "By the time I finished explaining it, we would already be there." She set off up the muddy incline without waiting for a reply.

"That woman's unnatural," Rémi muttered.

"She saw it," Bertrand wondered out loud.

"Saw what?" Rémi frowned at him.

Bertrand should have been disturbed by the magic he had just witnessed. Instead, all he felt was amazement. "I was with her. We...*flew* through the forest." He tried to recapture the feeling. All that remained was the sense of rushing headlong through the trees.

"I don't like any of this." Rémi gestured towards Salome. "This sort of thing is beyond me."

"Leave it for now, Rémi. She's found us a dry place to sleep. The rest can wait." Bertrand hefted his sack and trudged up the hill after Salome.

Rémi muttered a curse and stomped after him.

CHAPTER 24

18 October 1307

The Poacher's Hut

The hut was exactly where Salome had predicted. Built in the shadow of an enormous elm, the rough timbers were stained with age and moss covered the bottom of each plank. Some of the thatch in the roof had collapsed, although the dirt floor was only damp thanks to the elm's branches.

"We'll sleep here tonight," Salome said. "We can decide what to do in the morning."

Bertrand shivered. The temperature was dropping as night fell and his padded tunic and breeches were saturated from the rain. They needed a fire.

"If we're lucky," Rémi said, "they'll have left some dry wood inside." He ducked under the low eaves of the hovel and disappeared inside.

Salome placed a hand on Bertrand's arm. "Let's get out of the rain."

"How did you do that back there?" The feeling of their merging had become a vague, confused memory.

"Bertrand, you need rest." Salome guided him into the hut and helped him out of his armour. Water dribbled from his boots when he upended them.

Rémi stacked the pieces of kindling that he had collected from the barrow mound over some precious char-cloth. A pile of old, dry branches had been left stacked in one corner of the hut. Producing a dark grey flint from his tinderbox, Rémi struck it against the piece of fire-steel. It took him a few attempts to draw sparks in the damp air. Eventually, one caught in the char-cloth. Rémi blew gently until the spark took hold in the twigs.

While Rémi built up the fire, Salome filled a pewter bowl with rainwater. She searched through the supplies Rémi had gathered from the barrow and doled out portions of hard bread, now damp from the rain. Not much of the cheese remained. Bertrand's stomach growled as he ate slowly.

"I'll save the salted lamb for tomorrow," Salome said, removing her cloak. Underneath she wore a dark grey woollen dress divided on either side for riding. The damp wool clung to her willowy figure, especially around her hips where a leather ceinture, about three fingers thick, wrapped around her waist. Lean muscles shifted across her arms and back as she moved about.

No wonder she had been able to walk all day almost without rest. Bertrand wondered whether the rest of her body was covered in scars and belatedly realised he was staring. "What are you doing?" he asked around a mouthful of bread. She had opened a pouch that hung from her belt and was sorting through small cloth sachets.

"Making an infusion." Using the tip of her belt knife, Salome slit the thread of the sachet on one side and tipped the contents into the bowl of water. Dried herbs and withered flowers by the look of it.

"What's it for?" The fire glittered in Rémi's eyes as he watched Salome's preparations.

"It'll help you sleep and give you energy for the morrow." Salome tossed the empty sachet into the fire and stirred the water with one finger. Once satisfied the herbs were fully immersed, she pushed the bowl close to the fire.

"Then you won't mind drinking it first," Rémi replied.

"Of course not, but someone needs to stand watch. Are you offering?"

Rémi glanced at Bertrand. "Guess I am." His thick eyebrows bristled as he frowned in suspicion.

Salome shrugged. "Have it your way then."

"Aren't you going to eat something?" Bertrand asked. In all her preparations, Salome hadn't taken any food.

"You need it more than me."

That struck Bertrand as odd, although he was too famished to argue. Now that he was fed and warm, it was hard to resist the drowsiness stealing over him. His body ached, his muscles were stiff, and a chill had entered his lungs. Each breath felt wet and heavy. The sound of his rasping breath reminded him of Everard. Bertrand stared into the flames and recalled their final stand before the menhir.

Rain continued to fall. The fire crackled and wood popped. An odd gust of wind made the timbers of the hut groan. Bertrand's chin inched towards his chest, but he fought sleep. He thought of Everard, of Roland and Arnaud, and the others who had fallen. The pain of their deaths pricked the back of his eyes.

Why had the soldiers attacked? Was King Philippe truly imprisoning all members of their Order? And what was Salome's connection to the

Salt Lines? He needed answers to these questions and more before he could truly accept Everard's death.

"Here, it's ready." Salome knelt next to Bertrand and raised the edge of the bowl to his lips. She had fished out the herbs while he was brooding. The hot water was now stained dark red, like mulled wine. "Careful, it's hot." She had wrapped the pewter bowl in the hem of her dress, which exposed her calves. The faint, white scars that mapped the contours of her face were etched into her legs too.

Bertrand gazed into her dark, slanted eyes. When would she start to trust him?

Perhaps she sensed what he was feeling because she said, "Let me care for you, Bertrand. As you care for me. That's the way it has always been."

While he appreciated the sentiment, it only reminded him that he was not her first Shroud. *I am loss*, she had said. Already he believed her in a way that would have been beyond his understanding only a few days ago.

Bertrand sipped the infusion. It was hot but not unpleasant.

"More," Salome urged. "You'll thank me tomorrow."

He managed two more mouthfuls before refusing any more. The infusion simmered inside his stomach.

"What was that?" Bertrand asked.

"Herbs from my home," Salome replied. "You wouldn't have heard of them."

"Your home. Where's that?"

Salome sat back on her heels and balanced the bowl in her skirt.

"Not far from Jerusalem."

"Jerusalem! You're from *Outremer*?" Bertrand sat up straighter. "How did you arrive here? I heard the Mamlukes had closed their borders."

"The telling of that story will take some time. And it includes elements that I cannot speak of in front of Rémi. I'm sorry."

"Makes sense." Rémi jabbed the fire with a stick. "Don't want me asking difficult questions, eh?" He prodded Bertrand's foot.

"You're not part of the Salt Lines," Salome replied. "And I'm bound by ancient vows to only confide in a member of the original families."

"So, I can't be trusted. Very convenient." Rémi stood and retrieved his axe. "But you'll let me stand guard duty though."

Salome bowed her head. "I'll leave some infusion for you."

"As you like." Rémi tramped out of the hovel.

"That was unkind," Bertrand murmured.

"No, it was necessary." Salome sipped some of the infusion and left the bowl near the fire so that it would remain warm. She settled onto the ground and examined him with dark, bottomless eyes.

"Are you really from Jerusalem?" Just the name made Bertrand's pulse race. He had heard tales of the exploits of his ancestors in the Holy Land and had dreamed of perhaps one day emulating them. To actually meet someone from Outremer was almost as good.

"Not the city, but from Judea." An errant strand of charcoal hair had fallen across Salome's face. She tucked it behind her ear without a hint of self-consciousness. The simple gesture fascinated Bertrand. He couldn't drag his gaze from the lobe of her ear and the gleam of firelight on her hair.

"You're not a Muslim, are you?" That might explain her exotic features and her confident manner.

She laughed with an edge of bitterness. "Hardly." She picked up a black stone the size of her thumb and ran the tip of her finger over it. "Bertrand, is that really what you want to ask me?"

The question sent a flush of heat shooting across his cheeks and down his neck. No, it was not. He was far more interested in the present. In her.

He shifted position and the hilt of Everard's sword poked into his thigh. The memory of Everard's body laid out next to Roard in the barrow slid through his mind and he felt guilty for wanting her.

"No, your past can wait." Bertrand considered all the questions that jostled for priority in his mind. "Those soldiers that attacked our camp: they were after you."

"Yes." Salome placed the stone back exactly where she had found it. Folding her hands neatly in her lap, she waited.

"Why? What have you done?"

"It's not what I've done, Bertrand. It's what I know." A smile hovered about her face, not quite alighting. Beneath that smile, he sensed a great sadness.

"I'm sorry. I didn't mean to upset you." Bertrand was not sure why he said that, yet it felt appropriate.

"There's no need for you to apologise. I've inflicted far more harm upon you. And it's only just begun," she added softly.

Bertrand shied away from the topic of Everard. "What knowledge could possibly justify the slaughter of my brethren?"

"A great secret. An ancient secret. One the Salt Lines have protected for generations."

Bertrand resisted the temptation of asking what the secret was for fear she would refuse to tell him. No, that was not quite right. He felt that he had not yet earned the right to ask. At least not yet. And if he was truly honest, he feared the answer. "And these soldiers—the King—he wishes to possess it."

Salome sighed. "I doubt Philippe knows of my existence. However, his treasury is all but exhausted and your Order is wealthy beyond compare. I doubt it took much coaxing to convince him to seize your assets."

"Then who ordered the attack?"

Anger tightened Salome's mouth. "The Keeper of the Seals, Guillaume de Nogaret."

"Nogaret? Isn't he the King's right hand?"

Salome leaned forward. "Nogaret answers to no master. He's been hunting me for years, even before he became Keeper of the Seals. Somehow, he learned of the secret I carry. I don't know how, although I can speculate." Her expression darkened. "Regardless, he knows about the Salt Lines, Bertrand. He knows they orchestrated the creation of your Order in partnership with the Cistercian monks. This latest attack is far more sweeping than the skirmish that took place back at the Marne, no matter how grievous our losses. A secret battle is being fought for control of nothing less than the human soul."

Bertrand absorbed this claim in astonished silence. Was Salome mad? Could she be deranged yet still appear outwardly reasonable?

"According to Scripture, that battle is being fought daily," Bertrand said carefully.

"I'm not talking about sin." Salome pressed the black stone into the ground.

"Then what *are* you talking about?"

"Why do they always need to start at the beginning?" Salome rolled her eyes. "Very well." She settled into a comfortable position with her legs turned to one side.

"Long ago," Salome said, "the ancestors of your forefathers buried their dead in mounds such as the one we arrived in. They built great stone circles to chart the passage of the seasons and menhirs, which marked the meeting of ways as I've already told you. In those ancient times, the seers retained an understanding of the world that we have lost. Using sacred geometry and maps of the heavens, they charted lines across the face of the earth. Each meridian was spaced at regular intervals and ran either north-south or east-west. Through calculations I don't understand, they derived the total number of meridians that comprised the entirety of our world."

"Meridians?" Bertrand repeated.

"Or salt lines, if you prefer. They determined three hundred and sixty-six wrapped around the earth. One for each day of the celestial year. And the first of these runs through Jerusalem, the navel of the world."

"So the Salt Lines were originally a form of astronomy, not families."

"They were far more than that, Bertrand." Salome dropped her voice. "This was the first and most important step in understanding the nature of Creation, in drawing back the veil that hides God's design."

"But the Scripture says—"

"Forget what you've been taught to believe, Bertrand. Only yesterday I shifted us more than thirty miles south using a meridian. Except it's not yesterday anymore. Not only did we move through space, but we also moved forward through time. Three days have passed since the battle at the Marne."

"Three days? But that's impossible." Even as he protested, Bertrand remembered how the spear that killed Roard had slowed before it sped forward.

"Not impossible, just improbable," Salome replied. "After all, if we can move from one place to another, what fixes us in time?"

"This is your secret then," Bertrand asked.

"No, it's but an example." She pinched the bridge of her nose and closed her eyes. Watching her reminded Bertrand of his own weariness.

"Ever since the rise of Christianity," Salome continued, "the people who inherited knowledge of the salt lines have been pushed out of their traditional homes. The ancient monuments were torn down. Believers in the old faith were branded pagans. Christ was the only path to redemption and the Church became the one and only source of His truth. Seeing how they were being marginalised, the most powerful remnants of the old ways decided to preserve their knowledge beneath a veneer of Christianity. Coming together from the fringes of the British Isles, Gaul and the frozen lands of the Norse, they settled in Champagne and Burgundy. Thus the salt lines became families and they preserved their heritage in secret."

Bertrand fought back a yawn. The pull of sleep was becoming increasingly difficult to resist. "So the Salt Lines—even my family—are pretending to be Christians. In secret, they believe in something else, is that it?" He was too tired to be shocked.

"They believe in Baphomet," Salome whispered.

"What's that?"

"In essence, the wisdom of the ages." Salome held up a hand to forestall his next question. "Few agree on the form or location of Baphomet, but all agree it's God's Will made manifest. The keystone of Creation, if you prefer."

Again, Bertrand didn't know how to respond. It all seemed so fantastical, although much of the Old Testament contained stories that could only be considered miraculous. "And you know where this keystone is."

Salome folded her hands in her lap. "I know how it can be found. That's why you mustn't let them take me, Bertrand. You must help me reach England where the Salt Lines still hold sway."

Drowsiness dragged at his eyelids. He wanted to ask her something important, but his tongue lay thick in his mouth. He wondered if his sleepiness was due to her infusion.

"Hush now, my Shroud. You must regain your strength." She bent down and placed a gentle kiss on his forehead.

The softness of her lips ushered Bertrand into deep sleep.

<hr />

Salome emerged from the hut to find the rain had slackened into a constant drizzle. The smell of wet earth and mould was rich and cloying. This land was so different from the one of her birth. After the warmth of the fire, the frigid air was like a slap against her skin.

"I take it you heard everything," Salome said into the darkness.

Moonlight glinted on metal as Rémi emerged from his listening post. He cradled his axe casually in the crook of one elbow.

"Most," he admitted. "Not that it made any sense, mind you."

"Bertrand warned me that you're much smarter than you let on."

"I'll not let you ruin the boy." Rémi patted the head of his axe. "Not after shepherding him for so many years. Especially since I can return to my own family in two summers." A look of shock spread across his broad face.

She couldn't help but smile. "Don't worry, Rémi. People usually say more than they intend around me. Tell me about your family."

"I don't—" Rémi searched for a response. "Damn you to hell, woman. It's none of—" He clamped his jaw shut and glared at her.

"Just tell me." Salome didn't bother to hide her sudden weariness. This slow coaxing of trust had become all too familiar and the loss of Roard was still raw.

"Two sons and a daughter." Rémi said it through his teeth. "Would've had more but I was playing nursemaid to the cub. Not that I minded."

"Bertrand's father," Salome guessed. "He paid you to act as Bertrand's bodyguard."

"An annual stipend," Rémi admitted. "Paid each year to my wife until Bertrand reaches one and twenty. At first it was just a task." Rémi shrugged. "But he's a rare one. I'm closer to him than my own now."

"And he doesn't know," she said. "About you being paid, I mean."

Rémi grimaced. "He has an inkling. The Baron was always harder on Bertrand than his other sons. Not sure why. Watching him grow into a man has been an honour."

"Thank you, Rémi. That's what I needed to know." She rubbed her arms to ward against the chill.

"Curse you for making me say that out loud."

"Never be ashamed of speaking what's in your heart." Salome met the anger in his face. "Life is fleeting at best. Why fill it with regret?"

"Reckon you could take a measure of your own advice."

"Perhaps." She glanced up at the cloudy night sky. "You must understand. Bertrand and I are bound. You can't part us. To protect his life is to protect mine. They're one and the same now."

"Is that what you told Roard?"

She bit back the retort that sprang to her lips. "Yes," she said in the most even voice she could muster. A pang of loss slid through her ribs and lodged in her chest.

Roard, my love. I'm sorry.

Rémi stared at her with a shrewd expression. Finally, he said, "Let's hope we never have to put our loyalties to the test, eh?"

"Amen." Salome turned to re-enter the hut.

"There's one other thing," Rémi called softly.

She waited with her back to him.

"I recognise where we are. Come morning, Bertrand will too."

"And where would that be?" she asked over her shoulder.

"About twenty miles north of Bertrand's family estate and east of a small chateau called Fontette."

She turned and frowned at him. "Is that supposed to mean something to me?"

"It will to Bertrand." A smile widened across Rémi's broad face. "It's the home of someone he used to court. A widow by the name of Justine."

A widow? She had sensed the wounds left by a woman when they had merged, but Bertrand's exhaustion had been her primary concern. "Will she help us? Provisions? Horses?"

"Perhaps if you ask nicely." Rémi's smile became malevolent.

"I see. Good night, Rémi."

Salome ducked back into the hovel. The fire was burning low, so she added some of the precious dry timber. Bertrand looked so young in the soft glow of the fire. Tight brown curls framed a smooth-skinned face with a long forehead that gave him a thoughtful appearance. He had beautifully sculpted lips that she could easily become lost in, but his strong jaw hinted at the man he might grow into…given the chance.

She squatted next to her latest Shroud and twined a finger around one errant curl. "Bertrand," she whispered. She liked the feel of his name upon her lips.

This one was so different to quiet, brutally competent Roard.

The loss of Roard was already losing its edge as her bond with Bertrand deepened. This was the nature of her curse, although knowing this did little to lessen her guilt. Bertrand would change her, as she had already changed him. There was little point in dwelling upon the unfairness of it. It simply was.

Salome lay down next to Bertrand. Despite his youth, she sensed strength and determination in him. But did he possess enough for what lay ahead?

Closing her eyes, she hunted the answer in her restless sleep.

CHAPTER 25

19 October 1307

East of Fontette

Bertrand coughed. The wet, hacking sound startled him into wakefulness.

It took him a moment to recall where he was. He sat up and squinted in the dim light of the hut. The fire had dwindled to embers and the air was cold and damp. Bertrand shivered. He drew his legs up to his chest and wrapped his arms around his knees.

Rémi rolled over on the dirt floor and opened one eye. "What's wrong?"

Where's Salome? Bertrand wanted to ask. Another bout of coughing rattled through his chest and he spat out a gob of phlegm.

"Bertrand?" Salome's silhouette appeared in the doorway. Mist curled between the trees outside. For a terrible moment, he thought they were back at their camp near the Marne.

Rémi nodded at Salome. "She's been keeping an eye out while I napped." The grudging tone in his voice suggested he blamed Salome for needing to sleep.

Bertrand stood and a bout of dizziness set him back on his heels. He sat down unsteadily.

Salome pressed a hand to Bertrand's forehead. "You feel feverish. Rémi, is there any firewood left?"

"Of course there isn't. Do you think I'd let him freeze if I had a choice?"

"I'm fine." Bertrand brushed Salome's hands away. Her touch made him uneasy. He coughed again and brought up more phlegm.

Salome frowned at Bertrand. "He has fluid on the lungs. I need a fire."

"And I told you there's no dry firewood to be had anywhere in this forest." Rémi rubbed his eyes angrily. Bertrand sensed this was not a new argument. How long had he slept?

Salome shot Rémi a cool look. "Then how I am supposed to help him?"

"Tell him."

Salome stilled.

Bertrand glanced between the two of them. "Tell me what?"

A look of uncertainty crossed Salome's face. Despite all they had been through, Bertrand realised it was the first time he had seen her hesitate. Another bout of coughing wracked his chest. Salome rubbed her palm in circular motions into his spine. The pressure was comforting, although he still felt awkward at her touch.

"Tell me what?" Bertrand repeated.

"Rémi thinks he knows where we are." Salome avoided his eye.

"I don't *think*, I know."

Salome ground her teeth together, obviously biting back a reply.

Bertrand paled. "Not my father's lands."

"No, cub. We're a bit further north than that."

"Then where?"

"East of Fontette," Rémi replied.

Bertrand froze. Surely, he had misheard Rémi. "Fontette. You're certain?"

"Without a shadow of a doubt. I recognised this hut last night."

Bertrand glanced at the dilapidated timbers. "I've never seen it before."

"Never had to come this way." Rémi shrugged. "No need given we always stopped at Chateau Fontette. I know this place from my youth."

"Are you absolutely sure?" Bertrand asked. "I mean, there must be countless places like this." Panic squirmed in his guts.

"I'm sure."

Salome squatted in front of Bertrand. The split of her riding skirts revealed her pale chemise. The linen was stretched tight by the curve of her thighs. Bertrand averted his gaze. "We need provisions and horses," Salome said. "Will this woman of yours help us?"

Bertrand winced at the description and shot an accusing glare at Rémi. "What in God's name have you told her Rémi?"

"Don't look at me." Rémi threw his hands up. "She already seemed to know."

"Is that true? Did you know about Justine before you chose me?"

Salome sat back on her heels, perfectly balanced. "Everard mentioned an indiscretion. But I sensed the mark she left upon you when we joined earlier." She tilted her head. "Bertrand, there's no shame in having loved, no matter what others say."

"Love isn't something we shared." He fought the cough building at the back of his throat. "I know that now."

Salome raised her eyebrows. "Yet the very mention of her name undoes you."

Bertrand sniffed. "She's unlikely to feel the same if that's what you're hoping for," he said in a voice thick with bitterness.

"Whatever the case, you have the ague," Salome said in a brisk tone. "Unless we find somewhere warm and dry, it will only worsen. Already your limbs tremble. Soon you won't be able to travel at all. We have no choice but to seek shelter from this Justine."

Hearing Salome speak Justine's name invoked a complex knot of emotions: desire, shame, defiance, even a misplaced pride. How could he possibly unravel them so they could be dealt with one at a time?

Justine had been at the centre of everything he had thought he wanted for so long. Even after he was shriven of his sins by the local Abbot — with a heavy penance imposed — Bertrand had been unable to let her go. If Salome knew of Justine, she already knew him better than most of his brethren had.

She was right, though. Without food or shelter, what options did they have?

Another round of coughing wracked his body. After he finished, Bertrand spat and wiped his mouth. Salome's brows had knit together in concern. Her expression was mirrored on Rémi's face. It seemed they had finally found something to agree upon.

"Very well," he conceded. "It's not as if we have a choice."

Rémi hoisted Bertrand's hauberk over one shoulder and gathered their meagre possessions. Salome helped Bertrand up with a strong grip and his legs only wobbled a little.

How would Justine react when she saw him again? Would she be happy or contrite? Or would she be coolly indifferent? And what would she make of Salome? Bertrand cringed at the thought of the two women meeting. No, it was best he kept Salome a secret.

CHAPTER 26

17 July 1099

The Tower of David

Diederic remained kneeling as Count Raymond considered his account of the battle for the northern wall. Two members of Raymond's personal guard stood on either side of Diederic. The edges of their swords glinted in the morning sunlight. Both men were mutes, so the secrecy of Diederic's account was assured.

Raymond had chosen to hold this audience at the top of the highest parapet in the inner citadel known as the Tower of David. The Egyptian commander had surrendered it to Raymond in exchange for safe passage to the port city of Ascalon.

"How do I know this story of yours is true?" Raymond stared at Diederic with his one good eye. "Perhaps it's an invention to explain how you failed to prevent Godefroi from entering the Holy Sepulchre."

"Messire, I'd be willing to swear upon the True Cross," Diederic replied.

"And invite Peter Desiderius and the rest of the clergy into this discussion?" Raymond snorted. "I think not." He strode over to the battlements and gazed across the city. A turbulent sea of tiled roofs, spires and domes spread out beneath him.

"I'm happy to provide whatever assurances you require, messire." Diederic lifted his chin. "The chevalier I mentioned, Achambaud de St Amand. He consorts with the forces of Hell. I saw him perform magicks that gave Duke Godefroi a fearsome appearance."

Raymond strode across the parapet and grabbed Diederic by a thatch of hair. His dagger pressed against Diederic's throat. "Don't spin lies to distract from your failure. I'm not a fool."

Diederic met Raymond's angry gaze without flinching. "Messire, I believed myself dead once already in your service. The threat of it again no longer scares me."

"Pah." Raymond released Diederic with a shove and sheathed his knife. "What would you have me do? Bring you before the Council of Princes and claim that a warlock serves Godefroi?"

"I'm willing to submit to interrogation, if need be." How could he convince Raymond? "Messire, I saw the transformation with my own eyes, even though they tried to hide it from me."

"Then why has no one else come forward? Where are the other witnesses to corroborate your story?"

Diederic hesitated. "I'm not sure. Perhaps—"

"Perhaps you're mistaken." Raymond folded his arms across his chest. "Perhaps you're known to serve Count Raymond de Toulouse, who would do anything to discredit his rival, Duke Godefroi de Bouillon. That's what they'll say, and I'll have no answer to it, save your fervent word."

"Isn't that enough?" Diederic couldn't keep the wounded tone from his voice.

"No, it's not enough you idiot." Raymond's upper lip curled. "Godefroi will denounce you as a traitor. Instead of protecting him, as you were sworn to do, you tried to kill him on the very steps of the Holy Sepulchre. He'll have ample witnesses attest to that."

"I'm not a traitor." Diederic half-rose. The firm grip of the mutes forced him back to his knees. "You instructed me to obtain his confidences and to prevent him from entering the church first at any cost."

"Exactly." Raymond gave him a slow, mocking clap. The hollow sound rang across the battlements. "And once you admit this before the Council, as you'll inevitably be made to do, any chance I have of becoming King will be lost." Raymond nodded at the guards.

"Wait!" Diederic tore free from the mutes and threw himself face-down. "I beg you. Let me kill the sorcerer. If I remove this evil from the earth, Godefroi's powers will weaken, and you may still prevail. Let me live and I'll perform this final service for you. Then I'll leave the Holy Land forever. I swear."

Diederic had squeezed his eyes shut, dreading a sword thrust. It never came. Raymond's voice, harsh and heavy with disgust, impaled him instead.

"Get up."

Diederic was hauled back onto his knees. Raymond leaned over him and said, "I should cut your tongue out, just to be certain." His right hand stroked the hilt of his dagger. "Fortunately for you, the first Council meeting is tomorrow, so I don't have time for you to recover."

Dust swirled through beams of sunlight slipping through the

crenelations. Raymond's fingers trembled as they threaded through the rays of light. "Time has ever been my enemy," he said softly. "We're all dust before it."

Diederic did not know what to say in the face of this sudden change in mood. Raymond appeared haggard, as if his long years had just tapped him upon the shoulder. His skin had a grey hue and his cheeks were hollow.

Raymond's gaze snapped back to Diederic. "Go. Kill this warlock, but don't involve me in any of it." He undid a pouch hanging from his ceinture and threw it at Diederic's feet. Coins clinked against the stone. "This is enough to buy your passage back to Provence, or whatever hole you choose to crawl into. If I ever see your face again, I'll not be so merciful."

Diederic gathered up the coins and Raymond's mutes hauled him down the stairs. It was only half-way down that Diederic's legs began to shake. In serving Raymond, he had lost both his honour and rank. Anger stiffened his spine and he shook the guards off.

He came to a decision as he tramped down the flight of steps. Once he had killed the sorcerer, he would slay Duke Godefroi as well. If he survived both encounters, God would show him what to do next.

CHAPTER 27

17 July 1099

The Latin Quarter

The heavy wooden door swung closed behind Hugues and his eyes took a moment to adjust to the dim sunlight.

"Ah, Brother Hugues. It's good to see you whole and well." Arnulf de Chocques did not rise from behind his desk. Instead, he beckoned for Hugues to join him. The hair at Arnulf's temples was damp with sweat. A large, leather-bound Bible sat open before him. Arnulf's fingers worried at one corner of the vellum.

Like Godefroi, Arnulf had claimed a large merchant's home close to the Holy Sepulchre. Considerably larger than Godefroi's residence, the house was built around an internal courtyard. Delicate marble decorated the floor and beautiful statues adorned niches in the walls. Unlike Godefroi, however, Arnulf had dispensed with all other Saracen fineries.

"I'm pleased to see you unscathed as well," Hugues replied. Arnulf, while not a Deacon yet, was dangerously ambitious and worthy of caution.

"Please, sit." Arnulf gestured to the single, hard-backed chair that faced him across the desk. "Are you hungry? Thirsty perhaps?"

"No, thank you. I ate with Duke Godefroi's household."

"Of course." Arnulf ceased worrying at the Bible and leaned back in his chair. "No doubt that would explain why I didn't see you during the service at Matins."

Hugues nodded, preferring to let Arnulf draw his own conclusions rather than offer him anything to work with.

"But it doesn't explain why you missed the service at Compline."

"That is true." Hugues bowed his head and placed his hands in his lap. "Duke Godefroi requested that I stay with him, as he grieved for the loss of so many Christian lives during the siege. The burning of the Jews in their synagogue also troubled him greatly. After all, the Lord Jesus was once a Jew."

Arnulf nodded and made a show of looking forlorn. "Of course the Duke's soul was troubled. What good Christian wouldn't be upset by the slaughter in this holy city?" Arnulf's concern faded into something sharper and eager. "And how did you console him, Brother Hugues?"

Hugues took a moment to consider his answer. He had anticipated this question, but he did not want Arnulf to realise that. "I assured the Duke that we are the instruments of the Lord's Will." Hugues spread his hands. "Didn't Bishop Adhémar remind us of this daily before he passed into God's care?"

"Indeed he did," Arnulf agreed in a pious voice. "It seems to me that Duke Godefroi has much need of your counsel lately. Do you think Godefroi's ambitions exceed merely serving God?"

Hugues pretended to ponder the question, although he had known that Arnulf would eventually guide the conversation here.

Not content to wait for an answer, Arnulf leaned forward and spread his hands on either side of the Bible. "Jerusalem is not a place to be ruled by Princes or even a King. It belongs to all Christians and should become a See of the Holy Roman Church. Surely you agree."

Hugues chose his words carefully. "Duke Godefroi hasn't confided his plans in me, although I know him to be a pious man." He gazed past Arnulf's shoulder, ostensibly deep in thought. "He wouldn't seek to offend God by claiming the city as his own. But nor would he see it undefended. Perhaps you can suggest a satisfactory compromise?"

He realised immediately that he had overplayed his hand. Arnulf sat back slowly, his eyes narrowing, as if searching for the meaning behind Hugues' words. The tip of Arnulf's tongue brushed against his top lip.

"Brother Hugues, our obedience is to God before any earthly ties." Arnulf patted the Bible for emphasis.

"Of course," Hugues replied. "Although if God is best served in advancing the cause of the pious, wherein lies the sin?"

Arnulf considered this in silence. His steady, unwavering gaze never left Hugues' face. Eventually, he took a deep breath and touched the open page with obvious affection. "Despite my urgings, the Duke of Normandy will not remain in the Holy Land. Now that his vow is fulfilled, he wishes to take ship home."

"But you wish to stay," Hugues suggested.

"Don't you? God's work is here, in restoring the glory to His churches and uncovering his greatest relics." Arnulf stopped suddenly, as if he had said too much.

Hugues leaned forwards and dropped his voice. "Duke Godefroi also wishes Jerusalem to be the spiritual crown of a new kingdom, but first he must counter the claims of Count Raymond."

"I don't see how I could help you there," Arnulf replied in a neutral tone. "Many of the princes already support Godefroi's claim, as does the Duke of Normandy."

"I'm pleased to hear it," Hugues said with a smile, "but this is Jerusalem. Surely, temporal and spiritual matters must work in harmony."

A calculating look flitted across Arnulf's sweaty features. "What do you propose?"

"Simply this: we know Peter of Narbonne supports Raymond. If you were to publicly support Godefroi, it would carry weight within the Council and amongst the common folk."

"And how does such an action serve the interests of...our Lord?"

Hugues smiled. Now it seemed to be Arnulf's turn to act obtuse. They were both familiar with the steps to this dance. "Godefroi seeks only to protect the Holy Sepulchre, not to rule it. If chosen as the city's defender, he would appoint a Latin Patriarch, not one from the Eastern Church." Hugues let the implication hang in the hot, still air between them.

"And you have no such aspirations?" Arnulf asked suspiciously.

"I do not." Hugues shook his head.

This admission clearly troubled Arnulf. He leaned forward and threaded his fingers beneath his chin. "Then what *are* you seeking, Brother Hugues?"

"I seek the freedom to walk in the footsteps of our Lord," Hugues replied with all the conviction he could muster. "My greatest hope is to achieve a moment of pure grace before I die." It was not a lie. If anything, it was dangerously close to the truth.

"Grace," Arnulf said with one raised finger, "is something that finds you, not the other way around."

Hugues ducked his head and chose not to debate the matter. The slow smile that spread across Arnulf's face suggested they had reached an understanding.

CHAPTER 28

18 July 1099

The Council of Princes

"It's not simply a question of primacy," Duke Robert of Normandy said to Count Raymond across the broad table. "No one is disputing that Bishop Adhémar travelled with you and valued your counsel. This Council must take many factors into consideration in choosing who should be King."

The day was still new and the most senior nobles had broken their fast together. The smell of freshly baked bread filled the dour audience chamber of the Tower of David. Despite the early hour, Godefroi was already weary of the bickering.

"The only factor that matters is who would be most pleasing to God?" Raymond glared at the Council members through his one eye. He had chosen his garb carefully this morning. None of the assembled nobles could rival the splendour of his pale grey *bliaut* chased in silver. Godefroi suspected it to be a gift from Alexius Comnenus, the Byzantine Emperor, who had so impressed Raymond on their march to the Holy Land.

Godefroi checked a fresh surge of irritation.

"Therein lies the problem," Baldwin said, picking up the thread of Raymond's conversation. "While the clergy might be anxious to rule this city in the name of the Holy Roman See, they won't be manning the walls when āl-Afdal of Cairo comes to take his vengeance."

"Baldwin's right," the Duke of Flanders said. "The Caliph will demand the return of this city. Especially now that his governor in Jerusalem has reached Ascalon filled with tales of the atrocities committed against his people."

A murmur of assent rolled around the table. Raymond's mouth thinned at the reference to his bargain with the Governor. "Guaranteeing his safe conduct in exchange for the Tower saved many lives," Raymond snapped. "And it has shown the Saracens that we have *some* honour." He leaned on the table. "Make no mistake. If we wish to remain in the Holy Land, we'll have to find common ground with Baghdad *and* Cairo."

"I agree with that, at least," Baldwin replied.

Godefroi hid his shock. His younger brother was supposed to be supporting Godefroi's claim, not agreeing with Raymond. It took an effort not to grind his teeth.

"Our situation in Edessa is delicate," Baldwin continued. "The Armenians have rallied behind the banner of Christianity. However, the Kurdish tribes still rule the plains. I can't fight them and the Seljuq Turks. Diplomacy is needed to give us time to consolidate our gains." Baldwin avoided Godefroi's eye.

"Exactly." Raymond's smile broadened. "Jerusalem needs a king who is not only acceptable to the clergy, and indeed to all good Christians, but a seasoned tactician and diplomat. I have already demonstrated that I can treat with the Saracens when we must." He leaned back in his chair.

Godefroi stirred. Hugues had advised him to stay silent for as long as he could during the Council. *It's better to allow others to speak for you rather than make Raymond's mistake and advocate for yourself.*

"It's the sword that forces an enemy to diplomacy," Godefroi said quietly, "not the elegance of the request that they do so." Many of the assembled nobles nodded at that.

Raymond turned to Godefroi. "More conquest, is that what you recommend? Continue our pilgrimage until our supply lines are extended so far that they're inevitably cut off. We'll die of starvation and thirst!"

Godefroi ignored Raymond and searched the faces of the assembled nobles. The Dukes of Flanders and Normandy were with him. Baldwin, despite his comments about Edessa, would ultimately support Godefroi's claim, if only because he was next in line to succeed Godefroi. A cluster of other nobles, mostly Provençals, still supported Raymond.

"I would see no man crowned king in the city where the Lord Jesus wore a crown of thorns and died for our sins," Godefroi said. Hugues had made him memorise the sentiment rather than the words to ensure he delivered them with conviction. "I vowed that all Christians should be able to pray, unimpeded, at the Holy Sepulchre. This I have done." Godefroi let those words sink in.

Raymond leaned back in his chair, his lean face a mask of polite disdain.

"Instead," Godefroi continued, "if found worthy by this Council, I would claim the title *Advocatus Sancti Sepulchri*." *Defender of the Holy Sepulchre.* "And I would dedicate the rest of my days to protecting this holy place from any who would seek to wrest it from us."

Arnulf stood. He was seated with the rest of the clergy along the east wall. They were not part of the Council, but bore witness to its deliberations.

"May I be heard?" Arnulf asked with exaggerated humility.

Raymond made to protest, but Robert of Normandy waved him on.

"Thank you." Arnulf took a step forward and gazed at the assembled nobles. "As Duke Godefroi has already said, no man may truly rule this holy city, save He who died for all of us. Surely no-one disputes that." Arnulf paused to see if any dared challenge his statement.

Having silenced the bickering nobles, Arnulf continued. "The Church recognises that we are beset by enemies, so we have great need for pious men who can defend all who seek refuge within these walls." Arnulf spread his hands wide. "After Duke Godefroi's gracious offer, it is clear to the Church who would be most pleasing to God." Arnulf bowed towards Godefroi.

Raymond's face flushed and he glared at Peter of Narbonne, his pet clergyman, but it was too late. Baldwin stood, followed by the Dukes of Flanders and Normandy. Almost the entire Council followed, save Godefroi, Raymond and his staunchest supporters. Those Council members who had risen from their seats bowed towards Godefroi.

Raymond rose from his chair at the head of the table and glared at the Council. "If that's your decision, then you can hold this city on your own." He stalked out of the chamber, followed by his remaining supporters.

CHAPTER 29

18 July 1099

āl-Aqsa Mosque

Hugues, Godefroi and Achambaud stood in the cool silence of the āl-Aqsa Mosque. Despite recent attempts at scrubbing the tiles, bloodstains were still visible where Saracens had fallen. Hugues suppressed a shiver of guilt and glanced at Achambaud. The chevalier's jaw was tight and his eyes narrowed.

"It's cool in here." Godefroi carried his helmet in the crook of his elbow. Dressed in his plain grey tabard, mail shirt and boiled leather, he almost looked like an ordinary chevalier. Achambaud wore his traditional dark armour, although he had dispensed with his shield in favour of a spear. Even Hugues had donned his mail shirt and carried a mace.

"A feature of the dome," Hugues replied. "Like a chimney with smoke, the heat of the day escapes into the sky." He glanced about the mosque with genuine interest. "Do you feel the slight breeze? The latticework on the east and west walls probably conceals shafts for ventilation. A clever design."

"Their places of worship are so different to ours," Achambaud observed. "They don't have frescoes or stained glass, yet there is grace here, nonetheless."

Hugues admired the complicated mosaics that covered the walls, the intricate tiles that bordered the places of prayer and even the stylised, cursive script of the Saracens. "I agree, Achambaud, although you'd best keep such sentiments to yourself."

Godefroi glanced around the mosque impatiently. "We should keep moving. The longer my personal guard remains outside, the more likely our presence will be noted."

"Agreed," Hugues said. "We need to find a way beneath the mosque."

"I noticed a set of stairs over there." Achambaud pointed with the tip of his spear towards a wide set of stairs at the far end of the main chamber.

"Too obvious." Hugues scrutinised the mosque. "If the Saracen clerics knew of Solomon's secret, they would have restricted access to its location. At least that's what our Church would do." He strode towards an elevated dais where the Saracen version of a pulpit had been knocked over. Hugues stepped onto the platform and gazed down at an imaginary crowd of worshippers, all prostrated on their prayer mats, facing Mecca.

"I thought you said it wouldn't be obvious." Godefroi pulled the mail coif back from his head, removed his leather cap and ran his fingers through thick blond hair.

"It wouldn't," Hugues agreed, "but there should be subtle signs for the initiated to find the path." Wherever he looked, geometric patterns leapt out: interlocking tiles formed subtle designs too large for the eye to encompass unless they looked down from the dome above. The arrangement of different prayer areas around the central one resembled squares on a chessboard.

"So what am I looking for?" Godefroi asked. "Stars and circles? A picture of Solomon's Seal?"

Hugues contained his irritation with difficulty. The mosque was littered with countless stars. Some had been painted on the walls in gold or silver, often accompanied by the crescent moon of Islam. Others had been embedded into the mosaics, picked out with coloured chips of glass.

Wherever Hugues looked, the ancient symbols of Solomon had been blended with the newer images of Islam. Perhaps that was the point? Rather than seeking an overt sign, or something at odds with the rest of the mosque, the message was one of acceptance, of integrating two traditions.

"The whole mosque is dedicated to Solomon's memory." Hugues stepped down from the dais. "The dome forms the circle of Solomon's seal. Stars can be found wherever you look. Even six pillars support the dome, just like the six points of Solomon's star."

"How does this help us find the artefact?" Achambaud asked with a frown.

"It doesn't," Hugues replied. "The intention is to overwhelm and bewilder."

"So what are we supposed to do now?" Godefroi demanded. "I have a coronation to prepare for."

"We go down." Achambaud had closed his eyes and leaned on his spear. "The mosque is the seal. We must pass through it."

"Achambaud?" Hugues touched him on the shoulder and the

chevalier startled and blinked.

"What happened?" Hugues asked. "Are you hearing them again?"

"The voice," Achambaud said. "The one that helped me before. It... showed me the way."

"To what?" Hugues demanded.

"I'm not sure." Achambaud frowned in confusion. "Some kind of...I don't know. It's dark down there. We'll need torches."

"What's going on?" Godefroi's brows had knit together and he gave Achambaud a dubious look. "What voice?"

"We're being helped." Hugues did not want to elaborate as Godefroi was unlikely to understand.

"By whom?" Godefroi glanced suspiciously between Hugues and Achambaud. "I thought you'd told me everything."

"Everything I know about the artefact, yes," Hugues replied. "This is an unexpected development."

"Don't evade the question," Godefroi growled. "Who's helping us?"

"Please keep your voice down." Hugues took a calming breath. "I think the Saracens have five sacred points, like us. One of their number is helping us."

"Why in God's name would they do that?" Godefroi demanded. "How do you know this isn't a trap?"

"I don't." Hugues rubbed one eye with the back of his hand. "I can only speculate, but I have the impression they've been waiting for us." He turned back to Achambaud. "I'll gather torches. Can you show us the way?"

Achambaud nodded. "Yes, I think so."

"Wait here." Hugues strode outside and obtained torches from Godefroi's men while fending off questions.

Achambaud had moved to the far end of the building and discovered a second set of stairs hidden behind a delicate screen of tightly woven palm fronds. Cut from rock, the stairs were worn smooth from years of use. The steps turned sharply after the first landing and receded into the darkness.

"These stairs have seen many feet," Godefroi said. "Are you sure this is the way?"

"Yes, I think so." Achambaud closed his eyes, obviously trying to picture the images again. "If I'm right, we'll find a long hallway that runs underneath this floor. Small chambers attach to it on either side. Another staircase leads deeper again."

Using a flint from his belt pouch, Hugues struck a spark. It caught in the tinder and Hugues coaxed the flame with gentle breaths. The torch bloomed into flame. "I have some candles as well." Hugues handed a torch to Godefroi and Achambaud.

Achambaud led them down the staircase. As predicted, it joined a long corridor. Christian soldiers had obviously discovered this place. The corpses of Saracen clerics lay on the floor and in the small sleeping chambers attached to the passage. After three days, the stench was terrible.

Delicate glass lanterns had once illuminated the corridor, but most had been knocked over or crushed during the sacking. Hugues nearly tripped on a metal brazier that had been upended.

Godefroi and Achambaud explored the corridor and found little of interest. The hallway ended in a second set of stairs that descended further into the ground.

"What's next?" Godefroi asked gruffly.

"I'm not sure." Achambaud leaned his spear against the wall, closed his eyes and massaged his temples. "I keep seeing a solid wall with holes in it. The room isn't large, yet it conveys a sense of enormous space." He shook his head with a rueful look. "I know that doesn't make much sense."

"None of this does." Godefroi glanced uneasily back the way they had come.

"Take us to this wall with holes," Hugues said. "We can decide what to do from there."

Achambaud forged ahead, his spear levelled and torch thrust forward to light the way. The second stairwell was hewn from rougher stone that was darker than the light, sandy stone they had encountered so far.

The steps spiralled down into the rock and Hugues lost sight of Achambaud. Even the glow of his torch receded.

Godefroi moved to follow Achambaud. Hugues caught his arm. "Wait. I don't want you trapped in the staircase if someone is waiting down there."

"All's well," Achambaud called. His voice echoed up the stairwell.

Godefroi clattered down the steps, followed more carefully by Hugues. How far underground were they now? Had they reached Solomon's temple or had centuries of human habitation, wind and rain buried it even deeper?

Hugues emerged from the tight staircase into another long corridor, much like the one above. This hallway was narrower and the ceiling lower. Moisture beaded on the walls and the air was cooler.

More cells attached to the passageway. Carved from solid rock, each contained only the barest necessities: a rude sleeping pallet, coarse woollen blankets, and the melted stubs of candles.

The passageway ended in another staircase that wormed further below ground. A metal grill had barred the entrance, but the gate had been torn from its hinges and flung upon the stone floor.

"Did you see this in your vision?" Godefroi asked in a low voice.

"No."

Hugues caught the uncertainty in Achambaud's reply.

"I'm not sure our soldiers did this." Godefroi shifted on his feet.

"It seems obvious that we must continue down," Hugues said in an even voice.

Achambaud led the descent. The steps ended in a long, narrow chamber. The ceiling was low enough to force Godefroi and Achambaud to stoop. Small columns of lighter coloured stone supported the roof. Hugues guessed they were recent additions to support the weight of the mosque. He raised his torch to get a better look.

While the upper floors had been swept clean, this chamber was covered in dust. A long stone bench ran the length of the chamber and low wooden stools had been tucked beneath it. Niches had been carved into the rock at regular intervals and sealed with beeswax to prevent moisture from spoiling their contents. Bundles of scrolls filled each cavity, along with jars of ink and quills. Ash puffed beneath Hugues' shoes as he moved forward to inspect the writings.

"Are we supposed to find further instructions in this scriptorium?" Godefroi asked.

"Perhaps." Achambaud pointed. "Certainly, this one died trying to protect his scrolls."

A Saracen elder, dressed in a black turban and flowing robes, was slumped against the far wall. He had taken a sword thrust to the stomach. Scrolls were scattered around his corpse, many of which had been ripped to pieces.

Hugues retrieved an intact scroll, broke the wax seal, and carefully unrolled the fragile papyrus. It was written in the cursive script of the Saracens, although images interspersed the words, similar to Egyptian hieroglyphics.

"Can you read it?" Godefroi asked.

"No." Hugues searched the dead Saracen's face for a clue to the man's intentions. "Maybe that's what they intended."

"What do you mean?" Godefroi peered over Hugues' shoulder.

Hugues bit the inside of his lip. "I could spend a lifetime deciphering these scrolls only to find that none of them mention the artefact."

"Then what are we doing wasting time down here?" Godefroi kicked the wall in frustration.

Hugues raised a placating hand. "I didn't say we were in the wrong place. Achambaud, is this the wall you spoke of? The one with the holes?"

Achambaud gazed at the russet stone wall. "Perhaps. Except in my vision, it was completely empty."

Hugues carefully examined the cavities. Each was a hands-breadth high and two wide. Spaced in regular columns, the niches formed a grid. Another geometrical pattern, just like the mosque's imitation of a chess board. Hugues quickly counted the columns; seven in total, each with five rows of cavities.

According to the Kabbalah, seven was the number reserved for God, six for the angelic orders, and five for men.

The old cleric must have been removing the contents from this wall when he died, because five of the cavities were empty. Hugues took a step back. The message the dead cleric had been trying to impart suddenly became clear.

"Achambaud, hold this for me." Hugues handed his candle to Achambaud and dropped his mace.

"What are you doing?" Godefroi demanded.

"Testing a theory." Hugues crouched before the empty cavity closest to the ground on his left and felt inside. Wax coated the rough rock. He probed the back wall and detected a spot where the wax had crumbled away. Instead of rock, his fingertip brushed against a metal disk. Hugues pushed the disk and was rewarded with the grinding rasp of stone on metal.

"What was that?" Godefroi demanded.

"The tenth sphere of God," Hugues explained, unable to contain his delight. "What the ancient practitioners of the Kabbalah called Malkuth. It symbolises the physical world our bodies inhabit."

Hugues moved to the second empty hole in the column on his right. Knowing what to look for this time, he quickly located the disk and pushed. The rasp of metal was followed by a thud as something heavy fell into place. He stood and grinned at the two warriors. "The ninth sphere of Yesod, the reasoning and ingenuity that lies within all of us."

"Hugues, are you sure you know what you're doing?" Achambaud asked.

He nodded. "Yes, I believe so. This is a puzzle only someone familiar with the five sacred points could solve."

The empty cavity at the top left was shoulder-height. Hugues stood on his tiptoes to reach the disk. The hiss of sand falling whispered through the scriptorium. "The eighth sphere of Hod, the sovereign reason that sets us apart from all other creatures."

Hugues moved across to the top right cavity and stretched to reach the disk. No sound emanated from the far side of the wall this time. "The seventh sphere of Netzach, the empathy and compassion of brotherhood."

"Stop," Godefroi commanded.

Hugues turned to face Godefroi. "What's wrong? We've found the path. We—"

"It knows we're here." Godefroi pointed with the tip of his sword towards the wall. The faintest suggestion of a tremor quivered through his blade.

Hugues had already deduced someone had preceded them from the broken wax seals. "It? What are you referring to?"

"I'm not sure," Godefroi said in obvious confusion. "I can feel it... tugging at me."

"Tugging?" Hugues repeated carefully. "Does it feel like you're being pulled from within, almost like a soft hook caught in your innards?"

"Exactly. I can feel the...a pull, where the star touched me at the Anastasis." Godefroi indicated his groin, the place where the mystic energy of Malkuth resided. It was all the confirmation Hugues needed.

"Messire, we *must* discover what lies beyond this wall." Hugues clasped his bare hands together. "This is why we've travelled so far. Don't falter now, not on the very threshold of success."

Godefroi hesitated, clearly torn. "You don't understand. It *knows* me...whatever it is."

"Yes," Hugues cried. "All of us have felt this, each in our way. It's a form of recognition, a way of—"

Achambaud stepped forward, dropped his torch on the stone floor and using the butt of his spear, rammed it into the last cavity. A shriek of metal tore through the scriptorium, the wall shook, and the corpse of the cleric fell onto his face.

The bottom section of the wall swung outwards to reveal a narrow crawl space that angled down into the darkness. Cold, musty air flowed into the chamber.

CHAPTER 30

18 July 1099

The fortress of Alamut

The wind gusted up the steep slope that guarded the approach to the fortress of Alamut, it whistled through battlements, and tugged at the turbans of sentries. The stronghold was an extension of the peak of Aluh Amut, not an addition. Defensive towers rose from natural rock spurs and the walls followed the spine of the ridge, forming a long, narrow fortress. It made sense then, for the Imam of Alamut to become known as the Old Man of the Mountain, for he was indeed old, far older than any could have imagined.

The Imam sat cross-legged at the top of his tower. Eyes closed, head bowed, his breathing was slow as his thoughts ranged far beyond his body. Apart from the wind whipping his grey hair and tugging incessantly at his robes, he could easily be mistaken for stone. The Imam seemed part of the mountain: timeless, immovable, and unyielding.

A pigeon battled to control its descent towards the battlements. The Old Man opened hazel-coloured eyes flecked with green. They were a source of speculation among his neophytes, so unlike their own dark brown eyes. While the path to Alamut was harsh, and demanded determination and courage, none of them had been brave enough to ask the Imam about his origins.

The Old Man watched the pigeon's struggles with stony-faced dispassion. The bird was clearly exhausted. Each beat of its wings was slow and laboured, and the incessant wind tossed it carelessly. Having gained sufficient altitude, the bird folded its wings and plummeted towards its loft, only pulling out of the dive at the last possible moment. It landed heavily on its perch next to the dovecote, wings flaring to control its balance.

The pigeon keepers rushed out of their small enclosure, each eager to claim the honour of bringing the Old Man news. The fastest—a beardless youth with wavy black hair—clutched the bird to his chest.

Fending off the other boys with his elbows, he hunched over his prize.

The Old Man lost interest in the squabble and his gaze shifted to the flat plateau of Qazvin, intent upon what lay beyond the horizon to the west. Alamut was isolated, a stronghold in every sense of the word. Its solitary nature suited the Imam, although he knew that events in the world could touch him, even here.

Soon it would be time to make his presence felt. With the threat of the Franj thundering through the Caliphates of Baghdad and Cairo, the region would be in a panic. And confusion created opportunities.

The boy had managed to strip the carrier pigeon of its message. Even now, he dashed through the long, narrow courtyard towards the Old Man's private tower. First, he would have to navigate the lush hanging gardens that wooed initiates. The paths were deliberately circuitous and crowded with dangling vines. They would slow the boy down.

The Imam rose and stretched, thrusting his hips forward and pulling his spine back. A man of his long years should not move so freely, although he had learned to command his physical shell long ago.

He clambered down the wooden ladder that provided access to his eyrie. With each step, the pace of his heart increased. He savoured the dry taste of anticipation in his mouth.

A staircase carved from natural rock descended into the main body of the tower. While thick carpets adorned parts of the fortress to cushion against the harsh winter, the Imam spurned such comforts.

The stairs opened onto a circular landing that formed the Imam's private chamber. A hearth gaped in the wall to his right and small fissures in the rock allowed the smoke to escape. A sleeping pallet had been placed close to the fire, little more than a bundle of lamb skins on a straw mattress.

His only possession that could be considered opulent was a faded blue kilim. Woven into the dyed wool in silver thread was a five-pointed star. The beams of sunlight that squeezed through arrow slits glittered across the design.

The Imam descended a second staircase to the bottom of his tower. Here, more familiar items associated with the status of emirs were in evidence: sumptuous cushions covered in bright silks, a rare porcelain jug with six matching cups for chai, and a delicate hookah of purple glass. Cracked leather spines of manuscripts surrounded the chamber. They were written in a multitude of languages: Ancient Greek, Phoenician, Hebrew, Latin and Arabic. The smell of old hashish lingered in the air.

A tentative knock sounded at the door. The Imam removed the thick beam that barred the entrance and pulled on the iron ring. The hinges groaned under the weight of the heavy timber frame banded with iron.

The young pigeon keeper stood in the doorway clutching a tiny cylinder of wax. His expression was impassive, although the subtle shift of his weight from foot to foot betrayed his nervousness. The Old Man held out his hand wordlessly. The boy handed him the message, his eyes downcast.

A gash marred the wax cap that sealed the tiny cylinder. The Imam held it up, showing the boy the damage. "Did you open this?" His voice was soft, at odds with his weathered visage.

The boy's face paled and his knees buckled for a moment. "No, honoured master. I brought the message to you as soon as it was received. Perhaps...perhaps it was already damaged?"

The Imam searched the boy's face for a hint of deception. He seemed honest. Certainly, he was terrified, as he should be. The Old Man was pleased at the composure in one so young, but he didn't let it show. "Tell me your name."

The boy blanched further, pale enough to number among the Franj. Everyone in Alamut knew the Old Man only asked your name if he had a task for you.

"W—Wasim," the boy stuttered.

The Imam nodded. "Wasim, you will return to the Keeper of the Dovecote and inform him that you must retire from your duties. You will then obtain weapons that best suit your skills from the Master of the Armoury. Finally, you will travel to the home of Raknud ibn-Dawala in Aleppo. When you find him, you will ask him whether the seal was damaged when he sent this message. If it was, you will take his life and return here. If it was not, and you are satisfied that he speaks the truth, you will go to the nearest mosque and kill the Imam during morning prayers. Be sure not to let them take you alive. Do you understand?"

Wasim's eyes widened. He bowed low from the waist.

"Now go." The Imam slammed the door.

Incompetence could not be tolerated, not even among his lowliest servants.

The wax cylinder rolled around the leathery palm of his hand. It was possible the pigeon had been intercepted, but unlikely. He removed the wax cap with his fingernail and upended the cylinder to release the tiny scroll. The message contained only three words, but they were enough to upset the balance that had held for so long: *Jerusalem taken. Instructions?*

A rare smile split the Imam's face. He began composing a mental list of nobles to be killed to destabilise the region, starting with the powerful Sunni centres of Damascus and Aleppo. These names would be sent to a variety of devotees scattered across the countryside. However, the most important list could only be entrusted to one of his brethren.

Taking a scrap of papyrus, quill and ink, the Old Man wrote the first, and most important, list: *ālim Sharif—āl-Aqsa. The Qādī, the Seer, the Alchemyst and the Physick— Khirbet Qumran.*

He blew across the ink, his dry breath sealing the death warrants.

Given time, patience and discipline, anything can be accomplished. This the Old Man knew from personal experience. Soon, the entire Holy Land would grovel beneath the heel of Severity.

CHAPTER 31

19 October 1307

The outskirts of Fontette

Night was falling when Bertrand, Salome and Rémi reached the outskirts of Justine's estate.

The day had remained cold and only drizzled for short spells, rather than the driving rain from the previous day. Bertrand's fever had worsened despite the milder weather. His legs were as stiff as wooden stumps and his balance had become increasingly unreliable. Often, he was forced to stop, hands-on-knees, as he coughed uncontrollably. Chills shivered through his flesh, followed by bouts of heat that left him slick with sweat.

Salome had insisted they approach Justine's chateau undetected, so Rémi had led them in a wide arc that kept them inside the tree line. As the day wore on, Bertrand recognised familiar landmarks: he stumbled up a particularly steep gully that was home to a rushing brook. In the distance, he caught sight of a knoll, bare of trees and crowned with a crumbling pile of old stones.

Dropping his head, he plodded after Rémi.

Bertrand's feelings about returning to Justine's estate varied as wildly as his temperature. On the one hand, it was a relief to be returning to a place where they could claim shelter and some measure of protection. Yet this was not how he had visualised his reunion with Justine. In his imagination, Bertrand had returned at the head of a Templar caravan, dressed in the full array of a chevalier, perhaps recently returned from a successful campaign in the Holy Land. Instead, they were creeping through the night, spattered in mud and little better than beggars.

"Don't fight the convulsions." Salome slipped her arm around his waist. Using her palm, she rubbed tight circles into his back. The pressure in Bertrand's chest loosened and he spat out vile gobs of mucus.

Straightening, he wiped his mouth and glanced sideways at Salome.

Was she regretting her choice of Shroud? Was she inwardly cursing at being saddled with such a weakling? If so, she kept it from her face.

They stopped at the top of a rise in a stand of poplars where a chill breeze wended through the trunks. Rémi searched the terrain for possible threats. "Almost there, cub."

"I know," Bertrand replied in a hoarse voice. He swayed on his feet and Salome steadied him. He hated this weakness. Roard would not have succumbed to a fever. The big chevalier would have led them through the forest without hesitation.

Salome turned Bertrand's face so she could stare into his eyes. Her fingers were warm upon his cheek. "Strength isn't measured by what befalls us, only by how we respond."

Bertrand nodded wearily.

After a moment, Rémi cleared his throat. "It's mostly flat the rest of the way. The trees thin out into fields on the other side of this ridge. There'll be no getting inside the walls without an invitation."

"No one must know we're here," Salome replied. "It's too dangerous."

"Well, you won't get to her ladyship without trusting someone." Rémi dropped Bertrand's hauberk and their supplies onto the ground, and rolled his broad shoulders in relief.

"Do you have someone in mind?" Salome asked.

"Huon." Bertrand leaned against a tree. All he wanted to do was lie down and sleep, which was not a good sign.

"Who?" Salome asked.

"Her ladyship's gamekeeper," Rémi replied. "Once the Baron decided to send Bertrand to the Commanderie, he wrote her ladyship a note of farewell. I delivered it to Huon, who passed it on."

"So we can rely on this man," Salome said. "Is that what you're saying?" Her arm around Bertrand's waist tightened protectively.

"He's our best option. Bertrand needs a roof and a fire."

Salome slipped Bertrand's arm over her shoulder and pulled him upright. "You're right. We must get him warm and dry as soon as possible."

"Huon it is." Rémi led them downhill, through the tree line and across a barren field. Reaching level ground, Rémi folded up Bertrand's hauberk and hid it in the long grass. "I'll retrieve it later," he muttered.

Nudging Salome aside, Rémi looped Bertrand's arm over his shoulders. "Not far now, cub."

Justine's chateau was a block of shadow to the west, a handful of torches fluttering along the parapet. The moat glinted around the foundations and Bertrand could just make out the main gate in the face of the east wall. The drawbridge was down and the glow from braziers was visible through the heavy iron portcullis.

Was Justine feasting with her household? Had she reconciled with his father, or been forced to remarry? As capable and experienced as she was, her land would be safer with a strong lord to rule it.

A pang of regret pierced Bertrand. If the fates had been kinder, that lord might have been him.

"Steady." Rémi glanced towards the chateau. "Don't worry. Her ladyship will see you when she's able."

A humble cottage squatted at the edge of the field. Candlelight gleamed through gaps in the doorframe and dogs barked at their approach. Thankfully, the hounds were leashed, as they didn't come bounding out of the gloom. Rémi half-dragged Bertrand to the doorstep and handed him back to Salome. He banged on the door.

"Who's there?" a deep voice called.

"Huon, you miserable cur," Rémi replied. "Open the damn door. It's freezing out here and his lordship has need of your hearth."

"Rémi?" A note of disbelief quavered in the man's voice.

"The door, Huon."

"You can't be Rémi. He joined a Commanderie in Brienne."

"Things change," Rémi replied. "Are you going to open up, or am I kicking your door in?"

A bolt rasped in its sheath and the door swung outwards, spilling warmth and light into the frigid night. Bertrand coughed violently, and his body shook as he doubled over.

"Who's that with you?" Huon's narrow face peered at them from the doorway. The gamekeeper was as tall as Bertrand but heavier through the waist. He wore a thick woollen tunic, brown in colour, with grey hose. A rush of relief surged through Bertrand at the familiar face.

They were among friends at last.

"Master Bertrand and a servant," Rémi replied. "Quickly, man! The cub's half-frozen to death and he's got the shakes." Rémi pushed past Huon who was too astonished to protest. Salome followed them inside, head down and face covered by her hood.

Bertrand offered a muttered thanks but found his voice had deserted him. The warmth from the fire was a relief. He just wanted to sink down before it, as close to the flames as possible. Huon's wife hushed their four inquisitive children. Despite knowing Bertrand and Rémi, she appeared nervous at their sudden arrival.

Salome settled Bertrand in front of the hearth. Dry rushes covered the dirt floor and Huon possessed only a few pieces of furniture: a low wooden bench, a few seats carved from broad tree trunks and softened with rough pillows stuffed with wool. A cabinet on the far side of the hearth contained a mortar and pestle and a handful of rough pots.

"I need thick quilts and hot water," Salome said to the goodwife. Her strong fingers tugged at the ties of Bertrand's padded tunic. Within moments, Salome had removed his saturated garments except for his breeches.

"But what are you doing here?" Huon asked. "You're supposed to be in Brienne. At the Commanderie." He glanced between Rémi and Bertrand in confusion.

"Like I said, things have changed," Rémi replied.

"Changed? How?" A worried look spread across Huon's angular features. "You're not involved in this business with the King arresting all the Templars, are you?"

"No." Rémi pointed a finger at Huon. "And we've no desire to be, understood?"

Huon glanced at his family in concern. "And what's a woman doing travelling with two brethren?" A note of accusation had crept into his voice.

Salome removed her hood and met Huon's fearful stare. The gamekeeper recoiled at the faint scars covering her face. His wife gave a little cry of surprise before herding her children behind a drape that separated the sleeping pallets from the rest of the cottage.

"Bertrand said we can trust you," Salome said. "We only need shelter and for you to pass a message to her ladyship. There's no risk to you or your family if our presence remains a secret."

"Who are you?" Huon asked.

"Best you don't know." Rémi dumped their possessions in the corner near the door.

"Where are those quilts?" Salome called.

"Here." The goodwife hurried over and timidly offered two quilts stuffed with wool. "These are the best we own."

"Thank you," Salome muttered.

Another shiver ran down Bertrand's naked back. Shouldn't he feel warm by now? Or had the cold taken refuge inside his bones?

Salome wrapped a quilt around him. "I still need that hot water."

Huon's wife bobbed at the knees and set about filling a battered pot with water from a jug.

Huon wrung his hands. "Rémi, in the name of all that's holy, what are you about?"

"The less questions, the better for us all." Rémi took Huon by the elbow and led him aside. "All you need do is take a message to her ladyship. Just like before. Nothing has changed, my friend."

Bertrand watched them with heavy eyelids. He lost the rest of the exchange to the crackling fire and the excited whispers of the children. The leap and dance of the flames were mesmerising. His extremities tingled and he knew from previous experience they would soon ache with returning circulation. He coughed again. Thankfully, this time it didn't rattle his bones.

Salome squatted in front of Bertrand with another of her mysterious infusions. He took a few sips and tried not to gag on the bitter aftertaste. Warmth spread through his chest and he sighed in relief.

Bertrand lay on the floor and Salome lifted his head into her lap. Holding back his eyelids took an enormous effort. She smiled down at him, her expression tender yet edged with concern. Her scarred fingers stroked his curly brown hair.

"Sleep, my Shroud."

So he did.

CHAPTER 32

21 October 1307
The outskirts of Paris

Roustan waited impatiently in the antechamber. While he had shed his travel-stained cloak and wiped the worst of the mud from his boots, his appearance still left much to be desired. Ordinarily, an audience with Guillaume de Nogaret would have demanded a far higher standard of presentation, but this visit could hardly be considered ordinary.

He rubbed his thumb against the scrap of parchment clenched in his fist. The communiqué from Châtillon-sur-Seine had arrived earlier than he had dared hope. As for its contents…well, it had completely reshaped the nature of the discussion he was about to have. Haste, not protocol, had become the imperative.

Fortunately, Guillaume was well known for keeping late hours.

Roustan rocked on the balls of his feet. How much longer?

One of Guillaume's valets gave him a curious, sideways look. Roustan scowled and the valet averted his gaze. No doubt he looked quite a sight: his hair was tangled and his clothing was spattered in mud. Two of Guillaume's household guard had insisted on accompanying him, even though he was unarmed.

Roustan smiled. Perhaps his appearance would remind Guillaume of the dangers he had endured in the King's service.

Jean-Pierre—Guillaume's Seneschal—slipped through the door of Guillaume's private chamber. He stopped to confer with the head valet. They glanced frequently at Roustan during the quiet exchange.

Jean-Pierre was in his twilight years and his lined, morose face gave him a brooding air that suggested he disapproved of everything. Noting Roustan's scrutiny, Jean-Pierre beckoned him over with an expression of distaste.

"And not before time." Roustan strode forward, flanked by the two edgy guards.

Jean-Pierre frowned. "Despite your unkempt state, Guillaume will see you now. I trust that your manners are more refined than your appearance."

Roustan sized up the dour old Seneschal. "If your comments are intended to offend a loyal servant, Jean-Pierre, then you're in danger of succeeding."

Jean-Pierre smiled without humour. "The days of my life have been largely spent, Roustan. If they've purchased any value at all, it's the wisdom to know whose opinion is worth courting." Jean-Pierre stepped aside and gestured towards Guillaume's chamber.

Roustan stopped in the doorway. "It appears your days have purchased a good deal of pride, too."

"Perhaps," Jean-Pierre admitted, "but at least mine was well-earned." He turned his back on Roustan and dismissed the guards with a flick of his wrist.

Roustan checked his anger. To antagonise the Seneschal any further would be foolish given he had Guillaume's ear. But this latest insult would not be forgotten. He stored his anger for a later date.

Guillaume's large chamber was located on the upper floor of his castle. Heavy drapes of burgundy velvet had been drawn against the bitterly cold night. Thick rugs of eastern design covered the wooden floor and in one corner, a porcelain vase rested on a plinth of marble. Despite these casual displays of wealth, it was the books that drew Roustan's eye.

Shelves lined the room, stacked so tightly with books only their spines were visible. Lettering of no shape or constitution that Roustan could decipher tantalised him with untold mysteries. The power of those books, the knowledge that they represented, was intoxicating. Roustan was proud of his ability to read and write. But standing here, in Guillaume's inner sanctum, reminded him of how ignorant he remained.

This was what he desired: the trappings of this room and all that it implied.

"Are you going to stand there all night, gazing like a fool?" a lazy, disembodied voice asked. "I was told that you needed to see me urgently."

Roustan startled at those words. Guillaume was not a man to be kept waiting. He glanced about the chamber. "I'm sorry for intruding, messire, but I bring news of some urgency."

"So Jean-Pierre said." Guillaume's bored tone suggested that he doubted it.

A banked fire leapt in the main hearth. Two high-backed chairs, swathed in cloth-of-gold, faced the fire. A low mahogany table had been placed between them. Sitting on the table was a half-full decanter of golden wine. A pale, elegant hand unstoppered the decanter, poured a measure, and disappeared behind the chair again.

"Stop skulking and stand where I can see you," Guillaume ordered.

Roustan moved around to face the two chairs. Guillaume sat in the chair on the left. He was dressed in dark grey hose and a tunic of black silk that was unlaced at the throat and loose about his wrists. His dark brown hair was dishevelled and one errant lock fell across his forehead just short of sharp, hazel eyes. A carefully manicured beard followed the line of his jaw and connected to his thin moustache. Guillaume cradled a wide glass of wine in one hand.

"Is this him?" an unfamiliar rasping voice asked.

"Yes." Guillaume toasted Roustan. "He's our man."

A second fellow was sitting in the shadow of the other chair. Roustan had failed to notice him at first because of his stillness.

"To whom do I have the pleasure?" Roustan couldn't keep the note of surprise from his voice.

"The pleasure?" The man laughed, although it was more of a snort, before taking a noisy gulp of wine.

Now that he looked closely, Roustan saw the stranger was dressed in rags caked with old mud and what looked suspiciously like dried blood. A few strands of lank hair hung from his largely bald head. Raw sores clustered at the corners of the beggar's mouth, which curved into a leer when he noticed Roustan staring. Unhealed lesions dotted his skull like liver spots on an old man. Roustan couldn't begin to guess at his age.

"Who is this you ask?" Guillaume smiled and gestured towards his companion. "Why this is my Master of Eyes-and-Ears and Plier-of-Tongues."

The peasant slurped from his glass and watched Roustan over the rim with his bloodshot eyes.

Was this some kind of jest? Had Guillaume found the most degenerate man in Paris and extended his hospitality as a bizarre experiment?

"He seems surprised to see me here, amongst all this finery," the beggar noted.

"Indeed, he does." Guillaume swirled his wine.

The pause in the conversation became uncomfortably long. Sweat prickled along Roustan's back. He was too close to the fire. Not knowing what else to do, he cleared his throat. "Messire, there is a matter I must discuss with you…in private."

Guillaume frowned. "Anything you have to say to me can be said in front of my companion. Indeed, he probably already knows what you wish to tell me."

Roustan glanced at the beggar. He certainly appeared smug enough. Could news of the witch's escape have reached Guillaume already?

"Messire, with the utmost respect, I doubt that's possible. I've come to you in the greatest of haste." Roustan gestured to his clothing for effect.

"Then let me try to guess." The beggar drew up his spindly legs and tucked his filthy bare feet under him. "You managed to flush out Salome from her hiding place amongst the brethren of the Temple. Naturally, you pursued her. A battle took place, and even though she was surrounded, somehow she escaped." The beggar gulped more wine and licked his lips. "Is that about the size of it?"

"I see you serve our lord most effectively." Roustan kept his tone cool but polite. "She did indeed escape by means that could only be described as witchcraft." Here he glanced at Guillaume to gauge his reaction.

"A menhir?" Guillaume directed the question at the beggar.

The grotty peasant nodded, although his gaze remained fixed on Roustan. Sweat oozed from Roustan's armpits and trickled down the small of his back. The room was too hot.

"So she may have travelled further north," Guillaume hazarded. "Beyond our cordon."

"Or anticipated that we'd expect that and done the opposite." The beggar sucked the inside of his cheek. "You know how she delights in being unpredictable."

Roustan watched this exchange with barely concealed shock. How dare this vagabond address Guillaume as an equal?

"You have more to tell, don't you, Roustan," the beggar prompted.

"For messire, yes." Roustan couldn't keep the disapproval from his voice.

"I've already commanded you to speak freely," Guillaume said softly. "I don't appreciate repeating myself."

"My apologies, messire." Roustan sketched a bow to hide his discomfort. This was not how he had envisaged his briefing with Guillaume. "We managed to capture one of the fanatical Templars. He was unwilling to co-operate, but I did manage to discover the identity of one of the chevaliers the witch escaped with. His family is from Châtillon-sur-

Seine, which means they're almost certainly part of the Salt Lines."

"And?" Guillaume waved him on with his glass.

Roustan made a point of not rushing. "The chevalier, one Bertrand, was only newly elevated to the white. I'm sure her Shroud, and the Preceptor guarding her, died from their wounds. So she is virtually unprotected."

"And you think this Bertrand will race home to his mother's skirts," the beggar said.

"No." Roustan allowed his mouth to curve into a smirk. "My spies have discovered Bertrand had an affair with a local noble woman. Her estate is in Fontette. Rather than endanger his family, I think Bertrand will hide there."

Guillaume pursed his lips. "You know, I think you may well be right." He rose from his chair. Even though Guillaume was barefoot, he was still taller than Roustan. Guillaume placed one hand on Roustan's shoulder and leaned forward to gaze into his face. "I'm not angry with you for failing me. Out of all the hounds I've loosed across the land, you've come closest to bringing her down. But it occurs to me now, given her obvious powers, that I haven't given you the necessary tools to capture such an elusive quarry." He squeezed Roustan's shoulder and moved to stand behind his chair.

Roustan glanced between the two men. Guillaume was in a strange mood and something about this exchange did not sit right. The two men appeared to be sharing a private joke of some sort.

The beggar interrupted his thoughts. "I can tell that you don't like me."

Roustan stared at the peasant.

"Perhaps it's because I remind you too much of your past?" The beggar stood and approached Roustan. Resembling nothing more than a collection of bones thrown together and wrapped in a sack of flesh, he was hardly intimidating. Yet Roustan's skin crawled at his proximity. The man reeked of old vomit.

Roustan took a backward step and inwardly cursed his weakness.

"After all, what are the likes of us doing in this place?" The beggar indicated the chamber with a sweep of one gnarled hand.

"I serve messire in whatever way he desires." Roustan's reply sounded hollow even to him.

"Correct." The beggar shuffled closer. "We serve. We go where those who must seem pure cannot. Are we not the same, you and I?"

Roustan glanced past the beggar. Guillaume was watching the exchange avidly, and his hands gripped the back of his chair.

"We appear to have little in common," Roustan said.

"I think you're wrong there. Here, let me show you." The beggar touched Roustan's face.

Roustan recoiled from his touch. At least he tried to. The beggar's finger stuck to his skin. Guillaume darted forward, a knife flashing in his fist. The blade sliced the peasant's throat open.

Instead of blood, a black mist poured from the terrible wound. Each breath the beggar took expelled more of the vapour. It rolled down his chest and spread up his arms.

Roustan yelped as he tried to shove the body away. Even though the beggar should be dead, the vile peasant seized him by the hair with his free hand. Roustan struggled, trying in vain to break free. He pounded the beggar's bony chest with his fists. Each blow only forced out more of the black mist.

Roustan stumbled. He twisted and tried to shake the beggar off. The peasant's palm was firmly attached to his cheek and they fell to the floor. Flames scalded Roustan's foot as it slipped beneath the fire-grate. He bellowed and ripped his foot from the fire. They tumbled across the floor, fog swirling about them.

The mist pressed against Roustan's face, blinding, smothering. Its touch sent needles of pain digging into his skin. He held his breath and fought wildly to break free.

The beggar should be dead. This can't be happening.

The vapour squirmed inside his nostrils and invaded his ears. The tiny needles became hooks, piercing his skin. He was suffocating. The weight of the mist was pushing him down, forcing him *inwards*, so that the messages from his body were becoming increasingly remote.

The beggar's ugly face had disappeared. Even Guillaume's exquisite chamber had faded. Thick banks of fog pressed in on all sides, choking out the light. Roustan's lungs burned for air, but the pain was on the far side of the veil that separated him from his body. His eyes bulged. Roustan willed his mouth closed but instinct took over. He gasped for air…and the mist surged into his mouth.

He tried to scream again, yet no sound escaped his throat. The mist was as thick and vile as stagnant water in a pond. It poured into him, filling every part of who he was. He was drowning at the bottom of a deep well, where awareness of the world was only a distant circle of light far above.

"I said you needed tools to capture her." Guillaume's voice echoed down the deep shaft. "Meet Gamaliel, one of the Lords of Severity."

Roustan understood then, although it was far too late to resist. He thought about the books he would never read, the properties he would never own, even the children he might have sired one day. All those ambitions would remain unfulfilled.

Unbidden, the memory of his mother suffocating in the darkness of Guillaume's dungeon revisited him, and he knew there would be no divine intervention. No mercy shown. Not for him.

Roustan scrambled at the sides of the shaft, but the weight of his sins dragged him deeper. Somewhere far above...this *Gamaliel*...was taking control of his body.

He screamed in despair. And the mist-that-was-Gamaliel, the Lord of Severity, peered over the edge and revelled in his misery.

CHAPTER 33

21 October 1307

The Gamekeeper's cottage

"**D**o you think he'll wake soon?" a childish voice whispered.

"He will if you keep talking," another child replied with the sarcasm only an older sibling can muster.

Bertrand groaned.

"Hsst," one of the children warned.

"He's waking up."

Tiny feet swished through the rushes covering the dirt floor. Bertrand groaned again. He blinked. A thick film of sleep had caked his eyelashes.

Impressions registered slowly: timber beams overhead, tightly woven thatch stained with wood smoke, the smell of ashes and a whiff of fever sweat. Rough woollen blankets rubbed against his skin. He caught the sound of low, regular breathing nearby. His back ached from lying down for too long.

How long had he slept on Huon's floor? The tightness in his chest had eased and fever no longer throbbed at his temples. Sharp pangs of hunger had taken up residence in his stomach instead.

Bertrand peered up at chinks in the thatch roof. It was dark outside, although he had no sense of what time it might be. Early in the morning or evening? He had the impression of having slept for a long time, but it may have only been a few hours.

He lifted his right hand. Salome's tiny rose still nestled in the webbing between thumb and forefinger.

Why hadn't he turned to God for guidance? Why hadn't he prayed instead of rushing to do Salome's bidding? Devotion was at the heart of their daily routine at the Commanderie. Yes, they had been attacked and pursued, but that did not excuse his lapse. He was a chevalier of Christ, yet he had forgotten what that meant in just a few short days.

No. That was not entirely true. He had not forgotten. The guilt souring his stomach told him as much. If he was honest, if he listened to the still parts of his soul, he knew the answer. The life that he had known, the place that he had earned, had been stripped from him not once but twice. In the very moment of his ascension to the rank of chevalier, the foundations of his new life had been uprooted. Everard was dead, Arnaud and Roland and his fellow brother-knights were slaughtered. He was an outlaw, a fugitive from the King. Clearly God had abandoned him. What other conclusion made any sense?

He rolled onto his side and dry-retched. Nothing remained in his guts to bring up. He was empty. Even the solace of his faith had abandoned him.

They had left him near the fire, swaddled in woollen blankets. Smooth cotton brushed against his face. The pillow beneath his head was filled with fine goose feathers. Too fine for Huon's family, which could only mean one thing.

Bertrand sat up and peered around the gloomy cottage. Dizziness sloshed inside his skull. Eventually, it agreed to settle if he remained still. He caught the whispers of curious children in the far corner of the cottage. A small head jerked back behind the curtain with a suppressed squeak.

He was weak. It would be days yet before he was strong enough to travel. And Justine couldn't afford to just give them horses. At best, they might secure a nag to carry their supplies.

Bertrand turned his back to the children. Salome lay on her side next to him, knees drawn up to her stomach and covered by her cloak. A strand of dark hair had fallen across her scarred cheek and the top of her lip. A desire to brush that lock aside seized Bertrand. The compulsion was so strong it made him shake. He drew in a fast, shallow breath and leaned over her.

Salome's eyes flickered open. Bertrand froze, caught between what looked like an attempt to kiss her and the belated desire to pull away.

"Bertrand." She breathed his name.

His gaze fixed upon the swell of her lips, the way they moved when she spoke his name. He felt he should say something, but every reply that came to him felt dull and inadequate.

"Our time will come," she said. "Protecting me will require it. But you're not well enough yet." Her gaze flickered in the direction of the drape. "Besides, I doubt you'd want such a young audience."

A flush burned through Bertrand. He drew his knees up to his chest to cover his embarrassment. "Forgive me," he said hoarsely. "I wanted to make sure you were well."

Her eyebrows lifted infinitesimally. "Really? That's...disappointing."

"Where's Rémi?" It was the first question he could think of.

"Outside, scouting." She sat up, demurely keeping her knees together and turned away from him. "I fear your loyal sergeant isn't made to sit still."

Bertrand relaxed enough to smile. "No, he's not. But we're safe here."

Salome's smile faded. "Nowhere is safe, Bertrand. Nowhere."

"We only just arrived," Bertrand protested.

She shook her head. "You slept for two nights and a day."

"Truly?" That would explain the hunger gnawing at his innards.

She rose to her feet, smoothed her dress, and shook out her cloak. Bending down, she touched his forehead. "Your fever has broken."

He stood and spots swarmed across his vision. Salome caught his arm as he staggered. "She knows that I'm here, doesn't she?" He nudged the fine pillow with his toe for emphasis.

"Yes." Salome tilted her head. "How do you feel about seeing her?"

There was no point lying as Salome probably knew the answer. "I don't know. Seeing Justine again in normal circumstances would've been difficult. Now?" He threw his hands up.

Salome took a step closer. "You should go to her without me. It'll be easier."

"For whom?" Bertrand instantly regretted the question.

"For both of us, I should think." Salome considered the matter carefully. "Mostly you," she said with a playful smile.

"I thought we weren't supposed to be parted." Bertrand knew he was being churlish, but he couldn't help it. She always made him feel so foolish and inadequate.

"We aren't. At least not for long. You'll know when it's time to return. I promise."

Bertrand caught movement from the corner of his eye. Huon, sleepy-eyed and dressed only in an under-tunic and breeches, had appeared from behind the drape. "Messire," he said with a bow.

"Huon, it's good to see you again."

"And you, although if you don't mind me saying, I've seen you look better."

Bertrand pulled a face. "How is she?" The question was accompanied by a pang of anticipation.

The smile slid from Huon's face. "Well enough. I don't think I'd be doing her a disservice to say she pined for you after they sent you to the Commanderie." Huon parted his herd of solemn children and warmed his hands before the fire. "Not that she said as much, mind. It's just—" He gazed at the flames and rubbed his chin absently.

"Just what?" Behind Bertrand, Salome had stilled to listen to the conversation. He noted that Huon had failed to acknowledge her.

"She came to visit after we heard the news. Of you joining the Order, I mean. She's never done that before. I think—" Huon frowned. "I think in her loneliness, see, she came here. Not for company o'course, but to be closer to her memories of you. Only the once, mind. And she seemed sad, not that we spoke much. She just asked us all to leave so she could have a few moments alone."

Bertrand pictured Justine standing alone in the cottage. He was pleased to discover that she had missed him, but that did not change the fact that she had manipulated him. Pinning down how he felt about their impending reunion was proving more difficult than he had expected.

Salome moved closer to the hearth. From just behind Bertrand's elbow, she asked, "Did you take the message to the Lady Justine?"

Huon's expression clouded over. "I did."

"And?"

"What did you tell her?" Bertrand asked at the same time.

"The truth." Huon shrugged. "That you and Rémi had returned, along with a...*companion*. Her ladyship asked about your condition. I told her that you appeared to have had a rough time of it. She wanted to send her physician, but in the end, she agreed that secrecy was best."

"And did she give you any instructions?"

"She did at that." Huon glanced at his feet, as if embarrassed. "She'd like to see you. In secret, of course, once you're well enough. I said that you'd probably need at least another day to make sure the ill-humours had passed."

Bertrand closed his eyes. He was going to see Justine tomorrow. Tomorrow! That was so soon and yet too long to wait.

"We'll need to get you cleaned up," Salome murmured.

"Thank you, Huon," Bertrand said. "For speaking to her ladyship and allowing us into your home. I wish I could reward you somehow."

Huon waved Bertrand's thanks aside. "No need. Her ladyship looks after me and mine. And I look after her interests." His disapproving stare alighted upon Salome and darted away again. "I'll see about some breakfast."

"Bertrand, take this." Salome pressed a hard object into Bertrand's hand.

He opened his palm to discover a ruby. Cut in a rectangular shape, it was bigger than his thumbnail. Firelight rippled along its polished edges so that it appeared as if a wick of flame prowled inside the jewel.

"Where did you get this?" Bertrand asked in astonishment.

"It doesn't matter. Just give it to Justine when you see her. We'll need three strong horses, food for at least two weeks and oilskins to repel the rain. Make sure you ask for a skillet, a block of lard and sheets of canvas for when we make camp. And don't forget thick blankets. It will only get colder as we head north." Salome cocked her head. "What? You look surprised."

"You sound like you want to leave as soon as I get back." Bertrand hated the plaintive note that had crept into his voice.

"We can't stay here, Bertrand." Salome dropped her voice. "The longer we do, the greater the risk to these people."

"I know. It's just good to be among friends."

Salome squeezed his arm. "This sense of safety is an illusion. If you really care for them—for her—you must take me away from here as soon as possible."

"Why? No one knows that we're here. Nogaret's men don't even know you're with me, so they've no idea where to look."

"Perhaps not yet," Salome replied grimly, "but they will."

"How can you be so sure?"

Salome moved to the hearth to warm her hands. "I don't know how, but they always seem to find me in the end."

Bertrand absorbed this thoughtfully.

"Rest while you can," Salome said. "Tomorrow will be difficult for everyone, I fear."

CHAPTER 34

18 July 1099

The Temple of Solomon

"**I** commanded you to stop, Achambaud," Godefroi said furiously. "No one gave you leave to break the final seal." The hidden crawlspace in the scriptorium separated the two men.

"I'm sorry, messire, but it's too late to turn back now." Achambaud bent down and picked up his torch. "It has been ever since we crossed the northern wall."

Hugues noticed Achambaud's torch was burning low.

"I am your lord." Godefroi's sword quivered with rage.

Achambaud dropped to one knee. "I'll always defend you, but in matters of the spirit, every man must follow their conscience."

"This has nothing to do with theology." Godefroi pointed his sword at Hugues. "This is your fault. You've turned a loyal servant against me."

"I've done no such thing." Hugues met Godefroi's accusing stare. "Achambaud's right. Our conscience must always be our guide."

"*I'm* the Defender of the Holy Sepulchre." Godefroi beat a fist against his mailed chest for emphasis. "You *will* obey me."

"Publicly, yes. But not here, in this place," Hugues replied. "I've told you before, each of us is part of a greater whole. No sacred point can be set above the other four." Hugues glanced at the mouth of the hidden tunnel. "I realise that it's easier to be angry than afraid, but you must face whatever waits down there. We can only locate the artefact by penetrating the tenth sphere."

Godefroi stiffened and the tip of his blade sank to the floor. "Very well." His expression hardened. "One day you might do me the honour of trusting me as much as you insist that I trust you." He sheathed his sword. "And I'm not afraid of facing anything." He dropped to his knees and examined the dark cavity with his waning torch. The tunnel was narrow and angled into the rock.

Using the torch to light his way, Godefroi crawled into the tunnel. He was soon swallowed by the darkness. Only the sound of his shuffling descent marked his progress.

"Do we follow?" Achambaud's torch was faltering. It would not last much longer.

"I've no intention of letting him go down there alone." Hugues took a moment to light one of his candles from Achambaud's torch before following Godefroi.

The tunnel was tight and Hugues was smaller than the other two men. After some experimentation, he found it easiest to slide forward on his stomach, using elbows and knees to propel him forward. The hilt of his belt knife pressed cruelly into his abdomen and the head of his mace banged painfully against his knee. Despite these discomforts, Hugues was able to protect the candle so that he continued his descent in a small pool of light.

The walls of the tunnel were unusually smooth and the tunnel echoed with the slither and scrape of their progress. It would be difficult climbing out again, especially if the artefact proved bulky. Hugues pushed the thought aside and continued his slow, controlled slide.

Moisture dripped from overhead and a bead of water trickled into the corner of his mouth. The bitter taste of minerals stung his palate. The passage seemed to go on and on. He had no choice but to continue. The tunnel was too narrow for him to twist around and climb out. What if this was a dead end? He shoved the horrifying thought away.

The tunnel ended abruptly, and Hugues slid down a short drop onto a level floor. The candle flame guttered and nearly went out, but he managed to protect the precious light.

His first impression of this new chamber was of space. Darkness and silence pressed in on all sides, but the claustrophobic press of rock had lifted. Hugues rose cautiously to his feet. The wall that he had emerged from was cut from solid rock, although it was unnaturally smooth. The feeble light of the candle was unable to reach the ceiling.

"He's here," a dull voice said from the dark. Hugues belatedly drew his mace from the loop attached to his belt.

"Godefroi?" Hugues raised the candle overhead. The hollow, despairing tone did not sound like the man he knew.

Hugues took a tentative step forward, then another. Sand shifted beneath his boots. Godefroi appeared from the gloom. His torch had gone out and lay discarded at his feet. He had his back to Hugues, so he couldn't make out Godefroi's expression. Nor could Hugues see what held Godefroi's attention.

"Godefroi? What is it?" Hugues inched forward as Achambaud slithered out of the tunnel.

"I don't want to fight," Godefroi said.

Hugues swung back towards Godefroi. He wished the reach of his candle was greater. How could Godefroi possibly see any adversary? Hugues moved forward and the darkness vanished to reveal a glorious dome curving overhead. Silver-tinted light illuminated the large chamber.

Hugues stared in astonishment. Stars winked in the dark vaults overhead, mimicking the constellations of the night sky. They shifted slowly, almost imperceptibly, as if circling the chamber.

He could not find any obvious source of illumination, yet the clarity of the light was so clear and pervasive, it did not cast any shadows.

It took Hugues a moment to notice the figure that awaited them. The man was a Saracen: that much was evident from his dark skin, sharp nose and glittering black eyes. The face beneath his tear drop helmet was weathered and lined. His long hair was white with age and had been bound in a queue. He wore a light chain-mail cuirass and carried a curved scimitar in one hand, and a long knife in the other.

Hugues took a step forward, hopeful the man might understand French or perhaps Greek. Godefroi's arm blocked Hugues. "Stop. Look." Godefroi pointed at the floor.

Ankle-deep sand lapped at the edge of a raised dais. Pristine white tiles, tinged silver by the mysterious light, covered the platform. Each was cut in the shape of a pentagon, interlocking with its five neighbours to form a seamless mosaic.

Godefroi placed one foot on the tiles and hesitated. A haunted expression flitted across his face. "You said each of us would be tested in different ways." He drew a short, sharp breath. "You didn't tell me I'd have to kill a man who feels like the brother I never had."

Hugues frowned. "There's no need for bloodshed."

Godefroi shook his head. "You know nothing about honour among warriors." He mounted the platform. The ancient Saracen smiled, revealing yellow teeth.

A circle of light pulsed beneath the old man's feet and Hugues was suddenly drawn from his body. He rose to the apex of the dome, amid the stars that shifted in the night sky. Looking down upon Godefroi and the Saracen, Hugues finally understood the true purpose of this place.

The Saracen stood in a circle at the foot of a symbol hidden beneath the tiles. A tree with three branches rose from the sphere beneath the Saracen warrior's feet. A knot of darkness further up the central branch drew Hugues' eye. No, it went deeper than that. It was an absence, an open wound that refused to heal. The emptiness drew Hugues towards it, pulling him down from the heavens, dragging him in, until...

...Hugues jolted back into his body. He staggered and caught his balance.

Beside him, Achambaud said in a wondering voice, "What was that pattern?"

"You saw it too?" Hugues asked in surprise.

Achambaud nodded.

"That was the Tree of Life, the holy tree that describes the ten spheres of God that He used to create the universe."

"And the Saracen is trying to defend it from us?" Achambaud asked.

"I'm not sure," Hugues replied.

Godefroi walked across the tiles to face the Saracen. He drew his sword and dagger. "Do you speak our language?" Godefroi asked.

The Saracen shook his head and said something in the thick tongue of his people. A surge of frustration shot through Hugues at having failed to learn their language. The Salt Lines had promised him that Hebrew and ancient Greek would prove more useful.

"Submit," Godefroi commanded. "No blood need be shed."

The Saracen smiled savagely and adopted a guard stance.

"Don't underestimate him." Hugues was suddenly deeply afraid for Godefroi.

Achambaud tried to mount the dais, but Hugues caught his arm. "You can't help him. This test is for Godefroi alone."

"Have it your way then." Godefroi entered the faintly glowing circle. The Saracen launched at Godefroi, springing through the air with incredible power. Godefroi caught the downward sweep of the scimitar on his sword just above his cross-guard. The force of the impact pushed Godefroi backwards.

The old warrior returned to his position in the centre of the circle. Godefroi approached carefully, his sword raised in case the man should leap at him again. The Saracen feinted with his scimitar, dancing forwards and back to test Godefroi's defence.

Godefroi parried a sudden lunge. With a bullish roll of his shoulder, he turned the scimitar aside. Capitalising on the Saracen's slight forward momentum, Godefroi lunged forward and stabbed with his dagger at the man's neck. The Saracen deflected the thrust with his knife, but he was not strong enough to completely turn it aside.

Godefroi's blade nicked the bottom of his ear.

The Saracen twisted away from Godefroi and swung the flat of his blade backwards in a blow that crashed into the side of Godefroi's helm. Godefroi stumbled, rolled across one shoulder, and crossed his blades to defend against the inevitable overhead blow that must follow.

It never came.

The Saracen returned to the centre of the circle. Breathing hard and ignoring the blood running down the side of his neck, he beckoned to Godefroi with his knife. A wild grin split his weathered face.

The Saracen was testing Godefroi, goading him, but he didn't seem intent on killing his opponent. Godefroi must have sensed it too because he said something in a low voice that Hugues couldn't catch. The warrior shook his head and gestured with his knife again, impatient this time. Godefroi strode back into the circle and unleashed a wave of ringing attacks. Blows were countered by ripostes, sweeping backhand strikes were blocked, defence surged into attack and back again. Knives darted between the swords as they came together, seeking a decisive advantage.

Godefroi scored at least three more strikes that drew blood from the lightly armoured Saracen. Every time the warrior struck back, it was either with the flat of his blade or turned aside by Godefroi's superior armour. Blotches of blood stained the Saracen's sleeves and abdomen, but he ignored the injuries.

"Fight properly," Godefroi screamed.

The grin that twisted the Saracen's mouth was almost manic. He nodded briefly at Hugues and Achambaud, and Godefroi glanced in their direction.

The Saracen chose that brief lapse to leap into the air. Twisting his hips, his blades flashed silver in the light of the dome. Godefroi caught the scimitar on his upraised sword and the force of the blow drove Godefroi to one knee. In desperation, he thrust his knife upwards, locking his elbow as the Saracen landed.

Both men held still for a moment. The old warrior staggered backwards, the hilt of Godefroi's knife protruding from his stomach. He said something to Godefroi and collapsed. Dark arterial blood pooled on the tiles. Godefroi stared incredulously at his left shoulder. The warrior's dagger quivered upright from his hauberk.

Achambaud leapt onto the dais and rushed towards Godefroi. Hugues hurried after him.

"Are you badly hurt?" Achambaud asked.

Godefroi rose to his feet with a confused expression. He dropped his sword and pulled the Saracen's knife from the links of his armour and padded tunic. Only the very tip had drawn blood. Godefroi threw it away in anger. The blade skittered across the tiles and was lost in the gloom.

"*Allāhu akbar,*" Godefroi said to Hugues. "What does that mean?

"I don't know," Hugues replied. "We can find out." He glanced at the dying Saracen and wondered what he was thinking. Relief softened the warrior's wrinkled face. The fierce light of his brown eyes, almost black in this light, was fading.

Godefroi knelt next to the warrior and took his hand. "Why?" Tears left tracks in the dust that covered Godefroi's face.

"*Allāhu akbar.*" The Saracen closed his eyes and sighed. With an obvious effort, he pointed towards the centre of the dais. Not long after that, his rasping breath stuttered to a halt and the grip of his hand grew slack. Godefroi bowed his head and moaned.

Achambaud and Hugues drew back out of respect for Godefroi's unexpected grief.

Hugues lifted his candle and carefully crossed the tiled floor. The Tree of Life had faded, but he could still picture it in his mind. He stopped where the absence had been in his vision. The tiles here were black and warped, as if scorched by a fire. A shallow bowl had burned into the floor.

Hugues knelt next to the cavity. Reaching down, he recovered a small wooden chest banded in copper. The five-pointed seal of Solomon had been burned into the polished walnut. The box was surprisingly heavy, and he wondered what lay inside.

This was not the place to open the chest. Not standing next to the emptiness of Daat, the source of forbidden knowledge that had undone men and angels alike.

Hugues hurried back towards Godefroi and Achambaud, clutching his prize.

CHAPTER 35

18 July 1099

Khirbet Qumran

A skitter of pebbles down the rock face was all the warning the man known as the *Qāḍī* needed. After all, great rockslides could begin with the smallest of stones. So it would be with this visit, he sensed. He let whoever it was approach, his eyes shaded against the westering sun. The Judean foothills rose sharply before him from the plain of the Dead Sea at his back.

He had hoped to pick out the first star of the evening, a solitary ritual he had enjoyed for too many years to consider counting. In times past, he would have made measurements and drawn conclusions from the celestial march. Not now. The future, once as distant as the stars, had finally arrived among them.

"Umayr," a slightly breathless voice called. The number of people who still called him by his original name could be counted on one hand. In his imagination, the ground trembled as boulders tumbled past. He took no pleasure in being right.

"Come and sit." He patted a worn rock that perched close to his makeshift platform. Like the stone, his hand was weathered and deeply veined. Despite the gifts bestowed upon him, the *Qāḍī* and his four brethren had not escaped the touch of time.

Umayr preferred to sit cross-legged, although Tahīr's body was not as supple as his. He would appreciate being able to stretch his legs, especially after the long climb to the top of Umayr's rocky perch.

"I thought I'd find you here." Tahīr sank onto the stone with a sigh.

Umayr glanced sideways at his companion. Despite the cooling air, sweat dripped from Tahīr's gaunt features. In his prime, Tahīr had been a jolly man, heavy of limb and torso. Years of toil, and the emotional demands placed upon him, had stripped Tahīr of flesh. Now he was all sinew and sun-baked skin. His humour had dried out too.

Like Umayr, Tahīr was dressed in light, pale coloured robes that blended with the rocky terrain. They wouldn't be warm enough, however, for a body slicked with sweat.

"You'll catch a chill." Umayr offered his cloak to Tahīr, who threw it about his shoulders with a grunt that passed for thanks.

They sat that way for a time, gazing towards the sunset, bearing witness as it turned from lavender to purple. The silence between them was an old companion and it sat comfortably between them.

The first star appeared in the heavens. Venus, the Romans had named it. Umayr sighed. This was probably the last time he would greet it from this sacred place. The repository was no longer safe.

"Tell me," he said to Tahīr with genuine reluctance.

The lines of Tahīr's face tightened into knots of pain. He placed a steadying hand upon the rock. "The Franj have taken Jerusalem. ālim Sharif is dead."

Umayr drew his knees in and cradled the pain to his chest. The news was as he feared. Coming from Tahīr, it couldn't be disputed. Tahīr was the fulcrum, the one who bound the other four together. If the Sharif had fallen, Tahīr would be the first to feel it.

"When?" Asking questions was far safer than confronting how he felt about this news.

"Earlier today," Tahīr replied. "I told Jalāl before I came to find you."

"Did he...can you tell if—" Umayr searched for the right words. "Was his passing easy?"

"Still thinking of others, I see." Tahīr placed a comforting hand on Umayr's shoulder. "My friend, we have a little time to grieve. It took me most of the afternoon before I could even venture out."

An old argument, this one. And less time remained than Tahīr believed. Umayr stood. After a moment's hesitation, Tahīr rose as well.

"If the Sharif has fallen, then the Franj will have discovered the tree. The Lords of Severity will know the tenth sphere has fallen. We must bring the Franj's Imam here, to retrieve the essence."

Anger flared in Tahīr's eyes. "Why should we help them? They bring destruction upon our people. Their ways are barbaric, their ignorance appalling." He pulled the cloak tight around his shoulders. "Couldn't we—"

Umayr made a quelling gesture with his open palm. "You're angry at the Sharif's death. I understand that it affects you most of all. Yet this is part of the cycle. Our time is over. Despise the Franj if you must, but they will inherit our sacred trust. Better that than have it fall into the hands of Severity." Full night had fallen and shadows pooled around the rocks. "They'll be coming for us soon." He failed to keep the shudder from his voice.

"What would you have me do?" Tahīr asked.

"Send a pigeon to Firyal. Tell her to expect us soon."

Tahīr's head lifted in surprise. "Jerusalem has been overrun. I assume you have a good reason for hastening our deaths."

Umayr smiled grimly. "As I said, we must find their Imam. Only an initiate of Hod can retrieve the essence."

"Very well." Tahīr's doubt was written across his familiar face.

"This is the last thing we must do before we can rest." Umayr embraced Tahīr, his lifelong brother. The loss of the Sharif finally overcame him, and he wept. He suspected it was only the first of many sorrows.

CHAPTER 36

18 July 1099

Jerusalem

By the time Achambaud reached the scriptorium, his legs burned with the effort of wriggling back up the narrow shaft.

Strangely enough, Godefroi's guards, who had been patiently waiting outside the mosque, did not question their extended absence. Indeed, the sun had hardly moved overhead. Surely, the bells to sound the ninth hour must have rung by now.

The walk back to Godefroi's quarters was a silent affair. Hugues had bundled the small chest in a rough woollen blanket, which he held possessively to his chest. Godefroi showed no interest in it whatsoever. His disgust over killing the Saracen had left him terse and withdrawn.

When they finally arrived, Godefroi tramped upstairs and retired to his chamber without a word to Godwera or Etienne.

Godwera was repairing a hole in Godefroi's hose. She placed her needlework on a bright yellow cushion and said, "You've upset him." The accusation was directed at Achambaud. Thinking better of it, she turned her accusing gaze on Hugues.

"I have. Deeply, I fear." Hugues sank to the floor with a sigh. He placed the woollen bundle next to him with great care. Etienne, who had been examining a parchment, set it to one side on the low table.

Achambaud was reluctant to join them. The old habits of independence and self-reliance were hard to shake. He was not immune to curiosity, however.

"Is what we've gained worth Godefroi's displeasure?" Achambaud asked.

"I sincerely hope so," Hugues replied. "It seemed wrong to open it down there."

"Down where?" Etienne asked.

Hugues quickly described their journey, Godefroi's battle, and his subsequent discovery.

"I must tend to his injury." Godwera rose to her feet, but Hugues caught her sleeve.

"It's best you leave him alone, for now. And the wound is only slight. A symbolic gesture."

"There's still the chance of infection," she replied.

"Later." Achambaud waved her back down. "Hugues has something to show us."

"Yes, I want to see what you've found." Etienne cupped his hands together. His lean face was flushed with excitement.

Hugues glanced towards the balcony where afternoon sunlight slanted through the open door.

"No one can see," Achambaud said. "Open it here."

"Without Godefroi?" Hugues asked.

Achambaud concealed his surprise. Hugues had never sought anyone's approval. "I don't think he cares at present." Achambaud checked the stairs to the ground floor to ensure they were unobserved.

"Very well then." Hugues picked up the bundle and weighed it in his hands. "As I've said before, each of us will be tested. The combat between Godefroi and the Saracen was only the first such test."

Godwera leaned forwards. "The test of Malkuth, the sphere that governs the physical world."

Hugues nodded.

"Godefroi insisted the man was waiting for him," Achambaud said. "Does that mean there are others?"

"Yes," Hugues said with a slow nod. "Four more."

"The voice on the Temple Mount," Achambaud breathed. "The one who helped me to block out the voices of the dying."

Hugues nodded. "It's the only explanation that makes sense."

Achambaud frowned. "But why would they help us?"

"They're not," Hugues countered. "They're testing us. Making sure we're worthy."

"Of what?"

"The artefact." Etienne's gaze was fixed on the woollen bundle.

Hugues unwound the blanket so they could see the walnut chest. The copper hinges and clasp gleamed in the sunlight.

"The next test relates to Yesod, the sphere of concepts and possibilities," Hugues said. "That's why you must open it, Etienne." He offered the chest. "This challenge is yours alone."

Etienne accepted the box and traced the seal that had been branded into the lid. "Yes," he said. "I sensed it as soon as you arrived."

Achambaud stared at Etienne. He realised he knew almost nothing about the slight, curly-headed engineer. "Open it," Achambaud said.

"Of course." Etienne examined the chest carefully, checking the hinges, testing the balance and weight, before touching the clasp.

"The mechanism isn't trapped or locked," Etienne murmured. "And the seal appears merely decorative. How then to explain the weight?"

"Perhaps the answer lies inside," Godwera suggested gently.

"Yes, of course." Etienne unfastened the clasp and opened the lid. His eyes widened.

Achambaud could not see inside the chest from where he crouched. "What is it?"

"I'm not sure." Etienne withdrew an object wrapped in thick purple silk. He carefully unwrapped it. The object that emerged was cylindrical in shape and slightly longer than a man's hand. It was a dull grey colour, apart from specks that glittered in the sunlight. The circumference almost matched that of a sword hilt. Shallow grooves scored the surface and markings similar to Hebrew ran down its length. One end tapered into a dull point. The other end was flat.

"Is this the artefact?" Etienne asked Hugues, a note of disappointment in his voice.

"I don't think so," Hugues replied. "This is probably another marker."

"It almost looks like a weapon," Godwera said.

"Is it metal?" Achambaud asked.

"I'm not sure." Etienne stroked the short, grey spike. "It's heavy enough, but it has a strange texture. Not rough like stone nor smooth like metal either. And I have the impression—" Etienne stopped and peered at the capped end. "There are markings here. Very faint, but I can make out the seal of Solomon. Except I don't recognise these other figures."

"Let me see." Hugues held out his hand.

Etienne handed over the spike.

Hugues squinted at the flat end. "I think these markings represent the five lower Sephirot, or spheres from the Tree of Life. They match the symbols Ephraim told me to look for in the Holy Sepulchre." Hugues handed the cylinder back.

Etienne's free hand fluttered in excitement. "I can't explain why, but I feel certain this object is hollow."

"Hollow," Achambaud repeated. "You think there's something inside."

"Perhaps." Etienne shook the spike, but nothing rattled to confirm his theory.

"Then open it."

"I'm not sure how." Etienne stared at the spike in frustration.

"In Christ's name!" Achambaud slapped his thigh. "After everything we endured beneath that mosque, we're still no closer to finding the artefact."

"Clearly, that's not true." Hugues gestured towards the chest. "You must have faith that everything is happening as it should."

"Faith," Achambaud repeated incredulously. "In what exactly? In you? In us? Or in Christ, whom you'd have us believe was just a man?"

"Achambaud—"

"No Hugues, don't treat me like a child." He stood and glared at the other three. "We're all going to burn as heretics."

"Achambaud, don't say that." Godwera rose from her cushion and stretched a hand towards him.

Achambaud moved beyond her reach. "I'm going out. Don't bother me until Godefroi returns." Achambaud turned on his heel and stomped downstairs.

<hr/>

A team of Saracens and Jews were pulling a cart laden with limbs and body parts down the street when Achambaud ventured outside. A group of pedites guarded them along the route to the large pyres established outside the city. The prisoners staggered beneath the weight of their grisly cargo.

It took an effort to rein in his anger at their appalling treatment.

The stench of decay reeked throughout the city. The smell was so bad Godefroi had issued linen head-cloths to his chevaliers. Achambaud covered his face and strode down the street in the opposite direction to the cart.

He did not have a particular destination in my mind. All he knew was that he needed to walk. If nothing else, wandering through the alleys created an illusion of progress. He feared that Hugues, who had always seemed so certain of their path, was beginning to lose his way.

Lost in his thoughts, he was surprised to discover that his feet had brought him to the northern wall. He turned down a narrow alley that ran parallel with the parapet. Dusk was painting the rooftops and the shadows were deeper here with the high wall looming over his left shoulder.

How had he lost faith in Hugues so quickly? Perhaps he had expected too much of the priest? Achambaud believed Hugues when he said they would make amends for the slaughter of the city, but all they had to show for that promise was another dead man and a useless spindle of metal.

So much death for what? The pent-up misery unfurled inside him like black sails on a boat.

"Tell me what to do," Achambaud yelled at the heavens. He sank to his knees on the cobblestones. "Help me understand your Will."

No sign was forthcoming.

His shouting did cause a sudden exodus of peasant women. They bundled up their washing and children and fled inside the small homes they had claimed. The alley was empty by the time Achambaud wearily rose to his feet. Not that he could blame them. Armoured men weren't to be trusted, even if they were Christian.

"I must seek confession," Achambaud murmured. "I must—"

He paused, assailed by a sense of threat. Achambaud barely had time to twist aside as someone rushed him from behind.

A blade squealed against Achambaud's mail shirt. He spun and grappled for his assailant's wrist. An elbow crashed into the back of Achambaud's neck and he stumbled, using his grim hold on the man's arm to keep his feet. Letting go now would be his death.

His assailant's strength was prodigious as they grappled for control of the knife. Achambaud stamped on the man's foot and won a grunt of pain. The attacker tried to jerk his hand free again. Rather than resisting, Achambaud pushed in the same time direction. Taken by surprise, the man stumbled and fell. Achambaud landed heavily on top of him. Before the man could recover, Achambaud smashed the back of his head into the man's face.

Something cracked at the impact, probably the man's nose. Seizing his advantage, Achambaud wrested the dagger free. A thick forearm wrapped around Achambaud's throat. Achambaud retaliated by reversing the blade and stabbing downwards. The man squirmed away from the blade so that it only scored his leg. The hold around Achambaud's neck tightened.

Achambaud tried to break the chokehold with one hand and stabbed with the other. The dagger ground against armour before it pierced flesh. Teeth sank into Achambaud's unprotected neck. Achambaud thrashed in an attempt to break free, but it was useless. He struck again with the dagger, this time angling the blade beneath him. The blade struck something hard, perhaps a rib, and the man gasped in agony.

Achambaud tried to roll away, but his attacker wrapped his legs around Achambaud's waist. Using his free hand, he grabbed the hilt of Achambaud's belt knife and plunged it into the hole in Achambaud's mail shirt beneath the armpit. The blade was short but pain jolted down Achambaud's arm and he almost lost his grip upon the dagger.

Abandoning his attempt to escape, Achambaud lurched to the right and used his weight to pin the man's knife hand between his arm and body. Switching the dagger to his left hand, Achambaud rammed it into his opponent's stomach.

The man cried out as blood splashed against Achambaud's side. The iron grip around his throat weakened and Achambaud finally broke free. As he rolled away, his attacker wrenched the belt knife from Achambaud's armpit and stabbed his thigh. Achambaud collapsed to the ground. He backed away, gasping for air and dragging his injured leg.

The man's face and chin were covered in blood. Even so, Achambaud recognised him.

"Diederic?"

The Flemish warrior feebly plucked at the blade jutting from his gut.

"Why?" Achambaud gasped.

"Sorcerer." Diederic spat blood at him.

An old accusation, and one he could not seem to shake. A fierce anger stirred inside Achambaud. He heard his father's taunts as he was locked in the cellar as a boy.

Breathing hard, Achambaud set it all aside. "I...forgive you," he panted. "As...Christ...taught us."

Diederic blinked. Horror froze across his ruined face. He shook his head with a grimace. "No. You...can't."

"Who...sent you?" Achambaud demanded.

Diederic closed his eyes. "Ray...mond." Silent sobs wracked his body as death closed in.

Achambaud crawled over and sat next to the fallen chevalier. "You're not alone," he murmured. They stayed that way until Diederic's breathing stilled and he passed into God's kingdom.

This was not an evil man, only one who had lost his way, thought Achambaud. Perhaps they had that much in common.

Blood trickled from the wounds in Achambaud's sword arm and leg. He took the linen cloth Godefroi had given him for the stench and tied it around the gash in his thigh. It quickly became saturated with blood.

Achambaud tried to stand but his leg couldn't support his weight.

"Help," Achambaud bellowed. "I'm Duke Godefroi's man. Help me."

None of the peasants emerged from their houses.

Achambaud crawled down the alley. His strength was ebbing and shadows crept in from all sides. How many men had he killed? How many sins would come to claim him?

He fought to remain conscious. The sky and stone walls traded places. Hallucinations rose up from the dust and spoke to him. One of them coalesced into a Saracen dressed as a monk. The figure squatted next to Achambaud and the wizened visage that gazed upon him was kind. She had expressive brown eyes framed by dark lashes. Her wrinkled mouth was pursed in concern.

What was an elderly Saracen woman doing wearing a habit?

She gently touched his face. Without moving her lips, she said into Achambaud's head: *What have you done to yourself?*

"I know...that voice," Achambaud murmured. Or at least that was what he intended to say. The sky plummeted towards him. Any moment now it would crash into him.

The Saracen woman smiled.

He smiled back and the world tilted.

CHAPTER 37

22 October 1307

Chateau Fontette

"**S**tay here," Huon said to Bertrand. "And avoid talking to anyone if you can help it."

Bertrand ducked his head. "I will. You'd best get going."

Huon gave him a curt nod and strode out from beneath the eaves of the stables. He glanced back at Bertrand once before crossing the main courtyard of Justine's chateau.

Bertrand was dressed in one of Huon's patched tunics. The threadbare garment was the right length for him in hem and sleeve, but tight across his shoulders and chest. An old cloak protected him against the chill.

He knelt down next to Huon's two wolfhounds and stroked their rich coats. Anyone who glanced his way would recognise the hunting dogs. Hopefully, they would simply assume Bertrand was minding them.

Huon disappeared into an outhouse attached to the kitchen. At this early hour, only servants were about their daily business: drawing fresh water from the well, carrying firewood or ferrying chamber pots outside.

His breath curled in the chill air as he stroked the wolfhounds. A little over a year and a half had passed since his last visit, yet he felt like a completely different person to the boy who had played at being a man with Justine. He was a chevalier now. He had killed men in battle and buried fallen comrades. And he was bonded to Salome.

In every sense of the word, he was a man. Yet his heart pounded beneath his ribs, just as it did the first time he had visited this chateau. Would Justine see the difference? Would she look upon his face and see the experience written there?

Bertrand hawked and spat. He did not need her approval, just horses and supplies. He touched the pouch tied to his belt. And he had the means to pay for them, thanks to Salome. There would be no need to beg.

You've replaced one mistress for another. Where is the honour in that?

Bertrand scowled at the unwelcome thought.

Huon reappeared from the outhouse and waved him over. Bertrand crossed the cobblestones with the dogs in tow. He kept his head down and shuffled like a serf.

"She's expecting you," Huon murmured. "Follow the girl waiting at the servants' entrance. She'll take you inside. I'll wait in the courtyard for as long as I can. If your visit takes too long," Huon said with the ghost of a smile, "ask her ladyship to smuggle you out. I'll see you back at the cottage."

"Thank you, Huon." Bertrand handed the leashes to him. "I'm in your debt."

"Just do right by her and that'll see us even." He strode back towards the stables. One of the wolfhounds whined at leaving Bertrand behind.

Bertrand scraped the mud from his boots on three metal spikes embedded in the ground before entering the outhouse. His heart thudded against his ribs. He was never nervous like this in his imagined reunions with Justine.

A small, pale serving girl dressed in a shapeless smock was stacking dirty linen. A demure lace veil covered her dull brown hair. She stopped her folding as Bertrand crossed the threshold and bobbed at the knees.

"No need for that," Bertrand said in a soft voice. "Take me to her and forget that you ever saw me."

She nodded once and turned without a word. Next to the outhouse was a scullery filled with sour-faced servants scrubbing a pile of pots and platters. None of them paid any attention to Bertrand as he shuffled after the girl.

They entered the main kitchen. The chatter was punctuated by the chop of knives on wooden blocks and the bubble of pots boiling beneath open flames. Heat rushed across his bare skin and the mouth-watering smell of baking bread drifted from the main oven. Bertrand kept his head down and avoided eye contact.

They moved through a short passage and into another chamber. This one contained jars of preserved fruit sealed with wax. The girl led him through a side entrance and into the feasting hall. A pang of nostalgia pierced Bertrand: he had feasted here when he arrived to collect the tithe. The arched ceiling and rich, old tapestries covering the stone walls reminded him of his father's chateau in Châtillon-sur-Seine.

The girl hurried across the flagstones to the far end of the hall and turned left. Bertrand's eyes adjusted to the dim light. She avoided the main staircase and walked past the wide steps, stopping at a small door.

"Through here, goodsir." She pulled the door open. Bertrand ducked his head as he passed through the low opening. An older maid was waiting for him on the far side.

The door clicked behind Bertrand and the girl's footsteps hurried away.

"This way." The heavy-set matron turned and marched down the servant passage. They ascended a set of tight, spiralling steps. The landing opened onto another narrow corridor.

The matron stopped in front of a small door. "One moment, if you please." She knocked. A muffled voice called, "Come." The matron stepped inside and closed the door behind her. A further exchange took place, although the voices were too low for Bertrand to catch.

He took a deep, steadying breath. What if Justine had changed? In all his worrying about how he had grown, he had not stopped to consider that. He bit the inside of his cheek.

The matron reappeared and held the door open for Bertrand. "The Seigneuresse will join you soon."

"Thank you." Bertrand entered the small sitting room. A fire crackled in the hearth. The drapes had been drawn back and a tentative, watery sunlight squeezed through the narrow window of thick glass. The main door on the far side of the room was closed. Two worn but comfortable looking chairs had been arranged before the fire. They were turned towards the hearth, not each other.

Bertrand thought about sitting down and immediately dismissed the idea. Instead, he removed his dirty cloak and tried to smooth the worst of the creases from his tunic. He turned the chairs to face each other.

The far door opened and Bertrand turned slowly.

Justine stopped in the doorway. Her expression was composed, almost wary, but it softened when she saw that it was truly him. Her dark brown hair was unbound and spilled over her flowing gown of cream-coloured linen.

His nervousness crumbled and fell away. Beneath his anxiety was a sudden, unexpected need to preserve this moment in all its purity and exquisite anguish. He remained still, afraid any movement might give away his inner turmoil.

"I can't believe it," Justine whispered. "You're truly here." She moved forward, her blue eyes scrutinising his face.

One of Justine's ladies, a rosy-cheeked girl with a concerned expression, closed the door behind Justine.

"I never thought I'd see you again," Justine murmured. A mesh of white lace shot through with gold thread held the long tresses back from her face. More grey strands nestled in her hair than he remembered. She was tall for a woman, like Salome, but with a fuller figure. He could not help but remember how well their bodies had fit together.

He cleared his throat. "In truth, I feared the same." Bertrand wanted to take her hands in his. He wanted to kiss her. He wanted to blurt out the entire story of his suffering and then find solace in her embrace. But he was not that boy anymore. And his vows to the Order did not permit such intimacy, even if he had forsaken them to become Salome's Shroud.

She took a step closer and looked up at him. "Forgive me. I know your vows forbid this, but I must know for certain." She reached up and touched his cheek. Bertrand caught her fingers before they could escape and pressed his lips against them. Justine closed her eyes and they remained still for a moment, prisoners of the past.

Bertrand released her hand and drew back. "Is it true? The affair with my father? Was I just a means to spite him?"

The joy on Justine's face withered at those words. She sank into one of the chairs and smoothed the fabric of her gown across her knees. "Oh, Bertrand." Her eyes filled with tears. "Is that what you believe?"

"What else is there to believe? You convinced me to lessen the tithe, which I see now is what you wanted all along. And in return, I was banished to the brotherhood."

"I am sorry for that, truly I am." Justine's expression hardened. "However, you must try to understand my perspective. Your father's taxes are more than I can afford. With my estate in debt, and your father's unwelcome advances scaring off any viable suitors, I did what was necessary to survive. But you, sweet Bertrand, were not a calculation. You were an unexpected delight. Surely, you must know this in your heart."

He wanted to believe her. Desperately so. Yet he knew she was not being entirely honest with him. "You took advantage of my affection, and my naivety."

"Yes," she admitted in a small voice. "And I have regretted it every day since."

The ugliness that lay between them was finally laid bare. Bertrand sank into the opposite chair. The relief he felt caught him by surprise.

"What is done, is done. Perhaps it would be fairest to say we both made mistakes."

"You have changed." Justine's tone was wary, despite the honesty they had just shared.

"Yes." And then because that was not nearly enough, he said, "Perhaps not all to the good."

Her lips quirked and he finally saw the woman he remembered so fondly. "Ah, well…life has a way of humbling us."

He smiled. A genuine, unguarded smile. "Then you'll forgive the circumstances of my return?" He gestured at Huon's rags.

She pulled a face of mock distaste but grew serious again. "I certainly understand your need for secrecy given recent events."

The smile faded from Bertrand's face. For a brief moment, he had forgotten about his predicament.

Bertrand leaned forward. "Rémi and I have had no news in days. What's happening in the towns, in Paris? How has the King justified his attack on my Order?" The questions came out in a rush after being bottled for so long.

"It's said the King is acting on the Pope's behalf," Justine replied. "Your Order has been accused of all manner of heresies, including sodomy and the worship of false idols. All possessions and properties have been seized across France. Don't you see what that means?"

Bertrand slumped in his chair. "The King cannot prosecute us without the permission of Pope Clement. And I refuse to believe His Holiness would sanction such a course. Not without a hearing or inquisition."

Justine shook her head. "It doesn't matter what he should or shouldn't do. It's already done. The Commanderies have been seized. The Temple in Paris fell without a blow."

"Impossible."

"But fact just the same." Justine touched his hand. "I'm sorry, Bertrand. I know you held those who wore the white in high regard. Whatever transgressions have been committed by your Order, I'm sure you're not part of them."

It troubled Bertrand that she was willing to accept the Order's transgressions without any evidence whatsoever.

"There's more." Justine's gaze slid away from his face. "Every member of the Order is to be delivered to the King's Guard. Especially senior members and chevaliers. Harbouring or aiding them is considered treason."

"No. They can't do this." Bertrand stood. "They've no right, no justification."

"I fear that's for the canon lawyers to decide." Whatever she saw in his face forced her to glance away again. "I doubt his majesty would have acted so decisively if he wasn't sure of the legality of his actions."

"So, you're obliged to—" Bertrand stopped as the implications sank in. "And if you don't, you'll be considered guilty of treason." Bertrand sank to one knee and gathered in her unresisting hands. "Justine, I'm truly sorry. If I'd known, we wouldn't have endangered you by coming here."

"I know that." She withdrew one hand and trailed the back of her fingertips across his cheek. "And that's what I loved best about you, Bertrand. Yours is a generous heart. Perhaps too much so."

Bertrand drew back. "What do you mean?"

Justine shifted her gaze to the fire. "As a woman, I've been forced to do things to hold this estate, some of which I'm not proud. I've not had the luxury of honour, like you." She turned to him, her blue eyes pleading for forgiveness. "I know how you feel about your family, but this makes you vulnerable. Anyone cunning enough to offer you acceptance and inclusion instantly wins your loyalty."

"You think the brothers manipulated me by offering me a new home."

Justine sighed. "Did you choose the path of an outlaw? Did you decide to abandon your brothers in the Commanderie?"

Bertrand swallowed an angry retort and released her other hand. "It's true that I didn't choose to return under these circumstances. Far from it. But I was placed in a position where I was forced to make a swift decision. Surely, you can understand that."

Justine frowned. "Bertrand, decisions can be overturned. What seems right in one moment may not in the next. You were part of the Order for a little more than a year. Whatever sanctions are imposed upon your leaders, they'll hardly apply to you. Beg for the King's mercy and you'll emerge a free man. Vindicated even. I'm certain of it."

Bertrand searched her face. Her words made sense. And he knew her concern was genuine. But he couldn't ignore her underlying assumption that he had been misled. "You doubt my ability to make the right decision," he said at last.

"Bertrand—"

"Do you really think I'd take such risks for no reason?"

Justine wrung her hands together. "Please. I know you well. I know how you have always yearned for a purpose that would call you out from the shadow of your father. In the past, that idealism was charming. In the present, it could prove deadly."

"Deadly? To whom?"

"To anyone who cares about you."

Bertrand looked away. Hadn't Salome given him the same warning? "You don't understand."

"Then help me to."

Bertrand pinched the bridge of his nose. Why were they arguing? This was not what he wanted. "Something important has been entrusted to me. Something from the Holy Land. My Preceptor died to protect it and I swore on his body to shoulder that responsibility. I can't give up that burden, no matter who asks me to."

Justine's mouth thinned and she threaded her fingers together in her lap.

He recognised that gesture. "What?"

A long pause grew between them. "It's what you've *not* said," she replied at last. "You should not play me for a fool."

"I don't understand." He frowned in puzzlement.

"This piece of Outremer that you speak of. Does she have a name?"

An empty pit opened inside Bertrand's stomach, and all of his anger and outrage dropped into it, leaving him hollow.

"Did you think Huon would keep her secret from me?" Justine's lips barely moved. "Whom do you think Huon serves? A young lordling who has a kind word for him or the woman that owns his land and protects his family."

"Please, let me—"

She held up one hand to silence him. "Don't deny her existence or I'll have you in chains to protect you from whatever lies have bewitched you." She trembled with anger.

"Her name is Salome."

Justine bit her bottom lip. "And? Is she your lover?"

"No! She was a guest of our Commanderie."

"I don't believe it. Everyone knows women aren't allowed inside their walls."

"Yet the fact remains that she was," Bertrand replied. "My Preceptor, Everard de Chaumont, was protecting her. She's the reason we were attacked."

"Chaumont, you say." Justine's expression became thoughtful. "I heard a rumour the Chaumonts belong to a group called the Salt Lines." Justine caught his reaction. "I see you've heard of them."

Bertrand nodded. "What do you know about them?"

"Very little, although one can hardly live in this region and remain ignorant of them." Justine gave him a shrewd look. "I want no part of what you're mixed up in, Bertrand. You should take this to your father and be done with it. But you won't, will you?"

"No." Bertrand shook his head. "I won't run home like a child who skinned his knee."

This meeting had become far too complex. He had never intended to discuss Salome or the Salt Lines with her. He rose to his feet. "I'm sorry to have brought this upon you. Truly. All I need is three strong mounts, a pack horse, food, and blankets, and we'll be gone." He fumbled at his pouch and withdrew the ruby Salome had given him. "This should be more than adequate." It appeared his relationship with Justine had descended into barter. Keeping the sadness from his face, he offered the gem.

Justine took the ruby and examined it. "More than adequate," she murmured. "Where did you get such a fine jewel? Did this *Salome* give it to you in the hope of purchasing my assistance? Does she buy everything that she needs?"

Bertrand ignored the barb. "I had hoped for your assistance regardless." He hated retreating into exaggerated courtesy, but it was his only course. "The gem is merely intended as fair payment."

"I see." Justine closed her fist around the jewel. "You do understand the danger you've placed my entire household in, don't you?"

"I do now, but I swear I was ignorant of it when we first arrived."

Justine rose to her feet. "I believe you. But if this Salome of yours is a fugitive...surely, she must have known, yes?"

He nodded. Salome had been honest enough to warn him. However, admitting this to Justine only made matters worse.

"Bertrand, please think carefully about what you do next." Justine pressed her free hand against his chest. "I cherish what we shared, but I have responsibilities I cannot ignore. Don't make me choose." Her eyes were moist as she swept out of the room.

Bertrand gazed into the fire. He felt numb. The place Justine had always occupied inside him ached with emptiness.

Salome. This was her doing. Her arrival had stripped away everything he valued. And it had opened a gulf between him and Justine that might never be bridged.

I am loss, she had said. He believed her now.

CHAPTER 38

22 October 1307

The Gamekeeper's cottage

"**N**o need to ask how it went judging from your sour looks." Rémi was perched on a stump outside Huon's cottage honing the edge of his axe on a whetstone with long, rasping sweeps.

Bertrand leaned against the stone wall of the cottage. "It was horrible. Worse than I could have imagined." He sank into a squat, his back pressing against the wall.

Rémi grunted but said nothing. The rhythmic rasp of stone on iron continued.

Bertrand picked at the ground. "She knows about Salome. And she thinks the brotherhood has manipulated me." He glanced up at Rémi. "Would you believe she even talked about imprisoning me for my own good?"

"Maybe that's her way of keeping you close." Rémi inspected the edge of his axe.

"No, I don't think so. We've put her in danger by coming here. I see that now."

"We might at that. So she has a point."

"What? You think the safest place for me is locked in her cellar?"

"No. I meant about being manipulated."

"Oh."

Rémi put his whetstone aside and tested the edge of his axe with a calloused thumb. "After all, what do we really know for sure? Salome's a sorceress, no doubting that. And she knows how to make a man dance to her tune. Look at poor Roard and the Preceptor." Rémi squinted at Bertrand. "And you're too sharp to think you're any more special to her than that lot."

He knew Rémi was right. Salome was slow to trust, so why shouldn't he be the same? Besides, he had no right to expect anything from Salome. How could he when his heart refused to yield Justine?

Yet some traitorous part of him desired Salome's affection too. He knew it was sinful, but he would not lie to himself. No, it was simpler being angry than trying to find a way through the maze of his feelings.

"What would you have me do?" Bertrand asked. "Hand her over and be done with it? Break my oath and dishonour Everard's memory? Is that your counsel?"

"I'm not offering counsel," Rémi growled. "Just making you think. And keep your voice down. Huon's whelps are noisy enough, but she'll hear you before long."

"I don't care." Bertrand ground one heel into the earth.

"Listen close." Rémi pointed the head of his axe at Bertrand. "This business about honouring the Preceptor's wishes is all in your head. He never asked you to even sneeze on her, right? You decided to don that mantle. As for your vow to Salome, an oath don't bind a man if he's unfairly forced into it. There's no need to make a noose and put your head into it as well."

"Is that what I'm doing?" Bertrand considered what Justine had said. Was he turning Salome into the great purpose he had always dreamed of?

"Rémi, do you believe her? Salome, I mean. Do you believe she's protecting some sacred artefact?"

"Cub, I wish I could say." Rémi ran a hand through his bristling hair. "All we know is that someone is willing to kill us to get to her. Reckon they must have their reasons."

The sky had turned to the colour of slate and the day was growing dim. Another downpour was not far away.

"We've tarried too long," Bertrand mused.

"We'll not get far on foot."

Bertrand shrugged. "I've made my request and offered Justine fair payment. What more can I do?"

"Await her ladyship's pleasure," Rémi replied with a leer.

"This is hardly the time to jest."

Rémi snorted in amusement and resumed sharpening his axe.

An unpleasant thought occurred to Bertrand. "There's something else we should discuss. I would have raised it earlier, but there hasn't been time." Bertrand shrugged awkwardly.

Rémi's rasping sweeps of the whetstone paused.

"My father paid you to be my wet-nurse, didn't he? Just like Justine, he doesn't believe I can take care of myself."

Rémi laid his axe on the ground and squatted in front of Bertrand. "Now listen close. That arrangement was agreed upon when you were twelve. Twelve, you hear? No, look at me." Rémi grabbed Bertrand by the chin and glowered at him. "In two summers, you'll see twenty-one. What does that tell you?"

"Your friendship is well paid for."

"Dung head!" Rémi rapped him over the skull with his knuckles. "It means your father has an eye to your welfare, doesn't it? Besides which, I didn't have to stay on for nine years. So what does that tell you?"

Bertrand scowled back. "You're stubborn *and* greedy."

Rémi cuffed him and returned to his stump. "Why do you always have to fight the whole world?" He shook his head. "It means I want to be here. In the name of all that's holy, I'm closer to you than my own young ones."

"You have children?" Bertrand blinked in astonishment. "I thought they died of fever back in my thirteenth winter."

"One did." Rémi's expression darkened. "Renier, Aude and Gueri survived. My family lives off the annual stipend from your father. They enjoy a better life than I could ever offer them working in a field."

"Why didn't you just tell me then?"

"Every time I think you can't become a bigger idiot," Rémi snapped, "you prove me wrong. I'm telling you now and look how you're taking it."

Bertrand supposed he was right, but he couldn't shake the feeling of betrayal. "Leaving all that aside, Châtillon-sur-Seine isn't far. You could take a message to my father. Not that I want his help. Only... well, he should know about...what I'm involved in. And you could return to your family."

Rémi chewed the inside of his lip. "Cub, I'm proud of what you're trying to do, but are you sure that's wise?"

"Which part? Sending you home or contacting my father?"

"Both."

"If Justine won't help us—"

"Then this is over before it has even begun." Rémi waved his protest aside. "Might as well choose between the King's mercy or submitting to your father's will. Neither offers freedom."

Rémi was right, of course. They needed to escape to the uncertain shores of England. Salome had no future in France. Perhaps the Salt Lines had once ruled Champagne and Burgundy, but no longer.

"It seems you don't want to see her captured." Bertrand smiled in triumph.

Rémi stood. "I said no such thing."

"Not in so many words. However, it sounded like good counsel."

"Perhaps," Rémi said with a reluctant nod, "but the advice was given to Bertrand de Châtillon-sur-Seine, not Salome the sorceress."

"What about your children? Don't you want to see them?"

"Course I do, but the wife takes care of them. Besides," Rémi shrugged, "it's only two more summers."

Bertrand did not know how to respond to that. Even Rémi looked uncomfortable for once.

A branch snapped in a nearby thicket. Rémi leapt onto the stump and peered into the trees. Bertrand caught the rustle of dead leaves and Rémi raced towards the noise, brandishing his axe in one fist. Bertrand dashed after him.

Despite his stature, Rémi was quick over short distances. He soon outpaced Bertrand, sprinting between trees and leaping over fallen logs.

Bertrand did his best to keep up, but his breath rattled in his throat and his legs trembled. He forced his body to greater effort. A rock turned beneath his boot and he skidded into a low branch. He twisted to take the impact on his shoulder and nearly fell. Gasping for air, he reluctantly conceded he hadn't fully recovered from his illness yet.

Bertrand gave up the chase and leaned against the bole of a large beech. The sound of Rémi's chase was loud in the still forest. What had the sergeant seen to make him dash off like that?

There was little choice but to wait. Bertrand's heart slowed and he was finally able to take in deep, steady breaths.

Eventually, Rémi reappeared through the trees. His face was flushed and he wore a murderous scowl.

"What did you see?" Bertrand asked.

"Someone...spying...on us," Rémi said between breaths. "Quick... bastard."

"I'd run fast too if you were chasing me with that axe. Did you recognise him?"

Rémi shook his head. "Couldn't...get close...enough."

"Someone knows we're here." Fear scrabbled at the inside of his ribs. It was possible Justine had sent the spy, but what if she hadn't?

"You have to...force her hand," Rémi said. "We need...horses."

"Yes." They could no longer afford to wait. "I'll have Huon take a message." They hurried back through the quiet forest as the storm rolled towards them.

CHAPTER 39

23 October 1307

The Gamekeeper's cottage

Bertrand stood inside the Chapel of St Anne. Flames leapt up the walls and the panes of stained glass behind the altar shattered. Laurent approached him in vestments soaked with blood, his hands clutching a hacked Bible. Shards of glass crunched beneath the Chaplain's feet as he murmured a sermon. Bertrand was straining so hard to catch the words that he failed at first to notice Laurent's eyes had been plucked out and his throat slashed.

Bertrand startled awake as Laurent clutched at him. He shivered beneath his blankets. Something terrible had happened back at the Commanderie. He knew it with a deep, unsettling certainty.

He sat up and rubbed his eyes. Huon's small cottage was crowded. The children had overcome their initial timidity and circled around Salome, begging for stories. How he managed to doze off in the first place was a mystery.

Driven out by the noisy chatter, Bertrand pulled his cloak around his shoulders and slipped outside.

It had rained heavily throughout the night. Mist blanketed the ground, but the distant turrets of Justine's chateau were just visible. After the heat of the cottage, the chill air was refreshing. Bertrand drew in deep, cleansing breaths.

Nothing moved amongst the ghostly looking trees. Even so, he touched the pommel of Everard's sword at his hip. Questioning Huon had failed to reveal the identity of the spy. If anything, it had made the gamekeeper as uneasy as they were.

Was Justine right? Had Salome manipulated him? The answer was likely yes. Yet it changed little. Despite Rémi's protests, he still fervently believed that Everard's dying wish had been for him to protect Salome, even if this meant setting himself against the throne.

"So you've made your choice," Bertrand murmured into the stillness. "For good or ill."

Salome emerged from the lintel of the cottage where she had been standing. Although she made almost no sound, he was aware of her. Always and inexplicably.

She stood next to him, almost touching his shoulder. "Are you ready to talk?"

"There's not much to say." He shrugged. "I've changed. She hasn't. We no longer enjoy the understanding that we once did."

Salome waited.

Bertrand grimaced. Could he keep nothing from her?

"Justine does care for me. However, she thinks of me as easily swayed and overly naïve." He sighed. "She took the ruby, although I'm not sure she'll help us. The King has commanded all members of the Order submit to his authority. Sheltering us places her in jeopardy."

Bertrand looked at Salome. She was peering into the mist, her face rigid like stone. In the greyness of dawn, she could have been a statue carved from pale marble, her scars veins in the rock.

"I'm sorry that I've set the two of you at odds," she murmured.

"That happened before you and I met."

Salome sniffed. "You should know it's almost impossible for a Shroud to lie to me."

"Almost?"

"It only works when I don't want to hear the truth." She rubbed her upper arms to ward against the chill. "She'll come." Salome turned and patted Bertrand's shoulder. "Justine won't make a decision without confronting me. It's what I'd do."

Salome returned to the noisy cottage. Bertrand remained where he was, staring at the battlements. Yes, Justine would come. But with whom?

◆———————————————◆

"*M*aman!" One of Huon's brood, a dishevelled little girl called Ameline, burst into the cottage. "Horses, Maman!" She jumped in excitement.

Salome rose to her feet. Huon stood as well, a worried look pinching his narrow face.

"Are you expecting anyone?" Bertrand asked Huon.

"No." Huon rounded up his children. "Out with you." He ushered them through the back door along with his wife, speaking in a low but fast tone. Bertrand caught the word 'woods'.

"Salome, help me into this." Bertrand picked up his chainmail hauberk and slid one arm into the sleeve. She took the weight while he slipped his other arm in and fastened his stays with brisk efficiency.

Rémi had already donned his leather armour. He moved to the front entrance and peered through a crack in the doorframe.

"How many?" Bertrand's pulse was racing.

"Half a dozen," Rémi replied. "Definitely soldiers."

Salome secured the last strap. Bertrand cinched his sword belt around his waist and strode over to stare outside. The horsemen were cantering across the open field. He squinted, trying to identify individual riders. As they approached, Bertrand realised the lead rider was sitting side-saddle.

"It's her," Rémi said.

"I told you she would come." Salome remained in the centre of the cottage. Her dark, almond-shaped eyes were unreadable. Salome smiled at Bertrand. "Shall we greet our visitors?"

Despite their situation, a thread of anticipation coiled through Bertrand and tightened in his groin. Salome was utterly calm, even regal, like a queen about to face her conqueror. How could he not admire her?

"I doubt we have much choice." Bertrand turned to Huon. "Stay with your family. I don't want you caught up in this."

Huon hesitated.

"Go," Bertrand ordered.

"May the Lord keep you safe." Huon made the sign of the cross before he disappeared out the back.

Salome slipped into her cloak and pulled the cowl over her head. They stepped outside and waited. The sun was high overhead. While the day was still cloudy, the mist had burned away.

Justine's entourage included six mounted guards in light armour. She reined in her horse a few yards short of the cottage and dismounted. Passing her reins to one of her men-at-arms, Justine strode forward to meet them. A soldier flanked her on either side. Bertrand recognised Durand, the captain of her household guard, but he ignored Bertrand's nod.

"Is this her?" Justine indicated Salome's cloaked figure.

"Good morrow to you," Bertrand replied.

Justine's blue eyes narrowed. "This is not the time for pointless courtesies, Bertrand."

"Then what *is* it time for?" Bertrand gauged the soldiers' disposition and equipment. The guards seemed wary but uncertain, as if they had not been given clear instructions.

Justine lifted her chin. "I've considered your request, yet it seems to me that you're not the one petitioning my aid." Justine turned her stare upon Salome. A slight frown formed above her eyebrows when Salome failed to respond.

"If we must have this discussion," Bertrand said, "perhaps it's best done in privacy." He stood to one side of the door and invited Justine inside Huon's cottage.

"Very well." She took a step forward.

"Seigneuresse." Durand caught her arm. "Is that wise?"

"Let go, Durand," Justine commanded in an icy tone.

Durand hastily released her.

"Bertrand would never harm me and his...servant," she said, indicating Rémi, "will remain outside. Isn't that right, Bertrand?"

"Of course. The cottage is empty."

"Call out if you need me," Durand said with a frown.

Justine swept past Bertrand and entered the cottage. Salome turned and followed her. Bertrand nodded at Rémi and joined the two women inside.

Justine untied her cloak and draped it over one of Huon's crude stools. She wore a riding dress similar to Salome's, except Justine's was cut from summer blue cloth and adorned with lace at the sleeves, hem and collar. A simple lace veil covered her hair, which had been tied into a bun.

Justine removed her riding gloves one finger at a time. "I see you're afraid to show your face," she said to Salome.

Salome lifted her cowl. "Not without cause, I think you'll agree."

Justine paused in loosening her left glove, taking in Salome's scars. "So you're the woman Bertrand is risking his life for."

"Yes."

"*Yes.* That's all you have to say?"

"What more needs to be said?" Salome imitated Justine by slowly removing her cloak.

Justine glared at Bertrand, as if Salome's insolence was his fault. He glanced between the two women. Salome was taller and leaner than Justine. While Salome appeared younger, her bearing was a match for Justine's. If it was not for Salome's scars, her beauty would have outshone Justine's. But seeing them together, he realised there was a remoteness to Salome that could not be easily broached. Justine's feelings were much closer to the surface and she seemed warmer because of it.

Justine drew her shoulders back and lifted her chin. "Perhaps you can tell me what's so important that you send Bertrand to ask me to defy the King's decree?"

"I'm not asking you to defy anyone," Salome replied. "I've simply offered payment for the horses we need."

"It's far more complicated than that." Justine twisted the gloves in her hands.

"It need not be," Salome replied with a faint shrug. "Give us what we need and have fairly paid for. That's all I ask."

"Aiding your escape would be considered treason by some."

"Perhaps," Salome agreed, "but only if they knew of my presence here. I'm sure your guards can be trusted and there's no questioning Huon's loyalty. We can be gone before you've returned to your chateau."

"And what if you're captured in the next town?" Justine countered. "My life would be forfeit if they discovered I helped you escape."

"Justine," Bertrand interrupted, "you know I'd never let any harm come to you." Just having to say this made him feel sick.

Justine rounded on him immediately. "You've already brought great danger to my very walls. If you're tortured, Bertrand, how long do you think it will be before you mention my name?"

"Have you decided to arrest us?" Salome asked.

Justine's angry gaze shifted back to Salome. "I have no choice."

"I've heard that before," Salome replied, "usually when someone is about to act against their conscience."

Justine gave Salome a cold look. "Do not think I am here to banter with you."

"Then why speak with us in private?" Salome gestured to the guards outside. "Perhaps you haven't truly decided?"

"She's smart, Bertrand." Justine's smile was tight-lipped. "I hope you realise that." She turned back to Salome. "I was hoping you could offer me a reason that would justify letting you go. Can you give me one?"

Salome bowed her head. "I could, but it would only place you in even greater risk."

"More evasions." Justine's shoulders trembled with the force of her anger. "Can't you see that, Bertrand? How can you trust her counsel over mine?"

"I believe she's telling the truth," Bertrand replied. "From what I've seen, you would be safer not knowing anything about her or our destination."

"Bertrand, there's no escape from the King." Justine took a step towards him. "You'll be captured, branded a traitor, and tortured. My name will be wrenched from your agony and the same fate will befall me. If you truly care for me, relinquish this woman. I'll keep your involvement a secret. We might even be together again, in time."

Salome looked up. "Well, Bertrand? You must decide. Once and for all."

He glanced between the two women. Justine gave him a pleading look. Salome's expression remained impassive.

"Justine, my Preceptor gave his life to protect Salome." He clenched his hands together. "And I've vowed to do the same. It might seem like madness to you, but I know, in my soul, that this is my path. I can't turn aside from it. Not for anything. I truly wish I didn't have to make this choice."

Justine paled. "If I tried to take her from you, would you draw your sword against me?"

"Never," Bertrand replied immediately. "Nor would I ever allow any harm to come to Salome. I don't see why either must happen."

"Just tell me why?" Justine insisted. "Why throw your life away like this?"

"I told you before." He shook his head in the hope that he might shake the right words loose. "I didn't seek this responsibility. It found me. I promised Everard, my Preceptor, that I would keep her safe. Who are we if we fail to keep our most solemn promises?"

Tears brimmed in Justine's blue eyes. "You'll die, Bertrand. Horribly...and alone."

"No," Salome replied. "Not alone. And not without purpose."

Justine glanced between them. "I don't know you at all, Bertrand."

"I am the same man." He remembered what Everard told him in the Lodge. "Only now I see that sometimes virtue must outrank love."

Justine searched his face. "I don't believe you," she whispered.

He had no reply to that. They both saw it.

"Take the horses that you've purchased then," Justine said to Salome. "Keep your secrets as well. I'll not speak of this encounter, but don't expect my blessing either. Not when you subvert good and generous men."

Salome curtsied deeply. "There is an Abbot, Guillot by name, in a Cistercian Abbey south-east of Fécamp. He can get word to us...if you wish it."

Justine absorbed this offer in silence. She studied Bertrand, her gaze both angry and bewildered. He had the impression she was branding his face into her mind. Then she turned and swept out of Huon's cottage without a word.

Bertrand took a half step. This was not the way he wanted them to part. Grief settled inside him like a heavy block of ice with a numbing ache to match.

"Thank you," Salome said. "I had thought I could not ask any more of you than I already had. I see now that I was wrong."

Bertrand closed his eyes. "Why *am* I doing this?"

"Because I must not be captured." Salome replied. "The consequences are too dire to contemplate. You may not understand this here," Salome said touching his temple, "but you know it in your heart."

Bertrand drew back. "I think I've earned the right to the full truth."

Salome nodded. "Yes, you have. But we must leave. Now, before she changes her mind. Tell Huon we're leaving. I'll have Rémi collect the horses she promised."

Bertrand nodded. He needed action, movement. Anything to keep him from dwelling upon this moment.

Goodbye, Justine.

This time it really felt like forever.

CHAPTER 40

23 October 1307

East of Fontette

"We'll need to make camp soon." Rémi nodded towards the sky where thick black clouds loomed on the horizon.

Bertrand grunted. He had been silent for much of their ride east. Salome had sensed his mood and kept her distance, so it fell to Rémi to pick a way through the forest.

They had made good progress at first. As their shadows lengthened in front of them, the land began to rise. The ground was soft, and mud spattered the horses' fetlocks. A chill breeze wove through the trees and tugged at their cloaks.

"Bertrand?" Rémi called. "Did you hear what I said?"

Bertrand glanced up. "What?"

"It will rain soon. We'd best make camp."

They had reached the summit of a natural rise that looked back west towards the valley of Fontette.

"Let's cross the ridge first," Bertrand said. "We can make camp on the lee side."

"Now you're talking some sense. I'll find a spot." Rémi spurred his mount ahead.

A natural clearing appeared ahead. It was too exposed to make a good campsite, so Rémi had ridden on. It did, however, afford a good view of the valley below. From this elevation, the distant lights of Chateau Fontette twinkled along the walls in the deepening twilight.

Bertrand dismounted, and absently rubbed the nose of his roan. It nudged his shoulder, hoping for some grain.

Salome entered the clearing and followed his gaze towards the distant lights. She dismounted and observed his silent vigil.

Bertrand wondered what Justine was doing. Did she regret the manner of their parting as much as he did? Or was she cursing him for blindly following Salome? Perhaps both.

The sun dipped below the horizon and the velvet cloak of night dropped across the land.

"Bertrand."

He ignored Salome.

"We should make camp." She ran her hand down his shoulder blade and concern radiated from her. But he did not want her sympathy. He just needed a moment to himself.

"I know. I was just—" His voice trailed off. What was the point of explaining when she could sense what he was feeling?

"I understand. But Rémi will worry."

"You mean grumble."

"That too." He caught the echo of a smile in Salome's voice.

"Then we'd best keep moving." He was about to remount his horse when he noticed a distant glow.

"What's that?" Bertrand squinted, trying to work out how close it was to the chateau. Had someone lit a bonfire in the fields on the far side?

Salome stared. "It's a fire."

"I can see that. Where is it coming from?"

"I can't tell."

Bertrand peered anxiously at the growing blaze. A cloud of smoke with an orange underbelly spread over the battlements.

"The chateau is on fire." Bertrand was numb with horror. "What's happening down there?"

"I'm so sorry, Bertrand." Salome twisted her reins around her fingers. "Truly, I am."

A horrible certainty settled over him. "Nogaret's men tracked us to Fontette. How?" He remembered the spy Rémi had chased through the forest.

"I don't know, Bertrand." Salome's shoulders slumped and he sensed an immense weariness from her. "I told you before. They always find me in the end."

"Justine was right." Bertrand trembled as he imagined the screams. "She said you knew the risk you were placing her in." The flames rose higher. Was Justine trapped inside or had she managed to flee?

Salome blocked his view. "Bertrand, look at me." She grabbed him by the chin when he refused to meet her gaze. "We had no choice but to seek her help. And we would've left sooner if Justine hadn't taken so long to provide us with horses. I'm sorry for what's happened. You know I am. This is why you must take me to England."

Bertrand wrenched free. "We have to go back. We have to help them." He tried to remount his horse but Salome forced his foot from the stirrup. Bertrand's roan tossed its head and stamped its hooves in warning.

"No," Salome said in an eerily calm voice. "That's exactly what they want."

He shoved her hard. Salome stumbled and caught her balance. A burning sensation flared in his hand and Bertrand gasped at the fierce pain. He stared at the webbing between his thumb and forefinger. The rose scar had become an angry red.

"What have you done?" Bertrand demanded.

"You can't help her," Salome replied. "The agents of Severity have no honour or compassion. All that you can achieve down there is a futile death."

"I'd rather die than let them hurt Justine."

"I'm sure you would. Trust me, surviving takes far more courage."

Bertrand stared at the inflamed mark on his hand. He had vowed to protect Salome but his obligation to Justine ran just as deep. Just thinking about what might be happening to her was an agony. "I can't just watch this. Not when it's my fault."

"The fault is mine, not yours." Salome straightened. "And the guilt is mine to bear."

He stared at the burning chateau. The fire intensified as he watched, the fierce orange glow illuminating the pall of smoke. Surely, this was a glimpse of hell.

"You swore an oath, Bertrand. Only death can release you from it."

He massaged his hand. "An oath secured through falsehood isn't binding."

Salome's mouth became a flat, angry line. "I've told you nothing false."

"Nor have you told me enough for it to be considered truth." He stabbed a finger at her. "Do you think I can't tell you're hiding something from me?"

"I've told you as much as I dared." She gestured towards the chateau. "That's twice we've barely avoided capture. I'll tell you more when it's safe to do so." She took a half-step towards him. "If you've become so attuned to me, surely you can feel that I would never intend you harm."

"I don't know what to believe," Bertrand replied, edging beyond her reach. "The only thing I know for certain is almost everyone I care about is gone." His voice had risen into a shout. He brought his voice under control with an effort. "If you expect me to endure this, I need a reason."

The pinched, angry lines in her face eased into sadness. "I understand, but Bertrand, how long do you think it will be before someone mentions our presence? Unless it rains hard tonight, our tracks won't be difficult to follow. They may already be on their way."

Bertrand glanced back towards the valley. He knew Salome was right, but he ached to help Justine. No matter what Salome might say, they would never have attacked Justine if not for him.

"So, we continue to run and let our conscience atone for the destruction we've wrought. Is that it?"

Salome's mouth twisted into a bitter smile. "Yes, Bertrand. I wish I could tell you it becomes easier, but it doesn't." Sadness and regret poured through the link he shared with her. It was so strong Bertrand wanted to wrap his arms around her.

Justine was right: Salome *was* manipulating him. And yet her pain felt genuine. Bertrand pressed his palms into his eyes. He did not know what to think or how to feel.

Making soothing noises, Salome caught her mount. She swung up into her saddle and followed the path Rémi had taken.

"When will we stop running?" Bertrand called after her.

Her reply floated back through the thickening darkness. "When we reach England. There will be an ending there, I promise."

Bertrand remained where he was, watching the distant flames. His imagination tortured him with grisly scenes, and in every scenario he saw the savage face of the commander with the neat black beard. Bertrand knew, with unshakeable certainty, that he was down there. The man was like a pitiless crow picking through the remains of Bertrand's life.

He fell to his knees and begged for forgiveness, both from God and those who had undoubtedly lost their lives in the fire. Most of all, he prayed fervently for guidance. All his life he had dreamed of fighting for a noble cause. Instead, he had brought down disaster upon those he cared about.

Justine's face haunted him, and her warnings scalded his conscience. Was she dead?

Tears streamed down his cheeks. He felt trapped, caught in a snare that only tightened every time he attempted to escape.

Everard's sword—his now—rasped from its sheath. Bertrand held the blade by its quillons. "There will be a reckoning, Justine. I promise. And for you Everard, and the rest of my brothers. I swear it." Bertrand kissed the Beauseant on the pommel of his sword.

Fighting back tears, he remounted his horse. Salome had disappeared over the far side of the ridge. He could ride back down to what remained of the chateau. She couldn't stop him, no matter how much the rose burned his hand. But if he did, Everard's death and those of his brothers would be in vain. Worse still, he would never know why Everard had sacrificed them. Not truly.

But what of Justine? Could he really claim to be a chevalier if he just abandoned her?

"Lord, please. Give me a sign so that I may serve Your Will."

Wind tugged at the branches.

The roan shifted uneasily beneath Bertrand.

An owl hooted in the distance.

In his mind, he reached out to Justine, but he could only recall the anger of their parting. It was Salome who nestled in the back of his head. It was Salome's concern that answered his silent cry. Choking back a sob, he turned his mount and followed his two companions.

CHAPTER 41

24 October 1307

Chateau Fontette

"**B**ring the prisoner," Roustan ordered.

The captain ducked out of the tent and the smell of charred timbers wafted through the open flap. Roustan ate slowly, dipping pieces of hard bread into a warm stew of vegetables and venison. His troops were feasting upon food seized from the larder of Chateau Fontette before they put it to the torch.

The captain returned with a dishevelled looking noblewoman. She was tall for a woman and shook off the captain's grip on her arm when he stopped to present her. Soot smudged her cheeks and her gown was spattered with mud. Her long brown hair was unbound, giving her a wild look, and her blue eyes flashed with outrage.

Roustan did not speak until he finished dabbing the stew from his beard. "Do I have the pleasure of addressing Seigneuresse de Fontette?"

She pressed her lips together, as if curbing her initial reply. Taking a deep breath, she said, "By what authority do your attack my chateau without cause or provocation?" Her voice trembled with the effort of keeping her anger in check.

Roustan smiled and leaned back in his chair. "I am afraid I will be asking the questions today. Are you Justine de Fontette or not?"

She gave a tight nod.

"The lover of Bertrand de Châtillon-sur-Seine?"

Her face visibly paled.

"Thank you, captain. You may wait outside." Roustan waved him out.

"Yes, sir." The captain withdrew after a puzzled glance between Roustan and Justine.

"Please, sit." Roustan indicated the chair facing him on the other side of the table.

"How dare you offer me my own chair." She quivered with rage.

"You'll find I dare a great deal," Roustan replied. "Besides, you and

I have much to discuss, so it only makes sense to be comfortable." He leaned forward. "Or do you wish to be uncomfortable? I have talents that lie in that direction as well."

Justine searched his face. He saw fear in the tight corners of her mouth and eyes, but not as much as he might have expected given the circumstances. After a tense moment, she sat rigidly in the chair. "You didn't answer my question."

"And you're not listening." Roustan threw a leg over the padded armrest. "Do you deny receiving the King's proclamation that all members of the Ordre du Temple be surrendered to the King's Guard?

"I fail to see why that justifies the sacking of my estate."

"And do you deny having recently harboured your lover Bertrand, a chevalier of the same Order?" Roustan lifted a lazy hand. "Before you answer, it might be helpful to know that I have witnesses that saw him and his sergeant lodged in your Gamekeeper's house."

"I had no idea he was there, if what you say is even true." Justine met his gaze squarely. "As far as I am aware, Bertrand was assigned to a Commanderie near Brienne."

Roustan grinned. "I can tell you Seigneuresse, with considerable confidence, that is no longer the case. We razed that Commanderie in much the same manner as your chateau." He picked at some dirt lodged beneath his fingernails. "Ordinarily, I would thoroughly enjoy playing this game with you. However, I am in some haste. So, I offer you a choice: continue denying your knowledge of Bertrand's presence and I will execute the surviving members of your household until someone tells me where he is. Or you could take revenge on the man who brought destruction upon you."

Justine blinked. "Revenge?"

Roustan swung his leg back over the armrest and leaned forward. "I think it unlikely that you invited him to take shelter with you. Your brief affair was well known, after all. An intelligent woman would have realised inquiries would eventually lead back to you."

Justine hesitated. "Why ask such questions if you already know the answers? And why slaughter my household if you know I'm blameless?"

Roustan arched an eyebrow. "Would you have told me the truth if I merely asked? No. The King will no longer tolerate those who would usurp his authority, be they wedded to cross or salt."

Justine stilled. She was so pale now the blue veins in her face and neck were clearly visible.

"That's correct," Roustan said in a low voice. "I am familiar with the

Salt Lines. So, you have no secrets left to keep, bar one. Where are Bertrand and the witch going?"

"I don't know," Justine replied, hunching over. "I wanted them gone as soon as possible."

"Why continue to protect him when he has inflicted such misery and pain upon you? Is this the act of someone who loves you?" Roustan's gaze narrowed. "Although, in the end, this is her doing, not Bertrand's. She is a temptress, a sorceress of the worst kind. A young fellow like that needs to be protected from *her*, not me, a loyal servant of the King." He gave her a moment to think. "Is there anything you can tell me?"

Tears filled Justine's eyes and her bottom lip trembled. "I swear I don't know. I gave them horses and food—he is the son of my liege lord, after all—and bade them depart as soon as possible. That's all I know."

"I confess I am disappointed." Roustan sat back in his chair and drummed his fingers on the armrest. "You leave me no choice."

"What do you mean?"

"Well," Roustan said with a shrug, "if a fox steals your chicken, and you cannot catch the fox, you have no choice but to destroy the den."

Justine clenched the armrests of her chair. "You wouldn't dare."

"Then you have underestimated me again." Roustan shook his head slowly. "If you can't give me Bertrand, then I must ask his father and brothers instead." He stood. "You will accompany me to Châtillon-sur-Seine where I will serve the King's justice upon the Baron and his remaining sons for treason. After that, you will have no home or liege lord to shelter you." Roustan raised his index finger. "And before you rail at me, consider who it is that really brought you to this. I am merely the instrument of your rightful King. Would a man who truly loved you leave you to such a fate?"

"You can't blame the Baron," Justine cried. "He's not part of this."

"Then tell me who I can blame," Roustan shouted.

Justine fell silent.

Roustan stood and leaned over the table. "By rights, I should send your head back to Paris as well. It would send the right message, after all. Instead, you will accompany me to witness firsthand the cost of Bertrand's betrayal. Perhaps that might jog your memory."

CHAPTER 42

22 July 1099

Godefroi's quarters

"Father, apologies for disturbing you." The breathless guard stopped at the top of the stairs of Godefroi's quarters. "They've found the missing chevalier."

"Achambaud?" Hugues lurched to his feet. The parchment that he had been reading slid onto the carpet. Achambaud had vanished five days earlier, and despite an extensive search commissioned by Godefroi, they had found no sign of him. Diederic's corpse was discovered near the northern wall, and given Diederic was Raymond's man, it was possible the Count was responsible for Achambaud's disappearance. If so, he was beyond reach, as Raymond had refused to relinquish his hold on the Tower of David.

"Are you sure?" Hugues snapped. "You saw him with your own eyes?"

"That I did," the guard nodded. "He's pale and thin, but there's no mistaking him. Come see for yourself."

"You mean he's downstairs," Hugues exclaimed in astonishment. "Right now?"

"With a monk I've never seen before," the guard replied. "Come, I'll take you." The guard turned on his heel and raced back down the steps.

"Gondemar," Hugues bellowed. "I need you."

Godefroi was absent, having decided to visit the Duke of Normandy before the ceremony of acclamation at noon that would determine who ruled Jerusalem. Etienne had accompanied Godefroi, ostensibly as his scribe.

Godwera emerged from her chamber and peered down the stairs. She was dressed only in a linen shift that exposed the curve of her hips and her pale, narrow ankles. Dark tresses fell past her shoulders. Hugues had never seen her in a state of undress before. He was surprised to discover he was not immune to her beauty.

"What's wrong?" she called.

Even though the bells for Terce could not be far away, she had obviously been sleeping. Hugues realised he was staring and glanced away.

"They say Achambaud has returned," he said. "Put on your habit and join me downstairs. He may need your healing skills."

Hugues' leather sandals clattered on the steps as he hurried downstairs. A crowd of Godefroi's guards had gathered around a small cart tethered to a donkey. The press of bodies made it impossible to see anything.

"Out of the way." Hugues shouldered his way forward. An elderly monk stood next to the cart, which contained a pale figure with dark, matted hair. Hugues brushed the strands aside and turned his head.

Sweat lathered Achambaud's face and neck. He moaned at Hugues' touch.

"Careful," the monk said in strangely accented French. "He's still weak."

Hugues lifted the blanket. Achambaud had been stripped of his armour and his linen undertunic was stained with blood. A bandage had been wrapped around his right armpit and drawn tight across the opposite side of his neck. A second wad of bandages circled his thigh. Both were stained with old blood.

Hugues peered at the monk. "Who are you? What happened to him?"

"A friend," the monk replied. "Take him to your physick. I can't do any more for his wounds."

Hugues squinted at the monk. "What's your name? Whom do you serve?"

"Perhaps I can answer your questions inside." The monk gestured to the knot of guards watching them.

"Yes, of course," Hugues replied, realising his mistake.

Godwera appeared at the top of the steps. She had donned her habit and drawn the cowl over her head. She would need privacy to tend to Achambaud properly.

"You four." Hugues pointed to the closest guards. "Carry him into Godefroi's chamber."

"Wait. I have something more comfortable," the monk said. From the cart he unrolled a sheet of canvas. The monk inserted two timber rods into a sleeve stitched at each end of the canvas. Hugues noticed the monk's hands were quite wrinkled and dark in colour, as if he had spent long years beneath a harsh sun.

Under the monk's direction, the guards carefully placed Achambaud onto the stretcher. He did not stir as they carried him up.

Godefroi's room was the most spacious of the sleeping chambers. It became quite stuffy during the day, so Hugues threw open the window in the hope of catching a breeze.

Hugues dismissed the guards once they had placed Achambaud on the bed. Godefroi's clothes were strewn across the floor and his travelling chests had been haphazardly shoved against the wall.

The monk lifted his cowl and Hugues gaped in surprise. The ragged tonsure, the hollow cheeks and the careworn expression were a mirror to his features.

Hugues took a step back. "What is this?"

Godwera glanced up from where she leaned over Achambaud and gasped.

The likeness wavered and melted away, revealing a lined face beneath the glamour. The once black hair lengthened and turned grey, while the monk's skin darkened to the colour of caramelised honey and his lips became fuller.

"You're a woman," Hugues said in astonishment.

Care-lines gathered about the corners of her tilted, brown eyes as she smiled. It did not require much imagination to see that she must have been striking in her youth.

"And not a Franj," she replied calmly. "My name is Firyal."

"What have you done to Achambaud?" Godwera demanded.

Firyal gave Godwera a searching look. "It is good that you are part of their cabal." Her gaze flicked to Hugues. "Your seer is deeply troubled by the wanton slaughter, which does him honour." Sadness pulled at the corners of her mouth. "Not all of his injuries are physical. As the leader of your cabal, you need to help him heal."

"Cabal," Hugues repeated. "You mean the sacred points."

Firyal waved the distinction aside. "Call it what you will."

"Was the warrior below āl-Aqsa part of your...cabal?" Hugues asked.

"Yes." Tears gathered in her eyes. "He was my brother in all but blood."

Hugues grimaced. "I don't understand why he fought Godefroi. If you're trying to help us, why—"

Firyal raised an open palm. "Remember what I am about to say: it will serve you well during what is to come."

Hugues nodded.

"Accept that everything you build will be torn down," Firyal said. "It is the way of things. But knowing this should not prevent the building. Do you see?" She searched Hugues' face.

"Yes, I think so."

"What of Achambaud?" Godwera shot a furious look at Hugues. "You still haven't explained what happened to him."

"He was ambushed by one of your people. They fought and Achambaud defeated the other soldier." She shrugged, as if the explanation was obvious.

Hugues stared out the window. Did Raymond know of this? Had he commissioned it?

"What of his wounds?" Godwera pressed. "The bandages are stuck to his skin. I need to understand how grievous they are before I remove them."

Firyal moved to Achambaud's side. "He suffered three injuries," she said. "The first was to his head. I examined his skull and found no fracture."

"Has he woken since the attack?" Godwera's lips were pressed together in a thin, unhappy line.

"Only fleetingly," Firyal replied. "He lost a lot of blood." Firyal touched the bandage that covered Achambaud's right armpit. "He took two knife wounds. The first, under his arm, is not deep but bled greatly."

"Is the wound clean?" Godwera gently lifted Achambaud's under-tunic to probe the extent of the injury.

"Of course," Firyal replied. "I am not a fool. However, fever burns through his body." She moved to the bandage wrapped around Achambaud's thigh. The linen was crusted with dried blood. Achambaud moaned as her careful fingers probed the bandage. "This is his most grievous wound. It runs deep. The bleeding has stopped, although the wound is bloated and hot to the touch." She gave Godwera a blunt look. "He will die unless you use your power to banish the ill humours."

Godwera recoiled from the Saracen woman. "What power?" Godwera glanced at Hugues. "What do you know of such things?"

"Please, no need to pretend," Firyal replied with a wave of her gnarled hand. "Our physick shares your abilities, although is undoubtedly more skilled."

"I see." Godwera gave Firyal an uncertain look. "Hugues, I need fresh water. Make sure it's clean and boil one flask. I'll also need clean linen compresses and a dagger heated until it glows. Get my needlecraft from my chambers too." She thought for a moment. "Has he taken water?"

"A little," Firyal replied, "but not as much as I would like."

"Hugues, get a carafe for the water as well." Godwera placed her hand on Achambaud's brow and frowned. "He's hot. We'll need to cut away the old bandages. Can you remember all that?" She shot Hugues a look.

"Of course. I'll fetch them immediately."

"No." Firyal clutched at Hugues with a bony hand. "You must come with me now if you wish to complete your test."

"My test?" Hugues asked.

"Don't pretend," Firyal replied in a sharp tone. "Your cabal has mastered Malkuth and retrieved Solomon's Key. Three parts remain before you can obtain the wisdom eternal."

"Hugues," Godwera cut in, "Achambaud doesn't have time for such things. You must fetch what I've asked for."

"Wait," Hugues snapped at Godwera. "What three parts?" he asked Firyal.

"The essence, the resting place and the will," Firyal said. "All five are required to recover the wisdom eternal." She glanced between Godwera and Hugues. "You must make a choice, Hugues de Payens." Her expression was hard like granite. "Come with me now to retrieve the essence or remain with your brother and surrender your claim."

"Hugues," Godwera pleaded. "I can't leave Achambaud's side in his condition. There will be questions, and without you, I will be discovered. This could discredit Godefroi and place his position in jeopardy."

"Why now?" Hugues asked Firyal. "What's to stop me from imprisoning you until Achambaud is recovered?"

"Time," Firyal replied. "The Lords of Severity are stirring. It won't be long before they stalk us both. Besides which..."

...*you've been expecting this for some time*, she said directly into his head.

Hugues took a step back at the sudden intrusion.

"Hugues, I need you here," Godwera pleaded. "Besides, how can you trust her?"

"She brought Achambaud back to us." Hugues chewed the inside of his lip. "I have no choice, Godwera." He hated the idea of leaving Achambaud like this, but it was Godwera who possessed the ability to heal him. "I'll have servants bring you the things you've asked. They serve the Salt Lines and will keep your identity secret."

"Don't leave me." Godwera left Achambaud's side and seized Hugues by the arm. "I can't do this on my own."

Hugues kissed Godwera on the forehead. "Yes, you can," he said, "and you must. I'm sorry, but Achambaud's life is your responsibility." He prised her fingers loose. "Tell Godefroi...tell him that I'll return as soon as I can. And that I had no choice."

"Come." Firyal drew the cowl over her face. "The *Qādī* awaits."

"**M**essires," Arnulf called in a loud voice to counter the murmur of voices. "Messires," he repeated. The voices of the chevaliers and nobles that had assembled in the broken courtyard outside the Holy Sepulchre slowly fell silent.

Godefroi stood to the left of Arnulf and the cluster of priests that had taken up position immediately before the main apse of the Anastasis. Baldwin remained at Godefroi's shoulder, aloof and disdainful as usual. Gaston and a handful of other minor nobles from Lorraine had joined them, although Godefroi missed having Hugues and Achambaud at his side. A messenger had arrived just before the assembly commenced, advising that Achambaud had returned, but was grievously injured. It went on to say that Hugues had left in some haste with the monk who had brought Achambaud back.

On the far side of the courtyard, Raymond's party of Provencals was noticeably smaller than the host it had been outside the walls of Byzantium. Between the two groups, the Dukes of Normandy and Flanders, and their attendants, acted as a buffer.

Once Arnulf was satisfied that he had gained the crowd's attention, he continued. "All men of noble blood have been gathered here to state their preference for whom should protect this holy city."

Next to Arnulf, Peter of Narbonne shifted on his feet, his expression carefully neutral. Peter the Hermit stood on Arnulf's other side, dressed in his customary rags with dishevelled hair that resembled a nest of twigs.

"After much discussion amongst the council and clergy," Arnulf said, "two candidates have emerged whom all agree are worthy of acclamation."

The silence deepened as Peter the Hermit took a half-step forward.

Where Arnulf's voice was ponderous with self-importance, Peter's speech was lighter in tone. His voice held a melody to it that some claimed was mesmerising. "If it is pleasing to God," Peter said, allowing a noticeable pause, "let Raymond St Gilles, the Count of Toulouse, step forward to participate in this rite of public acclamation."

Cheers from the Provencal camp broke out as Raymond accepted the invitation. Dressed in his magnificent grey and silver bliaut, Raymond approached the cluster of clergy with a bowed head.

Peter the Hermit raised both hands overhead, motioning for quiet. "If it is pleasing in the sight of God, let Godefroi de Bouillon, the Duke of Lower Lorraine, submit to this rite of public acclamation."

Godefroi strode through the assembled nobles of his camp, cheers ringing around him. Everything seemed distant, as if a veil had fallen between him and the events unfolding about him.

Hugues and Achambaud should be here.

The thought was an unwelcome guest; uninvited, it lingered nonetheless. This was Godefroi's moment of triumph. Why then did he feel so hollow? In a way, it was not Godefroi de Bouillon they were hailing. At some point he could not identify, the man he was and the man he had imagined he would be, had diverged.

Allāhu akbar. God is great.

Try as he might, Godefroi had not been able to forget the sense of kinship he felt for the Saracen warrior he killed—no, murdered—beneath āl-Aqsa. That act had stained his soul and he felt unworthy of the acclaim he was receiving.

Godefroi stopped in front of the priests. He had known he could never match Raymond in elegance, so he had elected for simplicity instead. Dressed in a black bliaut and matching hose, the only splash of colour was the silver ceinture he wore around his waist.

"Messires," Arnulf said with elaborate courtesy, "please remain still so that the people you wish to govern may choose their leader."

Godefroi searched the sea of expectant faces and spotted Baldwin. His brother's expression was pained, almost resentful. It seemed he took no joy in his older brother's candidature either.

It struck Godefroi that if he were elected, he would be utterly alone. Every overture, every request, would have a purpose behind it. His favour would be solicited for personal advantage, not in honest friendship.

At least as a duke he had had peers in the other princes. Even Raymond, despite their differences. As a ruler, he could trust no one. Especially now that Achambaud stood at the very gates of death and Hugues had abandoned them.

Peter of Narbonne, the only remaining Bishop since Adhémar's death, moved between the two princes. In his hands, he held a simple circlet of gold. The centrepiece of the crown had been fashioned with rubies arranged in the shape of a cross in honour of those who had shed their blood to return the city to Christendom.

"Behold the crown of Jerusalem." Narbonne held the circlet over-head, so that all who had gathered could see the prize. "I ask you now, in the sight of the Most Holy and in good conscience, whom you would have as ruler?"

Peter waited for the gravity of his words to settle. "If you would have Raymond St Gilles, declare for him now."

As a single body, the Provencal camp went down on one knee, acclaiming their lord and master as the rightful ruler of Jerusalem. Some of the nobles attached to Flanders and Normandy bent their knees, although most remained standing.

It was obvious to Godefroi that he had the numbers. Arnulf must have agreed, as he grunted in acknowledgement.

"If you would have Godefroi de Bouillon, declare for him now." Raymond's supporters rose to their feet while Godefroi's offered fealty. For a moment Baldwin was isolated amid the nobles of Lorraine. With a tight smile and a nod at Godefroi, he bent his knee.

Arnulf and the two Peters took a moment to confer among them-selves.

Raymond shot a look of hatred at Godefroi. Out of the side of his mouth, he said, "I won't cede the Tower of David. It's mine by right of conquest. And if you try to force it from me, I'll withdraw my forces to Jaffa and you can face āl-Afdal's counter-attack on your own. It will be a short reign, Godefroi."

Godefroi's gaze skimmed across the assembly awaiting the formal decision. Not even Raymond could provoke him into strong emotion. He felt numb. This was a hollow victory, at best. "Would you truly risk everything we've accomplished out of spite?"

Raymond did not get the chance to reply as Narbonne turned back to address the assembly.

"We are in agreement," Narbonne called out. "By the power invested in me by the Holy Roman Church, and by clear public acclamation, I name Godefroi de Bouillon, *Advocatus Sancti Sepulchri*."

The defender of the Holy Sepulchre.

Godefroi knelt and Peter placed the golden circlet on his head. The assembled nobles erupted into cheers. Raymond made a stiff bow and swept away, his most loyal nobles following in his wake.

In a daze, Godefroi knelt on both knees as the priests anointed him. Their rites were a deluge of words that cascaded over him. Eventually, the clergy were done with him and he rose as King of Jerusalem in all but name.

The Dukes of Normandy and Flanders were first to offer their congratulations. Godefroi responded as graciously as he could, although his responses did not really register. Glowing faces offered their fealty. The clergy broke into a hymn of praise. Everywhere about him was noise and celebration, yet none of it touched Godefroi.

The procession continued: Gaston de Bearn, Engelbert de Tournai. Chevaliers from every country and faction offered their fealty.

Finally, Baldwin knelt before Godefroi and took his hand. "Your majesty, you've done our family proud. What, I wonder, will be your first command?" Amusement tugged at the corners of Baldwin's lips.

"Baldwin." The presence of his younger brother was an anchor in the strangeness that had overtaken him. Godefroi gripped him by the elbow and forced him to rise.

"Yes, your majesty," a voice called from among his supporters. "Tell us your bidding."

Godefroi glanced around his allies and suppressed the first command that came to mind: *find Hugues de Payens*. Instead, he said, "I claim the āl-Aqsa mosque as my palace. Let no man enter that place without my permission."

The crowd bowed, even the clergy. After years of preparation, Godefroi had finally honoured his pact with the Salt Lines. Why then, was he plagued by a sense of incompletion? And why had Hugues chosen now, of all times, to abandon him?

CHAPTER 43

22 July 1099

Jerusalem

The room they had locked Hugues in was small and dark. Little more than a cell, the only source of light was a narrow strip of wan sunlight beneath the door. The bare earth floor stank of human excrement.

In the dark, all he could do was wait. And worry about Godwera and Achambaud. The stricken look on her face still haunted him.

At least he had been vindicated in his assumption the Saracens had their own sacred points. Judging from the number of shadows flickering past the door, a good deal more than five were assembling in the town house Firyal had taken him to.

The building appeared modest from the front, squeezed as it was between two grander residences. Once inside, however, the house extended further back from the alley than Hugues had expected. He noticed sleeping pallets in the front room and rudimentary bowls and cups before Firyal handed him into the care of two wiry Saracens.

Firyal had spoken to them in rapid Arabic. They had nodded and dragged him down the corridor. Protesting would have been pointless.

Harsh voices echoed down the hall. Hugues cursed his inability to understand them. They sounded excited. Feet pounded down the corridor and Hugues caught the distinctive sound of blades being drawn.

What was going on? Surely, they weren't going to execute him?

A heavy thud shuddered through the walls and men shouted in alarm. Hugues jumped to his feet. Another thud, followed by the sound of splintering wood. The shouting intensified and a man screamed in pain.

The bolt on the door of his cell squealed against stone as it was flung open. Firyal stood in the doorway, panting slightly. A second figure, presumably male given the size of him, stood behind her, guarding the hallway.

"They've found us," she said. "Come."

Without waiting to see whether Hugues followed, Firyal moved to the back of the town house and entered a chamber on the right. The sound of fighting echoed down the corridor.

Firyal's bodyguard shoved Hugues in the back. The man stood half a head taller than Hugues and was so broad that his shoulders almost brushed either side of the hallway. A thick black beard covered the bottom half of his face. He pointed in Firyal's direction. Hugues noticed a silver ring, with the Pentemychos engraved in it, adorned his right hand.

The warrior shoved him again, harder this time. Hugues decided not to resist and hurried after Firyal. The bodyguard followed him inside and bolted the door in three places. Like Hugues' cell, this room was devoid of windows. There was no way out apart from a trapdoor in the floor.

Firyal had already disappeared into the shaft. The glow of a candle was visible from below. The Saracen pointed at the tunnel.

"Yes, I understand," Hugues muttered.

The descent lacked a ladder or steps, so Hugues had little choice but to hope his landing would be soft. He sat on the edge of the shaft and then pushed off, raising both arms overhead as he dropped into the cavity. He fell at least a body length, maybe half again, before landing on hard packed earth. The impact drove him to his knees. Thankfully, he landed evenly and managed to avoid rolling an ankle.

"Quickly." Firyal motioned for him to follow her down the tunnel.

"Who's attacking us?" Hugues asked.

"Assassins," Firyal snapped. "Now move."

"What about your man?"

"Artuk doesn't need help."

Even as Firyal responded, Artuk's legs dropped into view. The Saracen's leather-clad feet braced against the sides of the shaft, suspending his weight in an impressive display of strength. Hugues backed away from the dust and dirt that skittered down the hole. The sound of the trapdoor slamming closed echoed through the confined space, as did the bolt Artuk rammed into the stone bracing.

"That won't hold them long," Firyal warned.

They scrambled down the tunnel. The ceiling was so low Hugues had to bend his knees to avoid striking his head. He could only imagine the difficulty it presented to Artuk.

"Stay silent," Firyal whispered over her shoulder. Being smaller and obviously familiar with the tunnel, she set a fast pace.

Hugues hurried after her, using the walls to guide his steps where the meagre candlelight was insufficient. The tunnel was rough but relatively even.

Who had attacked the town house? Had Godefroi sent them?

The tunnel narrowed as it sloped upward. Artuk's gait behind Hugues changed to a shuffle. He was forced to worm his way up the tunnel on hands and knees. Firyal's pool of light halted. She turned to face Hugues, a single finger across her lips. In the candlelight, she appeared astonishingly calm. The tunnel ended in a flat rock face. Crude handholds had been cut into the stone.

Hugues pressed his mouth next to her ear. Her hair must have been oiled because it smelled faintly of jasmine and honey. "Where are we going?"

Firyal shook her head. She withdrew a knife from her robes and blew out the candle. Artuk whispered something in Arabic. Firyal did not reply. Instead, she climbed up the shaft in the darkness. Artuk growled at the back of his throat. Hugues guessed that he wanted to go first. Artuk squeezed past Hugues in the narrow passage and climbed after Firyal.

Left alone in the darkness, Hugues pondered his options. He could escape if he turned back now. However, if what Firyal had said was true, he would never find the artefact without her help. Or was that just a way to lure him in? Then again, if they wanted him dead they had been given ample opportunity.

He was still breathing, so that decided the matter.

The climb up the shaft was difficult. He had to navigate by touch, although the handholds were cut at even intervals. The shaft was even narrower than the tunnel. He wedged his back against the opposite wall as he made sure of each foothold. After a few feet, he emerged into another home.

This room was larger than the cell of the previous house. Hugues gripped the edges of the trapdoor and hauled his body out of the shaft. His fingers encountered something sticky. He snatched his hand away when he realised it was blood.

A body lay on the floor. A Tafur, judging from his rough woollen clothing. The man's throat had been cut.

Where were Firyal and Artuk?

Hugues crept to the doorway and glanced around the corner. This room opened onto a much larger chamber, not unlike Godefroi's quarters except not quite as fine. The furnishings showed signs of abuse; pillows had been slashed into ribbons and feathers were scattered around the room. A beautiful wooden divan had been splintered in two.

Artuk rose from the far side of the divan. Blood dripped from the short, curved blades he held in each fist. A figure twitched at his feet. Hugues spotted the body of another Tafur, a woman this time, where she had fallen near the divan.

"They chose the wrong house," Firyal said behind him.

Hugues stilled as Firyal pressed a knife against his side. Perhaps he had made the wrong decision after all. "Why didn't I hear the fighting?" Hugues asked. "Artuk almost demolished the room."

"You, of all people, should know how susceptible we are to suggestion," Firyal replied. "I simply encouraged anyone in hearing distance to ignore what their ears wished to tell them." The tip of her knife pierced his habit. "Now, remain still."

Artuk strode over, turned Hugues so that he faced the wall, and efficiently bound his hands together behind his back.

"There's no need for this," Hugues protested.

"There is every need," Firyal replied. "We're dead if you change your mind."

Artuk pulled him away from the wall and dragged him towards the back of the house. Firyal followed, limping slightly. How old was she? And how had she learned to confuse people's senses? Her gift, it seemed, had something in common with Achambaud's.

After the gloom of the tunnels, the flood of sunlight that greeted them as they emerged into a small, inner courtyard was blinding. Hugues blinked back tears. They passed through a gate that opened onto another alley. The stench of putrid flesh filled the air, so strong Hugues almost choked.

A Saracen youth rushed over from a cart left in the shadow of a balcony. He embraced Firyal and spoke rapidly in Arabic. Artuk gave the boy a friendly cuff across the back of the head. The boy released Firyal, sniffed once and scrubbed tears from his cheeks. He gave Hugues a hostile look.

The boy had obviously been left behind to guard the cart. A donkey flicked its tail irritably in its tethers. The dray had been piled with garments thick with crusted blood. Hugues caught sight of partially decomposed hands and feet where they had been left in sleeves and shoes. Flies buzzed madly around the grisly remains.

Hugues' stomach heaved in protest. He took a deep, steadying breath through his mouth. In the harsh sunlight, Firyal looked even more ancient.

"I'm pleased to see that you're offended by the terrible toll your people have inflicted upon this city," she said, gesturing at the cart. "You can imagine what it costs men like Artuk and Kamil to aid you."

"You're going to hide me in the cart." Hugues' gorge rose and he swallowed.

"Along with Kamil, who'll happily cut your throat if you make the slightest sound."

"Artuk will never pass for Christian," Hugues protested. "Nor will you."

Firyal grinned. "The guards at the gate of Jehosaphat will only see what they've been seeing for the past five days." She glanced at Artuk, who hid his weapons under the ghastly pile of clothing. "Defeated Saracens, hauling the remains of their unfortunate brethren outside the city walls."

"Who attacked us?"

"Members of your church have been following you for days," Firyal replied. "You would have known that if you hadn't lost Achambaud. The thing to remember is I've sacrificed my people to collect you." The world darkened as she pulled a hood over Hugues' head. Strong hands, probably Artuk, pulled him across the courtyard and lifted him onto the cart. The stench was appalling. With his hands bound, he could not escape the rotting pile.

"Where are you taking me?" Hugues cried.

"Not another word." Firyal stuffed a foul rag into Hugues' mouth.

Soiled clothing and chunks of decaying flesh tumbled over Hugues. He gasped for air and the smell of rot filled his nostrils. Hugues twisted, trying to force his head closer to the surface. Something moved next to him and the tip of a knife pricked his flesh. A low voice said something in Arabic. He did not understand the words, but the meaning was clear.

Remain still.

It must be the boy. Kamil.

Kamil adjusted his hood so that a thin trickle of air reached Hugues. He was still blind, but no longer suffocating.

The cart lurched down the alley. Hugues lay still, breathing shallowly, and prayed for strength.

CHAPTER 44

22 July 1099

Godefroi's quarters

"Tell them I've retired and don't wish to be disturbed," Godefroi ordered.

"Yes, your majesty," Gaston de Bearn replied. "Should I make any exceptions?" Gaston glanced at Godefroi's household who had assembled on the ground floor of his residence. Their honest faces were flushed with pride. Outside, revelries celebrating Godefroi's acclamation continued into the night. Godefroi had made an obligatory appearance, downed more wine than was sensible, and accepted the good wishes from a mass of faces that had blurred with each successive toast. The experience had left him drained and impatient.

A smile softened Godefroi's features. "No, Gaston. No exceptions." He placed a friendly hand on the tall noble's shoulder. "I just need some rest. And to do that, I need someone with enough seniority to turn everyone away, bar his Holiness the Pope."

Gaston laughed at this weak jest. "I would be honoured to act as Seneschal for your household, your majesty." He gave a slight bow. "Even if only in a temporary capacity."

"Thank you, Gaston. We can discuss more permanent arrangements after I've rested." Godefroi gave him a nod and mounted the stairs. A bout of dizziness caught him by surprise. He placed a steadying hand against the wall.

"Do you need assistance, your majesty?" Worry laced the edge of Gaston's tone.

"It's nothing," Godefroi replied over his shoulder. "Just too much to drink." The giddiness passed as abruptly as it had arrived. Godefroi walked upstairs, annoyed that everyone had witnessed his moment of weakness.

He hurried through the pale green chamber and continued up the second flight of stairs to the sleeping quarters. At the top of the landing, he cracked open his door. Pockets of candlelight glimmered in the room. Achambaud lay on Godefroi's broad bed. The rise and fall of his chest were almost imperceptible. Godwera lay on the divan opposite the window. A blanket hid her figure, although wisps of dark brown hair had escaped her cowl. He removed his shoes and padded across the floor.

Achambaud's breathing was shallow but regular, and some of his colour had returned. Beads of sweat glistened across his face.

"Be well," Godefroi breathed. "I need you more than ever." He moved to Godwera's side and knelt on the floor. Candlelight played across her smooth skin. The desire to touch her hair, to press his lips against hers, was a heavy weight in the centre of his chest.

Despite what she had said on the balcony when they first took the city, Godefroi knew she needed him too. He sensed the effort of her denial whenever she was near.

Godefroi brushed a strand of hair from her cheek. Godwera's eye-lashes fluttered and he froze. She sighed and her eyes opened. Godefroi watched as her expression changed from confusion to wariness.

"You're back." She blinked away sleep. "How is his majesty?" The soft smile that she offered with the question told him she was teasing.

"How is Achambaud?" he countered, steering them into safer waters.

Godwera's smile gave way to a frown. "He must be forced to take water. He doesn't move and only murmurs in his sleep. I fear he's weakening, not recovering."

Godefroi forced back a suffocating grief. Achambaud must not die. He would do anything to see him well again. "Is there nothing you can do for him? I'll get anything you need."

"Only one thing remains, but it's dangerous." Godwera's gaze dropped to the floor. "We could both die."

"Both of you?" The thought of losing both sent fear squirming through Godefroi's innards. "I couldn't bear that."

Godwera propped herself on one shoulder and gazed at him anxiously. "Is my lord well?"

"Well enough," Godefroi replied. "I rule this city. I have honoured my vows to the Salt Lines, yet I take no satisfaction from these things. Hugues has vanished. Achambaud draws near the veil that lies between worlds. And you—" Godefroi touched her face with trembling fingers.

"Please," she said in a warning voice.

"But I must. We need each other. Hugues even said so. Don't you *feel* it?" He sat back on his heels, wobbling slightly. The drink had loosened his tongue, but he was beyond caring. "Do you know what it's like to bite into your heart's desire only to find it hollow and bitter?"

"I think I do," Godwera replied. The shadow of old pain flitted across her face. "You must learn to fill it with other things."

"I would," Godefroi said passionately, "if only you would let me."

"Oh, Godefroi." Tears gathered in her eyes. "Don't you see? I've given myself to God."

"Am I not doing God's work? Am I not His humble servant?"

"You know it's not the same," Godwera admonished.

"Please," Godefroi whispered with all of his need for her.

"How can you ask this of me?"

"Don't you wish it for yourself?" he countered.

She sat up abruptly. An expression he could not name twisted her features. "It's too much," she whispered. "I can't." She rubbed her eyes with the heel of each palm. Godefroi was unsure whether she was trying to scrub away the sight of him or her tears.

He gently claimed her wrists and pulled her hands away. The look she directed at him had moved from sadness to something fierce.

"We can have this," he said. "We can."

She twisted one hand free and grabbed a fistful of his hair. Staring into his eyes, she pulled him into a deep, lingering kiss.

Desire flooded through Godefroi and he wrapped her in his arms. The tension in her body evaporated, as if in surrender. Joy lit him up from within.

And then Achambaud moaned in his fever.

Godwera pulled back from the edge they teetered upon.

Godefroi held his eyes closed for a moment longer, holding onto the feel of her lips, the taste of her breath. Already the sensations were fading. He opened his eyes with a sigh.

"Are you happy now, Godefroi de Bouillon?" Godwera asked angrily. "You've forced me to admit something I vowed to never acknowledge." She rose and pushed him away as he tried to hold her around the waist.

"I don't understand," Godefroi complained. "If you want this—"

"How *could* you understand?" She furiously smoothed her rumpled habit. "You've always been free to choose the path of your life. *My* life has been spent at the whim of others. When I won free from Baldwin, I swore never to submit to anyone again but God." Her heaving breaths threatened to break into sobs. "And no matter how I protest, you keep asking me to break that vow. Can you understand the price you're asking? Can you?" She hit him in the shoulder with a fist. The blow was a shock rather than painful.

"Godwera." Godefroi spread his hand helplessly. "I love you."

"And that's what makes it so hard, curse you." She fled the chamber, her bare feet slapping on the tiles.

Godefroi slumped on the floor, bewildered at this turn in their relationship. Achambaud moaned again in his delirium. He thought about going after her but decided against it. Instead, he sat on the edge of the bed and watched over Achambaud. How could such a mighty victory feel so empty?

CHAPTER 45

22 July 1099
Judean foothills

Hugues could not tell how long they had travelled before the cart finally jerked to a halt.

"Where are we?" Hugues whispered.

No response.

He tried again in Greek, followed by Hebrew. The boy—Kamil—must have left. Hugues wriggled onto his side with difficulty. With the hood still covering his head and human remains piled on top of him, it was impossible to tell the time of day.

Surely, they wouldn't just abandon him?

"I need water," he called cautiously. They must have travelled a safe distance from Jerusalem by now. "Water," he called again in a stronger voice.

A burst of Arabic erupted nearby and rough hands hauled him from the cart. Hugues stumbled to his knees and someone laughed at his weakness; a short bark that held neither amusement nor pity.

His captor gave Hugues a shake.

"Give me a moment," Hugues muttered from beneath his hood.

His body was stiff and aching. However, the rush of clean air was well worth the tingling pain of returning circulation. Hugues inhaled deeply. He was not sure he could endure that vile cart again.

Sharp commands were issued in Arabic. It took a moment for Hugues to realise the voice was female.

"Firyal? Is that you?" Hugues turned his head blindly, trying to judge where she was.

A strong grip yanked him to his feet. Hugues found he was able to stand this time. The hood was wrenched from his head and he blinked rapidly, his vision adjusting to the moonlight.

"Here, drink this." Firyal placed a skin of water against his mouth. Hugues swallowed greedily.

"Enough." Firyal withdrew the skin, even though Hugues had barely slaked his thirst. "We've a long way to go yet." She had changed her monk's habit for the robes and mail cuirass of a Saracen warrior. The few Saracen women Hugues had seen always covered their faces.

"Where are we going?" Hugues glanced around the terrain. The donkey had been untethered and was chewing contentedly on a bag of feed. Three Saracens were pushing the cart into a cave that nestled at the bottom of a cliff. As he gained his bearings, Hugues realised the cliff was part of a deep, narrow chasm. The moon and stars seemed an eternity away.

"East," Firyal replied.

Artuk stood at Hugues' shoulder but did not intervene when Hugues turned to follow Firyal's gaze. At least a dozen Saracen warriors were grooming and watering their steeds. Their robes blended with the arid, rocky landscape.

"Can you ride?" The moonlight had transformed Firyal's face into a wrinkled map of peaks and shadows. Hugues stared, thinking he could almost read the journey of her life if he looked closely enough.

"Yes, I think so," Hugues replied. "Although it would be a challenge with my hands tied behind my back." He tried for a smile and was rewarded with a twinkle of amusement in Firyal's dark eyes.

"Come, you must meet the other members of my cabal." Firyal motioned for Hugues to follow as she approached a group of men sitting in a loose semicircle on the ground. The hulking figure of Artuk trailed at a distance. Despite Hugues' jest, his hands remained bound.

Like Firyal, the three men were much older than the Saracen warriors making preparations to break camp. They had spread their saddle blankets across the rough ground. Hugues noticed a resemblance to Firyal in their weathered, proud features.

"This is Tahīr, our physick," Firyal said. The man she indicated was heavy-set, with a broad face, short grey hair and an open expression. He wore a light cuirass beneath his robes. The scimitar and helmet resting next to him had clearly seen hard use.

"Jalāl, our alchemyst." The second man was bird-thin with a narrow, bearded face. His dark-eyed gaze was more disapproving than Tahīr's. He gave Hugues a curt nod, before his gaze shifted to a point beyond Hugues' left shoulder. For some reason, Hugues was strongly reminded of Etienne. Perhaps it was the air of distraction that surrounded both men.

It was the third man, however, that held Hugues' attention.

"And this is Umayr, our *Qādī*."

The man Firyal indicated rose fluidly to his feet and approached Hugues. Up close, Umayr was of similar height and build to Hugues. His eyes were unusual for a Saracen: somewhere between green and grey, they reminded Hugues of the ocean on a stormy day. A long scar ran down the side of Umayr's neck, starting just behind where his left earlobe should have been.

"Qādī," Hugues repeated. "I don't know this word."

Umayr continued his silent, unnerving scrutiny of Hugues.

"You don't have an equivalent in your tongue," Firyal replied after an uncomfortable pause. "It's somewhere between judge and master of the law."

"He's your leader then?" Certainly, this Qādī" possessed a commanding presence. Hugues felt as if they had met before, although that was impossible.

"No," Firyal replied. "All elements of the soul are equal."

"*Deus vult,*" Umayr said in a dry, inflectionless voice. *God wills it.* "Do you really think so?"

Hugues had assumed Firyal had been sent to collect him because she was the only one who spoke French. Obviously, that was not the case. "I do." Hugues met the Qādī's gaze squarely. "Are you their priest?"

Umayr sniffed in disdain. "Not in any sense you might conceive. Our people haven't glorified the process of worship to the point that it's set above Allah Himself. You insult me by comparing our ways."

"You speak of Allah," Hugues replied. "Is that whom you pray to, or do you know Him by another name?"

Umayr's gaze narrowed. "We can debate that topic another time. For now, you may think of me as the keeper of knowledge." He glanced towards the horsemen. They had saddled their mounts and were watching the exchange. The cart was now concealed inside the cave.

Umayr seized Hugues by the arm. Despite his age, his grip was strong. "I am the only path to the essence of wisdom. Without me, you'll never find it. Remember that."

Hugues fought to retain his balance. "So you're prepared to help me then."

"That remains to be seen." Umayr frowned. "The object you seek is incredibly dangerous, even more so in the hands of the ignorant. It would be a mistake to think you deserved it."

Firyal cut across the two men. "Save the arguments for later, Umayr."

Tahīr grinned, as if he gleaned the nature of the exchange. Jalāl glanced at them for a moment, but his attention shifted to the Judean hills looming over their valley.

Firyal nodded to someone behind Hugues and a knife sliced through the rope binding his hands. Hugues turned to find Artuk had narrowed the gap between them without him realising. The warrior moved silently for such a big man. Blood tingled through Hugues' fingertips as he rubbed his chafed wrists.

"I know you won't try to escape," Firyal said grimly. "However, if you attempt to leave a marker or a trail for your people, I'll have you beaten senseless, stripped, and tied across the back of the donkey. Do we understand each other?"

"Completely." He did not doubt the threat was sincere.

Artuk shoved him towards a horse. Hugues mounted with some difficulty. In all, their party numbered over a score of riders, although it was hard to count in the moonlit shadows with the horses milling about.

They trotted through the ravine at a reasonable pace. The ground was even but littered with stone. Hugues glanced around, hoping for distinguishing landmarks. Firyal said they were travelling east, but without a clear view of the stars, he had no way of verifying that. In the moonlight, each barren foothill looked much like the next.

After riding for some time, the ravine narrowed to a bottleneck some twenty yards across. A third of the riders had passed through before a cry went up amongst the horsemen. Near the head of the column, Firyal called out what sounded like a warning.

A shower of arrows rained down from above. Riders either side of Hugues tumbled from their saddles. An arrow whined past his ear and he dropped to the ground, clutching the reins of his mount to present the smallest target possible.

Wheeling on horseback in the confined space, the remaining warriors returned fire. Hugues saw a figure on an upper ledge plunge down the side of the ravine without a sound, smashing into the rocks with a sickening thud. Arrows thrummed through the darkness and more men fell on both sides.

On the far side of the pass, Jalāl cried out. The men accompanying them huddled against their mounts as Jalāl hurled a burning object high into the heart of the pass. An arrow struck him in the chest as it arced through the air. Jalāl stumbled backwards as a blinding white light suddenly exploded above the ravine.

Hugues belatedly raised an arm to protect his eyes from the searing light. His terrified mount reared, jerking Hugues off his feet. Pink and green dots swarmed across his vision.

The light faded and night rolled back into the ravine. Hugues rubbed his eyes furiously. The dots became blurry as tears filled his eyes.

Something slithered down the side of the ravine and coiled on the ground nearby. Pebbles and small stones skittered down the steep slope. Hugues blinked away the tears: their ambushers were dropping into the ravine on ropes.

A thump sounded nearby. Hugues scrubbed at his eyes, desperate to clear his clouded vision. A figure in sand-coloured robes and matching head scarf had landed only a few yards away. He was dressed much like Firyal's men except for a red band tied around one arm. For a moment, Hugues dared to hope he might be an ally.

The man released his rope and drew a curved knife. Hugues crouched down and felt across the ground, pretending he was still blinded. His fingers tightened around a rock. The assassin rushed forward and lunged with his dagger. Hugues sprang to one side, pushing off with both feet, and swung the rock in a short arc. The blunt edge struck the man's temple with a sickening thud. Hugues was the only one to rise again.

The ravine was littered with men struggling through the shadows. Blades clashed and the smell of sulphur coiled through the air. Hugues retrieved the fallen knife and kept to the deeper shadows near the wall.

Who were these newcomers? They appeared to be Saracens as well. Another faction, perhaps? But how did they find Firyal's party?

The chill in the night air deepened until Hugues' breath clouded in front of him. Frost spread across the ground and crunched underfoot. Shadows oozed from the sides of the ravine and spread overhead, blocking out the stars. Men cried out in fear. Hugues moved away from the rock face, suddenly terrified of what might emerge from it.

The liquid darkness dripping from the walls of the ravine solidified into jutting spines. One shot out and impaled an archer wearing a red armband. Hugues watched in horror as black hooks threaded through his body. The archer screamed as he writhed in their grip. Seven tiny wheels of light appeared along the man's spine. Starting at the crown of his head, they ran all the way down to his groin, spinning furiously. Black threads wove through the spokes of each wheel and ripped outwards. With a final, agonised scream, the seven wheels were torn from the archer's flesh and his lifeless body flopped to the ground.

More spines hooked men from both sides. Hoarse screams and the crack of broken bones filled the ravine.

In all the battles he had witnessed, Hugues had never seen anything like this. Surely, the gates of hell stood wide open. The cold dread was a physical weight too great to bear. His arms dropped, his legs collapsed, and Hugues fell to his knees, shaking uncontrollably.

A man strolled through the carnage, or at least the semblance of a man. Wrapped in coils of mist, the figure moved through the battleground unscathed. Hugues caught a whisper of its voice. Its speech was harsh and unfamiliar. As it spoke, the shadows bent to its will.

The demon turned towards Hugues. Eyes bright like emeralds flashed and it uttered a harsh command.

Hooks burst from the shadows and sank into his flesh. The fiery agony of each puncture was enough to snap his paralysing fear. Hugues screamed and struggled to break free. Ribbons of darkness wrapped around his face and neck, and tiny needles pierced his skin and set his spine alight. He screamed again, momentarily blinded by the agony.

The demon whispered to the night and Hugues' spine cracked as the ribbons pulled tight. He was hauled forward until he knelt before the dark figure. Its face was wreathed with mist so that only sections were visible. Blackened teeth grinned at him between blistered lips.

"You smell of death," it said. "No wonder it was so easy to find you."

Hugues was flung to the ground, the impact winding him. The tiny barbs snagged in his flesh tugged impatiently. With a lurch of terror, he knew he was about to be torn apart.

"Swear to serve Severity," the demon commanded.

Hugues clawed at the ground in a vain attempt to find purchase.

Before Hugues could respond, a scimitar flashed in the darkness, followed by an ear-splitting shriek. Hugues was tossed into the air and the hooks withdrew from his body.

Hugues gasped for breath. He had landed on his side, facing the demon.

Artuk slashed at the demon's neck and it spun away, the blade lodging in its shoulder. The demon snarled in its guttural tongue and ribbons of shadow wound around Artuk's sword-arm, binding him to the creature. He grunted in surprise and heaved at his scimitar, but it was stuck. The barbed threads descended, a nest of coiling vipers that wove through the seven wheels that lit up along Artuk's spine. He gave up on his sword and drew a dagger with his free hand. Artuk tried to stab the demon in the face, but it twisted away from the blade.

The demon made a wrenching gesture with its free hand. The hooks exploded outwards, tearing the spinning wheels from Artuk's earthly temple. His body collapsed, unmarked yet lifeless.

Artuk's sword still quivered in the demon's shoulder. Wisps of smoke curled from the edge and Hugues noticed the blade was encrusted in salt. The creature eased the blade out with both hands, screeching as the metal parted from its flesh. No blood ran from the wound, but the demon favoured its injured side.

Hope surged inside Hugues despite the fiery pain tingling across his skin. The beast was not invulnerable.

Light bloomed in the chasm: a brilliant column of sapphire, followed by a second pillar of glorious yellow. Inside each moving column stood a man, their arms raised overhead in supplication. *Tahīr and Umayr.*

The same instinctive pull Hugues had felt when he first met Umayr drew him towards the blue pillar. Tiny silver stars gyrated over the head of each man.

The demon roared in anger and limped past Hugues. Shadows surged from crevices in the walls of the ravine. They resolved into glistening black spines and barbs that stabbed and hacked at the two columns.

Raising both hands overhead, the demon brought them together in a thundering clap. The barbs and spines dissolved into two massive waves of darkness that crashed over the bright pillars.

The darkness became absolute. Hugues was blinded, far worse than when he had worn the hood. The darkness broke abruptly as it shattered upon the columns. The tiny stars hissed and fizzed as they shredded the dense shadows that had swamped them.

The yellow pillar wavered. Sensing weakness, the demon showered it with more spines and barbs. For every hook that was severed by Tahīr's stars, a second and third tore chunks from his pillar.

Umayr raised his head to the heavens and screamed an invocation. Pointing at the demon, a torrent of stars struck its mist-shrouded body. The beast staggered backwards and screeched again in pain.

Tahīr's golden column crumbled and winked out. He stumbled to his knees, gasping for breath. The demon hissed a command and a spear of darkness punched through Tahīr's chest. He fell backwards, arms and legs outflung.

Umayr cried out and another burst of stars hammered the demon, shredding its protective layers of darkness. Even the fog that hid its face began to burn away before Umayr's fury. It fled back down the ravine at a shambling run, its form disintegrating into wisps of shadow as it merged with the night.

The freezing cold dissipated and Hugues rose unsteadily to his feet. His back ached and he felt exhausted. Even so, he had never been so grateful for his life. Nothing the Salt Lines had taught him had prepared him for this.

Umayr's pillar of sapphire faded. Thankfully, the shadows remained still and the air was only chilly. He murmured a prayer of thanks as he walked past the bodies scattered across the ground. Umayr was weeping as he rocked Tahīr in his arms. Jalāl was sprawled on the ground nearby, the fatal arrow jutting from his chest. Firyal lay face-down on the ground tangled with the corpses of two assassins. Dark blood pooled about her body.

Hugues was reluctant to intrude upon Umayr's grief, but he had little choice. "Umayr, we must leave before it returns." His voice quavered.

Umayr looked up. "Do you know how long this man and I have been brothers?"

This was not the response Hugues needed, although he understood the naked grief in Umayr's face. "Longer than I have been alive, I suspect." He glanced in the direction the demon had fled. "Which is why he wouldn't want you to squander his sacrifice."

Umayr's eyes narrowed. "That's exactly what I would have said had our situations been reversed." He laid Tahīr's body on the ground and kissed his forehead. "Farewell, dear brother." Umayr stopped next to Jalāl and kissed him on the forehead too. He turned Firyal over, cradling her about the shoulders with her head in his lap, and gently caressed her face. Firyal's body was riddled with deep cuts. "Farewell, my fearsome one." Umayr said something in Arabic and kissed her on both cheeks, then he laid her back down and placed her sword in one limp hand.

Umayr rose with obvious effort, every movement laced with weariness. Tears glistened upon his cheeks. "It's not right that you should be left here like this," he said to his dead brethren. "Yet, as always, we are offered few choices."

"Umayr," Hugues said urgently. "We must go."

The Qādī turned and regarded Hugues. Gone was the proud dignity that had defined his features. With the loss of his cabal, all that remained was the haunted expression that Hugues had come to recognise amongst the survivors of hopeless battles.

"That demon was one of the Fallen." Umayr prodded Hugues' chest with a bony finger. "Escape is no longer possible once the Lords of Severity have marked you."

CHAPTER 46

25 October 1307

The meridian

"At last." Salome swung out of her saddle and landed lightly on her feet. Holding her reins in one gloved hand, she crouched over a mound of crumbled stone. A light rain was falling, so fine it could almost be called mist. Beads of moisture glistened on her cloak and dripped from the lip of her cowl.

"At last what?" Rémi remained in his saddle and frowned at Salome. His short black hair bristled despite the rain.

Bertrand pulled his cloak tight. Two nights had passed since he watched Chateau Fontette burn. Since then, he had only spoken a handful of words. They had continued travelling east, avoiding roads, and keeping to the forest.

"We've found what I've been looking for." Salome shifted some small, moss-covered stones.

"What? A cairn to bury ourselves under?" Rémi asked.

A rare smile lit Salome's face. "Rémi, in all my travels, I've rarely encountered someone with such a dour sense of humour. It must be all the rain that falls upon your land."

Rémi snorted.

Bertrand glanced between his companions. Despite his protestations, it seemed Rémi was warming to Salome. The realisation did nothing to improve Bertrand's mood. "What's so important about these rocks?"

Rémi gave him a sideways look.

"It marks a salt line," Salome replied. "One that runs east-west."

"How can you tell?" Bertrand asked.

"The trees." Salome gestured with her free hand.

Bertrand glanced about the glade. While many smaller saplings had sprung up, six large beech trees towered over them in a loose circle. Now that he looked closely, they did appear to be positioned carefully, almost standing guard.

Salome stood. "This was once a sacred glade with a menhir at its centre." She gestured at the crumbling pile of stone.

"Once," Rémi agreed.

"The majority of the stone is hidden under the ground. If I can connect to it, I can tap into the meridian."

"To what purpose?" Bertrand asked.

Salome raised her eyebrows. "To help us reach the coast, assuming I possess the strength."

Bertrand swapped a concerned look with Rémi. "This is the same thing you did when...we were attacked."

"Almost. Last time I only moved us south along a single salt line. This time I propose to move us further west, where we'll switch to the next salt line that will take us north."

Rémi cleared his throat. "I'd rather we stay on horseback, if it's all the same to you." He patted his mare on the neck.

Salome shook her head. "We'd never make it. Nogaret's men know roughly where we are. First, they'll form a loose cordon around this region. Then they'll send in scouting parties to flush us out." She nudged the crumbling standing stone with her boot. "This is our only means of escape."

Rémi rubbed his beard. "What's got him chasing your hem anyway?"

"I can't answer that," Salome replied. "Only a member of the Salt Lines—"

"No." Bertrand cut her off. "Answer the question."

"Bertrand, I—"

He slid off his horse and stabbed a finger at her. "Our brothers died in ignorance protecting you. Justine is probably dead, or worse, with no idea why. If Rémi and I are to suffer the same fate, I demand you tell us everything. We *deserve* to know."

Rémi dismounted and caught the reins of Bertrand's roan before it could wander off. Bertrand's gaze never left Salome's face. "Even though my family has all but disowned me, Rémi has one waiting for him. Explain to me why I shouldn't send him home right now."

Salome glanced between the two men. "This goes against—"

"I don't care." Bertrand tore the hood from his head. "Look at me. Look at me!" He grabbed her by the shoulders and shook her. "I've lost everything, do you understand? Everyone I cared about. Everything I believed in." The rose on his hand tingled in warning, but he was beyond caring.

He choked back a sob. "I need a reason for Everard's death, a reason why Justine burned." Bertrand's hands fell from Salome's shoulders and he dropped to his knees. What was the point?

Everard.

Justine.

Roland. Arnaud. Laurent.

Their faces gathered about him: lips moving, voices silent. They were warning him about the man with the neat beard. He was coming. Always dogging their heels until there was nowhere left to run.

Rain trickled through his hair and ran down his face. He felt adrift in the vastness of his grief.

"The cub's right," Rémi said. "He deserves an answer. A real one. Not your usual sleight-o-hand."

Salome knelt in the mud with Bertrand. "Yes, he does. You both do." She looked to the heavens. Thick, grey clouds blocked out the sun. She sighed. "The Fraternity is broken, so I suppose the old strictures no longer apply. And I'm too heartsick to fear rebuke from any who might remain."

Salome touched Bertrand's temple. Her fingertips were warm and the strength of their connection intensified. First came trust, a bright yellow feeling that suffused his body with confidence. A sense of relaxation followed, accompanied by a tremendous flood of relief. She was opening to him, unfurling at last. Old barriers within Salome crumbled, long-held disciplines unravelled.

She gazed deeply into Bertrand's eyes. His heart thudded in response.

"I'll explain as simply as I can," she said. "You'll have questions I won't be able to answer. At least not yet. The knowledge you seek has many layers, and it's dangerous to peel them back too quickly. Besides which," she said with a rueful glance to the west, "we don't have much time."

"Then get on with it." Despite his brusque manner, Rémi inched closer.

Salome took Bertrand's hands and drew him to his feet. In the dim light, Salome resembled a queen surveying her court. He felt a rush of—not love—but admiration, mingled with a tangled knot of guilt and desire.

Salome drew her shoulders back. "Scripture speaks of the tree of knowledge, of good and evil. This is an allusion to another tree, one that was first revealed to Moses. When Moses received the commandments, it is said he was also given secret knowledge: an understanding of the workings of all Creation. Originally, this lore was passed to his chosen descendants via an oral tradition. Later, it became what we some call the Kabbalah. Put simply, this mystical tree, this Tree of Life, is the key to all existence."

"And you know where this tree is?" Bertrand asked. "That's the great secret you keep."

"No." Salome raised her hand and gestured for patience. "The tree is not located in any one place, just as He who is Unfathomable is not confined to a single space. The roots of the tree are in the ground we walk. Its branches are the mountains we climb. Its leaves are the air we breathe."

"I don't understand," Bertrand said. "What does any of this have to do with us?"

"You've already seen a representation of the tree, Bertrand. Three branches with ten spheres."

He blinked. "I remember. Hidden in the stained glass of our chapel."

"Exactly." Salome gave him an encouraging smile. "Your Order takes its rule from Bernard, the founder of the Cistercian Order. Bernard was a leading member of the Salt Lines. He foresaw the need for a military wing of the Fraternity to protect the secrets it uncovered in the Holy Land, so he wrote the Rule for the Ordre du Temple."

"Wait." Bertrand thought rapidly. "Are you saying my Order was created to guard your secret?"

"In part, yes." Salome arched her eyebrows. "How else do you explain the tree in your chapel?"

Bertrand had no answer to that. "And Everard knew all of this?"

"Much of it," Salome agreed.

Bertrand digested this revelation in silence.

"Get to the part that involves us," Rémi said.

Salome inclined her head. "We are nearing it, Rémi. A little more patience if you please." She focused on Bertrand. "The two outer pillars of the tree are known as Mercy and Severity. In the Bible, they're called good and evil, yet this is a simplification. In the ancient tradition of the Kabbalah, they are presence and absence."

"If I wanted to be fed manure—" Rémi began.

"Wait." Salome raised her palm, although her eyes never left Bertrand. "Presence is life: it's creativity, it's freedom of thought and action. Absence is death: it's emptiness, rigidity and oppression. He who is Unfathomable wrought life where none existed. He manifested all Creation through the Tree of Life and the ten Sephirot that are the fruits of His labour. And the tree rests upon a keystone that has two facets. One is the essence of Mercy, the other Severity. In simplest terms, they are the two sides of human nature, locked in eternal conflict."

Bertrand searched her face. "And you know the location of this keystone."

Salome nodded. "Yes, I know the location of Mercy's half. Over time, it has acquired many names. Some know it as Baphomet. Others call it the wisdom eternal."

"And Nogaret wants it. What happens if he finds it?" Bertrand asked.

Salome's expression darkened. "The pillar of Severity claims the human soul. The angels that fell from grace walk free from their prison. All Creation is perverted."

Bertrand tried to make sense of what Salome had told him. Elements of her story reminded him of sermons warning of the Apocalypse. He turned his mind to more immediate concerns. "So that's why we're going to England. Nogaret won't be able to reach you there."

"No. Now that your Order has collapsed, nowhere is safe for me."

"Then why England?" Bertrand demanded. "Why not return to the Holy Land?"

"A place has been prepared for me. A special place, where I can forget all that I know. It's not far from Scotland, which remains outside papal control. I hope to find peace there."

Rémi grimaced. "Forgive me but—"

"Why doesn't someone simply kill me?" Salome asked.

Rémi shrugged his broad shoulders. "If your capture would mean such disaster, why not?"

"I cannot die without passing on my knowledge," Salome said. Her expression darkened. "Believe me, it has been attempted often enough." She rolled up her sleeve to expose her scars.

"And this is what you hope for in England?" Bertrand asked. "Death?"

"No, release." She sighed and her gaze dropped to the crumbling pile of stone. "There is a world of difference."

The rain eased and the patter of dripping leaves filled the forest. Even the horses were still. Bertrand thought of Justine, yet her presence was already retreating into memory. Salome, with her bowed head and a curtain of charcoal hair was all he could focus upon. Experiencing her sorrow, the loss of Everard pierced him anew.

"Bertrand, Severity gathers wherever I go. Take what you've seen these last few weeks and multiply it across a lifetime. *That* is my existence, and I can no longer bear the horror of it." The naked appeal in her dark eyes was impossible to ignore.

"I'm sorry for the pain that I've caused you," Salome said. "But surely, you see now that I had no choice. With Roard and Everard gone, you must shoulder their burden, regardless of whether you're ready or not."

"It's not a question of responsibility," Bertrand replied. "I've already accepted that. It's a question of trust."

"I understand," Salome replied. "Given what I have endured, perhaps you can see why I have become slow to trust. Please, we must leave now. Every moment is precious."

He did believe her. How could he not? Yet she had also admitted that she was not telling him everything. At least not yet. That would change, he silently vowed. And soon.

"What do we do?" Bertrand asked reluctantly.

"Stand as close to the menhir as possible." Salome waved Rémi over. "You too. You insisted on coming, didn't you?"

Rémi muttered under his breath as he brought the horses closer to the pile of stone.

"And the pack horse," Salome said. "Bring it in as close as possible. Yes, that's good."

Salome took Bertrand's hand. "When we arrive, I will be exhausted. Probably unable to stand. Don't be alarmed. This is natural, but I will need time to recover. If all goes well, we'll arrive on a hilltop surrounded by stones that look like broken teeth. To the south-west, you should be able to see a Cistercian monastery. The Abbot is expecting us. His name is Guillot. Ask for him by name. If the monks refuse you entry, insist they give their Abbot the following phrase: *The sun sets over the Anastasis.* Guillot will come in person if he receives that message. Repeat what I have just said."

Bertrand repeated her instructions.

"Good. Do not speak of me or mention my name. Now let's begin." Salome knelt next to the crumbled rock. "Rémi, keep a tight hold on the horses. They'll try to bolt when we arrive. Bertrand, place your hand against my neck and don't break contact."

Her skin was soft beneath his calloused palm. The unfurling that he had sensed before shifted. Now she seemed to draw inwards, building pressure as if she were holding her breath. The fine hairs on his body lifted and air seethed through the glade, charged like the still moments just before a thunderstorm.

"Remain still," Salome muttered. Drawing her belt knife, she nicked the side of her hand and smeared blood onto the remains of the menhir.

Bertrand's heart lurched beneath his ribcage and his breath came in short, sharp bursts. He tried to slow his breathing and closed his eyes, which helped a little.

Salome's free hand pressed against his and the pressure inside her shot downwards into the stone. For a moment, nothing happened.

Bertrand opened his eyes. A glowing image hovered in the air, just above Salome's head. He recognised the stem and circles from the attack at the Marne. Only now he noticed the similarity to the scar on his hand.

A pocket of charged air rose from the earth, expanding like a bubble until it surrounded them and the horses. He sensed a torrent hurtling underground, like a raging river, and the ground trembled.

"Now!" Salome cried.

The surface of the bubble shuddered, Bertrand's ears popped, and he stumbled. Salome steadied him and he tightened his grip on her neck. The ancient elms surrounding the glade wavered, as if seen through water. They appeared to lean inwards before…

…the glade lurched sideways.

The bubble surrounding them dropped into the meridian and the world contracted into a whirl of light, sound and sensation. With no anchor or point of reference, Bertrand let the salt line take him.

CHAPTER 47

23 November 1307

The Boudoir

Roustan stamped up the stairs of the inn. A burly soldier guarded the landing, his sword drawn.

"Put that away," Roustan snapped. "Guillaume sent for me."

The guard took one look at Roustan's grim, haunted face and sheathed his sword. "Still need to search you," he muttered.

"Again?"

The guard's expression became stubborn. "*His* orders," he said with a jerk of the head.

"Very well." Roustan raised his arms and let the man paw him in search of hidden weapons.

The soldier reluctantly made way for Roustan in the narrow corridor. In the past, Roustan might have asked for the guard's name in the hope of punishing his impertinence at a later stage. That Roustan was gone forever. Now, he had but one purpose. A single goal branded into his every waking moment.

Capture Salome.

Roustan shuddered violently. He would *not* think of the demon Gamaliel. It was bad enough to be spurred on like a horse. Why worry at the bit when the saddle was empty?

He stopped at the large door and rapped his knuckles against the oak. Was Guillaume a puppet too? Or had he managed to bargain with the demons for his safety? If anyone could manage such a feat, it was Guillaume.

Roustan ground his teeth. Curse that godless bastard! After all of the sacrifices Roustan had made to win Guillaume's trust, look what it had won him. Barbed coils stirred in Roustan's stomach and a wave of terrible heat rolled down his spine and discharged through the tender flesh between his legs. Roustan staggered against the wall.

The pain passed quickly.

Just a warning this time. He had dallied too long, thinking about things that did not relate to Salome's capture. He knew her name now, and much more besides. Gamaliel had shown him things. Things that Roustan was still trying to comprehend. She was no ordinary witch. That much was clear.

"I said *come*," an irritable voice called from the far side of the door.

Roustan turned the latch and entered the room. The chamber was large and decorated in the manner of a boudoir. Thick burgundy drapes kept out the light. A large bed, replete with a canopy swathed in silks, dominated the room. A woman lay face-down and unmoving in the bed. The sheets partially obscured her, although Roustan caught sight of black hair draped across a bare shoulder and a pale bottom. One foot dangled loose from the side of the bed. Blood dripped slowly from her toes.

"Over here."

Roustan turned towards the voice. A small divan covered in lurid red silk had been placed in the left corner of the room. Guillaume lay sprawled across it in a state of undress: his white linen shirt was open to the waist and his grey breeches were untied. Sweat had darkened the underarms of his shirt and drops of blood stained his cuffs.

"Peach?" Guillaume offered one of the ripe fruit piled next to him. "A late harvest has just arrived from Spain."

"Thank you, messire." Roustan bowed. "Perhaps later." Whatever curse Gamaliel had wrought inside Roustan, it allowed him to eat but not indulge. Roustan suspected a peach would be considered a luxury and hence result in excruciating agony. But did Guillaume know that?

"Pity." Guillaume glanced at the dead girl in the bed. "They're quite sweet. Particularly, the soft flesh either side of the crease." Guillaume grinned at Roustan. Was this Guillaume's natural depravity or the cruelty of demons speaking through him? Either was possible.

Roustan's innards quivered again in warning. Gamaliel's barbs had no patience for questions of morality. "Salome has escaped again. Our search parties failed to flush her out of the forest near Fontette."

Guillaume's hazel eyes narrowed and he bit into the peach. Juice trickled from the corners of his mouth and into his beard. Chewing deliberately, he said around the pulp, "That's unfortunate. Particularly, for you."

"We burned his lover's chateau to the ground. A few escaped, but this Bertrand made no attempt to interfere."

"Hardly surprising," Guillaume murmured. "Salome wouldn't let him intervene. What about his family?"

"The Baron of Châtillon-sur-Seine and his two sons were taken into custody. A brief trial was held as you ordered. Their public beheading was widely proclaimed, but again, no attempt was made to save them." Roustan sneered. "I can't say his father appeared surprised. Even he considered his youngest son to be something of a disappointment."

"Yet he's escaped capture nonetheless." Guillaume tore into the heart of the peach and spat out the pip. "Perhaps this Bertrand is too intelligent for bravery. Much like your good self."

Roustan ignored the taunt. "Or perhaps he was isolated and didn't learn of his family's fate in time."

Guillaume tossed the remains of his peach aside. "Either way, your strategy to capture Salome through her new, inexperienced Shroud has failed. She has eluded your net and is now travelling north as she intended all along." Guillaume stood and glared at Roustan.

"All major ports have been alerted," Roustan said. "We have reliable descriptions of this Bertrand and Salome dare not show her face. I have also set Seigneuresse de Fontette on his trail. She might lead us to him."

"Desperate ploys." Guillaume picked at his teeth. "Much as it pains me to admit it, she is nothing if not cunning." He chewed on his fingernail. "Perhaps it's time to stop chasing and lie in wait instead."

Roustan frowned. "That assumes we know where she's going."

"Yes, it does, doesn't it?" Guillaume moved to an ornately carved bureau and withdrew a leather satchel from it. He tossed the satchel to Roustan.

"Inside you'll find letters of introduction to members of the English court who are willing to help us," Guillaume said. "There's also a promissory note that will grant you enough gold to acquire a small army of mercenaries. Best not lose them, eh?" Guillaume gave Roustan a playful slap on the shoulder. "You can have ten of my personal guard as an escort."

"England." Roustan looked up at Guillaume. "So you *do* know where she's going."

"Yes, I believe so." Guillaume gave him a wintry smile.

"How?" The word escaped before Roustan's natural caution could prevent it.

Guillaume's expression hardened. "Like you, I host a Lord of Severity from time to time. His name is Sammael, and he has taught me much. Word has reached Sammael of a new cathedral just finished in Yorkshire. It sits on the junction of two salt lines. That can't be a coincidence, can it?"

Roustan shook his head. "No, messire." Gamaliel had whispered of ancient meridians beneath the earth, but that did not explain why someone would build a church over them. The very concept was heresy.

"It's not far from a town called Skipton," Guillaume continued. "Take your men there, capture Salome, burn the cathedral and kill anyone else you find. Leave no evidence behind. Do this and you get your life back, Roustan. Gamaliel will have no further need of you once we have Salome."

Roustan shuddered at the mention of the demon. Freedom from Gamaliel was more precious than anything Guillaume could offer. Roustan clutched the leather satchel to his chest. "Yes, messire. I won't fail you."

"I know you won't, Roustan." Guillaume sat on the bed and patted the dead girl's flaccid rump. "The Lords of Severity have little patience with those who fail to please."

The Salt Lines duology concludes with *The Final Shroud*.

CAST OF CHARACTERS

THE HOLY LAND, 1099

Hugues' five sacred points:

Achambaud de St. Amand	A knight and bodyguard to Godefroi de Bouillon.
Etienne de Champagne	An engineer and designer of Godefroi's siege tower.
Godefroi de Bouillon	Duke of Lower Lorraine and one of the principal nobles commanding the siege of Jerusalem.
Godwera de Bouillon	Former wife of Baldwin de Bouillon. Believed to have died while travelling south from Constantinople. Disguised as a monk called 'Gondemar'.
Hugues de Payens	Chaplain to Godefroi de Bouillon.

The Christian Nobility:

Baldwin de Bouillon	Younger, ambitious brother of Godefroi de Bouillon.
Diederic	A Flemish knight appointed to act as Godefroi's bodyguard during the siege of Jerusalem.
Gaston de Bearn	A minor noble charged with the responsibility of overseeing the construction of Godefroi's siege tower.
Raymond de Toulouse	Born Raymond St Gilles, now the Count of Toulouse. Godefroi's fiercest adversary in the struggle to rule Jerusalem.
Robert de Normandy	Duke of Normandy and cousin to Robert of Flanders. One of Godefroi's most important supporters.

| Robert de Flanders | Duke of Flanders and cousin to Robert of Normandy. One of Godefroi's most important supporters. |

The Christian Clergy:

Arnulf de Chocques	Chaplain to the Duke of Normandy.
Peter Desiderius	A priest who claimed to have divine visions. Supporter of Count Raymond.
Peter de Narbonne	One of the most senior ranking clerics. Made Bishop of Albara by Count Raymond in September 1098.

Umayr's Arabic Cabal:

ālim Sharif	An elderly Saracen warrior whose title translates roughly to "learned noble".
Firyal	An elderly Saracen woman known to her people as The Seer.
Jalāl	An old Saracen man known to his people as The Alchemyst.
Tahīr	An old Saracen man known to his people as The Physick.
Umayr	A mysterious Saracen known to his people as the Qādī, which translates as a combination of "judge" and "master of the law".

FRANCE, 1307

The Templar Commanderie:

Arnaud	A senior knight or chevalier.
Bertrand de Châtillon-sur-Seine	A newly made knight. Third, and much maligned, son of the Baron of Châtillon-sur-Seine.
Everard de Chaumont	Preceptor (i.e. commander) of the Templar Commanderie in Brienne-le-Château.
Laurent	A Chaplain at the Templar Commanderie in Brienne-le-Château.
Rémi	A sergeant and lifelong mentor to Bertrand.
Roland	A senior knight or chevalier.
Thibauld	Everard de Chaumont's Seneschal.

Characters in France:

Guillaume de Nogaret — Keeper of the Seals for King Philippe and the king's principal adviser.

Guillot — Abbot of a Cistercian Abbey.

Huon — A gamekeeper for Justine de Fontette.

Justine de Fontette — Former lover of Bertrand and widowed ruler of the estate at Fontette. Justine's deceased husband was a vassal of Bertrand's father, the Baron of Châtillon-sur-Seine.

King Philippe le Bel — Philippe the Fair, King of France, and fourth of that name.

Roard — A large knight and bodyguard to Salome.

Roustan de Toulouse — A ruthless agent of Guillaume de Nogaret.

Salome — A mysterious woman protected by Roard and Everard de Chaumont.

MERCY AND SEVERITY

The Lords of Mercy and Severity:

Gabriel — One of the five Lords of Mercy. Leads the angelic choir of the Cherubim.

Gamaliel — One of the five Lords of Severity. Opposes the archangel Gabriel.

Haniel — One of the five Lords of Mercy. Leads the angelic choir of the Elohim.

Lilith — One of the five Lords of Severity. Opposes the archangel Sandalphon.

Michael — One of the five Lords of Mercy. Leads the angelic choir of the Malachim.

Orev Zarak — One of the five Lords of Severity. Opposes the archangel Haniel.

Raphael — One of the five Lords of Mercy. Leads the angelic choir of the Beni Elohim.

Sammael — One of the five Lords of Severity. Opposes the archangel Raphael.

Sandalphon — One of the five Lords of Mercy. Leads the angelic choir of the Ishim.

Tagiriron — One of the five Lords of Severity. Opposes the archangel Michael.

GLOSSARY

Abaddon	Prison for the bodies of the Lords of Severity. Located in the seventh, and deepest, layer of Hell.
Adonai Melech	The divine name used to invoke the power of the tenth Sephirah called Malkuth.
Aloah v'Daat	The divine name used to invoke the power of the sixth Sephirah called Tipheret.
Baphomet	A mysterious term with a range of possible meanings, all of which derive their root from the ancient word for "wisdom".
Bascinet	A helmet, typically worn over the top of a chainmail hood. The knight would usually wear a leather cap to protect his skull from chafing.
Bliaut	An over-gown worn by men and women during the Middle Ages. Typically, the men's version was shorter in the hem, while women wore theirs to ankle length.
Ceinture	A thick belt worn around the waist, often with a bliaut.
Chevalier	"Knight" in French.
Compline	The evening devotion, usually held around nine in the evening. Forms part of the Liturgy of the Hours and is observed by monks and brothers of the Templar Order.
Elohim Tzabaoth	The divine name used to invoke the power of the eighth Sephirah called Hod.
Ein Sof	Translates roughly as "God the Unknowable" — that is, the aspect of God that is beyond human comprehension.
Franj	A collective term used by the Saracens to refer to all Franks and other Christian invaders.
Hod	Translates from Hebrew as "Glory" or "Splendour". Hod is the eighth Sephirah in the Tree of Life and corresponds to reason, abstraction, logic and communication.

Holy Sepulchre	Located in Jerusalem, this is the most common name for the church built over the sites of Christ's crucifixion and resurrection.
Jehovah Tzabaoth	The divine name used to invoke the power of the seventh Sephirah called Netzach.
Kabbalah	The word "Kabbalah" literally means "to receive or accept". Historians disagree over the timing of the emergence of the Kabbalah, but most agree that it derives its origins from rabbinic Judaism. Over time, the Kabbalah has been incorporated into Western mysticism.
Lords of Mercy	Five archangels who cleave to the Pillar of Mercy and fight for the restoration of the unity between Ein Sof and all His children.
Lords of Severity	Five archangels who cleave to the Pillar of Severity. Responsible for the expulsion of humanity from the Garden of Eden.
Malkuth	Translates from Hebrew as "the Kingdom". Malkuth is the tenth Sephirah in the Tree of Life and corresponds to the material world, practicality and stability.
Matins	The morning devotion held at dawn. Forms part of the Liturgy of the Hours and is observed by monks and brothers of the Templar Order.
Menhir	An upright stone often with carved markings. Menhirs were used in ancient times as markers for sacred sites or meeting points.
Messire	From Old French, translating roughly as "My sir" or "sire".
Milites	A Roman term the Franks borrowed to describe professionally trained infantry.
Netzach	Translates from Hebrew as "Victory" or "Endurance". Netzach is the seventh Sephirah in the Tree of Life and corresponds to intuition, emotion and sensitivity.
Pedites	A Roman term the Franks borrowed to describe foot soldiers. Typically, poorly equipped compared to chevaliers and milites.
Pillar of Mercy	The right Pillar of Mercy belongs to the Tree of Knowledge that Adam and Eve ate from. It represents life, purity, and abundance.

Pillar of Severity	The left Pillar of Severity belongs to the Tree of Knowledge that Adam and Eve ate from. It represents death, corruption, and absence.
Pillar of Unity	The middle Pillar of Unity is an aspect of the Holy Shechinah and represents the one true path to God.
Saracen	A term used by Christians during the First Crusade to refer to all Moslems.
Seneschal	A senior official, or servant, in charge of a noble's household.
Sephirah	Singular usage of Sephirot.
Sephirot	The Ten Sephirot are manifestations of God, often represented by medieval Kabbalists as spheres emanating outwards from Him through the Tree of Life. The Ten Sephirot are the source of life in the universe, moving from the abstract concept of Ein Sof that humanity cannot comprehend to the physical matter comprising our existence.
Shaddai el Chai	The divine name used to invoke the power of the ninth Sephirah Yesod.
Shechinah	The Holy Shechinah is the manifestation of God in the lower worlds separated from His direct presence, symbolised by the Pillar of Unity. In Christianity, the Holy Shechinah might correspond to the Holy Spirit.
Tafurs	Vicious peasants who participated in the armed pilgrimage to take Jerusalem from the Saracens.
Tipheret	Translates from Hebrew as "Beauty" or "Compassion". Tipheret is the sixth Sephirah in the Tree of Life and corresponds to individuality, personality and the mind.
Tree of Life	The Tree of Life is a pictorial representation of the Ten Sephirot, showing the process of Creation. The Tree of Life is divided into three pillars: the left Pillar of Severity, the right Pillar of Mercy, and the middle Pillar of Unity.
Vespers	Devotion held at sunset. Forms part of the Liturgy of the Hours and is observed by monks and brothers of the Templar Order.
Yesod	Translates from Hebrew as "Foundation". Yesod is the ninth Sephirah in the Tree of Life and corresponds to imagination, dreams and instinct.